I0648069

THE GLORY JUMPERS

THE GLORY JUMPERS

DELANO STAGG

CUTTING EDGE

Copyright © 1959 by Mel R. Sabre & Paul Eiden

The characters and events portrayed in this book are fictitious. Any similarity to real persons, living or dead, is coincidental and not intended by the author. No part of this book may be reproduced, or stored in a retrieval system, or transmitted in any form or by any means, electronic, mechanical, photocopying, recording, or otherwise, without express written permission of the publisher.

For Doro and Splook

ISBN-13: 978-1-957868-10-3

Published by
Cutting Edge Books
PO Box 8212
Calabasas, CA 91372
www.cuttingedgebooks.com

(To: THE BATTLE HYMN OF THE REPUBLIC)

"… There was blood upon the risers, there was blood upon
    the chute,
And his guts were pink and yellow on his bloody jumper's
    suit,
So they picked him up and poured him from his para-
    trooper's boot,

AND HE AIN'T GONNA JUMP NO MORE!

GORY, GORY WHAT A HELLUVA WAY TO DIE,
GORY, GORY WHAT A HELLUVA WAY TO DIE,
GORY, GORY WHAT A HELLUVA WAY TO DIE,
    AND HE AIN'T GONNA JUMP NO MORE!

(From the *Song of the Parachute School,*
Fort Benning, Georgia … Expurgated Version)

TABLE OF CONTENTS

CHAPTER ONE

D MINUS ONE,
0900 HOURS

"Double time ... *Harch!*"

The sweating, helmeted paratrooper company swung into a dogtrot at the captain's command. Lieutenant Thomas B. Edgerton turned from his idle scrutiny of the sentry-guarded barbed-wire fence, which surrounded the marshalling area, to watch the running men. He was grateful for the hard comfort of the jeep seat.

His glance was arrested by a squat and surly-looking non-com who stood near the jeep. The man had come up quietly and now relaxed in an easy slouch, reading the regimental numbers on the bumper. He was a staff sergeant and wore on his shoulder the alien patch of the 82nd Airborne. He ignored Edgerton and addressed himself to Purgatorio, the colonel's driver. "This buggy's from the Five-Oh-Zero, ain't it? Colonel Tighe's regiment?"

"Five-Oh-Goose," Purgatorio corrected him. "This is the colonel's jeep."

Edgerton felt a trace of annoyance. The man had not saluted him. He checked the reprimand that rose to his lips. This sergeant had a disturbing presence. He stood no more than five-foot-nine or – ten, and yet, enormous in his barrel-chested spread of flesh and muscle, he bore himself with a curious arrogance. His bullet skull was cropped and the short black hair bristled with occasional patches of gray, indicating either falsified records, or friends in high places to sanction his presence in an outfit where the maximum age for enlisted men was thirty-two. His flat-nosed face was seamed with scars. He had the sort of chin which, however closely shaved, would never look clean-shaven, and a mat of wiry hair protruded from his open-throated jump-jacket and lined the corded wrists that jutted from his sleeves. His eyes were black and sleepy as he let them drift over Edgerton indifferently before he fixed them on the driver again.

"Where's Colonel Tighe?" the sergeant's voice was brass-gong deep.

Purgatorio pointed to the Division Operations Tent. "Inside the war room. Hassling with the general and his staff."

The sergeant nodded. "Tell him Sergeant Mungo is reporting in. I got a jeep-load of casuals with me. I'll take them straight to Regimental."

He turned and walked away, almost pointedly it seemed to Edgerton, dispensing with the salute. Edgerton flushed and considered calling the man back. Something disquieting about the sergeant made him decide against it. He fixed his eyes on the company of troopers running across the Devonshire meadow.

Purgatorio turned and smiled at him, as though he had noticed Edgerton's failure to rise to what he probably considered a challenge. Edgerton continued staring at the jogging men. Purgatorio followed his eyes and said casually, "Hey, Lieutenant ... you noticed how many guys been falling out of the runs today and yesterday?"

Edgerton grunted and lit a cigarette. He didn't particularly like Purgatorio, and he was always on guard against any sign of familiarity from enlisted men. Unsolicited remarks from them always seemed to point up the anomaly of his position as regimental adjutant—an officer with no unit of his own.

The observation amused him nonetheless, and he meant to include it in his next letter to Grace. An unusual number of men had been dropping from the runs around the airstrip recently.

Colonel Tighe had insisted that on training runs, "Nobody falls out until he passes out." The men mocked the ukase, but they lived up to it. These paratroopers were stubbornly proud of their physical hardness and boasted that no officer could outrun them. Rather than face the ignominy of dropping out of ranks, they would plod along, glassy-eyed, mile after mile, to the limit of their officers' endurance.

The values of the men were obviously changing: it was no longer important to hang on to the end. Their attitude was easy for Edgerton to understand. Soon, probably tonight, the regiment would have its baptism of fire. In a very few hours these men would bail out into the hostile night over Normandy, and the prospect of battle reduced the runs to trivia.

Edgerton drew on his cigarette and tried to visualize what it would be like. Sticks of jumpers would crowd through the doors to plunge earthward, neatly spaced at first, then, as their chutes sprang open slipping rapidly apart, "like a string of pearls, breaking and spilling across the sky." That had been one of the most successful images in Edgerton's letters home to his wife. Grace was saving all his letters. Binding them, in fact. They planned that he would go into advertising copywriting for the first few years after the war, to remain independent of both their families while he wrote the first of his novels.

Edgerton clambered from the jeep. It would be wise to take stock of his impressions at division headquarters the day before the jump. A casual paragraph perhaps, but objectively detailed, for realistic color in the book he would someday write about men at war. The book would center on a sensitive young officer whose profound willingness to come to grips with life had brought him to the paratroops, instead of to one of the genteel Navy sinecures of his classmates.

The sensitive lieutenant gazed about him, cataloguing the scene. Division clerks in OD's hurried by, a faintly apologetic look in their eyes for not having to die as abruptly as the men in the line outfits might. A cluster of signalmen nearby were checking their radios and loading them away in canvas packs for jumping. Across the field, C-47's lined the landing strip, their crew chiefs and mechanics working over the motors. The squat brown transports crouched in the meadows, low and ugly, turning their motors sullenly and snarling a promise of aerial grace. Edgerton smiled at his own felicity of phrase.

Satisfied with the notes he had collected, he snuffed and field-stripped his cigarette. He wondered how much longer the colonel would be, and what effect his arguments were having. Tighe had shot up to the Divisional War Room almost an hour ago, to demand more men and planes from the divisional reserve, or, at least, permission to redispose his companies for the mission.

Tighe's anxiety concerned a recent report from British Intelligence regarding the deployment of enemy troops on the Cherbourg Peninsula. The British had advised that a mobile German division, the 352nd, previously located in reserve around St. Lo, had been moved to strengthen the Normandy coast in the Orne-Vire valley sector near Isigny. If the report was true, the Germans would have a division on Tighe's left flank, within striking distance of his proposed assembly area.

The divisional staff had chosen to ignore the report. They would not permit Tighe to alter their complex plans for his regiment's objectives and deployment—the timetable of phase lines, assault and holding missions—that impressive and vaguely ludicrous "overall plan" with which military staffs reduce imponderables to neat operational schedules.

The mission of the division had been outlined months before: to jump on the southeastern flank of Utah Beach, about four or five miles inland; to capture the vital exits from the invasion beach and block the flow of enemy reserves through the eastern approaches of the peninsula. Colonel Tighe's 500th Parachute Infantry Regiment was slated to secure the division's left flank.

It all looked very well on paper, and seemed feasible enough in sand-table planning. But if the British report was true, the German division garrisoned at Isigny could strike before the regiment assembled, roll the scattered battalions up, and even— it was Tighe's recurrent nightmare—seal the causeway exits from the beach, stopping the invasion cold.

Tighe had been in the War-Room tent too long now for an ordinary "yes" or "no." He must be putting up a hell of a battle. Edgerton could imagine the tone in which the driving, dedicated officer would try to force his arguments home against the bluff stolidity of the division staff.

He was reaching for another cigarette when the regimental commander emerged from the tent. The stocky colonel's face was claret-red with rage. His fists were clenched and his heels rang hard on the duckwalk leading from the tent. The guard presented arms, and the answering salute was a sharp, almost ferocious gesture. He motioned curtly at the jeep, and Edgerton bolted back over the side and onto the rear seat again.

Purgatorio had the engine turning and the wheels curling off in a mud-splattering turn toward the regimental area the instant Tighe's rump hit the seat beside him.

Tighe turned and glared at his adjutant as though Edgerton had just been caught polishing his boots with the regimental colors. "One lousy extra C-forty-seven," he snarled. "One lousy Goddamned airplane!" For a split second Edgerton thought the colonel was about to punch his face. "That's all they'll give me," the colonel roared at him. "And I have to supply the men myself."

He jammed a cigarette into his mouth as though he were skewering an enemy. Edgerton held his gold lighter under it, shielding the flame from the wind. "Isn't Division concerned at all, sir?"

"Oh, they're concerned all right," Tighe said, drawing hard on the cigarette. "They're concerned right up the line to First Army. They're even sending me a pigeoneer to fly back reports, in case the radios break down as usual." He laughed bitterly. "A pigeoneer, damn their eyes! But no one's concerned enough to give me a few companies from one of the other regiments."

Edgerton felt sorry for the harassed man. Colonel Tighe had prepared half his life for this first combat operation. His regiment was his life, and for two years he had driven himself tirelessly, training his men to a hard-edged pitch of combat efficiency. However superior Edgerton might feel to military skills, he knew that Tighe brought an artist's dedication and a saint's intensity to soldiering. It was ugly to think of the man betrayed by miscalculation in higher echelons of command.

"Have you decided what sort of outfit to use, sir?" Pity and respect tinged Edgerton's voice.

The colonel seemed not to notice the tone. "Oh, that was decided for me," he told the wind. " 'A reconnaissance patrol is all you're going to need, Tighe.' That's exactly what they told me." He punished his palm with a savage fist " 'Drop an outpost squad on that Isigny road between the Douve and the Vire. A squad's enough, Colonel, to call for an air-strike or support from the sea-borne artillery. Especially for an observation mission on a Kraut division that isn't even there.' Then the flyboys let me know that they can spare only one plane, anyway, and I'm damned lucky to get that." He shook his head in pained wonderment. " 'A Kraut division that isn't even there.' "

"They won't give you anyone from divisional reserve?" Edgerton asked.

" 'Divisional reserve,' " Tighe mocked bitterly. "They gave me the stockade. The bottom of the barrel—whatever we've got there waiting on court martial. And to beef up these foul balls, they're throwing me some casuals they just got on transfer from the Eighty-second. 'Empty out the guardhouse,' they told me. 'Everybody jumps tonight. It cost the government plenty to train those men as parachutists. And the government wants its money's worth.' As if I were a Goddamned taxpayer!"

Edgerton barely repressed a smile.

"I didn't want any screw-ups on this jump," Tighe said. "I wanted soldiers, damn it! Men with guts enough for discipline. And now I have to use the dregs of the division in the most crucial spot on my front." No puritan himself, the colonel believed with all his heart that the ideal soldier was a manly, clean-living, brave young American in his early twenties. Tighe had no use for the renegades and rebels.

"What have we got in the guardhouse, sir? I thought they cleaned it out before we left garrison."

"Oh, Christ," Tighe snarled. "The usual damned scum; the ones they haven't had a chance to sentence yet. A refusal or two; some hillbilly coward, started out as a draft-dodger and wants to finish in an army prison. There's that pair of misbegotten rapists out of D Company, too. All of them the sort that take the Army's money, as long as there isn't any danger."

Tighe crushed his cigarette and ripped it apart before he flung it out on the road. The jeep swung into the regimental area. Tighe went on with his guardhouse inventory. "Some fool kid from I Company, tried to crawl out of combat by slugging his officer. And then there's Nolan, out of Headquarters, First. You remember him … hell of a good first sergeant. They broke him for beating up some drunk last night. Damned good non-com. I warned Fitzpatrick to keep a tight rein on him—too handy with his fists."

"And those replacements from the Eighty-second, sir?"

"What the hell can you expect?" Tighe bellowed at him. "Would the Eighty-second be giving them up if they were any good?"

Purgatorio braked the jeep to a stop before the regimental headquarters tent. Tighe made no move to leave the jeep, and Edgerton waited patiently for him to descend. "There's one good man there though," the colonel said. "His name is Mungo. I think he's holding tech now."

"Staff," said Edgerton. "I believe I met him at Division, sir."

The colonel's eyebrows lifted. "Been up and down from private to master sergeant at least a dozen times. All soldier, too, that son-of-a-bitch. Served under my own father in Nicaragua." Sentiment softened the angry face. "He was in my platoon with the Fifteenth in Shanghai, when I was a kid lieutenant. One hell of a combat soldier—Mungo."

Edgerton was leery of asking irritating questions, but the inconsistency troubled him. He followed the colonel down from the jeep and asked, "Why did the Eighty-second ship him down then, sir?"

Tighe was looking at him with a cold, appraising gaze. He smiled as though he had come to a sudden decision. "Oh, Mungo? Well, he got into trouble on Anzio. He'd been with them all the way, too—Africa first, then the Sicily and Salerno jumps. His company had been in action for a month … one officer left, the company commander. Mungo figured he was screwing up and sent him back under guard as a fatigue case. Took over the company and ran it for a week—he wasn't the ranking non-com, either. They'd have shot him, I suppose, but he did a good job. Mungo always does."

Edgerton was shocked. "The captain let him get away with it?"

Tighe nodded. "National Guard man," he said simply. The adjutant was certain that if the colonel had been addressing another West Pointer instead of an O.C.S. product, he would have added, "of course."

Tighe made no move to enter the tent. Edgerton fidgeted nervously; there was still a pile of loading manifests to check, and the details of emplaning by sticks to arrange. He'd hoped, too, for time to write a final letter to Grace before the jump. But the colonel stood there staring at him, his hands cocked on his hips.

The hard brown eyes crinkled just a little at the corners. "Remember those speeches of yours, in the officers' club at

Mackall? One of your pet theories, as I recall it, about yardbirds making the only real soldiers."

Edgerton felt his cheeks flush; he hated to be patronized, even by his colonel, and he answered almost hotly. "No, that wasn't quite the argument, sir." He'd had a few too many that night and had been carried away by the sound of his own voice.

"I only maintained, and I still insist," he went on with legalistic precision, "that at certain times—in extreme situations—it doesn't hurt a soldier to have a trace of the outlaw-desperado in his make-up. A certain rebelliousness, a tough self-reliance. You remember General Butler's phrase: 'Give me a regiment of brig-rats—' Once you accept that single premise, you can make great soldiers from the scum, the outcasts. The Chinese have an expression, sir, that puts it rather neatly: 'The poorest iron for nails; the worst men for soldiers.' "

All humor seemed to leave Tighe's face. Perhaps the colonel had misunderstood that last phrase—the wording had been a bit unfortunate. Edgerton tried to recover the ground. "What I think the Chinese really mean ..."

"I don't speak any Chinese," Tighe snapped, "but I damned well hope you're right. Because I need an officer in charge of those men, and I don't need an adjutant. You've got yourself a job, Edge. Keep the jeep and round up those Eighty-second men, and that Goddamned pigeoneer. Get the guardhouse roster from the M.P.'s and send somebody to the company supply tents for your yardbirds' gear. Then get back here and I'll brief you on your mission. It isn't going to be an easy one."

Edgerton gaped at him, shocked into silence. The colonel was obviously in dead earnest.

After a long moment he realized that Tighe was waiting to be saluted. Falteringly he brought his hand up.

CHAPTER TWO

D MINUS ONE,
1200 HOURS

Dana drifted out of his doze again, sluggishly resisting the return of consciousness. His bare back squirmed against the scratchy canvas cot, as though hoping that, cocoon-like, it might fold around him, shutting out the sunlight and the dangers of the day. Sleep receded further down the corridors of his mind.

Stubbornly he held his eyelids closed and reviewed the sequence of sensations to be faced. The momnet had a flat, familiar taste. He had opened his eyes too often before on a dreary succession of jailhouse ceilings, stared at from iron, impersonal beds.

The details would be different now: both bed and cell were canvas, and the ceiling would be the steeply-pitched, weatherproofed top of an army pyramidal tent. The tent top would be bellied in, as though beneath a weight of heat; the color would be green—that curious, translucent, underwater green of canvas under sunlight. But the feel would be the same: the sense of closeness and confinement, the desolate sensation of trapped impotence. Canvas backed with bayonets serves just as well as concrete for a man whose past has taught him the tone of jailhouse waking.

The air hung hot and stale around him, smelling of creosote. Of all the tents in the assembly area, this one alone had the side-flaps dropped and the top-vent fastened shut. Dana cursed silently the systematic pettiness behind the M.P. mind. Every breath he took was choking-hot and heavy. His chest and arms were clammy with sweat.

The tent had been cooler, even chill, last night when the M.P. lieutenant led him in and lanced a flashlight beam to indicate the spot where Dana was to set up his cot. There had only been four others in the tent then; an hour later they brought Nolan in, swaggering and sullen, glowering beneath the welt on his forehead. He did not shoulder the bundled sticks and canvas of his guardhouse cot, but carried them effortlessly under one thick arm.

Dana had caught his breath at Nolan's entrance, and made a preparatory shuffle of his legs to free the fold of blanket around his feet. Inwardly he tensed for action, but he kept his facial muscles soft and relaxed as though in sleep. Through barely parted lashes, he watched Nolan set the cot up, expecting that as soon as the lieutenant left, Nolan would be charging across the tent to fall upon him in the darkness. He knew that he didn't stand a chance against the brute power of the towering first sergeant. He wanted only to be on his feet, to stand against the first attack and go down swinging.

The M.P. said, "All right, you men." His flashlight swept around the room to drive the lifted heads back against their folded fatigue-suit pillows.

Dana's eyes moved with the light, examining each face in turn. He saw them for the first time, sharply etched against the shadows: the handsome, curly-headed Greek who called himself "Cadillac," turning away with an insolent half-smile; the pale, blond, adolescent Hollister, who had been explaining all morning now how he had come to hit his platoon leader; and the two prisoners from D Company, the settled inmates, with the broad white "P's" already stenciled to the backs of their fatigues. Those two met the flashlight with the hard, set, jailhouse masks of every renegade since Cain—smouldering, rebellious, but carefully impassive in the presence of authority. Waiting faces, closed and calculating.

He had carefully avoided Nolan's face, and even the lieutenant's beam had never focused there.

He didn't want to see Nolan's face now, or any of the others, but while his eyelids shuttered off the glare of day, nothing would stop the shrill monologue that grated in his ears.

"He's been riding me that way since basic training," Hollister was saying in his boyish voice. He just took a dislike to me, I guess. He jumps me for screwing up, all the time. And I don't screw up more than anyone else. Really, I don't." Behind the voice an anxious tremor begged for reassurance.

One of the men grunted non-committally.

"Well, you guys don't really know me, do you?" Hollister said with an apologetic laugh. "But what I mean, this Lieutenant Gordon—they call him 'Flash'—do you know what he used to do?"

There was a hopeful pause while Hollister waited for someone to ask what Flash Gordon used to do. No one asked.

"Well, he used to holler, 'Forward March', and then he'd yell, 'Hollister! Get in step!' without even turning around to look at me, and the whole platoon would laugh. He screwed around with me that way until, hell, I almost didn't have any buddies—though, still, I got some damned good buddies in my squad—but I mean, who wants to start buddying around with a guy that's right on top of the lieutenant's crap list?"

"You hear this kid, Reb?" The question was dropped lazily in a drawling voice which Dana knew already as that of Swampy James, the shaven-headed D Company man. Dana had heard him telling a disinterested Nolan at breakfast that they were facing a general court martial for raping some Land Army girl. Reb grunted sleepily. "So how did you come to hit him, kid?" Swampy asked.

"Well, yesterday, just before they called off the jump, they had us running all over the airstrip. My side hurt bad and I got to thinking, *what the hell, I may be dead tomorrow. Why am I running?* So I fell out—first time I ever fell out on a run. I tried to explain but Flash Gordon wouldn't listen. He just ate me out in front of the company."

"Go on," Swampy nudged him.

"He said that I was yellow. He said that I'd never jump over Normandy—that I'd freeze in the door. And that's when I hit him. Wham! Like that. Without thinking. One minute the whole company sitting on the ground there, all looking up and laughing at me—all the real screw-ups laughing the most—and then when I looked back at them, their mouths were hanging open. And I realized, 'Oh, God, I hit an officer.' "

This time a silence fell when Hollister left off, and after a moment he said into it soberly, "I turned around again and there was Flash Gordon, still on the ground, up on his elbows with blood on his mouth. And his helmet with the gold bar was rolling on the ground. Then Captain Reynolds grabbed me and said, "What do you think you're doing, soldier? You can be shot for this.' "

Swampy laughed. "Hell, kid, you ain't going to get shot for that. You got yourself a damned good deal in this here guard tent. Three square meals, no runnin' your ass off, and you don't have to jump no combat tonight. You're gettin' a break."

"You think so?" Hollister asked, with painful sincerity. "It's not that I'm scared of making that jump though. I don't want them thinking that I chickened out. I'll bet some guys in my company are saying that right now—that I slugged Lieutenant Gordon to get out of combat."

"You really think so, dad?" The soft voice came from the foot of Dana's cot. That would be Cadillac, smiling drowsily, his long, curved lashes veiling his eyes and a cigarette perched on his lips. "You really think they dig you're hip enough for that?"

"I didn't mean that," Hollister blurted. "I mean, well, in your case, if you refused to jump that's your business. It doesn't mean you're yellow. But those guys, you know how they talk ... because they're scared themselves, they have to yell 'chicken'."

"Sure, dad, they're always scared, the muscle-apes. That's why they raise all those muscles. The voice was a rough purr, like a street-bred cat's: "You got to be scared to swallow the con. That's the way the Army gets its heroes, man."

Hollister circled around the statement, begging to be shown a new direction. "Well, hell, it takes guts to refuse a jump—cold, like that—just telling them 'no'."

"Not guts, dad. Brains. Just enough brains to see around that glory hype they lay on you."

"Hey, Cadillac, how come you in the troops now, boy?" That would be Reb's voice, flat and toneless. It was the first time Dana had heard him speak.

"The threads man—you know how they flip the chicks. I dig the wings and the real sharp boots. It's just the blood and glory bit I don't make. Not my scene, man; not my scene at all."

Hollister said, with sudden conviction, "Well, to hell with those guys. Let them think whatever they like. If they figure I chickened out, screw them all.

"Forget it, kid," Swampy's voice answered him harshly. "After they jump, there won't be nobody to care what you done. There won't be nothin' but corpses on that drop zone, and nobody livin' to remember why you're in here."

"You think so? You think it'll be that rough?" Hollister asked. "Well, I sure hope that bastard Gordon gets it. I hope he gets it good." He hesitated for a moment. "No, I don't wish that on anybody. What I mean is, if anybody gets it, I hope it's Flash Gordon."

" 'If anybody gets it'," Swampy mimicked him. "He'll get it, don't worry. They'll all get it, kid. Up at Division they got 'em written off, you hear?" Dana knew that he was savoring the dismal fate awaiting all officers in the flame-spitting Normandy darkness.

Hollister nudged the image with his mind, and ricocheted sharply to more familiar ground. "You know what he did the day I got to Toccoa, when I was assigned to the Five-Oh-Goose?"

A new voice, sudden, harsh, and final as a bullwhip boomed through the tent. "*Shee—yit!*" The peremptory word, delivered in an angry snarl, was both an indictment and a crisp command. Sergeant Nolan wanted silence, and a strained and waiting silence fell.

Dana opened his eyes to Nolan and the savage bleakness of reality, and swung his legs around and off the cot. Every eye was fixed on Nolan, and his own gaze centered there.

Nolan sat on the cot just across from him, his fatigue shirt yawning open on his huge, arched chest, his gray eyes narrowed and sardonically amused, and his puffed lips twisted into something like a smile.

He still wore the stripes and lozenge of his first-sergeancy, and unlike the others, the legs of his fatigue pants were still bloused over his jump-boots. "You sucker-punching little bastard," Nolan said. "You decided to quit playing possum now?" His cheekbone was red and the lump on his forehead, thickly painted with gentian violet, seemed to glow in the faintly filtered sunlight.

Dana sucked in his breath and stared, wanting the beating now, wanting it quickly, the way a punched-out fighter wants the knockout and oblivion.

"Screw you, Nolan," he said flatly. "I should have killed you when I had the chance."

CHAPTER THREE

D MINUS ONE,
1215 HOURS

The hush in the tent was a palpable presence now. Four pairs of eyes went flickering from Nolan to Dana and back. They sensed impending drama and its resolution, an explanation for the fall from grace of the most feared man in the regiment. That the slighter, soft-spoken man was responsible came as a shock to all of them. The glances, drifting back to Dana, held each man's own degree of pity or vicarious ferocity.

Nolan nodded slowly, enjoying his hate. "That's right, you should have killed me, Okie. You should have left me dead and six feet under. Because when I start taking you apart you're going to wish your old man was a queer."

The stinging curses rose to Dana's lips and died there, unspoken. What was the use? Nolan could not be provoked into rushing him now. Nolan's temperament was geared to vengeance but he enjoyed planning and waiting for it. The beating would be bad enough when it came. That he must wait for it, trapped by the army and M.P.'s and stockades until Nolan chose to exercise his wrath, only added another dimension to his dread.

He shrugged and disengaged his eyes. He would not permit himself the rush of self-pity. "Just remember," he said, fixing Nolan again, "when you come for a piece of my ass, you won't be getting no virgin."

He made a calculated business concealing the tremble, of searching through the pockets of his fatigues for cigarettes. When he found one and put it to his mouth and lit it, his feet were up on the cot again and he was staring once more at the green canvas roof. *The hell with it,* he told himself. It had to come—his clash with Nolan.

For a year and a half he had known it had to come. The first time he had seen him, across a barracks square, taking the measure of a company of men, he had known that Nolan was the kind who liked to wait. There was in the first-sergeant's eyes the look you saw in the cold, flat eyes of the meanest cops—the kind who shoved their bats into their belts and pinned your arms with effortless strength and eased you in the wagon without striking a blow. The citizens watching from the curb smiled at them, admiring their restraint. And you knew all the time that they were nursing their wrath until they had you in the backroom cells, with all the time and help they wanted.

All his life, it seemed, there had been Nolans in his path. They were set there to rob him of his right to live. Even before he left the farm in Oklahoma, with his feet still flapping in his father's shoes, he had known about it and fought his Nolans for it . . . the right of a small and shabby kid to hold his head as high as his neck allowed, and to walk the earth without apology. In the squalor of the Hoovervilles where he grew up, following the fruit crops around the weary circuit, he'd preserved this quality against assault by foremen, railroad bulls, deputies and cops. His antennae had grown sensitive to any threat; his resistance swift, reflexive.

The war had brought him, for the first time in his life, a steady and comparatively well-paying job. The world became less hostile and his anger less intense. When the draft-board notice reached him, to tear him from his refuge, all the ancient anger flared up again. Dana dodged from sight and hid, and when they tracked him down, he tried to flee to Mexico. They caught him at the border and returned him to his native state. A compassionate judge had given him a choice—the army or Leavenworth. Dana chose the army and was delivered straight from the courtroom to the induction center, still in handcuffs.

Although he found the discipline distasteful, soldiering was easier than following the crops. The specter of poverty still haunted Dana. After his infantry basic training he volunteered for the paratroops—the fifty dollars extra jump-pay monthly was a strong inducement. At Fort Benning he was trained as a communications man and took pride in his specialty. He was raised in grade to Technician Fifth and assigned to the 500th Parachute Infantry Regiment.

Integrated for the first time into a social organism, actually endowed with rank and status, he was finding the army almost tolerable—until Nolan became his first sergeant.

In a regiment where athletes were commonplace and brute-strength standard, Al Nolan's physique was legendary. Six-two high and well over two hundred pounds, he was the biggest of nearly two thousand good-sized men. His body had the hard, sculptured lines of a dedicated weight-lifter.

On the day he took over, Nolan brought to the orderly room two men caught filching laundry bundles, and beat them into whimpering submission. He used his hands thoughtfully, punching to the guts and kidneys, carefully measuring his blows. He left no marks, but for several weeks one of the men's urine showed traces of blood.

The company commander looked the other way, for his discipline problems were solved. There was a tacit understanding that Nolan would always be able to show extreme provocation. The beatings became ritual—a risk you ran if you got in Nolan's way—administered to AWOLS, company drunks, and even an anarchist who attempted one pay day to spoil the company's perfect record for voluntary war-bond deductions.

Dana kept his nose and carbine clean and soldiered by the book. For eighteen months he managed to steer warily clear of

Nolan. But his hackles rose whenever Nolan was near, and he never forgot the lessons of the past: that the club of authority strikes everyone in turn, and when the stiff behind you falls, you're probably the next.

The night before, his luck at last ran out. Carroway, "The Preacher," had precipitated the trouble. He was a slim, frail boy, a sort of company mascot. Pious and abstemious, he was said to be a minister's son, and although he wouldn't drink or swear, he asserted his freethinking independence by reference to Freud and the other iconoclasts whose works he kept in his overseas bag.

Somehow, with a combat jump impending, Carroway had been persuaded to share in the consumption of a pint of gin, smuggled into the marshalling area. For the first time he found himself completely, wildly drunk, and at last in possession of the vital insights into his first-sergeant's character. He had broken away from restraining hands to find Nolan and deliver the revelation.

Dana chased after him and found him near the slit trench behind the tents, in the center of a knot of four or five men. Carroway was on his knees, bleeding from the mouth, and whimpering softly with anger and shame. Nolan stood over him, his fingers curled in the boy's hair, holding his head back and demanding over and over with strained intensity, "What else do you know, you smart son-of-a-bitch? What else you got to tell me?"

Running swiftly through the darkness, Dana heard one of the men say, "Cut it out, Sergeant. He's drunk," and heard the others join him in a tentative but angry mumble.

Nolan clamped his steel-boned fingers around the boy's thin neck. Carroway yelped in pain. "Tell me some more of them big words," Nolan spat. "I want to find out what's wrong with me."

Dana caught the thickly muscled forearm with both his hands and levered it away. "Leave up, Nolan. I don't want no trouble with you. Just leave up on him, damn it!"

Nolan shook his arm free, slit-eyed, nodding with the stylized gestures of movie hard guys. "That's right, Okie. You don't want any trouble with me. I'm a sadist, Okie. I just found out. Your Goddamn fairy college-professor buddy here just explained it to me."

"Nolan ... you're gonna leave up on him now," Dana said. *The hell with it*, he thought. *If you make me, you big son-of-a-bitch, I'll kick your balls through the top of your head.*

"And do you know what he is?" Nolan asked, prodding Carroway with his foot. Carroway was down on his hands and knees, struggling to rise. Blood dripped loosely from his mouth, crimson in the lantern light and brown against the grass. "He's a masochist," Nolan said contemptuously. "You know what a masochist is, Dana? That's a guy who gets his kicks getting kicks." He drove his heavy foot against the back of Carroway's thigh. Carroway shrieked—it must have caught his groin.

That should have been the end of it. Nolan was plainly finished with Carroway. He was turning away from him, smiling sardonically. Without willing it—perhaps it was the smile that did it—Dana drove his fist into Nolan's mouth.

The big man rocked back and came up counterpunching. His fist swept through a blurring arc and exploded against the side of Dana's head. Dana felt himself lifted from his feet. The ground came up and crashed against his back.

He rolled to his knees and shook his head. The world was a roar, a shimmering blur that would not come into focus. He saw the lantern that marked the slit trench, the entrenching-tool pick that had been used to dig the trench, and he wondered vaguely when Nolan's cabled hands would come down and snatch him to his feet. He didn't have a chance. The top-kick was a fighter and incredibly strong.

He knelt, peering vaguely around for Nolan, grateful for every second allowed him towards recovery of his senses. There was shouting, the sound of blows and curses, and he saw a man lying beside Carroway. A second thrashed wildly in Nolan's grip. A third was running off. He realized then why Nolan had not rushed him. He was not alone—the others had revolted too, come wading in to help him.

Even as he regained his feet, Dana saw Carroway and Novak rising groggily, and Nolan clubbing Bannion into the ground with a vicious, looping left. Novak rushed in low, driving for Nolan's knees. Nolan stopped him stiffarmed. He drove upwards with his knee and brought a crushing rabbit-punch down on Novak's neck. Novak dropped to the grass without a sound, and Nolan, turning, roared, "Come on, you gutless bastards. I'll take all of you at once!"

Dana knew that the big man could do just that, and he checked his headlong rush. It was then that he snatched up the stubby pick. He collapsed it in a single motion, slipping the handle from the loose-fitting ring, and charged at Nolan with the weapon shoulder-high.

Bannion's body bowled into him, staggering back from Nolan's juggernaut uppercut. Dana caromed off and came driving into range, and brought the hickory club down in a whistling, full-armed swing. The impact stung his arm and all but numbed his shoulder. The sound was flat, like the *chunk* of a baseball thudding against canvas.

Time shuddered to a stop. The night was hushed for a breathless instant. Then Nolan bellowed wildly with pain and rage, and wide-eyed, backed two steps away.

His face contorted, he charged Dana blindly, with his arms up to protect his head. Dana dodged aside and swung for Nolan's ribs, slamming the pick-handle hard against his side. Nolan dropped his arms and grunted.

Both hands tight on the pick-handle now, Dana stepped in and brought it high and hurtling down on the thick black mass of Nolan's hair. Nolan roared, and slowly, with a soft, collapsing motion, sat down on the grass, shaking his head ponderously from side to side.

"Get up, you bastard," Dana told him. "I'm going to split your frigging head wide-open."

Nolan ran his hand across his scalp and peered, unbelieving, at the blood on his palm. His eyes grew wide again, then slitted as he stared at Dana. He said nothing, but his movements were cold and deliberate as he gathered his feet under him and rose up, crouching, his arms spread wide in a wrestler's stance. Blood ran in a trickle into his eyebrow and spilled over down his cheek.

He circled Dana watchfully, measuring the distance, while the smaller man turned with him, on the balls of his feet, waving the club back and forth, slowly, like a snake's head.

Feet were pounding toward them and a voice yelled hoarsely, "Corporal of the Guard! Post number three!" A rifle fired twice, but neither Nolan nor Dana disengaged his eyes.

Then two helmeted troopers were thrusting between them, their rifles at port arms. "Drop that club, guy," one of them warned Dana, and he let it slip through his fingers.

"All right, get out of here," Nolan told the guards, his chest heaving massively, his eyes still on Dana. "This was just a little fight. It's all over now."

The troopers eyed each other questioningly. Dana could see that both of them were willing to let the matter drop. He knew no line soldier pulling guard duty wants to get anyone in trouble. But the sergeant of the guard came sprinting up sleepy-eyed and angry over being awakened. He was a tough platoon guide out of A Company, with little love for Nolan. He would have to explain to the officer of the day just why two rounds had been fired. "All right, Nolan, just shut your mouth," he said, "until I get the O.D. over here."

"I was just breaking up a fight, Mack," Nolan told him, wiping blood from his cheek with the back of his hand. "This is my company—just company business. You forget about it."

"Balls," the guard sergeant said. He pointed at Carroway. "This man has blood coming out of his ear. He may have a skull fracture. It's got to be reported."

They hustled Dana away under guard, on charge of assaulting a non-com.

He wondered now if Carroway was seriously hurt, if that was the reason for Nolan's arrest. He pinched the spark from his cigarette and tucked the butt away and closed his eyes.

"Don't go to sleep, you chicken-gutted Okie," Nolan said. "Don't ever go to sleep when I'm around. I might just decide to cold-cock you in your sack."

"Screw you, Nolan," Dana told him, not opening his eyes. But his muscles tautened and his ears were straining for the sound of Nolan's rush. He would always lie tensed now when Nolan was there; there would be no respite.

"You studs must have tangled." That was Cadillac's voice—soft, indifferent, and just a little bored.

"Not yet," Nolan said. "Preliminary skirmish. When we tangle, you'll know it by the guts on the ground."

"You spill guts, sergeant? Break heads and all that? You hassle rough that way?" His tone was light and drily unimpressed.

"You want proof, trooper?" Dana heard the cot creak as Nolan swung to face the slim and arrogant city-boy.

"No proof, Sergeant. I take your word. I was wondering if that's why you're in the slammer. They put you here for breaking heads?"

You never asked a prisoner what landed him in jail, until he volunteered to tell. That was the one, inviolate, unwritten law of prisons. Dana had a feeling that Cadillac knew it, that he was somehow trying to relieve the pressure, to divert the top-kick's wrath.

The cot creaked again as Nolan settled back. The question seemed to please him. "They put me here because I told them to go frig themselves. I dropped some fairy's ass and they busted me. I told them that I wouldn't jump in combat as a private. They want to make me change my mind. But they won't keep me long—you better believe it."

"Going to bust out, Sergeant? Just split like that?"

"Going to walk out, trooper, with my stripes still up. When the captain gets through to Colonel Tighe. There ain't but one man can run that company right, and the captain knows it. The colonel knows it too, so I'll just be waiting around a while."

"You so hot to get out of here and make that jump?"

The question came in a nasal drawl from the far corner of the tent, and carried with it a trace of Reb's own indecision.

"Frigging A," said Nolan. "I'm hot to get out." His inflection hardened. "But I got a little business in here first."

Dana sensed, almost tactilely, the thrust of Nolan's eyes, and this time, heartened by Cadillac's intervention, he opened his own and returned the stare. Swampy whistled, and Nolan turned to look at him. "I tell you boy, that ain't for me—that barrel-assin' into Normandy." Swampy's wet cackle was echoed, a little hesitantly, by his partner.

"What do you know, Sergeant—they got no eyes for combat." Cadillac directed Nolan's gaze from falling back on Dana. "These cats are lovers, man ... they ain't fighters." He rose gracefully and pointed at the snickering Swampy and his sullen friend. "Let me introduce you, Sergeant. These are the James boys from Company D and the swamps of Mississippi. Reb and Swampy James—no relation, except by disease—and they'd rather frig than fight."

"Why, hell," chortled Swampy squatting on his cot, "Ol' Reb here is a fighter born. Why that mean ol' coon-ass is the bare-hand pisshouse champion of lower Mississip'. I'll back him in a men's room against anyone you name, long as he can keep 'em kinda squeezed between the piss-bowls." He whinnied loudly and turned to his sidekick, " 'member them honkytonks in Hattiesburg, hey boy?"

Reb grinned back at him and spat at the floor. "Any two men in any ol' pisshouse," he affirmed.

"Now don't you believe that jazz, Sergeant," said Cadillac. "I'll hip you, man ... these studs are lovers. Lovers, nothing else. Why it was love that brought them here. Now, lay it on him straight, men."

Swampy doubled up with laughter, crackling through his nose. "Love, it was," he said. Nolan stared disgustedly and Dana smiled.

"Go, man—make it," Cadillac prompted. "Tell the sergeant here about your flaming passion." Swampy grinned modestly and launched into the details of the rape for which the two of them would be court-martialed. Nolan listened idly with a scowl of contempt and Cadillac winked at Dana. Dana felt himself yielding to a flood of relief—at the tacit alliance which Cadillac offered, at the half-formed hope that as the minutes fled, they might come to take Nolan back to his company, before he consummated his revenge.

The story was a rambling one, which Swampy recounted with obvious pride. They had met two girls in a local pub, and while Reb disposed of their escorts in the men's room, Swampy had hustled the girls outside. One was frightened and broke away, but the other, having drunk more beer, accompanied them to a field on the outskirts of town. Then, sobering probably, she had tried to break away from them.

"All of a sudden she acts pretty scared, like she wants to head on back. But ol' Reb, hell, he made her change her mind." Swampy's voice broke off and he and Reb exchanged a reminiscent smile.

Nolan, curious despite himself, asked curtly, "Well? And afterwards?"

Swampy said it slowly, his eyes soft with nostalgia: "Afterwards it was pretty nice, now wasn't it, Reb, hey boy?"

"Red pants she had, that l'il ol' babe," said Reb and chuckled softly. "We kept them awhile, and then we throwed 'em away."

"I asked you what happened afterwards," Nolan said.

"Weren't nothin' happened," Swampy said reproachfully. "We headed back to garrison and didn't say nothin'. Then a couple-three days later they had this formation. And the babe comes up with two M.P.'s and some brass from division, and they walk her up and down. She's got this here veil on so you can't see her face, or it might have been embarassin' for her."

"On account of them l'il red pants," Reb said, and snickered.

"That jive's a little different from the tale the M.P.'s tell," said Cadillac to Nolan. "The way I heard the bit, the chick is all veiled up because they got her taped in bandages."

Reb replied defensively, "Well, Swampy was in a hurry. We didn't hardly get enough beer in the babe. If we'd have waited a while at the bar like I said..."

"Well, hell, you ol' coon-ass," said Swampy, and pursed his lips contentedly. "It was worth it now, weren't it? And we got out'n this combat jump."

Cadillac turned again to Nolan, like a circus impresario demanding applause for his featured performers. "You dig, man?" he smiled over an upturned palm. "The lover boys. That's their kick: *they got to club it down.* No one hipped them you can get it any other way."

Nolan made no comment, but stared across the tent with ice in his hard, gray eyes. "You smiling, Okie, with that crap-eatin' grin? Something strike you funny?"

Dana heard him rise, and he opened his eyes. The sergeant was advancing toward him with slow, measured steps. "I don't ever want to see you smile again. You hear me, Okie? Nolan swept his arm to brush Cadillac from his path, and the gesture slowed him just enough for Dana to spring tensely to his feet.

He had dropped his guard too easily, been lulled to forgetfulness while Cadillac baited the James boys. He backed against the cot, his eyes intent on Nolan's. Nothing in his face betrayed his inward panic, but he groped back with his hand for the wooden cross-slat at the head of his cot, and calculated swiftly his chance of working it loose before Nolan launched himself.

Nolan feinted abruptly with his left, and Dana, springing back, tripped over the cot and sprawled across it awkwardly.

Cadillac said suddenly, "Hey, guard, come here," and Nolan whirled to face the entrance. A helmeted head came through the flap and looked questioningly around the tent.

"About time for chow, Kirby. How about it?" Cadillac said with nonchalance. "I was wondering when we scoff."

"You feed when we feed you, Kadillius," said the guard, and he stared at Nolan and the prostrate Dana. "What the hell's going on?" he asked.

"Nothing that you need to know," Nolan spat. "Get your lard-ass out of here."

The guard was an M.P. from Division, aware of Nolan's size but not his reputation. He measured the big man with a thoughtful gaze and shifted his rifle to a high, aggressive port. Like most airborne M.P.'s, he was tall and hard himself. "A busted top-kick, and he's lipping off. You forgetting where you are now, soldier?" He moved inside the tent and took a step towards Nolan.

"First time I ever blew the whistle in my life," Cadillac said softly to Dana, helping him up. "Hope I didn't bug you, man— hollering for fuzz." Dana grinned.

Nolan faced the guard and drove the words like bullets. "I told you once to take off, sonny. Now move out fast, before they drag you out." His hands were on his hips and his deep chest labored heavily with anger.

The guard stood his ground, trying to face Nolan down. "You're a yardbird now," he said. "A prisoner. You're not a ser-geant and you're not a jumper. Now take them trousers out of your boots." Nolan's face grew red with rage. "Go on, move," the guard insisted.

"Take them out yourself," said Nolan, thrusting one foot forward. "Go on, sonny. Try it."

Except for Cadillac, the others sat on their cots, straining forward tensely. Cadillac touched the guard on his shoulder. The guard spun around and glared at him.

"About this chow scene, dad," said Cadillac. "Maybe you've forgotten ..."

"Shut your mouth, wise guy," the guard snapped, and turned back to Nolan.

Nolan's voice was velvet-soft now, and his eyes were narrow slits. "Go on, touch my boots, boy. Just touch them with one finger and I'll take that popgun and ram it up your tail so hard, they'll plant you at attention."

It might have been the softness, or the look in Nolan's eye, but the guard drew back and shuffled his feet and retreated toward the entrance. "We got ways to handle guys like you," he said. "We got ways to cut you down to size."

Nolan laughed and sparked a roar of laughter from the others. The guard's eyes swept nervously around the tent.

"Now, about my question, Kirby—" Cadillac began.

"I told you to shut your mouth," the guard snarled.

Outside they heard the tinkle and the clash of messgear. "Never mind," said Cadillac. "Forget it. You're dismissed."

The guard backed out of the tent, looking warily back at them.

CHAPTER FOUR

D MINUS ONE, 1300 HOURS

"All right," the M.P. corporal said. "You've had your chow. Now wash those mess kits and hand them to the guard." Kirby stood beside him with another M.P.

Dana led the group down the row of twenty-five-gallon drums. As prisoners, they brought up the rear of the chow line, and the water now hovered near the boiling point. One by one they dipped their kits into the steaming disinfectant and handed them to Kirby.

Nolan was the last in line. As he thrust his gear at Kirby, the guard bellowed, shot back and did a little one-legged dance of pain, clutching at his kneecap. Beneath his shaking hand the wet patch of trouser leg emitted tendrils of steam. The mess kits in his other hand crashed to the ground. Nolan had brought his canteen cup out of the last drum, filled with scalding water.

The corporal glared at Nolan and then at the dirty gaggle of gear on the ground. Nolan's bruised lip curled mirthlessly. "All right, Kirby," the corporal said, "now wash that gear yourself. I got to get these yardbirds over to the adjutant."

He swung back to the prisoners. "Uh—right *face*. Foe—warrrd…. *Harch!*" The short column moved off toward headquarters, the scowling corporal in the lead. Nolan smiled to himself as he walked a step ahead of the other M.P. who bore his rifle at a watchful port and eyed him with distrust.

They were halted at the entrance to the operations tent. "Prisoner detail for Lieutenant Edgerton," the corporal said.

The sentry disappeared inside the tent. The corporal, redundantly, gave them "at ease". Except for the eager Hollister, there was no one standing at attention.

Dana gazed around him with country-boy interest a line soldier always manifests at Regiment or higher commands. A hum of earnest talk drifted to him from the clustered tents, and beneath the rolled-up flaps he could see the boots and jump-suit trouser-legs moving busily around the sand tables.

A trailer jeep was parked a short way down the street, its occupants watching them curiously. A clumsy, round-faced man leaned against the trailer and examined them with nervous eyes. The man behind the wheel of the jeep seemed to find the prisoners amusing. Beneath his helmet, the strange Eurasian face split in a sudden grin. He said something softly to the trooper beside him.

The other nodded with a brief, pre-occupied smile. He was trim-built, tall, with clean good looks. Dana liked him on sight.

All three were strangers and wore on their shoulders, instead of the Screaming-Eagle patch, the Double-A of the 82nd Airborne.

Swampy shifted nervously from foot to foot. "What's the deal?" he asked of no one in particular. We got no more business with the Five-Oh-Goose. We're supposed to go to the Litchfield Stockade."

"How about it, Sergeant?" Cadillac said to Nolan. "What's it all about?" For the first time his fine-boned, insolent face betrayed some lack of ease.

Nolan shrugged and stared ahead of him at the operations tent.

The sentry finally emerged from the tent followed by a first lieutenant. The corporal barked, "De—tail. Ten ... *hut!*"

Lieutenant Edgerton nodded and said, "At ease." He coughed into his hand. *Should he smile at them winningly right away, or save that for later and eye them sternly with a martial no-non-sense glare.* All morning Edgerton had steeled himself for this, telling himself firmly that this guardhouse crew would act like any other group of men, that he must not invest them with an aura of evil. But now in the six pairs of eyes that met his, he was sure he faced a wall of hard recalcitrance. He groped for a way to begin.

He drew a breath and plunged forward. "Well, you men, I've got good news for you. You're going to jump with your buddies after all!"

He offered them a smile of encouragement. Only Dana and Hollister seemed to react, and their faces were not exactly radiant.

Edgerton shifted his approach to the James boys. "That's right, men. You're getting another chance. And if you come through like real troopers, I think I can promise you that ... uh ... the slate will be wiped clean. Your past indiscretions will be forgiven. Forgiven and forgotten."

Edgerton put his hands behind his back and rocked on his heels, still beaming cheerfully at the wooden faces of Reb and Swampy. "I bet it will be a big relief to get those "P's" off your backs, eh, boys?"

A faint stir, which Edgerton chose to interpret as a sign of gratitude and hope renewed, moved through the ranks. He clasped his hands in front of him and rubbed them together briskly. "As of this moment, all of you are restored to duty and to jump-pay. We've drawn your jump-suits and weapons and packs. You can blouse your pants again and hold your heads up, and even ..." He made a reedy noise to indicate the laughter of complicity. "... even start saluting again."

Edgerton waited for the laugh that never came. He had planned that last line as the ice-breaker. The men stared at him stolidly except for the big first sergeant, and he wondered dimly if the sergeant's lip was curled that way by bruises only.

"Very well," he said in a firmer voice, falling back on the curt military intonation. "You'll be jumping with me on a special mission." He saw a shorter, thicker shadow move up beside his own on the-ground. That would be Mungo, the hugely squat, direct-eyed staff sergeant from the 82nd, coming from the tent to stand beside him.

A small sound of surprise escaped from Nolan's lips. The adjutant threw a hurried glance at Mungo from the corner of his eye. Mungo merely stood there, massively at ease, his heavy belly forward and impassive eyes fixed on the men.

"We'll be a small group," Edgerton went on. "Only a reconnaissance patrol." He tried the line which, in his mind's rehearsal hall, had elicited the second, enthusiastic laugh. "So you see, there'll be plenty of glory for everyone."

The faces in front of him were six wooden masks, betraying no reaction. He'd imagined it differently—a confused image of manly laughter and even cheers. He brushed off an odd and unfamiliar feeling of inadequacy, noticing that the eyes of the men were no longer front, but fixed on Mungo. Well, the sergeant did have a certain magnetism. "And here," he said abruptly, "is Sergeant Mungo, to brief you on the details."

Dana watched the slim officer turn gracefully and accept the sergeant's casual salute. Lieutenant Edgerton, known as Edge the Adj, had that well-groomed, moneyed-father, campus look that set Dana's teeth on edge.

The sergeant was something else again. The power that you felt in him was his alone, and not dependent on his status or the system behind him.

He stood there, relaxed, almost indolent, measuring the men. His arms were long, his hands enormous. From the squat bull-neck, down the bulky, sloping shoulders, to the ponderous, fat-armored gut that hung above his belt, there was nothing of the athlete about Sergeant Mungo. And yet, when he swung forward to approach the men, he moved with a sort of hulking grace that bespoke absolute control and even speed if the occasion should demand it.

Not even Dana's status-conscious mind could correlate Mungo with a civilian caste. This was a soldier—nothing more.

Nolan moved to meet him with a broad, delighted grin. "Hell, if it ain't old Mungo." He clapped the other ringingly on the back. "I've soldiered with this bastard all over the Phillipines," he roared. "Never thought I'd find you in the jump troops, Mungo. I thought you were in the straight-pants infantry."

Mungo fixed him with a flat and lazy gaze. His eyes were veiled and neutral. They drifted over Nolan with no flicker of interest or any sort of feeling. Nolan said, with his grin a little frozen, "Hell, you remember me, Sarge, from the old P.I. days."

"I remember you," Mungo said. "Take off them stripes." His voice was a rumbling bass without inflection. He turned to the M.P. corporal and guard who hovered near the group. "You two," he said tonelessly, "take off running. We don't need you anymore." They nodded, edging back, and then moved off hurriedly down the regimental street.

Mungo's black eyes moved, with indifference it seemed, over each of the men. Dana found it hard to meet that hooded, sleepy stare. "All right, you men," Mungo told them softly, "draw your gear and weapons from that trailer over there. Fall back here in ten minutes with your field equipment on."

"Hold it, Sergeant." Cadillac strolled forward with an amiable smile. "Someone got their signals crossed. I told them I'm not jumping."

Mungo looked at him impassively. "You qualified?" he asked.

"Parade-ground jumper, Sergeant. I'm the cat who chickened out. I'm a refusal—waiting on a General Court."

Mungo took a quick step forward, drove his big fist suddenly—you hardly saw the movement—into the pit of the slim boy's stomach. As Cadillac, grunting, doubled forward, the sergeant cuffed him, bearlike, with an open palm. The sound was sharp, like paper slapped against a wall, and Cadillac went spinning to the ground.

The men were shocked and silent; nobody moved. The blinding speed with which the big, sluggish-looking man had struck, awed them as much as the brutality.

Then Dana bent to help Cadillac up. Mungo ignored them both and continued: "The people with the trailer are going with you. They'll show you what to take and get you squared away. When you're back in formation here, I'll brief you on the job. It's no dry run, so get your asses moving."

"Wait a minute, Mungo," Nolan said, in a hard and grating voice. "You think you're going to jump me as a private?"

"They busted you, didn't they? That's your rank."

Nolan started to say something, but Mungo cut him short. "I need an assistant, Nolan. You're a jawbone corporal, as of now. Now get these Geronimos over to the jeep and see they put their pants on frontwards, and then get them back to the operations tent." Without waiting for an answer, Mungo turned on his heel and walked away.

Cadillac, with his hand to his stinging ear, watched the sergeant's broad, retreating back. He grinned sardonically at Dana. "The top gorilla, man," he said. "They really pick 'em hairy in this club."

"Looks like you're jumping, buddy," Dana said.

Cadillac shook his head. "Not this cat, dad." His eyes were narrowed and his features set with resolute assurance. "They can haul me to the plane, but they won't get me in. No muscle-ape is big enough to get me in that plane."

"All right, damnit," Nolan bellowed, happily in authority again. "Get over to the trailer and get into your jump-suits. You heard what the sergeant said, so move your asses."

Dana followed the others over to the jeep. Their faces were still blank with astonishment at the brutal suddenness of Mungo's act. It absorbed what should have been the greater shock, their abrupt removal from the guard tent and assignment to a combat mission.

The 82nd men climbed down from the vehicle and joined them at the trailer. Bundled jump-suits lay scattered on the trailer bed, each ticketed with its owner's name. Webbing, packs and weapons were similarly labeled, the men in the companies having been careful to prepare whatever their absent friends might need, with that tender solicitude that field soldiers show toward a buddy in the guardhouse.

Dana rummaged in the trailer and found his combat clothing. Two jump-suits were there; one of them, which he had turned in several weeks before, was stiff and acrid-smelling with an unfamiliar chemical. He held it up distastefully. Beside him, Reb demanded in an outraged voice: "What in hell's this whore-smelling stuff on my jump-suit?"

"Gas-impregnate," said the slight, oriental-looking trooper. "You're supposed to wear both suits in case the Krauts are using gas."

"Both of them? To hell with that," Reb snorted angrily. "You ain't wearin' no pregnant suit."

The trooper shrugged, his helmet cocked back on his head. "You're supposed to," he grinned indifferently, the tone implying: suit yourself. All but Hollister threw the foul-smelling second suits back into the trailer.

The grinning trooper watched Dana tear away the label with his name. "You Bob Dana?" he asked, handing him his musette bag.

"That's my name."

"Mine is Sacco. Got a message for you from the people in your section." His voice was light, but easy, and totally assured. His slightly slanted eyes had a constant twinkle-quizzical, amused, as though some secret inner merriment colored his every perception of the world. His skin was olive and his nose snubbed; the broad, high cheekbones, and tilted almond eyes gave his face a quasi-Asiatic look.

"What they have to say?" Dana asked, in a carefully uncaring voice, removing his boots to slip his feet into the stirrups of the baggy jump-pants. Inwardly he felt a rush of warmth at the thought of hearing from the men in his company, who, in eighteen months of field and barracks kinship, had come to represent both home and family to him.

Sacco's face bore the faintest suggestion of a smile. "They said to tell you Carroway'll be all right. Also they said to thank you. They sort of like you over there. Something you did for all of them."

Dana nodded, repressing a sentimental grin. He zipped up his jacket and buckled on his webbing, already hung with his canteen, bayonet, first-aid kit and entrenching tool.

"There was something else," Sacco said, handing over the ticketed M-1 rifle. "They said to kill the bastard—put a bullet through his head." This time Dana smiled.

"The 'big mean bastard', I think they said. That him over there?" Sacco pointed nonchalantly at the massive Nolan who, already in his jump clothes, was shrugging into his webbing with the unneeded help of the round-faced trooper who had earlier been squatting near the jeep.

Dana said, "That's him, all right. That's who they mean."

"Looks big," said Sacco. "Is he all that mean?"

"He's mean," said Dana. "What's the story on this guy Mungo?"

Sacco's face was inscrutable, but something brightened the glint of secret amusement in his eye. "Mungo," he said, "he's a different breed." He cocked his helmet even further back on his head. "He's rugged, now. He isn't mean. When he walks, he walks; when he sits, he sits. He doesn't wobble. After you know him you'll see what I mean."

"Know him pretty well, do you?" Dana bent to ladder-lace his boots.

"I was with him all the way in the Eighty-second. He bounced a captain at Anzio and took over his company. He sent him to the rear with his hands tied behind his back."

Dana couldn't conceal his surprise. "Took over a company?"

Sacco's crinkled pixy eyes betrayed a puckish admiration for the ways of Sergeant Mungo. "Well, it was something that he figured ought to be done. They gave us both a hard time about it later. Shipped us out of the outfit."

"Why you?" Dana asked.

"I was the guy he had boot the captain all the way to the rear."

"Sounds like quite a man, this Mungo," Dana said, a little skeptically. He could not erase the memory of the burly sergeant's vicious punch at Cadillac. One Nolan riding his back was enough. If anything, this Mungo seemed more domineering, more brutally assertive of authority.

Sacco grinned at him. "Quite a man," he said laconically. "When he's around, you know about it."

Dana said nothing. He slipped his helmet on and slung the rifle over his shoulder. He tightened the canvas cartridge belt. Although he would not have admitted it to anyone, and least of all himself, the strong, taut weight of weapon and equipment slung around his body, was pleasurable. After his spell as a prisoner, it was almost like buckling on his manhood again.

Both of them turned at Swampy's indignant yelp. The gangling southerner was rummaging angrily through the discarded fatigues in the trailer. "All right," he howled accusingly, "Who lifted my canteen?"

The blond, good-looking 82nd man, whom Dana had seen earlier talking to Sacco, pointed out a canteen on the pile of impregnated jump-suits. "It ain't mine," insisted Swampy. "I want my own canteen."

Cadillac laughed. "What's the matter, Swampy? Afraid of catching some disease?"

Swampy's face was screwed up in rage and he brandished his rifle as he snarled at the group. "All right, which one of you beetle-headed jokers light-fingered my canteen?"

The men looked at each other, perplexed by his anger, until Hollister, unhooking his canteen from his belt, said, "Maybe this is yours." He looked at it. "Yeah. I was wondering why the fellers filled it up."

Swampy snatched it from him and hefted it, then shook it up and down. "Yeah, that's mine," he said reproachfully. "You watch yourself boy. Don't be screwin' with any of my stuff."

Dana noticed that he carried it around the jeep and squatted on the far side, away from the men, to unscrew the top and smell the contents. He seemed satisfied and even gay when he rejoined the group.

The men were dressed now, and a single question seemed to occupy their minds. Hollister was the first to voice it: "Hey, what kind of a guy is this Mungo?"

The round-faced man, helping Nolan slip the stubby 45-caliber cartridges into his Thompson magazines, answered the boy but seemed to direct the words tentatively at Nolan. "I don't know, kid. He acts pretty tough. But he's getting old, I figure, and he kinda runs to fat. I think he does a lot of bluffing." His eyes appraised Nolan as though probing for complicity, nervously gauging the big man's reaction.

"You can always spot the bluffers, can't you Uhlan?" Sacco asked him drily.

The round-faced trooper thrust his heavy jaw forward. "I was only telling the kid what I thought. The top-kick here can tell you. He knows Mungo from way back."

"First of all, I'm not a top-kick anymore," said Nolan gruffly. Dana noticed that someone in the company had already removed the stripes from Nolan's sleeves before sending the jump-suit over. "And Sergeant Mungo is a damned good non-com. You frigging well better do what he says. And to get it straight right now, I'm here to back him up, all along the line."

"Oh, sure he's a good non-com," Uhlan said quickly. "Used to be a first sergeant, too, I've heard. All the good top-kicks get busted now and then." He glanced at Nolan with a nervous smile, but Nolan ignored him, stolidly stowing his clips away in the magazine pouches on his belt.

"How about it, man?" Cadillac addressed the question to the trim, blond trooper who had not said anything up to then. "You known this gorilla very long?"

"I don't know much about him," the boy answered quietly. "Only met him in the casual pool down here. I haven't been with the outfit since Sicily."

Uhlan laughed harshly. "Since before Sicily, is what you mean, Carr. You never even got a look at Sicily."

Carr fixed him with his frank, blue eyes, which looked like motionless pools that stand without a ripple, yet are troubled in their depths by powerful, silent, underwater battles. His face was calm, his mouth creased with little lines of resolution or concealed hurt. "That's right, Uhlan," he said. "I never saw Sicily." He turned back to Cadillac, adding briefly, "I think he'd be a good man to follow in combat."

Cadillac laughed mirthlessly. "I ain't going into combat. Not behind that gorilla or anybody else. He's not snowing me with that muscle bit."

Carr shrugged his shoulders and turned away. Sacco slapped him lightly on the back, and Carr looked at him with a calm and thoughtful face.

"All right, you men," roared Nolan. "Let's cut out the yakking and get back to the tent. You got your equipment now, so let's get mobile." He turned and led the way back to the war room.

The blond boy's reticence intrigued Dana. There was something in Carr that attracted him, but his life had taught him to respect a stranger's silence and to guard against thrusting his friendship on anyone. "What's the story on that boy?" he asked Sacco as they walked together toward the tent. Somehow you felt that you could ask anything of Sacco, as though nothing, in his eyes, could be serious or sacred, or worthy of more than a quizzical smile.

"Lord Jim, you mean?" asked Sacco. ,

"That his name?"

"His name is Wall Carr. He's a radio man. He was born to be a hero but he got fouled up—cheated out of the chance. He needs a fresh deck, that's all. He'll come out on top. Good man to have around."

Dana nodded, feeling somewhat better about the forthcoming jump. He would have preferred, of course, to go in with his own company, but these men around him ought to measure up. He seemed to have found a friend in Cadillac—although that one, he reflected, was determined not to jump. And except for the sycophantic Uhlan, he liked these troopers from the 82nd. They had all seen combat, but surprisingly enough, didn't throw their weight around to impress the still battle-green Five-Oh-Goose men. Best of all, his problem with the vengeance-bent Nolan seemed to have been suspended for the moment, superceded by more serious considerations. As for Mungo—well, what the hell, he'd learn soon enough what sort of man the hulking sergeant was.

Mungo was waiting for them at the entrance to the war room, his squat bulk resting easily on wide-spread, chunky legs.

CHAPTER FIVE
D MINUS ONE,
1340 HOURS

Mungo's eyes moved with deceptive negligence over the men and their equipment. "All right," he said to Nolan. "Bring them inside and we'll get the party rolling."

He turned and brushed aside the canvas flap. Nolan led the men inside the long green tent. A large sand table stood at one end, and the walls were lined with detailed operation maps, their acetate overlays heavily grease-pencilled with unit symbols, arrows and perimeter lines. The faces of the men were suddenly solemn, impressed with the chill military fixtures—intricate, abstract and terribly distant from the world of flesh and flaming metal which these antiseptic symbols represented.

Lieutenant Edgerton and a captain were standing at the maps. Mungo called the men to attention and the captain waved them "at ease."

"This is Captain Stork, the regimental S-2," Edgerton said. "He's going to brief you on the overall plan—sort of give you the big picture, so you'll know where we fit in."

"Let's keep it quiet, men," the captain said. "you can smoke, but pay attention."

All but Cadillac stared at the maps, awed by their admission to high, strategic secrets. Cadillac leaned casually against a tent pole with a bored and placid look. He gazed idly about him, the plumes of smoke curling thinly from his nostrils.

Edgerton walked briskly to the door and drew the canvas flap shut as the captain lifted a long wooden pointer and moved to the largest 1/200 map.

"This is Normandy, men—the Cotentin peninsula. That's Cherbourg on the tip up north and here are the invasion beaches. Utah Beach, the one that we defend." The pointer traced a circle inland, a flat area delineated by a curving river. "Here is where the division drops—to seize the roadways inland for the seaborne troops, to establish a defense line all along this river, and to keep the Krauts from pushing reinforcements to the beachhead."

The captain moved to another map: a large scale blow-up of the land behind the beaches. The overlay was penciled with unit symbols—their own, and some in red with unfamiliar numbers. The pointer moved along the river. By now they recognized its curve. "Now our regiment will be on the flank, holding the whole southeastern bend of this Douve River line. This map will give you some idea of what we're coming up against."

His pointer flicked across the area. "This is what we figure the Krauts will have against us here. The Seven-Oh-Nine in static beach defence. Don't worry about them; they're low-quality foreign troops. They probably won't put up much of a fight. The Ninety-first. Now that's another matter. They're good troops. New in the area. Probably have a battalion of tanks."

There was a quick, reflexive sucking in of breath. The captain smiled and went on in a casual tone. "Well, we'll find out if those bazookas are worth anything. Now, further west, between Utah and Omaha..."

His pointer danced across the Douve, down a roadway, across another river—Dana read the name "Vire" and committed it to memory—to a little town called Isigny. "Across here, we don't know. The Three-hundred-fifty-second Kraut Division may be waiting there. It's a tough division, one of their best. It may be somewhere else, in reserve down south where it won't give us any trouble. Even if it is at Isigny, it may turn northeast to Omaha Beach and give them headaches there. But it may—now, this concerns you men—come west along this road towards Utah, and hit us on our flank, cutting the regiment right off."

He paused a moment while the men tried desperately to assimilate the details. "Now, supposing we move over to the sand table and let Lieutenant Edgerton explain the mission of your own patrol."

Silently they filed across the room and formed around the table. Dana stared at the contoured sand, the geometric network of sparse, straight roads. He focused on the road that ran south from the invasion beach, west across the Douve, and then across the Vire to Isigny. *"A division that may or may not be there ..."* He guessed how much that would mean to them in the dark night which lay ahead.

Lieutenant Edgerton cleared his throat and the pointer danced across the table. "Now you'll notice, men, that behind the beaches the land is flat, below sea level. Swampland mainly, and the only way across it is on these roads and causeways. That's why it's so important that we take them right away—both to deny them to German reinforcements, and to give our seaborne troops an egress from the beach. The Five-Oh-Goose will hold them, and hold this river line, and seize the locks on the Douve, right here, so the enemy can't flood the area." He noticed, not without a certain pleasure, that this time the men seemed utterly absorbed.

"Now, across the Douve—listen carefully—" His pointer traced the road westward to the Vire and centered there. "There may be, as the captain said, a strong enemy concentration about here. If they came down this road, where, as you can see, they'd hit the causeways between us and the beaches, roll up the flank and cut the Five-Oh-Goose to pieces.

"Now, to guard against this, the regiment needs a reconnaissance patrol. To keep that Isigny road under observation, far enough east of the Douve to give the warning in time." The pointer jumped back to the bridge across the Vire. "Right here, about eight miles from the regimental drop zone."

Even on the miniature sweep of the sand table, the distance seemed enormous ... eight miles out from the nearest friendly troops. Dana could guess what was coming next. The pointer kept circling around that bridge. "And that's our job, men. There's a little village here, Sainte-Madeleinesur-Vire, and an old stone bridge where the causeway hits the river. Just southwest of the village there are empty fields and hedgerows—that's going to be our drop zone. We'll set up an outpost in the village and make sure that nothing comes up that road without Regiment and Division knowing about it. Nothing can move through the swamps around the village or the hedgerow country to the south, so whatever comes through, it will be on that road."

Mungo seemed to stiffen. He took his eyes from the table and stared flatly at the lieutenant. Edgerton, unperturbed, went on: "Now, we'll be in radio contact with Regiment, and have another set netted in with Division. The job is so important that we'll even have a pigeoneer for messages back to First Army." He paused for a moment to let the significance of that sink in.

"What's that village, again?" Dana whispered.

"Sainte-Madeleine," Sacco said. "Bound to be all right. She's the patron saint of whores."

Edgerton continued: "Now, that division may not be there— but if they're at Isigny and moving west, our report will get the Air Corps on them, and the seaborne artillery, and even ..." He paused impressively. "Even naval gunfire from off-shore battleships."

He stopped talking and enjoyed the hushed solemnity of the men. After a moment he finished briskly: "That's it, men. I have to get back to Colonel Tighe. While I'm gone, I want you men to study the terrain until you're sure you'll know your way around in the dark. Sergeant Mungo will brief you on your individual jobs and answer any other questions you might have."

Mungo called the men to attention, but although technically under arms indoors, he did not bother to salute. Edgerton and the captain left the tent, Edgerton carefully pulling the tent flap closed behind him.

"All right," Mungo said, in his deep and toneless bass. "You heard what the lieutenant said. Now let's be sure you got it straight. You there, Hollister. Do you remember what our mission is?"

The wide-eyed soldier swallowed nervously. "To jump near this bridge, about eight miles from the regiment, and to see that nothing comes down the road without getting word to headquarters."

"No," said Mungo flatly. "Let's make it simple. We're gonna see that nothing comes down that road."

He stepped closer to the table and beckoned the men around him. "Now, this is how we're gonna do it …"

CHAPTER SIX

D MINUS ONE, 2000 HOURS

The weather had broken, the clouds were low, and in the lingering, rain-hazed English dusk, the marching men were bathed in an opalescent light, like figures under water.

The mile-long, double column ahead of them curved around a hill, then reappeared in the distance, snaking down the winding Devonshire road. All along its length men were chattering and smoking. Dana had never seen a route march like it. The regiment was noisy, exhilarated. Even the officers who marched between the columns were laughing and bantering; there was shouting back and forth between platoons and companies as they moved toward the airstrip.

As the bulbous cargo planes came into view, specially painted for the mission with broad white recognition stripes, companies began peeling from the column. Men broke ranks to dash over for a last quick handshake with a friend, a meaningful tap on the shoulder.

Dana felt a resurgence of loneliness, a longing for the faces of Headquarters Company, First Battalion. The past eighteen months had been spent acquiring the feel of that outfit. He knew the men and understood them; those he could count on and the ones he must support. Now he was cut off from them, perhaps forever, with only Sacco's laconic message to assure him that he was remembered. He was marching to the planes, and to the dark ordeal of battle, with a bastard patrol. He felt like an orphan among strangers, and he ached with a lonely nostalgia that he had not known since childhood.

Mungo had fallen the patrol in at the tail of the marching regiment. A bubble of isolation surrounded the dozen men with whom Dana hiked into the war; as palpable as the walls of the guard tent, it had settled around them since the briefing, sealing them off from the regiment and all community with other men. They were linked together now, on this maverick patrol, by stronger bonds than friendship or familiarity.

The planes on the airstrip stood far from the road, and Dana somberly marched past his outfit without recognizing one face in the gathering dusk. There was no one to call to, no one to whistle and wave back at him. If he died tonight, he would die among strangers.

He wondered if the others felt the loneliness, too. Sacco marched ahead of him, making soft and desultory conversation with the quiet, blond boy, Carr, whom he called "Lord Jim." Cadillac, behind him, had said nothing on the march, except for one clipped comment as the planes appeared in view: "Hell, I'll make it for the walk. I aint getting in no plane."

On Dana's left, the gangling, shaven-headed swampy was singing thickly to himself. Dana recognized the rhythm of the infantry chant: "You had a good home, but you *left*—that's *right*, you *left*." Swampy kept shuffling his feet and missing his step to capture his own cadence.

In the rear, Uhlan aimed a steady monologue at Nolan. "Well, now these rookies are going to earn their pay, eh, Sarge? They're going to find out what soldiering means. Right?" Nolan grunted sullenly, "Yeah, that's right." Uhlan, reassured, went on, "Yeah, they got to face it now. The Krauts are going to separate the men from the boys, right?"

Reb marched, head down, silent. Beside him Hollister's eager voice addressed itself to no one and everyone: "Hey, what did you think of Colonel Tighe's speech, fellows? I mean, some of it was crap, I guess, but it made me feel pretty good. He's right, too. We *are* the 'best-trained, bestarmed, best-led, toughest fighting men the world has ever seen.' And that part about the German army—they can't be so tough. Colonel Tighe is right. We're only jumping on a bunch of guys whose grandfathers didn't have the guts to immigrate to America like ours did." Reb cast him a dour, disgusted look from the corner of his eye.

The last company before them was turning off the road now, to a final squadron dispersed on the hard-stand. Mungo led them further down the road to a solitary C-47, crouched like an afterthought on a strip of perforated landing-mats.

His wide back rolling as he walked, like a trailer truck swaying on its springs, Mungo barked, "Column *right ... Harch.*" His commands of execution snapped out sharp and clear as a drummer's rim shot, moving their feet for them.

As they wheeled toward the plane, a few faces in the last file of the preceding company swiveled back and stared at them—unrecognizing, blankly curious. No ganglia of friendship or of shared experience seemed to connect a single man of their patrol to the organism of the regiment.

Mungo rumbled, *"Dee-*tail—*Halt!"* He pointed to a row of parachutes lying under the wing of the plane. "There's your chutes," he said. "Get into 'em." He turned to stare up at the plane, his hands resting lightly on his hips. A neatly-spaced row of machine-gun punctures ran up its fuselage and over the rounded top. One of the engines seemed to sag from its cowling. The men eyed the ship uneasily. It was the most decrepit C-47 any of them had ever seen.

Then a roar of outrage rose from Swampy. "Look at these damn chutes!" he cried. "They're all friggin' rejects!"

Startled, Dana stooped and picked up one of the heavy T-7 parachute assemblies. On the red pasteboard rigger's tag dangling from it, the bold printing read: TO BE REPACKED. The curses around him indicated that all the chutes were similarly tagged.

Mungo ambled over to Reb and glanced briefly at the tag. "Shut up!" he bellowed, and the men were hushed. "The riggers put those tags on all chutes. It's S.O.P. They repack every chute once a year or so, just to keep busy. They just didn't get around to this batch yet." His eyes moved lazily over the men, and his smile was almost gentle. "This ain't no honor-guard patrol, remember. They dreamed it up late and they scraped it from the bottom. So we take whatever they give us."

Holding the chute by the shoulder straps, Dana shook it dubiously. There was nothing to be learned about the state of the chute without opening it and going through the laborious business of repacking it.

"Pick 'em over and leave the worst one for me," Mungo said contemptuously "but get into them right now." He turned his back and moved to where the crew chief and the two young pilots stood, peering out the plane door at them.

"Hell," said Nolan, effortlessly hoisting a chute to his shoulder. "Cram one into a barracks bag—I'll jump one any old way."

It was an old familiar paratrooper's boast, but the others picked deliberately from amongst the chutes.

Mungo stared up at the Air Corps men. "This is your regular plane?" he asked. While he seldom used the "sir" in addressing any officer, these Air Corps lieutenants he patently regarded as something less than soldiers.

"No, we're casuals," the first lieutenant answered. He laughed nervously, as though apologizing for something to this rock of an infantryman.

Mungo nodded, indifferent. "Ever jump troopers?"

"Not yet, Sergeant. Flown some supply drops, though."

Dana heard Uhlan whinny despairingly. *Scraped from the bottom—on everything,* he thought.

"Okay," Mungo said. "I'll check you out on it." He reached up to the doorframe and vaulted lightly into the ship. The flyers, startled, leaped out of his path.

Dana laid the parachute pack carefully on one of the stringers of the improvised landing strip. He was surprised to see that a bazooka and two 30 caliber light machine guns lay near the stacked chutes. Nothing had been said in the Operations tent about taking heavy weapons with them. Theirs was to be a reconnaissance patrol, designed to gather information, not to inflict casualties.

Alongside the guns was a large supply of metal ammo boxes and two thickly-padded equipment bundles with their attached chutes. Apparently Lieutenant Edgerton had had some second thoughts about his patrol.

The folded antennae of two heavy SCR 300 radios jutted from the tops of two leg packs near the weapons. Dana hoped that he would not have to jump one of the awkward, bulky packs.

He field-stripped his rifle and stowed it away in the padded Griswold case. He noticed then, that Cadillac was merely dawdling with his gear. He stood there idly, his eyes cast down, turning his chute over with the toe of his boot.

Dana slipped on the deflated Mae West and hooked his musette bag across his belly, where the small reserve chute would lie across its straps. He lifted the parachute pack onto his back and worked his shoulders under the constricting arm-straps. He slipped the bellyband through the loops of his reserve chute and hooked the rifle container to his shoulder strap.

Mungo bounded out of the plane and came bulling his way through the cluster of men. "The belly racks aren't functioning," he announced. "We'll toss the bundles out the door." He swung to Sacco. "Did you get me that oh-three, Fortunato?"

"All organized, with rifle grenades. And two dry thirties, too."

Mungo bobbed his bullet-head approvingly. "You steal like a real soldier. I'll make a thirty-year man out of you yet."

"Balls," Sacco said. "I'm going to spend my life in a Japanese monastery."

Mungo had a cigar clenched between his teeth. He lifted each of the machine-gun barrels from their tripods, and worked the actions back and forth. He grunted satisfaction. "Doing what?" he asked Sacco.

"Sitting," Sacco said. "The regimental S-4 gave me some other stuff. Linseed oil and cocoa, for blackening our faces."

Mungo snorted. "All right, put this crap on, all of you. Won't do any good, but it'll keep the lieutenant happy."

"Here's something else," Sacco said, stretching out his hand. A dozen toy crickets lay in his hand—little metal noisemakers, painted with bullfrogs and grinning Donald Duck and Mickey Mouse heads. "I picked the prettiest ones for us."

"What the hell?" Mungo asked.

"You put them in your jump-knife pocket," Sacco said. He zipped open the little hidden pocket near the collar of his jump-jacket, dropped a cricket inside and clicked it briskly several times, squeezing it through the cloth. The sound was audible at a considerable distance, and it could not be readily imitated. "S-3 wants them used instead of a password for drop-zone recognition. If you see someone, click; if he doesn't click back, shoot him." He squeezed the gadget in his collar once again. "The paratroopers' mating call," he said.

Mungo looked at the cricket Sacco had dropped in his hand wonderingly for a long moment, shaking his massive head. "Okay, you men, draw your Mickey Mouses from Sacco here!"

Mungo snatched up the Springfield and worked the bolt. He caught the weapon by its balance and slipped the slung Thompson sub-machine gun from his shoulder. He looked around and seemed to notice for the first time that only Cadillac stood without a chute. "You, Kadillius. Come over here."

Cadillac moved warily toward him, his head high, his eyes intransigent, waiting for the showdown.

Mungo thrust the Thompson at him. "Put your M-1 with the stuff for that equipment bundle."

Cadillac stood blinking with his hands at his sides. "You want me to carry your Tommy-gun?" he asked.

"Yeah. It's yours now."

"Why?"

"You look like a Tommy-gunner to me."

Cadillac lowered his rifle slowly and took the proferred Thompson. He hefted it and began to smile. Nolan, who carried the group's only other Thompson as a badge of non-comissioned caste, walked over to the pair. "Wait. Have you been familiarized with that gun, Greek?"

"I'll familiarize him with it, if he ain't," Mungo said. His eyes probed Cadillac's. "What about it, Kadillius?"

Cadillac held the gun by its magazine, the butt against his hip. "I've fired them before," he said.

"Good," Mungo said. "You're our Tommy-gunner. Just bursts of three, remember. No James Cagney stuff. I'll teach you how to clean it later." He grinned at Cadillac and added, "Sometime in the morning."

Dana checked the rip cord of the emergency pack and snapped the cover closed. He noticed then that Cadillac was slipping morosely into his harness. Dana grinned at him. "Going for the ride?"

Cadillac shook his head. "No use hassling with that muscle-ape. I'll wait until we load, when he's got no time to argue." Cadillac strapped the Tommy-gun across his back, muzzle down. "I ain't getting into that plane."

Mungo called: "You're chuted up, Dana. Bring that empty leg-pack over here." Dana carried the padded sack and its coiled rope to where Mungo squatted over the loose equipment. He watched as the sergeant stuffed it with rifle grenades, coils of fuse and gray plastic oblongs of composition C-2. He wondered why a reconnaissance patrol would take explosives along. He framed the question, but looked at Sergeant Mungo and kept it to himself.

Mungo's hooded eyes flicked methodically over each of the men in turn. "Dana, you'll operate the radio on the regimental net. Carr's got the set for division." He closed the cover over the folded aerials and set the pack down.

Dana slid the pack onto his foot, and fastened the strap around his knee. Deftly, Mungo attached the rope to an eye on Dana's harness. Dana clumped a few tentative steps to see how the pack would ride on his leg. Now, in addition to his other woes, he would have this bulky forty-pound burden dragging on his leg when he fought his way to the door of the plane to jump.

On the drop he would be occupied not only with maneuvering his chute for the safest landing, but must also be careful to release the pack, kick it free of his leg and lower it down the length of the rope before he hit the ground. That meant he would be dragging a free-swinging anchor beneath him in the dark. If it curled around telephone or high-tension lines, he would be brought crashing down from a height of fifty feet or more.

Dana opened his musette bag for a pack of cigarettes and passed them to Sacco and Carr. He liked these two transfers from the 82nd, particularly the quiet, strong-seeming Carr. The handsome blond trooper had an air of self-containment, a sort of calm resolution that attracted Dana. He was certain the signalman could be relied on, and the phrase had a new intensity of meaning in the solemn moment of impending combat.

CHAPTER SEVEN

D MINUS ONE, 2100 HOURS

"Here's your rations for the next three days," Mungo shouted. "Don't eat it all at once." He threw several chocolate D-ration bars to each of them in turn, and they packed them away in their musette bags with the previous issue of three K-ration boxes. "And a little something extra you'll find more useful." He flipped a round object through the air to Dana. Dana grabbed for it and stiffened as the live fragmentation grenade hit his palm.

Mungo sent two of them sailing to each man. Uhlan fumbled and dropped one on the ground. He flung himself away from it. Nolan caught his arm, his voice contemptuous. "Take it easy, trooper. They're not armed until the pin is pulled." Uhlan's nervous gesture, like a spastic tic, was intrinsic to the man. It was somehow too embarassing for general laughter. Dana took his eyes away and looked back at Mungo.

The sergeant was back under the belly of the plane packing the equipment bundles. Swampy sat alone beneath the far wing, sucking from his canteen and humming to himself. Nolan walked over to watch the loading of the guns, Uhlan slouching behind him.

Uhlan craved reassurance that the Army meant to carry him through this D-Day ordeal safely. It gnawed at him that Edgerton was not here yet. The absence of higher authority filled him with superstitious dread. The adjutant's presence would prove to him that the general staff had not forgotten Pfc. Uhlan. Anxiously he asked Nolan: "Where the hell *is* that lieutenant?"

Nolan glanced at him uneasily. At first he had been flattered by the sycophancy of this round-faced, rugged-looking ex-fighter, seeing in it a tribute to what he thought of as his "quality of leadership." But the feeling had grown on him that Uhlan's fawning somehow lessened his stature.

Nolan found Mungo duck-walking out from under the plane, the cigar still clenched between his teeth. "Hey, Mungo. When's he getting here—Edge the Adj?"

The sleepy eyes seemed preoccupied. "Who cares? Who needs him?"

Nolan's jaw dropped. "Well, Christ—don't you? He's leading the mission, isn't he?"

Mungo paused to relight his cigar. "He's going along, if that's what you mean. You know the mission, don't you? Do you need a lieutenant, Nolan?"

Nolan shrugged his shoulders. "Yeah, what the hell" he drawled, larding his voice with casual indifference.

Uhlan drifted out to where Dana was sitting with Carr and Sacco under the wing tip. An old sense of peril swelled in Uhlan's chest. The dangers which loomed so large to him seemed to leave these other men unimpressed. They lacked something with which Uhlan was cursed; was it foresight? Imagination? The anxious knowledge of all that might go wrong? Not even Nolan had been willing to discuss the dire implications of Edgerton's absence.

He wondered if Nolan had penetrated him, seen something shameful and loathsome in him as so many others seemed to do.

Uhlan bit his lips and searched again for something inside him that would brace him as these other men were somehow braced. Hell, he was a veteran, and these kids were green. It was monstrous that these poor, dumb recruits should treat him with contempt just because he had seen more war than they. Even the doctors called what had happened to him 'battle fatigue.' Uhlan's self-pity turned instantly to wrath. They treated him, a seasoned combat soldier, as though he were a coward. And there was Carr, a proven coward if ever there was one, chatting comfortably with Sacco and that Okie.

The words were pressured out of him before he even willed them. His lips curled in a sneer, his tone was acid: "Are you going to jump tonight, Carr? Are you going to jump in France or hit that channel again?"

Dana saw the creases form around Carr's mouth, the look of careful self-containment grow somehow concentrated. Carr raised his eyes to Uhlan and stared at him, unblinking, gathering his feet under him slowly.

"Screw you, Uhlan," Sacco said. "Get out of here." The hand that fell on Carr's arm must have felt a stiffening of muscles. "Take it easy, Wally," he said.

Uhlan turned to Dana, raising his voice righteously. "He don't want to let you know about this guy. Carr refused the Sicily jump. He was transferred out of the Eighty-Second for being yellow!"

Dana could sense activity coming to a stop around them, and he knew every man in the patrol was listening to Uhlan. "Your lives might depend on him," Uhlan said. "You've got a right to know about him. He bailed out over the Mediterranean on the way up to Sicily. He saw the fleet down there, and he knew they'd pick him up. He didn't have the guts for a combat jump."

"Is that right, Carr?" Nolan towered over the seated men, his hands arrogantly on his hips.

"He sounds like a pretty hip stud to me." Cadillac grinned and winked at Dana.

"Shut up, Greek," Nolan growled at him. "I want this man to answer for himself."

Dana felt the old familiar rush of blood to his temples, and hot words formed inside him, forcing their way to his lips. Carr said softly to Nolan, "That's the way it was, more or less."

"All right, Carr." Nolan hammered out his words as he might have hammered nails into a cross, and Dana saw Carr's cheeks grow flushed. "I'm going to have my eyes on you, all the way. Make up your mind to it right now—you'll jump. You'll jump or I'll boot you out of the plane. That's the way I run an outfit."

"You ain't running this outfit, you muscle-bound fink," Dana spat at him. "Get off of him. Worry about that yellow streak you've got running down your own back."

Nolan bent swiftly. His big hands caught Dana's shoulder straps. He straightened, and his bent arms held Dana, parachute, equipment and all, in the air. Dana's toes were inches above the ground. Only the bulging cords of Nolan's neck betrayed the strain. "You draft-dodging Okie bastard, I'm going to put some fear in you!"

Dana's punch was constricted by the shoulder straps. Nolan jerked his head away from it. Dana hawked and spit a thick glob of phlegm into the snarling face below him.

Nolan dropped him on his heels with a bone-jarring thud. His hand balled into a huge fist. "You've got no pick-handle now, Dana!"

Mungo stepped between them with a look of bored impatience. His parachute still dangled from one gigantic paw. The heel of his hand struck Nolan's shoulder, rocking him off balance. He swung the parachute into Dana contemptuously. The smaller man almost fell under the blow.

"There's going to be no fighting in this detachment," Mungo said. He did not raise his voice, but his tone was flat, emphatic. "When they pull us back you can beat his head off every day, Nolan, and twice on Sundays. But not while we got a job to do."

He stood between them with his hands on his hips, watching them lazily, waiting to see how much resistance he must crush.

Dana's arm was numb where the heavy weight of the chute had crashed against it. Very suddenly, he was afraid of Mungo.

Nolan popped his huge fist into his palm and cracked the knuckles deliberately. "Fair enough, Mungo." I'm good at waiting."

"All right, Fortunato," Mungo rumbled. "These heroes want to know all about Carr. Tell 'em!"

Sacco looked up at the men with his usual faint smile. "Carr's all right," he said. "He's a friend of mine."

"What about that Sicily jump?" Nolan challenged.

"The jump was rough," said Sacco. "You heard about it, maybe. The Air Corps fouled up on their recognition signals with the Navy. Flew us over the fleet and the swabbies panicked. Shot down something like a third of our planes. In our ship we were standing all hooked up, ready to jump if the ack-ack caught us. Same in Wally's outfit—he was standing in the door. He must have seen a dozen planes go flaming down around him. Seems that his plane took a minor hit. He didn't know it was minor. He jumped. Anything else you want to know about him? His batting average? His grades in school?"

Embarrassed, the men looked at Mungo. Mungo took his cigar stub from his mouth. "Carr's a good soldier," he said, and walked away.

The men began to break away, when Sacco said drily, "Wait a minute, Uhlan. This is get-acquainted time. Tell the men why *you* left the Eighty-Second."

"Not for being yellow," Uhlan said sullenly. "You know damned well it was battle fatigue." He seemed to be pleading a case before a tribunal, appealing the judgement that his own soul had rendered. "I'd seen too much combat. My nerves went bad."

"Where'd you see all this combat from, Uhlan?" Sacco prodded. "A balcony seat?"

"I went all the way through Sicily," Uhlan protested.

"Sure. On a private tour. You missed the fighting. Why don't you tell them about Anzio beachhead. What were you aiming your carbine at?"

"I dropped it in the mud. The captain was a liar. I was only checking my sights."

"While you were changing your boots?" His oddly-tilted eyes seemed almost compassionate as they examined Uhlan's face. "You weren't trying to trade your big toe for a discharge, eh? The captain had you wrong?"

"Go to hell, you Goddamned Jap-Wop bastard," Uhlan blurted. He tore his way through the circle of men and walked toward the tail of the plane.

One by one the men drifted off, and Dana found himself alone with Sacco.

Dana sat on his helmet again and lit another cigarette. After a while he asked: "Was that true about Carr?"

Sure."

"You figure he's—well, okay now?"

The spark of Sacco's cigarette waxed and waned, and his face was etched in red against the dusk. "He was always okay. He got mousetrapped once—he has some yardage to make up. Lord Jim is going to be a heller in combat."

"And how about Uhlan?"

Sacco shook his head ruefully. "He's pretty hopeless. But Mungo's the man to make him soldier."

Dana nodded thoughtfully. He couldn't understand Sacco's rapport with Mungo. The burly sergeant seemed worse than Nolan—the perfect embodiment of brute authority.

Sacco seemed to read his mind, and grinned that enigmatic grin. "You still can't figure Mungo, can you Dana?"

"He's rougher than a cob," Dana said, massaging his arm.

"Look," said Sacco. "Mungo's rare. He doesn't recognize an enemy within him. There aren't many like him."

Dana squirmed uncomfortably. "Oh, Christ ..." he said.

"There's something in the Bagavada Gita. A lot of Sanskrit, pretty stuff, but what it all boils down to is, well ... 'if you're going to soldier—then soldier.' Mungo wrote the book. He's whole, complete—an atavism maybe, but a perfect product."

Dana understood little of the unfamiliar words. "What's the Bagavada Gita?" he asked.

"One of my relatives," Sacco said. Dana stared at him and Sacco grinned. "On my mother's side," he added. "She was Hawaiian. In my father's family they peddled fish. When they weren't climbing up on crosses."

Dana said, "You snowing me? That don't make any sense."

Sacco let a laugh escape him. "Sense?" he said. "Nothing makes any sense. What are we doing here with knives in our teeth, setting out to slaughter us some strangers? What the hell is anybody doing? In this world you expect sense?" He waved his hand impatiently, dismissing the concept, then joined his fingers, wriggling them through the air. "You got to live it out, man, that's all you have to do."

Dana's puzzlement showed on his face. "What the hell are you talking about?"

"Nothing," Sacco said. "Let's get back to Mungo—there's a man to talk about. He never tires, you know. Never runs down. Hell Dana, he's not a man, he's *Man,* roaring out of his cave, swinging his club. It's a pleasure to watch him function."

"Yeah, with a club." Dana found his argument. "He's got to do it with a club."

"You're still pissed off about him hitting Cadillac." Sacco struck his hand. "Wham! Like that, with no preliminaries. Well, think it over, Dana. Cadillac had to be hit. He wouldn't soldier—he refused his role. The thing is that Mungo didn't reason it out. He saw and he reacted ... instinctively, by reflex."

Sacco seemed to relinquish all hope of prejecting the idea. "Never mind," he said softly. "Just remember this: all of us, the whole damned human race, we're descended from females who liked babies and males who liked to fight. That's the way to understand Mungo."

Dana shook his head and said, "He should have been a cop." Sacco smiled, abandoning the subject, and turned to watch a racing jeep swing off the road and onto the airstrip.

It stopped near Mungo, its wipers clacking busily against the rain streaming down the windshield. Lieutenant Edgerton climbed down grinning, visibly straining to radiate confidence. Another man, a small and spectacled T/S, dismounted after him.

The patrol gathered around the jeep.

"I've got our pigeoneer," the lieutenant said. "Franklin, this is Sergeant Mungo, the squad leader." Mungo nodded indifferently.

Franklin, frail and very earnest, wore a First Army patch above the American flag sewn to the sleeve of his jump-jacket. "Hi," he said to Mungo, and then, bobbing his head around the circle of men, "I'm glad to be going along with you. Heard a lot about the Five-Oh-Goose."

"He's got a lot of spirit," Edgerton told Mungo, and walked to the equipment bundles.

"I was the last jumper left in the First Army pigeon loft," Franklin said brightly. "I was afraid I wasn't going to get to jump." Mungo grunted and chomped on his cigar.

Edgerton's voice rang out sharply. "Sergeant Mungo! What's all this?" He pointed perplexedly at the weapons bundle. "Our loading manifest doesn't call for heavy weapons."

"Figured we might need them," Mungo said. "Don't worry about it. They aren't signed for."

"But we're going on reconnaissance. We have to be mobile."

"We'll be mobile all right. Don't worry about it."

Edgerton stared at the bundles for a moment, then shot his sleeve back to look at his watch. "Damn! Nine-thirty. Better come over here—there's still a lot to go over with you."

Franklin was struggling with a bulky cage attached to an oblong parachute pack. Nolan brushed the T/S aside and plucked the cage out with one hand, and with the other tossed two personnel chutes on the ground. "Take off," he told the driver, and the jeep spun away.

Mungo followed the lieutenant up into the plane and stood over him, silently working on his cold cigar. Edgerton seated himself and drew a penciled list from his map case. "I made up a tentative jump roster, Sergeant."

Mungo took it from him and read it slowly. Edgerton, smiling, kept his eyes on him. He had given a lot of thought to the order in which the men would jump. He wanted to impress Mungo with his savvy. It was important to him.

Mungo shook his head. "Can't do it this way," he said flatly. "We'll use one stick, not two."

"The men will be wearing a lot of equipment." Edgerton's voice rang more sharply than he meant it to. "One stick means a lot of crowding."

"So they'll be crowded," he said. "Twelve men ain't a big stick. The big thing is to get them out that door damned fast."

Edgerton was silent. The sergeant was obviously right.

"Why did you lead off with Carr and Kadillius?"

"Kadillius is a refusal," Edgerton said, rallying. "And you know Carr's record. I want them both up front. They can't freeze in the door with a dozen men pushing behind them."

Mungo shook his head with swift finality. "Carr's okay. Forget about him. And Kadillius isn't scared—just smart. He won't refuse in any plane I'm on."

Edgerton found himself nodding inanely. "You're sure of Carr?"

"Dead sure. He's a good man. Get your jump roster, lieutenant, and I'll tell you how we'll do it."

Edgerton fumbled in the map case for the blank, mimeographed sheet. It was comforting now, to leave details to the sergeant. While he held his pencil poised above the sheet, Mungo told him curtly: "You're the jump-master. First in the door. Uhlan right behind you..."

"Why Uhlan?"

"He's scared. He's going to need a lot of push behind him."

"Scared? How can you tell?"

"I can smell it on him."

"Smell it?" The lieutenant stared. That was an attribute of animals—to recognize the scent of fear.

Mungo's eyes were just a little condescending. "That's right. There's a smell to fear." He rolled the cold cigar stub around in his jaw. "You. Then Uhlan. We'll jump the pigeoneer next. He has to toss his cage out before he jumps. Then Nolan—he's strong and I want him to help with that cage." Mungo scratched his ear and said rapidly: "Swampy James, Reb James, Hollister, Dana, Sacco, Carr, Kadillius. And then me. I'll be last man standing in the tail just in case Kadillius tries to run past the door."

The heads of Dana and Franklin appeared over the bottom edge of the door. They slid the pigeon crate with its cargo parachute into the plane. They stood aside while Edgerton climbed out, a vaguely disconcerted look on his face.

The two men climbed up and knelt beside the pigeons. Dana lifted the cargo chute so that Franklin could check the attachment of the risers. They heard a little rustling and a chorus of cooing. Franklin smiled. "Lots of GI's can't appreciate how important pigeons can be."

Mungo grunted non-committally and turned away. He carelessly unfastened the straps of his gas mask and slung it into the dark depths at the tail of the plane. Then he swung himself outside.

Franklin pulled two small folds of olive-drab nylon from the pocket of his outer jump-suit. He raised the door of the cage and felt carefully inside. His hand emerged with a frightened blue and white bird.

Dana watched him zip the nylon cover over the pigeon so that only the head and tail of the bird emerged. He hooked the bird to the straps of his chute, and reached into the cage for a second. Dana could not help smiling. It seemed so bizarre to attach birds to parachutes.

A starter whined, and hesitantly one cold motor began to warm up. The second motor coughed, then roared, and both props were spinning. The floor of the cargo plane shook beneath his feet. Dana felt a premonitory tug of dread in his belly, and saw Franklin's face lose some of its color.

Dana put his head out of the plane. All down the line the C-47 engines were rumbling into life. He could hear the wild, brave cheering from the men of the regiment. The men of his own patrol looked silently at each other. Here and there were tentative smiles. Dana, dropping to the ground, felt an emptiness inside him, and longed for the men of his own company.

The planes fell silent down the length of the field. The silence seemed eerie after the roaring of the engines and the cheering. Dana noticed that even the rain had stopped. With Sacco's assistance, he was struggling to fit the radio pack to his leg. A dark figure came up beside them and juggled the gas mask under Sacco's chute. Mungo.

"Didn't you get rid of it?" the sergeant asked.

"I wanted to, but I didn't want to take any static from that lieutenant."

"Balls," Mungo said. "It's only extra weight." The blade of his jump-knife glittered in the darkness as he sawed through the strap of Sacco's mask, and flung it off into the night.

Sacco said to Dana, "How about yours?"

"I'll keep it," he said.

"You don't need it."

"Let him haul it around if he wants to," Mungo said. "Give me your morphine syrette, Dana."

"We're all supposed to carry one," Dana told him.

"You'll get it back if you need it."

Dana removed the syrette from the special paratroop first-aid kit on his belt and handed it to Mungo, who added it to a half-dozen others in his hand. He dropped them inside Sacco's jacket. "That's the last one. You got half of them, Fortunato. They couldn't spare an aid man, so you're elected."

"By appointment only," Sacco grinned. "Except for those delicate female complaints."

Behind them, a wobbly baritone thundered into song:

"… So they picked him up and poured him from his para-trooper's boot,
   Annnnnd, HE AIN'T GONNA JUMP NO MORE."

Swampy sat on his helmet, grinning happily. He sucked in his breath and bellowed out the chorus:

"Gory, gory, what a helluva way to die,
   And HE DON'T HAVE TO JUMP NO MORE!"

Swampy looked around at the startled faces and laughed with alcoholic glee. Mungo crossed to him and slipped his canteen out of the holder. Too late, Swampy tried to snatch it back. Mungo unscrewed the top and raised the canteen to his mouth. He held it there until it was empty. He tossed it back to Swampy. "Well, Goddamn it, you could have brought whiskey. What the hell you saving your money for now?"

Edgerton looked up from buckling his leg straps. "Sergeant Mungo, has that man been drinking?"

"Yeah," Mungo told the thunderstruck officer. "Gin."

"Gin!" The lieutenant stared around him, outraged. "Where did he get it?"

"Must have had it in his canteen back in his outfit, while he was in the stockade."

"Well, why didn't you stop him?"

Mungo shrugged. "He can still jump. And if he needs it, what the hell."

"I'm okay, lieutenant, buddy," Swampy said earnestly. "Don' you worry 'bout me. Go any Goddamn place you will." Edgerton looked helplessly at Mungo. Mungo wiped his lips. "He's okay. Got that jump roster?"

The lieutenant handed it to him. *"Fall in,"* Mungo roared. He gazed stonily up and down the line. "You too, Kadillius."

Sullenly, the Greek boy joined the formation, slipping next to Dana. "Coming with us?" Dana whispered.

"Let him try to make me," Cadillac snarled, from the corner of his mouth.

"We're jumping in one stick," Mungo announced. "Lieutenant Edgerton is jump-master. He'll be in the door. Get in the plane as I call your names."

One by one the men filed into the plane. Dana followed Hollister. "So long, dad. Good luck," Cadillac called after him. The crew chief extended a hand and helped swing him up into the airplane. He marched up the steeply slanting, slippery aluminum floor, past the faces of the men already in the plane, the familiar bucket seats, the rows of plastic windows with their rubber gun ports, the gauge of the ship's skin and the maker's name stamped repeatedly over the walls.

Cadillac's was the last name to be called. The slim Greek youth shuffled slowly up to where Mungo waited at the door of the plane. His eyes avoided the lazy, probing gaze. He stopped and shrugged, then looked at Mungo. He raised his hands to the edge of the door frame and swung himself inside.

CHAPTER EIGHT

D MINUS ONE,
2221 HOURS

The plane turned onto the runway, swung its tail slowly and began its run. The engines throbbed louder, straining for flight. The men felt a bump, another, and then imperceptibly the tail began to rise. The talk in the cabin died abruptly. The men unconsciously strained forward in their seats, waiting for the moment when the wheels rise, the instant of severance of identity with the earth. The plane lurched again. The dark tents were fleeing by them, receding. They were airborne.

"Unfasten safety belts," Lieutenant Edgerton shouted. "Smoke if you've got 'em." He beamed a smile and fumbled for his cigarettes. He was startled at the slight tremor of his hand, and grateful that the darkness hid it from the others. A conviction of inadequacy had been gnawing at him since he stepped out of the jeep. His mind whirled with the responsibilities that would be his when they touched the soil of France; he felt a cold trickle of sweat run down from his armpit.

He turned his face away from the men and looked out the yawning door at his side. *"Get hold of yourself,"* he whispered fervently. *"You can handle this."*

Opposite him, Mungo scratched a wooden match with his thumbnail and held the flame to his inch-long cigar stub. The soaked butt would not light. He took it from his mouth and looked at it regretfully for a moment. He flipped it to the wind whipping by the door and folded his arms across the reserve pack on his chest. Mungo was glad to be leaving England, getting back to the field again. His slow, steady eyes swept once over each man in the plane. Their faces were blackened for night camouflage now. Then he let his lids drop. In less than a minute, he was asleep.

Uhlan gripped his knees hard to still their tremor. He, too, was grateful for the gloom of the cabin. He listened to the thunderous beat of his heart and hoped his pose looked relaxed to the others. They could joke about combat—they didn't know. They'd never seen men die. The chill knife of terror began to probe his guts.

Technician Fifth Grade Francis Franklin stroked the head of the pigeon clipped to his chest strap. He had names for all his birds. This was Pickles. He sat stiffly in his seat and gazed around him with shy pride. He was sure he was the youngest here, except for Hollister. And he was the second-ranking non-com, too. Franklin shut his eyes and drifted into a revery. In it, every kid he knew was sitting awed in a movie theatre watching a newsreel of Francis Franklin flying off to storm Fortress Europe with a planeload of hard-bitten paratroopers. Tears glistened in the eyes of Nancy Hooker, the prettiest girl at Evanston Township High School. Franklin smiled to himself.

The wings of the plane rocked suddenly. The floor bucked and the equipment bundles went spinning drunkenly down the fuselage.

The weapons bundle with the bazooka strapped to it slid heavily past Edgerton's legs toward the nose of the ship. Nolan sprang to his feet and caught it. Dana left his seat to help him. "Sit your ass down, Okie," Nolan snarled. "Save your strength for where you're going."

He hauled the heavy pack back to the tail, nodding at Edgerton's "Good work, Nolan!" He sat again, his iron fists clenched on his thighs, and glared at the other men. *Kitten-feeble little bastards,* he thought. *And they call themselves troopers.* There wasn't a real man among them, save for Mungo, and he was getting fat. Everyone of them was smoking, sucking poison into his tissues. They'd all be as drunk as Swampy, too, if they could have gotten their hands on the booze.

Well, they were going to learn soon that it paid to live clean and develop your body. Too late for most of them, but they'd find out now. They were a bunch of shiftless, lazy slobs without the character it takes to train with weights, like a real man.

This was the pay-off—war, by God. In battle, a real soldier, *a real man,* could not help but win recognition. *I'll come out of this war a captain,* Nolan promised himself. *A major, even.*

He'd show them all right. Especially that draft-dodging, yellow little Okie bastard, Dana.

Swampy hiccupped and giggled happily. I-God, he was doin' it, after all. He was goin' to France. Well, now he'd find out if all those crazy stories Pap and Uncle Jim told about the French girls were true. Pap claimed there were still ten thousand deserters in France from the last war. Swampy snickered. If the stories were true, there would soon be ten thousand and one. He slapped his sidekick on the back.

The heavyweight pisshouse champion of the world, Reb thought angrily. That's what Swampy always called him. That was the way he had described him to these men. He wondered if they thought he was a clown like Swampy. He would have to be a clown to be proud of a title like that.

He wasn't like Swampy. He wasn't like anyone else in the world. He was just a no-good bayou rat, a back-road slut's bastard, with a whole county to claim for a father. Reb bunched his muscles and spat on the floor, feeling the wild, indiscriminate rage welling in him.

He had felt like this when he smashed that English girl's face. It was the same black rage that had led him to break heads in every honkytonk in Mississippi. There would never be an end to it, until his own head was busted. Maybe it was coming in France, in an hour or two.

Hollister took a fresh cigarette from his pack and lit it from the butt of the last one. Chain-smoking. He cast a hurried glance around the plane, wondering if any of the others had noticed. He didn't want to look nervous, make them feel they had any cause to worry that he might not measure up. Actually, he was glad to be going, he told himself firmly. This would show the guys in the outfit that slugging Flash Gordon wasn't a put-up job to get out of combat.

Carr stretched his legs out into the aisle. It was odd, but the plane ride reminded him off the locker room just before a game, when you knew you were in the starting line-up. There was the same feeling of cumbersome equipment strapped to your body and of imminent action. He was facing much more of a test than a football game, of course.

He glanced briefly at Uhlan. He'd felt like slugging the big slob back there. He was glad now that he had not hit him; Uhlan was beneath his contempt.

Cadillac whistled, staring out the door. "Man, just dig that! Dig that scene!"

They had flown through the storm and a bright round moon had broken through the clouds. Below them were the moon-hazed waters of the Channel, and bobbing on the surface, as far as they could see, were miles and miles of invasion craft, stretching dimly off to the horizon. The seaborne troops had been embarked, were riding into battle, too.

"Man, you could walk to France on that. It's like a frigging bridge." The others rose and crowded to the door and stared down silently, in awe. Mungo, drowsily opening his eyes, rumbled: "Get your asses back. You're rocking the ship." Shaking their heads, impressed beyond measure by the sight of the armada bringing troops to support them, the men returned to their seats.

Cadillac sank down again and stared at Mungo, at his relaxed body and slumberous eyes. Well, the big gorilla had got him in the plane. Cadillac considered for a moment the possibility of hooking up and diving abruptly through the door. The Navy would fish him out of the water, just like Carr at Sicily. But the deal seemed corny; the Channel would be cold, and—what the hell—there was no reason to get wet.

He would play it cool: wait it out until the jumplight turned green. Then he would dive into the tail of the plane, fight the big bonehead off long enough to make him know that he would have to jump without Georgie Cadillac, or be carried miles from the drop zone.

Cadillac shut his eyes and saw himself leaning on a bar, his tailored civvies draped smartly, replying lightly to a naive question: "What? Jump in France? Man, you're coming on. A cat could get himself messed up that way!" He smiled tolerantly at the square. "Sure, I made the paratrooper scene, dad. Why not? If you got to make the Army, take the extra loot."

Beside him, Mungo grunted and opened his eyes. He turned a long, slow stare on Cadillac. His face was expressionless, yet Cadillac started just as though a policeman had tapped him on the shoulder. Somehow he knew he would not be riding back to England this night. Combat, now—a cat could really swing in combat, out on his own with a piece like the Thompson.

Some of them aren't bad, at all, Dana thought. *Sacco, Carr, Cadillac, and even Hollister. Good men to go into action with.* He would like to have them with him in Headquarters Company, 1st Battalion. This patrol was only a temporary detail. Maybe, with luck, some of them would be reassigned there with him.

But then Nolan would be his first sergeant again. That was a risk that must be taken. There could be no hiding from Nolan, no matter where he went. The big bastard would come for his revenge some day, in a way of his own choosing. *I'll handle him when he does,* Dana promised himself. *Some way.*

He looked at Sacco beside him. Sacco flashed him a grin. His hand made the fluttering motion of a goldfish swimming, and he winked at Dana.

An unfamiliar sound hammered up over the motors, like a motorcycle starting with faulty carburetion. Dana peered out through the celluloid window. Many-colored streams were rising slowly toward them: red and yellow, green and blue, arcing gracefully up from everywhere at once. The streams rose sluggishly, hanging in the air, then seemed to gather speed as they approached and flashed on past with blinding swiftness. For an instant Dana felt only a sense of wonder at the unreal beauty of a fireworks display witnessed from above. Then the sharp staccato clatter ripped along the wings, and Dana stiffened in his seat.

Hollister, beside him, gasped and clutched his arm. Carr stared stolidly ahead of him.

Then there was a tremendous tearing sound. The plane seemed to buck against the air, and the wingtip turned down sickeningly.

"Oh, Christ, we're hit!" Uhlan's voice was thin, but shrill enough to carry over the motor and the other, more terrifying, noise beneath them.

"All right, you Geronimos, let's relax." Mungo's strong, impassive voice boomed the phrases out. "Only coastal batteries. We'll clear them in a minute." The ship bucked and rocked and went straining through the darkness.

"Oh, my God, look at that!" It was Hollister's voice. He was staring through the round plastic window above him. Dana turned and saw a plane burst suddenly into orange flame and spin away toward the earth. A single chute came out of it, and then the silhouette was totally engulfed and became a plunging ball of fire. Only Carr refused to watch it—his face composed beneath the cocoa blackening, he sat there quietly and looked at nothing.

Dana had a brief and horrible awareness of what it must be like in the stricken ship: men aware of falling, struggling through the flames in a spinning, twisting cabin, towards a door that none of them could hope to reach. The ball of fire exploded a long way behind them as it bounced against the earth and broke into fiery fragments, then burned dimly in the distance. The one lone parachute drifted through the air, something lifeless dangling beneath it, the target for a hundred tracer streams.

Then a new sound ripped the sky around them: a series of concussions like rolling thunder. A blinding glare pulsed harshly against the clouds and waned, and then there was another and another. A rattling of ack-ack fragments beat against the fuselage. Off their port wing, another ship went down and their own plane shuddered, the motors snarling savagely. The plane dipped, then rose, and changed its direction. Dana heard the voice of Sergeant Mungo, cursing bitterly. "Evasive action, the yellow bastards. They're moving out of course—they'll never find the drop zone!"

Dana noticed that Uhlan's lips were moving silently, that Swampy stared around in drunken bewilderment, that Edgerton was standing and peering out the door and the others sat rigid.

At the door the little warning light glowed red. Edgerton's voice, impossibly hoarse, shouted: "All right, men, *stand up and hook up.*" Mungo and Nolan moved to the tail and wrestled the equipment bundles to the door. The others rose and clipped the snap fasteners of their anchor lines to the overhead cable. Dana found it almost impossible to stand beneath the weight of his equipment in the dipping, lurching plane. He hung hard to the cable and his mind went blank; its control was transferred to the automatic pattern of reaction to jump commands.

"Check your equipment!" the lieutenant ordered. Could that hoarse croaking be Edgerton's voice? Dana ran his hand over his buckles and over the chute of Hollister in front of him.

"Sound off for equipment check!"

"Number twelve okay!" roared Mungo from the door. He had not yet returned to his place in the stick, and Cadillac, awaiting the ritual slap from behind, was silent. "Goddam-nit, Kadillius, *sound off!*" Mungo bellowed.

"Number eleven okay!" Cadillac shouted and slapped Carr on the tail. Carr's voice was firm and steady: "Number ten okay!" Dana was grateful for Carr's presence in the plane; he would be even more grateful to have him on the ground below. "Number nine okay!" cried Sacco, and the shouting followed down the chain of men.

There was a heavy silence after Edgerton had croaked out "Number one okay." Dana shifted his feet uneasily, pressing against Hollister, dreading the return of thought. Mungo's voice boomed the jump-school ritual into the silence: "All right, you Geronimos—*Is everybody happy?*"

"*Yes!*" the ten men roared at once.

The wings rocked drunkenly, the tracers stabbed the sky around them. Dana wanted desperately to dive for the door, to go hurtling through the darkness, to get out of the plane.

"Get back in the stick, Nolan," Mungo snarled.

"Help you with the bundles," Nolan said. "I'll jump my position when they come by."

"*Get your frigging ass back in that stick!*"

Nolan turned and hooked up behind Franklin. Mungo, with his ponderous barrel-gutted strength, eased the equipment bundles forward, balancing the ammunition bundle in the door. He wanted the other one, with the machine guns, nearer to the stick when they hit the ground. He crouched behind the bundles and the wind whipped his jacket and set loose straps to fluttering.

Dana stopped breathing and felt his muscles tighten, the little empty places in his stomach coil up lightly. Then the motors seemed to change their pitch; the tail went up. *Green light on!*

Mungo bellowed, "Let's go!" He drove the first bundle out, kicked the second forward and out the door. Edgerton grasped the frame of the door, pivoted around and swung his body out into the prop blast. There was an instant of arrest as Uhlan faltered, but the men straining forward were massed behind him, and the desperate pressure drove him to the door. Mungo swung his arm like a club on Uhlan's back, and Uhlan, half-turned to look behind him with wide and panicked eyes, went disappearing through the door.

Franklin, behind him, screamed, "My pigeons!" The cage, with its parachute still unhooked, was lying just beside the door. Nolan shouted, "Screw them," and pushed Franklin through the door. As Nolan followed, he hooked the cage with his foot and kicked it out into the night ahead of him. The others, driving forward, went popping out behind him.

Dana saw only Hollister's back, moving toward the tail. The radio pack was bulky on his leg and he had to drag it clumsily, fighting his way, lurching up the inclined aisle. He saw Mungo's face, unblackened still, hurrying them on, and felt the pressure of Sacco's body behind him. An instant later Hollister's back disappeared—there was a screaming rush of wind as he stepped off into the night, and Dana, swift behind him, felt that awful moment that you never can recapture in retrospect, when the flame-spitting darkness yawns suddenly before you, the wind smashes at you and the dark ship lunges; and the world is a whistling, whirling groove through which you have to hurtle. With a wrenching movement of his packburdened leg, Dana went plummeting out through the door.

The prop blast snatched him and hurled him through the air at eighty miles an hour, twisting over and over. As he tumbled in the wash, he lost his sense of falling. He was spinning, helpless in a wind-battered world, dimly conscious of the tracers splitting the sky, of moon hanging absurdly beneath him. He put his hand on the reserve chute and ducked his head, waiting ... waiting for an endless and immeasurable time.

Like a bull whip cracking, the chute boomed open, jerking him so violently his breath smashed out of him and for an instant he blacked out completely. Then he was drifting, cradled in gentleness, twisting in his harness to avoid the stabbing streams of technicolor tracers that seemed to be probing for him, spitting up from a dozen flashing points below. Beyond and beneath him, the graceful blossoms of other parachutes were white in the moonlight.

Something plummeted by him. He heard a scream, blurred and muffled by the wind, and saw the dark body plunging down, trailed by the long, white, quivering plume of a chute that had not opened. Someone had caught a streamer and the stick had jumped too low for him to get the reserve chute into action. Dana's heart went cold as he wondered who it was.

Mechanically he released the leg pack and lowered it down the length of rope, waiting for the greater blackness of the ground to move up through the night.

CHAPTER NINE

D DAY, 0130 HOURS

Dana heard a thud below him and felt his body lift in the chute harness, as the leg pack touched ground. An instant later his heels hit the earth. A jarring shock ran up his spine. A gust of wind took the now useless chute and he was jerked onto the flat of his back like a doll at the end of a string. He seized two of the risers and fought them to spill the air out of his chute. Above him, machine-gun tracers ripped apart the night, and he heard a man still in the air screaming frightened curses. His own stomach was a cold ball of panic.

He was in a sitting position now, the chute collapsing slowly. His shaking hands tore at the fold of the bellyband, the catches of the leg straps. He got the chest buckle unhooked and then he was on his back, tearing the disassembled rifle from the Griswold container. The machine-gun fire ceased as abruptly as it had begun. The metallic *tick-tick, tick-tick* of a cricket came to his ear as he slapped the rifle together.

Dana jammed a full clip into the rifle, let the bolt shoot home, snapped the safety off and rolled onto his belly. Sweat was streaming down his face. He cradled the M-1 in his arms and began crawling down the length of rope to the leg pack. Ahead of him a cricket was clicking again. He stopped and pressed the cricket in the pocket at his throat. He crawled on to the bundle. Ahead the cricket clicked again. His nerves could stand no more. "Who it is?" he croaked.

"Me," came the answer. "Cadillac."

A figure darker than the night rose ahead of him and sprinted forward. Cadillac dropped beside him. "Man, I thought that was you had the streamer."

"Where the hell are we?" Dana asked. "Did we hit the drop zone?" Whose chute had failed? It had been someone behind him. If not Cadillac, who? Sacco? Carr? Mungo?

A C-47 roared overhead, only a few hundred feet in the air, hurrying for England. Instantly a dozen streams of machine-gun bullets probed upward for it.

"I hope they keep firing at him and leave us alone," Cadillac grated in his ear.

"Shh," Dana told him. In the instant before the guns began he had heard a far-off wail of fright. There it was again. "Off on the left," he told Cadillac. "We should go over." He gripped the M-1 tightly to still the shaking of his hands. He could make out a double row of trees fifty yards away now. He thought he saw an uncollapsed parachute at their bases.

"It might be a German trick," Cadillac said. Untying the rope from the leg pack, Dana felt a new thrust of fear. Maybe.

A shrill whistle blasted the air. "Five-Oh-Goose! Assemble here! Five-Oh-Goose!" a big voice roared.

"Mungo!" Cadillac blurted. He was on his feet instantly, sprinting toward the trees. Dana seized the leg pack and staggered after him. Strangely, the sound of the surly non-com's bellow had lifted his own spirits a notch. From the corner of his eye, he saw a huge figure lift itself from the ground and begin to run after Cadillac. He recognized it as Nolan's.

The high wail of fright was coming from behind the trees. Hollister! Shots rang out in the field ahead of them, and Hollister screamed again.

Dana saw Mungo then, standing in a sunken lane between the rows of trees, waving them on. He held the Springfield in one hand, the heavy leg pack in the other. "Fan out, damn you! Find him!"

Mungo, Cadillac and Nolan disappeared into the field.

Dana dropped the radio in the lane and ran after them. "Over here! Over here!" Cadillac called from a stand of trees on their right, and Dana turned toward them. Dana saw a parachute tangled in the top branches of a tall tree, the man in it dangling twenty feet above the ground. Below, shadowy figures whirled. The guns in their hands spat flame at Cadillac.

Dana saw Cadillac firing the Thompson from his hip on the dead run. He threw himself on the ground and drew a bead on one of the men. Cadillac's Thompson chattered. A German lifted in the air and flew over backwards. Dana swung his M-1 to the other man, and squeezed off three shots rapidly. The second German was running away; zigzagging between the trees. Dana heard a *ping* as the empty clip was ejected past his ear. Mungo crashed through the undergrowth on Dana's left, dropped to one knee and fired a single shot. The German went down.

The paratroopers were on their feet now, sprinting toward Hollister. Nolan stood above Cadillac's German and fired three shots into him from his Thompson. Then he bounded to the second. Again his sub-machine gun barked.

"Don't waste bullets on dead ones," Mungo shouted. "Get flat and keep your eyes open!" He was standing beneath the gibbering Hollister. "Get the saddle of your chute under your butt, boy, and open those leg straps. We've got to get out of here."

Hollister clung helplessly to the risers. "Th-they were going to shoot me."

"Shut up before more of them get back here," Mungo ordered.

"Why did they do it?" Hollister asked, not letting go of the risers. "I said 'Kamerad!' I tried to surrender to them."

"You've got one minute to get down or I'm leaving you here," Mungo said. "Do you want to stay here?"

Instantly, Hollister became silent. There was no doubting the tone of Mungo's voice. Dana watched as Hollister wiggled to get his rump over the saddle. Dana realized guiltily that he was not doing his part to keep them alive. He strained his eyes to the edge of the field, looking for the outlines of coal-bucket helmets.

"Now pull the rip cord on that emergency chute and climb down it," Mungo said. His voice was calm, reassuring. All around them the night shook with the roar of airplane motors and German guns snarling up at them. Hollister opened his chest strap and threw himself out of the saddle of the chute, grasping for the lines of the dangling emergency. A gasp of fright escaped him, and then Dana heard him sliding hurriedly down the nylon and dropping to the ground.

Mungo turned to Dana. "Did you abandon that radio?"

"It's back in that lane, Sergeant."

"Good. We're moving out. Follow me and keep a good interval." The orders flowed from Mungo rapidly, competently; they might have been on night maneuvers in North Carolina. They followed him into the lane.

Dana kept low as he struggled to fit the 300 radio onto his back. Mungo signaled for silence. He swung his head in a slow circle, the broad face intent, listening. "There's someone over there," he said at last. "I can hear his cricket. Come on."

Dana got to his feet and followed the crouching line of men back into the field where he and Cadillac had landed. He heard nothing but the chatter of far-off machine guns and his own rapid breathing.

Nolan and Cadillac were snapping their crickets as they moved across the field in short, jagged runs, dropping to the plowed, sweet-smelling earth to listen before moving on. Suddenly Mungo emitted an ear-splitting whistle.

"This is Mungo!" he bellowed, lying flat on the ground. "Where are you?"

"Over here," came the answer, far ahead to their left.

"That sounds like a German voice," Nolan said.

"It's Swampy James, damn it." Mungo waved them to their feet and jogged ahead. He ran with amazing speed for such a big man. He held the leg pack in one hand as lightly as if it were a pillow.

A paratrooper rose suddenly from the ground as they pounded up. Another lay at his feet. Dana recognized Swampy and saw that his drawn, shocked face was completely sober. A long roll of camouflage parachute-nylon was still harnessed to the man lying at his feet.

Mungo dropped to his knees and slid the helmet back from the man's face. "Carr, eh?"

"Christ!" Swampy said. "Look at him!"

Dana felt himself drawn forward, not willing it. He saw the jagged white ends of the thigh bones protruding from Carr's belly and turned away from the horribly twisted body.

"He was a good man," Mungo said. His voice was matter-of-fact.

Two machine guns suddenly burst into life nearby. The men flung themselves down. The guns did not have the rhythm of American Brownings, Dana realized.

The guns stopped, began again, stopped. Then each fired in turn, the sounds coming from slightly different angles. "Sounds like trouble with the equipment bundles," Mungo said. "They would have dropped over there." He glanced hurriedly around him. "Okay, we're going forward. Skirmishers right and left, on me. Spread out, but keep the men on each side of you in sight."

"Wait," Dana told him. He ran hurriedly to snatch up the top of Carr's parachute. He saw the suspension line that had wound around the canopy nylon, wrapping it into the paratrooper's dread 'cigarette roll'. Cadillac helped him fluff the chute over Carr's body.

"You'd better learn to save your energy, Okie," Nolan growled at him.

"Move out," Mungo said.

They went forward slowly, knees bent, ready to throw themselves down on their faces. Ahead of them, the Nazi guns hammered, making a deeper, faster noise than American machine guns. The tracers appeared as dancing specks, turning swiftly into orange streaks above them. Now and then, when one passed directly overhead, it made the same noise as a rifle fired close at hand.

Mungo halted them in a shallow ditch. Once again he whistled.

The answering hail came from a hundred yards ahead. "Mungo?"

"Yeah!" Mungo bellowed. "We're coming forward!" He turned to the men crouched in the ditch. "Keep your eyes open and don't shoot at anyone you meet unless you're Goddamn sure he's German. That was Sacco!"

They crept forward, hunched against the bullets flailing the sky above them, dreading the lowering of the German gunners' sights. Sacco rose up ahead of them when they had gone fifty yards.

"Carr's dead," Mungo told him succinctly. Sacco cursed. "You got anybody with you?" Mungo asked.

"Edgerton's up there with Reb and Uhlan and the pigeoneer." Sacco's eyes swept down the line of men with Mungo, counting them silently. "It's the same screwed-up deal as Sicily," he said. "There's a couple of mg's zeroed in on the blinker lights on the equipment bundles. Edgerton's all set to lead a bayonet charge."

Mungo snorted. "Let's go up and see what we can do," he said. He waved the line forward. Every few yards he sang out: "Edgerton!"

The Lieutenant answered at last. He waved them over to a shallow fold in the ground where he lay with three men. Dana saw Uhlan with his face in the ground, and Franklin, the eyes behind his GI spectacles wide and bewildered. Reb James had scooped out a little hole for the upper half of his body, and he lay in it, staring out angrily over his rifle sights. Dana raised his head and saw the two amber lights of the equipment bundles blinking in the field ahead. In the far corner of the field, he thought he could make out the squarish lines of a low building. Even as he looked, a machine gun somewhere near it opened up, spraying more bullets around their precious equipment bundles.

"Spread out, spread out," Mungo called quietly. "Don't bunch up. We may get mortar fire here. And dig in as much as you can—even an inch down makes you harder to hit."

Dana eased the radio off his shoulders and freed the folding entrenching shovel from his rifle belt. He saw Cadillac ten feet away from him, already scraping at the earth. "Man," Cadillac whispered in awe. "Did you see that Kraut go over on his back when I let him have it with the old chopper?"

"Sergeant," Lt. Edgerton said. "We've got to split into two groups and knock those machine guns out."

"No," Mungo told him. "We're not splitting up. We couldn't assemble again in this light."

"Did you hear me?" Edgerton demanded angrily.

"Yeah. But we got a damn small chance of getting either one of those guns and we'd wind up scattered all over the damn countryside."

"We've got to get those bundles." Edgerton's voice was shrill.

"I'll get 'em." Mungo was rummaging in his leg pack. He threw a coil of fuse aside, and Dana remembered the rifle grenades and the containers of C-2 he had seen the sergeant stow in the pack. If Mungo caught a bullet through that leg pack, they would all go sky high.

"Sacco," Mungo hissed. Sacco crawled over, and Mungo thrust the Springfield at him, and four or five clips of blank ammunition. Rapidly he stacked the rifle grenades. "We'll try for the bastard on the right," he said softly. "Wait for his next burst, and try to figure his distance. When you think you're on him pretty close, start rapid fire. Make him think there's a sixty millimeter mortar working him over." Sacco nodded, removing the clip of live ammunition from Mungo's gun, and inserting the blanks used to hurl rifle grenades. Dana watched him arm the first of the tailed grenades and slip it over the launcher.

Mungo turned to Edgerton. "Lieutenant, have these other men concentrate their fire on the gun on the left. They can see its muzzle blast. The idea is to pin those gunners down or scare them into running off." He grinned sardonically. "They're supposed to be low-quality troops, remember?"

Edgerton had begun nodding as soon as Mungo spoke to him. "Okay, Sergeant Mungo. Hear that, you men?"

"I'm going to make a run for those bundles as soon as it looks like I got a chance," Mungo said. He seemed to notice Uhlan for the first time. "Uhlan! Get your face out of the mud and man your weapon!"

"Oh, God, Lieutenant," Uhlan moaned. "Give up! We'll all get killed!"

Mungo wormed his way quickly across the ground to Uhlan, and punched him in the ribs. Uhlan raised his head, his blackened moon face contorted with pain and fear. "Get that rifle butt up to your shoulder," Mungo snapped, "and get ready to squeeze them off when the lieutenant gives the order."

Uhlan raised his M-1, his eyes never leaving Mungo's face. The big sergeant watched him until his hand closed around the slender pistol grip and his cheek rested against the stock. "Dana!" Mungo called. "You're pretty fast. When I holler, get up with me and head for those bundles!"

Why me? Dana thought resentfully, and then, *all right, you big bastard. I'll go anywhere you will.*

The enemy gun on their left coughed heavily. "That's your target, men!" Edgerton said. "When he opens up again, blast away! And keep blasting!"

A moment later the second gun hammered at the bundles. Dana laid his rifle aside and dug his toes and fingers into the soft earth.

"Sacco?" Mungo asked softly.

"Yeah," the other answered. He raised himself on one knee, the Springfield's butt jammed into the earth, his rigid arm holding it at an acute angle to the ground. He fired; the gun recoiled heavily. Seconds later they saw the flash of the exploding grenade in the field. "Over," Sacco and Mungo said together. Sacco ejected the spent shell. Mungo slipped a grenade onto the launcher, armed it. Sacco raised the angle of the gun and fired again.

The machine gun on the left sprayed the field again. "Fire!" Lt. Edgerton shouted. The guns of the patrol roared.

"Down some, Sacco," Mungo shouted above the din, readying another grenade. Sacco made a minute muscular adjustment and fired again. Dana thought the grenade hit even closer this time to the spot from which the German gunner seemed to be firing. It was almost impossible to judge in the dark. Mungo nodded and Sacco began firing grenades rapidly.

Dana kept his eyes on Mungo, set to spring to his feet. His ears rang with the firing. He realized that the voice of the machine gun on the left was absent from the din. Sacco's grenades began exploding in quick succession.

"Go!" Mungo roared, on his feet and charging straight for the blinking amber lights. Dana lunged after him. He felt, rather than saw, another man get to his feet and come pounding after them.

Mungo dove to earth behind the first bundle. He smashed the light out with the butt of Sacco's M-1. Dana dropped beside him. There was another thud, and Dana saw Reb on his right. The redhead's face still held its set, angry look. A burst tore at the air inches above their heads.

Mungo said, "Keep on the ground and roll this bundle out of that gun's beaten zone." Then he left them, crawling swiftly around the green canvas roll of the bundle, the rifle held in the hollows of his elbows.

Reb reached up and unfastened the cargo chute. "Let's go, boy," he told Dana. They began crawling back with the heavy bundle. It was hard, slow work. They dared not raise themselves more than inches from the ground and they had to fight for handholds on the tough canvas hide. All about them the night roared with small-arms fire and the German gunner's bullets cut the air above their heads. Dana was drenched with sweat and panting from the effort before they had gone ten yards.

The long nightmare crawl seemed to take forever. His arms ached. He and Reb were budging it only inches at a time now. They kept stubbornly on. How far had they run forward to the bundle? A mile? It seemed like an eternity of pulling this canvas-covered weight across a continent of soft, impeding earth. The insane German gunner continued to probe the night for their flesh, with Sacco's grenades crashing all around him. Dana wondered if Mungo was still alive, out in front of them with the second bundle.

Then Nolan dropped between them, pushing them roughly aside. He spread his arms and grasped the bundle by the thick white strap that connected the caps of the roll. He tugged it toward the line of men at an impossible rate of speed.

Dana rolled aside. He got his knees and elbows under him and crawled, drunk with fatigue, back to his rifle. He pointed it at where he hoped the remaining German gunner was and fired it as rapidly as he could. His own face held Reb's look of hatred now.

"Cease fire!" Lt. Edgerton shouted. Dana was ramming another clip into his rifle when Cadillac shook him.

"There's Mungo!"

Unbelievingly, Dana raised his cheek from the rifle stock. There was Mungo, fifteen yards ahead. He was on his knees, shoving the equipment bundle ahead of him. He kept steadily on until Nolan and Hollister raced out and pulled the second bundle back to their little fold in the ground. He lifted himself and ran, wearily, to Edgerton's side. Sacco kept lobbing grenades. Dana cursed and began firing at the far field again.

Cadillac shook him again, beating his back. Dana took his finger from the trigger. No rattle of gunfire came from the dark field. Far off they could hear a man screaming in pain. He saw Cadillac's grin white against his smeared face. The German! "That last grenade got him, man!" Cadillac said gleefully.

Dana let his cheek fall against the cool earth. It was heaven to lie like this, sucking air into his lungs.

Mungo was sitting up, his deep chest heaving. "Nolan," he rasped. "Get those bundles unrolled and pass out the guns and ammo. Every man carries an mg ammunition box, even the lieutenant! Sacco! Stuff what grenades you've got left into my musette bag!" He turned back to Edgerton. "We've got to get out of here, if we're going to make that village by daybreak."

"I think we're in the right drop zone, Sergeant," Edgerton said, nodding briskly. "I spotted the highway just before we went out of the plane." He pointed in the direction of the silenced machine-gun nests. "Over there."

Mungo sighed heavily and shook his head. "You're turned around." He pointed to the double row of trees on their right and swept his arm down to indicate the low bulding. "That's a French farm at that end of the lane. That lane must lead to the highway, or to a road that will take us to it." He jerked his thumb over his shoulder. "We go this way."

Edgerton had his map out, holding it close to his face to study it in the bright moonlight. "You're sure, Sergeant? The map—"

"I don't need any map. I looked at enough of them back in England. Mungo got to his feet, his stance solid, the weariness shaken off. "All right, Dana. Move your ass."

Dana repressed a groan. Getting to his hands and knees, he crawled to the unrolled equipment bundles. Franklin came crawling up while he was draping the bandoleers of M-1 clips over his chest. The frail pigeoneer was dragging a mass of splintered wood behind him. He seemed close to tears.

"Look at them, Nolan," he cried indignantly. "Every one of them dead!" Startled, Dana swung to him, and then realized that Franklin held the crushed remnants of the pigeon crate.

"You didn't hook their chute up before you pushed them out the door," Franklin said accusingly. "Why, Nolan? They're just poor dumb animals! They never did anything to you!"

Nolan laughed harshly. "Shut up, Bird-turd. You've still got two left. Me and Mungo need ammunition bearers, not pigeon nurses."

Franklin turned to Dana. "They never had a chance, Dana."

A fleeting sense of wonder at Nolan's casual, pointless brutality held Dana for a moment. But the image of Carr's mangled body was to awesomely fresh on his mind for him to show any concern over dead birds.

Nolan was still chortling as the patrol moved out, single file, across the field. Dana picked up the last ammunition case and followed him.

Mungo was waiting for them when they reached the narrow, two-lane highway. "Sacco, take Franklin down the road and set up opposite the bazooka team. We're going to see what can be done with this radio." He beckoned to Dana and led him across the macadam road to the center of a field where Edgerton waited.

The lieutenant sat cross-legged, studying an acetate-covered map. "Set up, soldier. I've got to get in touch with Regiment."

Mungo lifted the radio from Dana's back and set it on ground. He knelt a yard away, the Springfield's butt on the ground, his eyes searching the night. Dana socketed the long antenna and telescoped it out to its full length. He checked his calibration—Band 38—and held the phone to his ear. The air crackled with static. He could feel Lt. Edgerton's anxious eyes on him.

Dana flipped the butterfly switch and said softly: "Powderhorn. This is Powderhorn Special One. Come in Powder-horn. This is Powderhorn Special One. Come in Powder-horn. Over." Then he waited. No answer came.

"Are you getting anything, soldier?" Edgerton asked.

"Just some faint signals I can't read."

"Why don't they answer?" Edgerton demanded.

"It don't even pay to try guessing," Mungo rumbled. "We'll try later. We should be moving out for Sainte Madeleine."

"Try Division," the lieutenant snapped.

Dana reset the calibration of the set. "Whirlaway, this is Powderhorn Special One. Come in, Whirlaway."

No answer came from the division's headquarters. "Sir, all I'm getting is a bunch of confused signals," Dana reported. "Yeah, I figured," Mungo said, with no trace of rancor. "Another screwed-up deal like the Sicily jump. The Air Corps chalked up a snafu again. They spread the division all over the map. Let's go. We gotta get down that road."

"Try your spare batteries, operator," Edgerton said.

"Sir," Dana said, "I think Sergeant Mungo is right. Those planes broke formation as soon as the flak hit us coming over the French coast."

"As you were!" Edgerton snapped. "Try your spare batteries, operator!"

Dana found his eyes going to Mungo. The big non-com nodded.

Dana took the spare battery pack from his musette bag and transferred it to the radio. "Come in, Whirlaway. This is Powderhorn Special One. Come in, Whirlaway."

Lt. Edgerton waited silently for a moment. "Try Regiment, damn it!"

Dana reset his calibration to the regiment's net, checking his anger. After a moment, he said decisively, "Sorry, Lieutenant, but I can't raise them." "That's all she wrote," Mungo said. "Let's go."

"I want to be sure of our position," Edgerton said angrily. "I have to contact Colonel Tighe."

"I'm sure of our position," Mungo said. "You can call the colonel after we see what's in Sainte Madeleine." He stood and held the radio for Dana to slip on his back. "That's our job." He walked back to the road, his whistle raising the men to their feet.

The slim officer rose, folding the map back into his case, his eyes worried. Dana followed him to the road where Mungo waited. "I'm going up on the point with Cadillac," Mungo said. "I think we're about seven miles south of that village. No more than nine. Don't let the men bunch up." He jogged down the road to take up the lead of the little column. Very soon the whispered order came back, "Move out."

CHAPTER TEN

D DAY, 0530 HOURS

It took them more than three hours to reach the village. Progress was slow in the mud and darkness. Mungo called frequent halts while he and Cadillac checked ahead, probing turns in the road and the farm lanes joining it. The sergeant was tireless and his swift, reflexive mastery of scouting technique made him seem indifferent to his own safety.

As they moved down the road, the character of the countryside altered sharply. Trees and the thick, impressive hedgerows became fewer. The scent of hay and apples left the air and was replaced by that of seawater and then the putrid marsh smell of dead and rotting things. When they moved off the road to rest, the men found themselves in soft, foot-grasping swamps. Now and then, as the sky began to lighten, Dana caught a far-off glimpse of water.

"Getting close to the coastal marshes," Lieutenant Edgerton said.

At every extended pause in the march, he had Dana run up the aerial and call both the division and regimental headquarters. They met with no success. Not only could Dana make no contact with either the Whirlaway or Powderhorn net, but the frantic traffic he intercepted revealed that the American airborne landings behind the coast were in almost hopeless confusion. The air crackled with messages from isolated units striving desperately to make contact. Most seemed lost and completely disoriented, just beginning to accept the fact that Troop Carrier Command had reduced their plans to chaos.

A cold lump of fear settled in the men as the realization moved up and down the line that the regiment could not be reached. They were eleven lightly-armed men, alone in the midst of enemy armies. Intermittently, the distant roar of battle told of other paratroop units being snuffed out in the Normandy night. Their turn must come soon. They thought of the tenacious German gunner continuing to rake them with fire while Sacco's grenades fell all around him, and the men of the patrol shuddered. It was nearly dawn when Mungo halted them behind a low, crumbling field-stone wall. Dana could see the men crouched along it at intervals. "Here's your village," the sergeant told Edgerton.

"Why did you stop us here?" the officer demanded.

"There's Germans there," Mungo told him curtly. "Cadillac found wire running down the street to one of the houses. Single-strand—that's German field wire."

Edgerton snapped his fingers. "That's what Regiment is waiting to hear. Set up, Dana."

Mungo shook his head. "We don't know what strength they're in. They may be just an outpost. We're supposed to watch for a whole division—the Three-five-two, remember? We've got to go in there and see if they're around."

Dana raised his head far enough to peer over the wall. Dimly, in the somber morning light, he saw a single cobblestone street, no more than fifteen or twenty feet wide. He could make out the outlines of a half-dozen houses with barns attached behind them. Surprisingly, for such a small place, the spire of a church loomed at the far end of the street. No sound came from the village.

"All we've seen so far is telephone wire," Mungo said drily. "We're supposed to occupy this village. Before we report we better go in and hit whoever is there. If they hear you gabbing on a radio, you ain't going to surprise them none."

"Damn it, Mungo! Do you think you're running this patrol?"

Dana turned at the outrage in the lieutenant's voice. Mungo, unperturbed, studied the officer. "Are you going to run it right?" he asked.

"I'll make the decisions and I'll give the orders," Edgerton shouted. "Dana, set up that radio."

Stone chips flew up beside the lieutenant's head. From somewhere in the depths of the village, a Schmeisser machine pistol sprayed the wall. The men crouched low and thrust their weapons up and fired wildly at the buildings. Nolan shouted, "The second house!" His Thompson hammered on full automatic.

Dana put the M-1 on the top of the wall and fired a clip at the dark bulk of the building, trying to guess where the windows would be.

"Franklin, damnit, get that tripod over here!" Dana recognized Sacco's voice above the din. He lowered himself to feed another clip into his rifle. He heard Mungo roar. "Keep down! Don't run!"

The Schmeisser opened up again. The gun was incredibly fast. It made a noise like ripping canvas. Dana found a notch in the wall and fired steadily at the spot where he had seen the gun flashing. Sacco's machine gun burst into life on his right, and when he lowered his head to slip a bandoleer from around his neck, he saw Edgerton steadying its tripod and feeding the belt into the gun. A trooper lay at the lieutenant's feet sprawled in the utter relaxation of death.

Grenades were exploding in the village street now, and Dana heard the patrol's second machine gun join in the fire fight.

Then Mungo was barking, "Cease fire! Cease fire!" Up and down the line the guns fell silent. Dana saw Mungo crouched behind the wall, not far from him, listening intently.

"They're taking off," Mungo said. "That Kraut with the Schmeisser was just to hold us off while they saddled up."

Dana frowned at him disbelievingly. Then he heard the whine of a starter, and an automobile motor roared somewhere out of sight in the village. He rolled quickly into firing position, the stock of the rifle against his cheek.

"They won't come this way," Mungo said.

Sacco and Edgerton were kneeling over the dead man. Dana crawled down to them as they rolled the corpse onto its back, and he saw that it was Franklin, the pigeoneer. One lens of his GI glasses was broken and the face of the frail T/S was caked with mud. The Schmeisser bullets had crashed into his chest, pulping one of the pigeons that dangled from the clips on his chest straps. Edgerton unfastened the bloody jacket and jerked a dog tag loose from the thin chain around Franklin's neck. He unsnapped the live pigeon and handed the frightened bird, still in its nylon vest, to Sacco.

Mungo's eyes rested on the body briefly. "He was a good kid."

Edgerton crawled up to where Mungo was peering at the village through a crevice in the wall. Dawn was coming on fast now, and they could see that the houses were roofed with red tile. Rotting plaster crumbled from the brick walls—despite its church, the farm village was obviously a poor one. "What do you think we should do now, Sergeant?" Edgerton asked.

If Mungo remembered the officer's earlier reprimand, he gave no sign of it. "We push right in and take a look. It's probably empty now, but we better play it safe. I'll leave Sacco here to give us covering fire while we rush the buildings. He can have Uhlan as assistant gunner." Mungo scratched the wiry stubble on his chin. "Lieutenant, you take Nolan, Hollister and Dana and go around on the left. Grenade every house before you go in, and tell the men to be careful. We've got two casualties already."

The big non-com rolled over and sent his piercing whistle down the wall. "Uhlan! Nolan! Hollister! Come up here and keep your heads down!" He turned back to Edgerton. "I'll take the others around on the right. Give me a couple of minutes before you start firing and then go over the wall fast, Lieutenant."

Edgerton nodded. "Okay, Mungo."

Nolan and Hollister crouched beside him, as Dana fixed his bayonet to the rifle. Uhlan was lying flat beside Sacco, his eyes carefully averted from Franklin's body. Dana gathered his legs under him, tensed to spring. About twenty-five yards of open ground separated them from the cover of the houses. How many seconds did it take to cover twenty-five yards at a dead run?

"Now, Sacco!" Edgerton brought his hand down sharply. The light machine gun roared and spat. Sacco held his finger to the trigger, spinning the gun on free traverse, spraying the windows and the doors of the buildings.

"Charge!" The lieutenant's voice was cracked with tension. Dana bounded over the wall. Bent low, he ran heavily through the mud, waiting to learn what it felt like to be shot. Behind him, Sacco's gun never stopped; the lead shrieked overhead. Dana drove his legs like pistons, racing side by side with Nolan. Then they were against the wall of the first house. Nolan pulled the pin of a grenade and held it for a long time, his lips moving in a silent count. Then he flipped it through a window. The grenade exploded almost instantly.

Dana dove headfirst through the window. He skidded across the floor and tore the bullet shredded curtains from his eyes. Nothing moved in the shattered room. Nolan and Edgerton bounded in after him; Hollister climbed through a second window.

A cellar door lay flush with the floor. Edgerton snatched it open and dropped a grenade down, the handle flying from his hand. The boom was muffled beneath the floor, but the heavy door bounced and shuddered with the blast.

Dana ran for the stairs that led to an upper floor. Nolan flung him aside and raced up in the lead, his Thompson at the ready. All three bedrooms were empty. They heard Sacco's gun ripping into the buildings further up the street. Grenades exploded in the house across the street and they knew that Mungo had reached it with the James boys and Cadillac. When they came down the stairs, Hollister and Edgerton were emerging from the attached barn. "Nothing there," the lieutenant said.

Dana saw the faces of the men were drawn and tight with strain. Their eyes glittered. Dana knew he must look the same to them. He was aware only of his heart pounding in his chest and an overwhelming desire to finish the job fast.

From across the street he heard Mungo's voice, cautioning them all: "Let's conserve on those grenades now, but don't expose yourselves."

Nolan ripped a side door open and kneeled to spray the windows of the next house. He paused to change his magazine, then dashed across the intervening yard, Dana at his heels. They burst into another empty house. While Nolan led Edgerton up to probe the top floor, Dana grenaded the cellar. Grenades might be scarce, but he had no intention of exploring the dark depths in person.

He led Hollister out to check the barn. All the stalls were empty and the floor was clean. The manure pile in the corner looked several days old. Warily they walked the length of the barn and slipped out the back way. Sacco was no longer firing. They had advanced too far into the village for him to cover them.

The next building was the last house on their side of the road. Then would come the church. Dana spotted Edgerton and Nolan sprinting to the windows and he raced with Hollister to the next barn. He rolled a grenade inside the wide door. The huge timbers of its framing shook with the explosion. They pried the door open on more empty stalls. A few stalks of hay drifted down about them, shaken from the loft by the concussion. Nolan and Edgerton entered from the house, shaking their heads.

"Looks like they skinned out, all right," Edgerton said. He crouched in the barn door and pointed to a stand of dark green trees at the foot of a knoll of ground that humped behind the church. Beyond the trees, the early sunlight shimmered on the mist rising up from the Vire River. The knoll was high enough to give them cover even from the tower of the church. "We'll get down in those trees and work our way back along the river to the church. Let's go."

They gained the trees in one brief rush.

Dana could hear the bark of Cadillac's Thompson as Edgerton led them, single-file, along the slippery river-bank. Ahead, he saw a single-span stone bridge arching the highway over the Vire, onto a low-lying causeway that curved gracefully through the marshlands on the other side of the river. The marshes stretched out, pool-table flat, into the morning haze. They were thickly sewn with clumps of sea grass and a gray scum floated on the surface. Insects buzzed and swarmed around the men, biting at their faces.

Edgerton dropped, panting, onto the solid ground at the edge of the churchyard. Reb and Swampy were standing in the cobblestone street, recklessly smashing at a house door with their rifle butts. "If those two aren't drawing fire, the town is empty," the lieutenant said as Dana came up. Across the street Reb splintered the wood from the lock and walked arrogantly through the doorway, his rifle at his hip. Edgerton stood up and began walking toward the ancient, square-towered Norman church. Dana and the others followed him.

None of them saw the blast of the Schmeisser that opened on them from the church. A high thin snarl, and a row of mud spurts danced up on Dana's left. He threw himself to the ground and rolled himself dizzyingly back toward the river-bank. The Schmeisser ripped again and he heard a yelp of surprise.

He reached the embankment and dropped behind it with his M-1 in firing position. Hollister was lying at the edge of the churchyard, trying to raise himself with one arm. With his other hand he clutched his groin. His white, stunned face was piteous. "I'm hit, I'm hit," he said. He looked ridiculous.

Nolan yelled, "It came from the church!" He raised his Thompson and blazed away at the weathered shutters on the windows. Dana trained his M-1 on the apertures of the medieval bell tower. "Come on, Hollister," he pleaded, "get back here!"

Hollister stared at him numbly, his mouth hanging open. The proud booted feet thrashed pitifully on the ground as he tried again to rise. "I'm hit," he said again.

Nolan propped the Thompson against a tree trunk. "He can't move," he told Dana and Edgerton. "Keep firing at those windows!"

Dana pumped a shot into each of the four windows, reloaded and swung the muzzle of his rifle back down the row again. Nolan leaped with long steps to Hollister's side, bent and scooped him up effortlessly. Then he was back and sliding past Dana, dropping the boy behind the cover of the bank. Dana squinted at the bullet-pitted sides of the church, trying to detect movement behind the inch-wide gaps in the shutters. He heard Hollister begging, "No, don't leave me!" Then Nolan dropped beside him. "Get back and take care of him, Okie."

Somewhere down the street Mungo was bellowing, "Nolan! Edgerton! Where the hell are you?" Dana slid further down the embankment to where Nolan had dropped the boy.

Dana dropped to his knees beside the moaning Hollister. Blood had escaped through his jump-pants and made a wet and sticky patch above his groin. Hollister lay writhing feebly on the ground. His body gave off a foul odor.

Dana unbuckled the boy's rifle belt, whispering, "Take it easy, buddy. Try to take it easy." He opened the zipper of the jacket and slipped the suspender tabs from their anchoring buttons. Blood and liquid excreta welled thickly from a hole above the line of Hollister's pubic hair.

Sacco appeared further down the bank, on the other side of the roadway. He ran for the edge of the churchyard, straining with the weight of the machine gun. Uhlan plodded heavily behind him, carrying the tripod and the ammunition boxes. His face was sick with fear. Scattered shots came from the other side of the church.

Dana snatched the sealed bandage from the first-aid kit on Hollister's belt. He shook the powdered sulfa into the pulsing hole in Hollister's underbelly. He unwound the bandage; *"This side away from wound,"* he read. He laid the pad over the bullet hole and unrolled the long gauze strips. It was going to be difficult to tie it in place without assistance. He thought of calling for someone to help, and decided against it. The important thing was to knock the enemy out of that church before more of them caught it. Sacco's machine gun roared in four short bursts. One for each window, Dana thought automatically.

He knelt astride Hollister's legs. "Can you raise yourself, kid?"

The boy moaned and arched his back feebly. His head rolled on the ground. "It's going to hurt, Hollister," Dana said. *Why in hell had Mungo collected the morphine syrettes at the airstrip?* He slid his hands under the boy's hips and raised him, working his right arm along the small of Hollister's back, fumbling for the roll of gauze in his left hand. Hollister sobbed and cursed him: "Oh, you son-of-a-bitch!"

"Sorry, kid. I've got no one to help me." He had the gauze roll in his right hand now and he stretched it over Hollister's belly. A knot just above the pad anchored it over the wound. He had to raise the boy again, sweating with the effort while Hollister cursed him, to pass the other tie-strip under his crotch and around his buttock before knotting it at his hip.

Dana patted his shoulder and picked up the rifle. "You're okay now, kid. We'll move you inside in a minute."

Hollister's eyes opened, a new fear in them. "Don't leave me here!"

Mungo came plunging over the bank and dropped to his knees beside them. "How are you, kid?"

"I hurt bad, Sergeant." It was like a child pleading. "Don't leave me here alone."

"We ain't going to leave you," Mungo told him. "Come on, Dana. You're finished here."

Dana followed him over the bank and up to the edge of the churchyard. They dropped together behind a little fold in the ground. Nolan and Edgerton were crouched behind trees, neither of them firing. Sacco swung the barrel of his gun back and forth, his finger ready for any hint of a target behind the shutters. Uhlan lay beside him, his face pressed into the ground.

"Have any of you heard anything in there?" Mungo asked the group.

"No," Nolan said, his eyes never leaving the building.

"They might have taken off after they fired at you," Mungo said. "They had time to get out and into the marshes."

Dana saw a man sprint into the graveyard at the rear of the church, and drop among the headstones and crosses. He snapped his rifle up for a quick shot and recognized Reb just in time. Reb lay behind a marble headpiece and began firing into the windows on the opposite side of the church.

"He takes too many chances," Sacco said. "But he's got guts."

Mungo was surveying the church. "Once we're up against the wall underneath those windows, we're okay," he said. He glanced around at the others and nodded. Dana tensed, ready to spring forward. "Okay, Fortunato!" Mungo growled.

Sacco clamped his hand on the trigger. A heavy window shutter shook beneath the rain of bullets, and Dana saw splinters flying from it as they rushed the church. He crouched against the rough wall, rifle ready, with Edgerton beside him.

Mungo and Nolan stood before the big brass-handled door in the angle formed by the wall and the tower. Mungo tossed aside the ring of a grenade and nodded to Nolan. Nolan grasped the door handle and tugged experimentally. The door swung easily outward. Mungo hurled the grenade far into the depths of the church.

Nolan kicked the door shut. The grenade boomed inside. Mungo snatched the door open; they poured inside and threw themselves on the floor.

Their darting eyes saw no one in the gloom and quiet.

The church was a shambles. The leaded frames of the narrow, arched windows were empty. Light poured through the dozens of round holes in each wooden shutter. Ricocheting bullets had ripped long white scars in the time-darkened wood of the pews.

They rose slowly to their feet. The thick-walled little building was scarcely thirty feet wide inside. "Make a good fort," Mungo said.

Edgerton crouched at the open archway of the bell-tower, carbine ready in his hands. *"Raus mit!"* he shouted up the stairway. *"Handen hoch!*

No answer came. He bounded through the arch. "Hey, look!" he shouted back to them. Dana and Nolan crowded into the archway. Edgerton held a Schmeisser in his hand. There was a hint of small-boy pride on his face.

Their eyes went upward. A bannisterless flight of rude stone steps climbed the inner walls of the tower. Thick, hand-hewn beams supported the belfry platform. Through its narrow opening they saw stone fly as a bullet entered through one aperture and smashed against a corner of the tower. "That's Reb," Mungo said. "Go out and tell him we're inside, Nolan."

Dana followed Mungo down the single aisle of the church. Some superstitious awe held him back as Mungo stepped over the communion rail. The big sergeant threw open the door of the sacristy, the muzzle of his Springfield probing ahead.

"Well I'll be…look!" Edgerton shouted, and Dana whirled around. The lieutenant, his shoulder holding open the curtained door of the confessional, gaped ludicrously at something inside. As Dana watched, Edgerton reached in and drew out by her bare arm, a slender, dark-haired girl.

CHAPTER ELEVEN
D DAY, 0700 HOURS

The girl shrank back like a cornered animal. Her eyes flickered wildly over the men, glittering defiance and fear. "She thinks we're Germans," Edgerton said brightly. "She doesn't know about the invasion yet."

He smiled at the girl and turned to show her the American flag stitched to the right sleeve of his jump-jacket. *Nous... Américains—comprenez? Vous savez... Américains."*

The girl drew back against the wall. She gave no sign of understanding. She wore a bulky trench coat spattered with mud, and there were two streaks of dirt on her face. She was taller than Dana expected French girls to be; her face had a sullen, sensual prettiness.

Edgerton's smile faded. "Don't be afraid," he said. "We're Americans. *Americanos, sabe?* Damn! Do you speak French, Dana?"

"No, sir."

Mungo came back down the aisle. The girl's dark eyes darted over him and her chin came up. "Where did you find her?"

"She was hiding in the confessional," Edgerton told him. *"Nous... Américains, mademoiselle."*

"Do you speak English?" Mungo rumbled. The girl's lips tightened ; she shook her head.

"I'm sure she thinks we're Germans, Sergeant," Edgerton said. He laughed.

"Balls," Mungo told him. His hands swept over the pockets of the trench coat. He caught the girl's arm and turned her roughly around. He prodded the loose bulge of the coat above her belt.

"*Laisse-moi!*" the girl spat savagely. "*Sal 'ricain!*" She tried to jerk away as Mungo ripped her coat open; she managed only to slip out of the coat. Mungo caught her easily, the coat in his hand. He thrust his Springfield at Dana and slid his free hand up under the girl's tight skirt. She swung her fists against his temple. Mungo jammed her, kicking, into a corner. He ran his hand, slowly and carefully, up the inside of her thighs.

Edgerton threw his weight against Mungo, breaking his hold on the girl. His face was furious. "This is a Frenchwoman! One of our allies! What the hell do you think you're doing?"

The girl slid down the wall toward the door of the church, glowering with fury. Cadillac and Nolan stepped into the doorway. Cadillac's eyes lit and he threw his arms wide in a gesture of happy surprise!" The girl moved quickly to his side, clutching his sleeve, pressing her breasts against his arm. "Man," said Cadillac happily "Where did we get her?"

Mungo brushed the lieutenant aside, the sleepy eyes contemptuous. "Do *you* want to search her? Go ahead."

"Search her for what?" Edgerton demanded. "Get outside, Sergeant."

Mungo did not budge. His hands were examining the coat he held. "Search her. Period. There's a man outside shot in the guts by someone in this church."

"Hollister was shot by a German."

"Did you see him? Did you see him in here?"

"He got away."

"Did you see him get away?" Mungo's hand shot out and almost slapped the Schmeisser out of the officer's grasp. "Why in hell would he leave his piece behind?"

Sudden doubt crept into Edgerton's face. All eyes swung to the girl. Mungo dropped the coat and crossed to her, and Cadillac braced himself with one protective arm across her shoulders. "Watch it now, Mungo."

Mungo's stiff-arm shove sent him reeling into Nolan. He caught the girl's arm again and tugged at her blouse. The girl spat suddenly and brought up her knee in a flash of bare pink flesh and ruffled cotton. Mungo twisted and caught the kick heedlessly on his hip. His thick fingers knotted in the long, black hair and he thrust her against the wall, leaning on her. Nolan watched him with feverish eyes.

Mungo slipped his hand inside the loose green bodice. He laughed. He caught the collar of the dress and ripped it to her waist. A P-38 pistol hung between her breasts, the dark blue steel incongruous against her pale, pink-nippled flesh. Her full breasts shook and reddened under Mungo's rough mauling as he snapped the lanyard that held the gun suspended from her neck. He grinned at Edgerton and flung the girl aside.

Cadillac's eyes were on the high-tipped swell of her satin flesh. "Man," he breathed, "a way-out broad!"

"She shot Hollister," Dana told him.

"She's some Kraut officer's shack-job," Mungo said. "He left her behind to hold us up."

"Maybe she shot Bird-Turd, too," Nolan said. "Let me shoot the bitch, Lieutenant." There was a look of erotic frenzy on his face. Dana hated him more than ever.

"Good God, no!" said Edgerton.

"The orders say no prisoners until we meet the seaborne," Nolan argued. "We can't spare a man to guard her."

The color drained away behind the smears on Edgerton's face. His eyes looked trapped. "That order is for line companies," he said weakly. "It doesn't—doesn't apply to us."

Nolan, with a twisted smile, raised the Thompson's muzzle and pointed it at the girl. "We can't take her along. Let me blast her."

The girl was trembling as she rose from the floor and drew the tatters of her dress across her breasts. Her eyes sought Cadillac's beseechingly.

"Man, there's no hurry," Cadillac protested.

"Nolan, take a couple of men and carry Hollister in here," Mungo ordered. The big man lowered the gun and left, his eyes lingering on the girl. "Dana, you and Cadillac go down and pick up the bazooka and the radio. Leave the other machine gun there; we'll need it to protect our rear. Doubletime back with the radio. The lieutenant's going to try Regiment again."

Edgerton brought his mind back with a visible effort. "Yes," he said. "Yes. Get it up here right away, Dana."

"Things are happening too fast for that stud," Cadillac said as they trotted quickly out of the church. The morning light was full now and Dana saw by his service watch that it was nearly seven-fifteen. They had been in France for almost six hours. And two men dead already, possibly three.

"Things are going to fast for me, too," Dana said. "Let's go check on Hollister."

They started across the churchyard to the river-bank. Dana went on: "I think we're sunk. With the long antenna up, that SCR-three hundred will pick up signals twenty miles away in this flat country. We ain't heard anything from Regiment all night, and we're supposed to be eight miles out."

Cadillac's face sobered. "Jeez, as bad as that? Well, hell, we got a chance with Mungo leading us."

"Mungo?" Dana could not hide his surprise. "That son-of-a-bitch is another Nolan. Maybe worse."

Cadillac shrugged. "The cat's a swinging soldier though."

They slid over the embankment and found Uhlan and Nolan crouched with Sacco over Hollister. Sacco had stripped off one of Hollister's two jump-jackets. It lay on the ground now, the sleeves inside out, the zipper pulled shut. As they watched, Sacco slipped the first of two rifles into the armholes. The jacket made an emergency litter, long enough to hold a wounded man's upper body while his legs dangled over the rifles.

Hollister rolled his head feebly back and forth. "It hurts. Oh God, it hurts!"

"Take it easy, buddy," Dana said. "They're taking you inside now."

"Be a man, kid," Nolan told him.

Sacco adjusted the improvised litter. "Let's get him onto it," he said. Franklin's pigeon was still clipped to his pack strap.

"He needs a fix," Cadillac said. "Sacco, let me have a couple of those 'M' syrettes."

Sacco searched his face with an appraising glance. "One will do it, Cadillac," he said. "You're not feeling hung yourself?" His eyes had that familiar ironic glint.

"Screw you, Sacco," Cadillac said, but there was a guilty flush on his face. "Fix the cat. He's hurting."

Sacco had produced one of the morphine tubes from his pocket. He removed the cap from the needle and inserted it gently into Hollister's thigh. Hollister groaned and thrashed his legs weakly. Cadillac's eyes were intent on the face of the wounded boy. "Mainlining's better," he said to no one in particular.

"Let's go, Cadillac," Dana said. "Got to pick up that gear."

Cadillac, reluctantly, rose to his feet as Nolan and Sacco eased Hollister onto the stretcher. Hollister groaned and Cadillac said gently, before turning away: "Cool it, kid. When that junk hits, it'll groove you out." His tone was almost envious.

Nolan supported one end of the stretcher with Sacco and Uhlan paired at Hollister's feet. They moved toward the church. Dana and Cadillac started down the village street, toward the fieldstone wall at its western end. They walked side by side, the length of the village, their weapons at the ready and both of them searching the edges of the houses and the countryside beyond, for any sign of the enemy.

"Guess they've taken off," said Dana.

"Looks that way." Cadillac's mind was elsewhere. It was obvious that he wanted to talk. "Hey, how about that chick now, dad?"

"Well, what about her?"

Cadillac's fingers made a quick, approving gesture. "I think she kinda digs me. Did you see the way she came on to me when Mungo tried to strong-arm her?"

Dana smiled. "Cadillac, you're oversexed."

"Nah," said Cadillac. "I'm not oversexed. I'm Greek."

For the first time since the guard tent, Dana threw his head back and laughed. "You're Greek, all right," he said. "You're a screwed-up Greek. What are you doing here, anyway? I thought you weren't going to jump."

"Hell man, were you on the nod in that plane? Didn't you catch that flak coming up? Only a flip would want to fly back through that." He glanced at Dana sharply and grinned. "Anyway, I kinda changed my mind. Always wanted to see France."

"Mungo changed your mind for you, you mean."

Cadillac shrugged. "Ah, the big ape needed me. Thought I'd help him out."

Although the sun had been up for some time, the low-lying mist still wreathed above the swamp and was just beginning to rise. Behind the wall, half-hidden in the swirling haze, they found the crumpled body of the pigeoneer. The thin, soft face, already green, wore a look of pained bewilderment. The shattered chest was caked with coagulated blood. Empty machine-gun cartridge cases were strewn profusely near the body, and the sweetish smell of death still lingered in the air.

Dana said, "We shouldn't leave him lying here. We ought to..."

"No. There isn't time," said Cadillac. "Let's organize this gear."

Dana forced himself to ransack Franklin's body for the carbine clips and extra ammo and grenades. Cadillac shouldered the long bazooka and slung the rocket pouches on his neck. They gathered up the extra ammunition boxes and Dana set the radio on his back. Then, feeling just a little sick, he sat down behind the wall and lit a cigarette.

Behind them, running feet clattered along the cobblestones. They both turned anxiously, raising their weapons, and saw Sacco trotting down the middle of the street. He vaulted over the wall. "Figured you'd want some help with all that stuff," he said.

"What's happening?" asked Dana.

Sacco took the butt from him, dragged on it a moment, and then handed it back. "Got to conserve," he said. "We may run low. Oh, back there? Edgerton's got him a problem. Mungo figures the Krauts are coming back—that was probably just an outpost we routed. He wants a patrol out right away, and he can't spare anyone to guard the girl."

"Mungo want to shoot her?" Cadillac asked apprehensively. He was hoisting the bazooka to his shoulder again.

"Would it bother you, Cadillac?" Sacco grinned.

"Kinda wasteful, man."

They trotted back to the church together. On the edge of the churchyard, close by the near abutment of the bridge, Reb was digging a spider hole. He shoveled the dirt neatly onto a blanket, which Swampy carried off to dump behind the church. They were preparing a bazooka trap, concealing its presence from anything that might come over the bridge.

As they swung into the churchyard, Dana noticed that Sacco's machine gun had been mounted in the tower to sweep the causeway leading to the bridge. They went through the church to the sacristy, where Mungo's voice was booming.

"All right," he said. "So we do it your way. And supposing the kid passes out? He's weak and the morphine's working on him. Then we got this bitch with an M-1 rifle blazing at our backs."

"I won't pass out, Sergeant," Hollister said as they entered. "I feel pretty good now." He was lying on a pile of sacramental vestments laid out on a bench beneath the window. A folded cassock lay underneath his head and he held his rifle cradled weakly on his chest. His drug-glazed eyes were fixed on the girl, who crouched, still terrified, between the cabinets on the farther wall.

She had pinned the tatters of her blouse together somehow, but one soft breast showed whitely through the rent, the nipple pink and oddly pathetic in the harshness of the morning light. She was staring at Mungo, as though she sensed that whatever might happen, her fate lay with him.

Mungo turned away. His commands were brisk and immediate. "Sacco, get up in the tower and relieve that frig-gin' Uhlan on the gun. Watch the road; they'll be coming back. You'll have to cover me a little ways. I'm going up the road a piece with a couple of men to see if I can spot 'em. Dana, set that radio up." His eyes ran rapidly around the room, passing contemptuously over the girl, who shrank from them as though from a blow.

"Nolan, saddle up," Mungo continued. "Take Uhlan and patrol the road down the other way—back the way we come. We don't know what's behind us, so take it easy. Make about a half-, three-quarters of a mile. If you run into anything, get your ass back here."

"Uhlan?" Nolan asked scornfully. "Rather do the job alone."

"Get moving, Nolan. Uhlan's going with you. And pick up Reb James outside. Drop him at the gun behind that wall. He'll have to secure our rear." He slung his Spring-field over his shoulder. "Cadillac, tell Swampy to leave off on that digging and both of you come with me." He paused before he started from the door. His eyes were soft as he gazed at Hollister. "How're you doing, kid?" he asked. "Sure you can stay awake now?"

"I'm okay, Sergeant." The voice was weak, but Hollister's face was rigid with a kind of baffled anger as he stared at the cowering girl.

"If she gives you any guff, just drop her, kid. Let her have what she gave you."

Hollister nodded and shifted his rifle so that it pointed directly at the girl.

"Now, wait a minute, soldier," Edgerton said to Hollister. His voice was firmer than before, but his gestures were nervous and his face unsure. "I know you're bitter … you have a right to be. But we don't want you to shoot that girl. She might—" He faltered, searching desperately. "She might have valuable military information."

Mungo snorted and left the room, followed by Sacco and Nolan. Cadillac stopped in the door, looking back. "Grooving with it, dad?" he asked Hollister.

Hollister tried to grin. "There's hardly any pain now," he said.

Cadillac nodded. "Yeah, this army junk makes it. Wilder than that beat stuff the uptown pushers handle." He winked at Hollister and then his eyes moved slowly to the girl. His features seemed to soften and his long black lashes swept down, hooding his eyes. His gaze was fixed unwaveringly on the pink swell of her breast. Something of a half-smile came over her face as her hands went up and clutched the torn dress closely to her throat. "Yeah, baby, later. We'll save it for later." His voice was velvet-soft and he raised his lids to stare calmly, assuredly into her eyes. The girl tore her eyes away—with an effort, it seemed.

"*Goddamnit, Cadillac!*" Mungo's voice outside was a peremptory bellow. "Let's get moving!"

"Business, baby," Cadillac said. "The working people need me. I'll be back real soon, now. Keep it warm for me."

He turned and walked lightly out through the door. Edgerton, confused, cast a nervous glance at the girl, and then turned back to Dana. "We'd better get set up in the tower," he said.

Dana shifted the radio to his back and they climbed the stairs together, leaving Hollister, with the rifle in his arms, staring harshly at the girl.

Sacco was already up in the tower. He leaned on his elbows at the aperture and gazed calmly up the road. Dana caught a glimpse of Mungo and Swampy moving cautiously across the bridge. Cadillac trailed behind them. Nolan strode toward the other end of the village, leading Uhlan and Reb.

Dana socketed the large antenna, and pointed it out the western aperture. "Try to raise the regiment," Edgerton said.

Dana centered the regimental band. There was a confused crackling of signals; no voices were audible. He pressed the butterfly switch to send. "Powderhorn," he said, "this is Powderhorn Special. Come in Powderhorn." He released the switch to listen— there was only static—and again he repeated the call. Edgerton shifted impatiently. Dana raised his eyes and shrugged his shoulders. Just then a distant signal sounded in the earphone. *"Powderhorn, Powderhorn... come in, damnit!"*

"This is Powderhorn Special," Dana said. "Identify yourself. Over."

"...half of them lying wounded in the swamps. Where the hell is Regiment?" The voice was faint and frantic in his ear.

The readability was almost zero. *"...Third Battalion set...operator's dead...Colonel and the whole battalion staff...Scattered over hell and gone. Everything's frigged up..."*

Edgerton snatched the phone-piece from Dana. His face was strained as he listened. After a moment he handed back the phone. "Can't understand him. What in hell is he saying? Third Battalion scattered and cut to pieces? Can't you raise the regiment?"

"Trying sir," Dana said, then into the phone he repeated the tedious netting-in procedure. The distant operator, ignoring his signals, kept sending without a break: *"...cut off and surrounded... machine-gun fire... Where the hell is Regiment. Where is the regiment?"* The signal seemed to weaken. The voice trailed off. Dana looked up helplessly at Edgerton.

"Try for Division," Edgerton said. The strain of command was showing on his face. For the first time in his life, Dana found himself almost sorry for an officer.

Dana tried the divisional net. The signals on that band were even more hopelessly confused. There was static, the shrill piping of CW code, and a stream of barely audible voices, unreadably intermingled. After a time he found that he could isolate a voice transmission. A lone operator from the 82nd was lost in a swamp, somewhere on the beachhead near Pouppeville, and frantically calling for help. Dana held the phone up to Edgerton. "Can't raise anything much," he said. "Want me to keep trying?"

Edgerton refused the phone with an impatient gesture. "Might as well close down for a while. You sure you know how to operate that radio?"

"Try it yourself, sir," Dana said. He did not disguise the contempt in his voice.

Edgerton refused the phone again. "Well, we can't raise Regiment or Division. Anyway, it's good that we still have a pigeon for contact with First Army."

Sacco, leaning on the embrasure, half-turned in their direction. "What are you going to tell them at Army, Lieutenant?"

"We'll see when we get the information we're after." Edgerton's voice was sharply defensive.

"Yeah," said Sacco, drily. "It's good to have a pigeon with us." Dana stifled a laugh.

There was a sudden rattle of small-arms fire. Sacco crouched over his machine gun and stared intently up the road. "Mungo's run into something up there," he said. Dana sprang forward to help feed the belt.

Edgerton kneeled behind their shoulders. "Well, cover him, man," he said. "Give him covering fire."

"Fire at what, Lieutenant?" Sacco asked. "They're beyond the bend. I can't see anything."

They heard the rough staccato of Cadillac's Thompson, heavier than the German burp-guns. There was quiet for a second, then an intermittent volley of rifle-fire broke out. "Here they come," Sacco said. He edged his cheek against the handle of the gun and squinted down the barrel. "Use your rifle," he said to Dana. "I can handle the belt alone."

Edgerton, behind them, had unslung his carbine. Dana crouched at Sacco's side, with his M-1 centered on the road. They waited tensely while the volume of firing swelled.

CHAPTER TWELVE
D DAY, 0820 HOURS

Swampy appeared around the bend of the road and threw himself flat. He fired up the road. Cadillac, then Mungo leap-frogged past him. Mungo took the cover of a concrete marker while he sighted up the road past Swampy. Swampy sprang sharply to his feet and retreated toward the village with Cadillac. Mungo covered their withdrawal with his Springfield.

In the tower they could hear the clatter of footsteps as Cadillac and Swampy crossed the bridge and ran into the church. Mungo then crawled backwards past the curve of the road. He raised himself abruptly, and ran to the church. He lifted his eyes to Sacco in the tower and pointed back down the road. Sacco nodded and made a little circle with his thumb and forefinger. Sacco held his gun sighted on the road.

"Fire at whatever comes around that bend," Edgerton said foolishly.

"Sure, Lieutenant," Sacco said. His tone was soothing, as though he spoke to reassure a child. "That's exactly what I figure to do."

Mungo came racing up the tower stairs.

"Infantry coming. They got a little armor, mainly light stuff." His words were rapid but his voice was without alarm. He might have been reading a morning report at some garrison back in the States.

"Then we'd better pull out, sergeant," Edgerton said. It was obviously meant as a question.

Mungo was staring down the road with the sharply-patient eyes of a hunter. He did not look at Edgerton. "They'll pot us like rabbits if we try to move out through the marshes. And the vehicles could run us down on the causeway. We got a nice position here. Why the hell move?"

Sacco's voice was coldly professional, "What about that dead ground just around the bend?" he asked.

Mungo pointed off to the left where the ground rose up to form the knoll before it sloped away to the marshlands north of the village. "An LMG right there could sweep that stretch and keep them off our flank. The fields of fire would interlock just at that bend."

He was right, Dana saw. Sainte Madeleine lay on a tiny finger of land poking into the marshland all around it. A machine gun in the tower and another on the knoll would command the full sweep of the causeway from the east and the marsh on each side.

"There's no time to dig in now," Sacco said.

"That can come later—there's cover enough on the knoll." Mungo turned to Dana. "Go get Reb and that machine gun I posted at the other end of town. Hubba-hubba on it—they'll be hitting us soon."

Dana caught up his M-1 and started down the stairs. He heard Mungo saying to Edgerton, "Better set up in that house across the way, Lieutenant. I'll give you Swampy and Kadillius. They're pretty good men."

"What about Dana?"

"Need him on the gun with me. Reb goes on the bazooka."

Dana ran into the breathless Swampy in the doorway of the church. He had removed his helmet and his shaven skull looked antiseptically clean against the black smudge on his face. He was staring intently up the road to the east. "Where's Cadillac?" Dana asked him.

Swampy pointed to the sacristy. "Better get him," Dana said. "Mungo wants you both with Edgerton in that house across the street." He stepped past Swampy into the street. "What's he doing in there, anyway?"

Swampy grinned at him and winked. "He said he was goin' to check on Hollister."

Dana turned and ran down the street, feeling nakedly exposed to any fire that might break out from the road. But there was not time enough to hug the walls for shelter and work himself slowly to the other end of the village.

So Mungo wanted him on the gun! The decision surprised Dana. He felt an odd sense of pride that the surly non-com wanted him at his side in the coming fight.

Reb had already dismounted the gun. He had the barrel on his shoulder. He handed the folded tripod to Dana. "Heard the firin'," Reb told him as they jogged back down the street, the heavy ammo boxes clanking on their handles. "The Krautheads comin' back already?" Reb's face was lit with a fierce expectancy.

Dana nodded, too winded to speak. Mungo waited for them outside the church. He took the barrel and ammo from Reb and pointed wordlessly to the spider hole and the bazooka lying next to it.

"That hole ain't finished," Reb said.

"T. S." Mungo said. "It'll give you some concealment. Just keep your ass down. They might try to move some armor over that bridge."

Reb trotted off to the spider hole. "Let's go," Mungo said, moving rapidly across the road and up the sloping ground. He peered cautiously over the top of the knoll. Dana followed him with the tripod, keeping his head down.

Mungo chose a hollow in the crest and signaled Dana to drop the tripod there. Mungo slipped the barrel spindle into its socket and sighted the gun on the road. The knoll commanded an unbroken view of the stretch of roadway that was shielded from the tower by the shoulders of the curve.

The gun was set on free traverse. Mungo did not touch the elevating or traversing screws. Dana was opening an ammo case when Mungo announced, "Here they come!" Dana looked up sharply. A half-mile off, a crawling chain of blurred figures had detached itself from a woodland close to the roadway and started toward the village. The wind brought the sound of powerful motors.

Mungo prodded him. "Give me the belt."

Dana started and flipped back the lid of the metal box, uncoiling the cartridge-studded canvas belt with its two hundred and fifty 30 caliber rounds. Mungo fed the metal tip into the gun, worked the action once to arm the magazine, and then slapped the bolt home to drive a round into the chamber.

He motioned Dana down and stretched himself prone, loosening the clamps of the tripod to lower the gun. Then he rolled on his side and grinned at Dana. It was the first time that Dana had seen him smile. "I don't think they'll look for trouble until they round that bend," he said. "We can take them with a few belts of enfilading fire."

Dana nodded, his mouth dry. Mungo rolled back into position and checked the sights of the gun again. "Be nicer if we had us an emplacement here. We'll dig a gun pit. Sometime after lunch."

Dana gaped at him. Mungo's face was impassive; his eyes trained on the troops in the distance. With overwhelming forces moving infantry supported by armor, this man could talk about his plans for after lunch. Dana found that he could swallow again.

The motor sounded louder now and Dana raised his head again. He saw what seemed to be a tank, like a child's toy at that distance, crawling sluggishly forward on the macadam road. Infantry flanked it on either side. "Panzer," he whispered hoarsely to Mungo.

Mungo shook his head. "No. Just an armored car—Reb will take that baby out of action." He scratched the grizzled stubble which was already beginning to poke through the blacking on his chin. "This is a probing force. They won't bring up anything real heavy until they see what we've got here." He had an unlit cigar clamped in his mouth, and his back teeth worried it stolidly as he sighted down the barrel of the gun.

The specks swelled slowly, became men with weapons, wearing coal-scuttle helmets. Dana could even make out a figure leaning out of the turret of the car, bending to exchange words with someone in the walking files. The men were well within range now, but Mungo held his fire. Slowly, imperceptibly, the figures grew. The moment seemed suspended. The sun stood still. A soft breeze rustled the tops of the swamp grass and the tiny figures slid in front of the gun sights like shooting gallery ducks on a trolley.

Mungo tripped a sudden burst of half a dozen rounds. Three hundred yards away, with dreamlike slowness, the field-gray silhouettes were buckling to the ground. The machine gun hammered violently, raking the road. It bucked and chattered in Mungo's hands. He hosed the column carefully, traversing back and forth, on his face a cold, methodical deliberation.

The German infantry was scurrying off the road, in the frantic disorder of an overturned ant-heap. The armored car speeded up, the turret buttoned down, and disappeared around the bend toward the bridge. Some elements of infantry, running at full tilt, followed it. Dana knew they would be racing into the range of Sacco's gun.

Solitary bundles lay still on the road, and here and there were clumps of writhing men. Others had started through the swamps toward their knoll, firing desperate unaimed shots in the direction of the gun with which Mungo was destroying them.

The gun fell silent, and Dana swerved his head in an instant of sudden terror. Mungo winked and motioned for another belt.

Dana fed it to him, his eyes on the oncoming Germans. The gun began to snarl again. The first wave of infantry stopped dead in the marshland, collapsing, sinking out of sight amongst the clumps of weed. The hammering snarl of Mungo's gun drowned out all other sounds. In the intervals between his bursts, Dana could hear the cracks of rifles and the distant rattle of Sacco's gun. The men in the village were now engaged.

He saw two figures rise out of the marshland a hundred yards ahead of him and run forward, lumbering heavily in the knee-deep water. He released his steadying grip on the tripod and drew his other hand out from under the fast disappearing belt and seized his M-1. He sighted swiftly and his rifle bucked twice. It was impossible to miss at that range. Both of the Germans went down. Dana was vaguely surprised to see them hurtle backwards when the bullets took them. He had expected to see them clutch their bellies and sink slowly to their knees like movie extras in a battle scene.

He was aware of unfamiliar sounds—the harsh barking of a heavy Spandau and the quick high rasp of nearby Schmeissers. The scout car must be approaching the bridge. Back along Mungo's section of the road troops were fanning through the swamps to flank them. Mungo shifted the tripod and sent plunging fire down to his left. The firing in the village was more rapid and it disconcerted Dana. He felt sure the Germans must have penetrated there.

He crawled to Mungo's gun, to assist him with another belt. Mungo waved him back toward the village. "Get to the embankment overlooking the bridge. Support that frigging bazooka."

Dana pointed to the left, where a skirmish line of Germans had raced down the road and must be crawling toward the knoll. "I've got them stopped here, damn it," Mungo snarled. "Take off." Dana crouched low and ran along the knoll. He hit the ground as it sloped to the village and slid the last few yards.

Below him, he saw the armored car, its turret spitting fire, come grinding toward the bridge. It did not outrace its covering infantry, and darting figures leaped along on either side of it. They hit the ground and rose again, firing steadily. He heard Cadillac's Thompson from the house below him, the accompanying bark of a rifle and carbine. He caught a glimpse of Reb's unhelmeted red hair, where he crouched in the half-completed spider hole.

A stream of bullets from Sacco's gun hosed the road. The turret of the armored car swung around—it's gunner must have spotted Sacco. Chips of masonry flew from the embrasure; Sacco's gun was silenced.

Dana felt a chill, dread shock of apprehension. Had Sacco ducked or had the probing stream of lead from the car found him? Then there was no time for speculation. German infantry had reached the far abutment of the bridge and fanned out swiftly on either side. They came sliding down the embankments and into the river, leaving a squad to fight across the bridge behind the scout car. Fording the river, the enemy came slowly, wading chest-deep.

There were too many of them. Dana swung his rifle up and blasted out a clip, reloaded without thinking as the empty clip sprang out, and hammered snap shots at target after target. He shifted his sights with such desperate haste he was unable to watch the effects of his fire. He knew only that the enemy was coming, that some of them would reach the near bank of the river.

The armored car came clattering onto the bridge, riflemen crouching behind it. The turret Spandau raked the church and the house across the street from which Cadillac and Edge and Swampy were firing, but most of the automatic fire was directed to the tower of the church and Sacco's gun. The troops in the river were now out of sight, sheltered by the bank. Dana knew he would see them only when they mounted the embankment to sweep over for the final rush.

With maddening slowness, Reb rose from his hole. He had the bazooka on his shoulder now, and he knelt deliberately, squinting down the wire sights. Immobile, just beside the bridge, he must be visible to the Germans when they crossed it with the car. Dana saw a pair spring from behind the high solid rubber tire at the rear, raising their short machine pistols to blast Reb. Before he could bring the M-1 around to them, Sacco's machine gun roared, and the two *Panzergrenadiers* were slammed against the thick stone railing of the bridge.

The turret swung to the tower again, reaching for Sacco with a swiftly climbing chain of spattering, exploding stone. At that instant, as the car bumped up to the near side of the bridge, Reb's bazooka flamed. The flash behind him was a sheet of blinding flame. The rocket whammed into the car with an ear-splitting roar.

The car groped forward, its gun silenced, then crashed into the railing and toppled over on its side. The rocket-slugs ricocheting around inside, had gutted all life from the vehicle. Behind it, a handful of Germans, nakedly exposed by the collapse of their armored shield, tried to scatter back from the bridge. Sacco's machine gun chopped them down, and then came back over them, blasting the life out of them where they lay. A pitiful few vaulted over the railing and dropped into the river.

Cadillac and Swampy ran from the house and threw themselves flat on the embankment. Dana slid down the knoll to join them. Cadillac's Thompson was already thundering.

A figure loomed over the embankment just in front of him—a towering grenadier climbing from the river, a long potato-masher grenade jutting from the end of his upflung arm. Dana's slug took the German just under the chin. The huge helmet went spinning high, twisting thirty feet in the air. The German's feet seemed to leave the ground as he fell backward, sliding down the bank, a stream of bright red blood cascading from his head, curving in a graceful arc in the sunshine, like water gushing from a high-pressure fountain.

Cadillac crouched on the top of the bank and his Tommy gun rattled jack-hammer heavy, sowing death below. Swampy's M-1 thudded spasmodic rounds. Dana crawled his way to them and looked below. He saw only corpses swirling in the river. The huge grenadier lay head-down at the river's edge, blood still pulsing thickly from the top of his scalp, staining the brackish water.

The silence was suddenly heavy on the morning air. They heard a few quick bursts as the fleeing survivors ran into Mungo's range. Dana looked at the men beside him. Swampy was staring at the bodies with a strained, astonished look. Cadillac's face was expressionless as he released the magazine and slipped a fresh one into his gun. Meeting Dana's eyes, he smiled a strange slow smile. "Man!" he said. The word was like a single indrawn breath, a release from tension, and a summing up.

Reb ran to them from the bridge. A hot, triumphant light shone in his eyes. "One round," he cried. "One lousy frig-gin' round, and I stopped the damn thing cold!"

Footsteps sounded rapidly behind them. All four whirled and pointed their weapons down the village street. Nolan was running up, followed at a distance by the breathless, staggering Uhlan.

Reb grinned savagely. "You missed it, Nolan. Damned if you didn't miss all the fun." He pointed at the crippled car that lay across the bridge. "I knocked it over with one lousy friggin' round."

Nolan's eyes swept rapidly around the group, took in the corpses scattered on the bridge, in the river, and along the bank. "Where the hell is Mungo? Did they get him?" he demanded. In his voice was a curious mixture of dread and hope.

Dana gestured back along the knoll. Mungo was just coming along the crest, bare-chested, his jump-jacket wrapped around the hot barrel of the machine gun he held over one arm, the belt of cartridges draped around his neck. He held the tripod in his other hand and a row of ammo boxes under his arm. He gestured them all to the church with a jerk of his head. Dana saw his cigar was lit now, and Mungo was emitting contented puffs of smoke.

"Hey, Nolan," Cadillac crowed. He pointed at the German corpses in the river. "I've just been familiarized with this Thompson, dad. You been familiarized with yours yet?"

CHAPTER THIRTEEN

D DAY, 1000. HOURS

Mungo had disappeared into the sacristy. They heard his voice, "You feeling okay, kid?" and Hollister's weak affirmative.

When he came back his broad face held the barest suggestion of a smile. "You done pretty good," he said. "Pretty good for virgins. Next time, take it easy, and don't waste any ammunition." He drew heavily on his cigar and looked critically at its ash for a moment and then seemed to dismiss all memory of the fire-fight. "What did you find back down the road Nolan?"

"Ran into a little trouble," Nolan said. "Fired on by snipers a half mile back. Nothing heavy, but they may be building up there."

Mungo nodded. "They're sneaking men back through the swamps, all right. Outflanking the town. We'll keep a gun posted in the lower end of the village, because we're going to be surrounded pretty quick. Right now, I want a gun pit dug out on the knoll where we just set up, Dana. Take Cadillac with you and get started on it. That knoll gives us a field of fire going halfway back to Isigny. The Krauts will be back with armor, and that's the direction they have to come from."

"Wait a minute, Sergeant." Edgerton had come striding into the church. He waved a crumpled sheaf of papers in his hand. "I've been over those bodies on the bridge. I've found what we're after. It's the Three-five-two we're up against, all right."

"So what?" Mungo asked.

The Lieutenant faced him squarely and clipped out the words with the crisp ring of command. "We'll have to move out quickly to get the word to Regiment. Colonel Tighe will want to beef up those Douve River bridges against a motorized division."

"How do you know the Five-Oh-Goose is *at* the bridges?" Mungo asked. "We'd be able to raise them on the radio, if they were."

"That's one of their objectives. They have to hold the going to bring down artillery and hit us with tanks too big bridges. There's no place else for them to stop a German attack coming down on the beaches."

"Seems like a pretty good place right here. We stopped them coming over once already." A proud murmur of assent from the men followed Mungo's words.

Edgerton glared at them. "At ease!" he barked. "That was a probing attack, Sergeant. Any moment, now, they're to stop. They'll come pouring down this road on the regiment's flank. Col. Tighe has to be warned. Do you understand that, Sergeant?"

The men had gathered closely around them. They saw the black anger gathering in the depths of Mungo's hooded eyes. "You don't have to draw me any pictures. I remember the pictures on that situation map they showed us back in England. If the Krauts come down this road and hit the Douve, they can roll right over whatever we've got there. You tried with the radio and got nothing. Now when are you going to wake up? There isn't any regiment! Not until they get themselves regrouped. There's only a scattering of men like us, all fighting to stay alive. If the Krauts bust through here, they'll go through those little bunches of men like crap through a tin horn." Mungo wheeled abruptly on Reb. "Take off back to that house on the west end, again."

"Wait a minute, James," Edgerton said quietly, with steel under his voice.

"Okay," Mungo barked before the adjutant could speak. "You've got news to report to Regiment. Maybe tonight, and maybe tomorrow there'll be something you can call a regiment, but not now. The Air Corps flubbed the dub again and scattered the drop. If we stick it out here and block this frigging bridge, everybody's got a good chance. If we take off down that road, like you want to, they'll roll right over us before we've gone a mile."

"That's enough, Sergeant Mungo!" Edgerton's voice rose. "I don't want to hear your arguments. I've got my orders, and I'm going to follow them—to the letter. If you value those stripes of yours you'll do the same. I'm going to make one more try to raise Regiment on the radio. If I don't get them, we're taking off down this road until we contact our own people. Now, get your men ready to move out."

Mungo's voice had never been softer. "What about Hollister?"

"We'll do what we can for him. Let me worry about that." "Dana, come up in the tower with me and set up that radio. We'll try to signal Regiment again."

Mungo's sleepy eyes were blank and his belly hung forward as he thrust his massive head at Edgerton. "You're a yellow little bastard with crap where your guts should be."

"I've taken all I'm going to take from you!" Edgerton snapped. "You're relieved of your rating, Private Mungo. If I had the men to guard you, you'd be under arrest. Until then, damn you, you follow orders like anybody else."

Edgerton spun on his heel. "Nolan, you're acting sergeant, right now. Make sure you keep this man in line." Nolan's eyes flickered to Mungo's and away. His chin came up aggressively. "Get the men ready to move out in five minutes. We're heading back to our lines."

Edgerton nodded sharply at Dana. "Let's get set up in the tower, Dana."

Dana shot a glance at Mungo. "What about that gun emplacement you wanted dug?"

"Better go with the lieutenant," Mungo said indifferently. He walked to the sacristy and opened the door. Dana saw him looking in at Hollister as he followed Edgerton to the tower.

"Get that radio in operation," Edgerton ordered. Now that he had made his decisions the officer's manner was brisk and military again.

Sacco, leaning on his elbows, hunched over the embrasure, asked quietly, "What's the poop?"

"Mungo's a private, now," Dana told him.

Sacco glanced mockingly at the lieutenant and said, "Well, here we go again."

Dana called the regimental net. The signals were sparser and more blurred than ever. It seemed that the battalion commanders, if any of them were living, had given up hope of re-establishing communication by radio. He repeated his call sign, over and over, and received no more response than the crackling of static, and what seemed to be a dance band out of Luxemburg.

He turned to the division net and the signals were completely unreadable. He looked up at Edgerton and shrugged his shoulders.

"Let me have that set," the lieutenant said. "Go down and tell Sergeant Nolan we're pulling out."

Dana exchanged a brief glance with Sacco and then went down the stairs. The men were gathered near the sacristy. All but Mungo had their webbing on, their equipment slung for marching. Mungo slouched against the sacristy door talking quietly with Nolan.

"Hell with it," he said. "I'm going to stay with the kid. Maybe bluff the Krauts off till the dogfaces show. They can't be so very far away."

Swampy said, "Screwiest damn deal I ever heard of. Just when we kick the friggin' butts off the Germans, the Adj pulls us out."

Cadillac, eyeing the sacristy door wistfully, said, "Hey, Mungo, if you want me to stick around with you, I don't have eyes to split just yet..."

"You'll go with the lieutenant," Mungo said. He gazed sleepily at Nolan. "Well, it's your squad now, Nolan. Try to bring them back alive."

"You ought to come with us," Nolan said. "Maybe we could carry the kid." He stood taller now, with authority returned to him, and yet there was something hesitant, uncertain in his gestures.

Mungo said, "It's yours, boys. I don't want it anymore. You take the patrol back—if the first John gets it on the way, you'll probably get yourself a battlefield commission."

Nolan gawked at him. His eyes bored into Mungo's searchingly, their yearning dimmed with disbelief.

"I crap you none," Mungo said. "And if you stuck it out here with me and held up these Krauts until the dogfaces get here from the beaches, you could parlay it into a Congressional Medal of Honor."

"Bull," Nolan said, but with little conviction.

"Oh, use your head, Nolan," Mungo said disgustedly. "You know this is a big chance. They're going to hear about this village right up to Eisenhower's headquarters. You're too good a soldier to stay an enlisted man all your career, like me."

Nolan bit his lip. "But what in hell can I do, if the lieutenant orders the patrol back down the road?"

"That's your headache," Mungo said, turning away from him.

Nolan looked uneasily up at the tower where Edgerton was still attempting to contact the regiment, his face thoughtful. Then he turned angrily on the men. "All right, damn it. Get saddled up. We're going to get moving."

Edgerton came down the stairs, the radio in his arms. Sacco was behind him, lugging the machine gun and the tripod. Edgerton glanced swiftly around at the men and jerked his head approvingly. "Good work, Nolan."

"Sir," Nolan said. "I've been giving what Mungo said a little thought. Maybe we should set up here for a while."

"Not a chance!" Edgerton cut him off. "You there! Mungo! Get your equipment on! We're moving out!"

Mungo leaned against the wall chewing on the stub of his cigar. "Staying with the kid," he said. "He might get lonely."

Edgerton said curtly, "We're taking him with us. We'll rig up some kind of litter." He seemed to be remembering a lesson from the book—paratroopers always brought their wounded out.

Mungo spat a shred of cigar from his teeth. "You don't haul a gut-shot kid no eight miles through swampland. Not through enemy fire."

"What's that about enemy fire?" the lieutenant shot the question out with a quick and startled look. Mungo shrugged his enormous shoulders. "Ask Nolan," he said. "He patrolled through there. Caught a little fire down the road."

"Nothing much," Nolan said in a deeply virile tone. "A few snipers, is all. They've been filtering around us. If we go real careful, we can sneak right through them."

"Not with a wounded man along, you can't," Mungo said.

The men were clustered tensely around them, absorbed in the conversation. The gaiety that had followed the fire fight was erased from their faces, replaced by fatigue and nervous strain. "Aw, hell," said Swampy. "This Mungo just wants to stay and have that French broad all to himself."

A new consideration leaped to Edgerton's mind and was mirrored in his eyes. "She's coming with us," he announced firmly. "Mungo can stay here to cover our withdrawal—with Hollister if he wants to."

"Sure," said Mungo with indifference. He strolled across the room and sank calmly onto a pew. His cigar stub was dead; he lit it carefully. "Listen, Lieutenant, you better come here," he said.

Edgerton strode over to him. His voice was sharp with anger. "Damnit, Mungo, the only time you ever call me 'sir' or 'lieutenant' is when you're giving me an order!"

Mungo gave no sign of hearing him. "Sit down, Lieutenant. I want to help you out. You're going back down the road now—right?"

Edgerton stubbornly remained on his feet and glowered down at Mungo. "That's right," he snapped. "I have my orders. This mission is a reconnaissance patrol. We found out what we came for and—"

"Sure," said Mungo. "Now maybe I can give you a little advice. I was out on the flank when the Krauts attacked. I watched them scatter in the swamps. They been moving all around us to envelop the village. They got us pretty well sealed in."

"We'll get through them some way," Edgerton said.

"Well, you won't get far along the road. They're watching that, you know. Nolan drew fire when he tried to move on it. You'll have to circle them, south of the road, somewhere through the hedgerow country."

"That's where they were shooting from," Nolan said, swaggering over to join their conversation.

Mungo asked him: "Did you try the swamps?"

"There's a couple of lanes there," Nolan said. "Little footpaths. You can walk on them if you take it easy. You've got to keep low though; you've got to be careful."

"Be better if you made it after dark," said Mungo. He eyed the lieutenant appraisingly.

"There isn't time," Edgerton said with impatience. "They'll attack this village any minute, and we have to get our information back right away. Make your point, Sergeant. What do you have to tell me?"

Mungo paused and glanced sourly at the stub of his cigar. "All right. You're in a hurry. You want to move in daylight. You don't know how many troops the Krauts have got dug in along your route. You're going to try to infiltrate them, eight men and a prisoner, all of you loaded down with equipment." He paused and shook his head, then spoke very slowly and carefully. "I wouldn't just go barrel-assing out there, Lieutenant. I'd send me a patrol first, to check those footpaths. I'd make damn sure that I had a clear escape route, before I led my eight men out through Kraut-infested country." He stared at Edgerton, appraising the officer's uncertainty. "No matter how big of a sweat I was in," he added caustically.

"How about it, Nolan?" Edgerton asked. "How far did you get? What are the chances of sneaking through?"

"Well, there are those footpaths I told you about," Nolan said.

Edgerton hesitated. Mungo knew his business, even if he had no respect for authority. It might be suicide to lead the men out without reconnoitering the route.

Mungo smiled softly. "While you're thinking it over, why don't you give me Nolan and Uhlan. They been there before, they know the country. I'll take them out and check the terrain for you."

The final words were what decided Edgerton. Mungo had done enough for him. His authority, his pride, his very manhood demanded that he refuse the burly soldier's help.

"I'll take them out, myself," he said decisively. Mungo shrugged and looked away, making it clear the conversation was closed.

"All right, Uhlan," Edgerton said. "We're going out on a little patrol. We're going to find a route for our withdrawal."

Uhlan seemed to shrink; he backed away toward the altar. "I've just come off a patrol," he whined.

"That's why I need you. You and Sergeant Nolan know the terrain. Get rid of your equipment ... just your rifle. And Nolan—"

He was opening his map case and spreading it out on a bench in the sunlight that streamed through the door. "Better come over and check this map with me."

"Just a minute, Lieutenant," Nolan said. He leaned over Mungo, speaking very quietly so that none of the other men could hear. "You don't think we ought to withdraw?"

Mungo's eyes were completely disinterested. "You want to go eight miles through the swamps? With the Krautheads gunning for you every step? We're safe right here—we could dig ourselves in and it would take an army corps to drive us out. We got the armored car blocking the bridge, and nothing can hit us without they come over that bridge."

Nolan's eyes narrowed as he listened to Mungo. He ran his hand along the stubby barrel of his Tommy-gun.

"Let's go, Sergeant Nolan," Edgerton called. He and Uhlan were crouched over the map.

"You think this bastard wants to get us killed?" Nolan's question was an angry whisper.

Mungo gazed up at him dispassionately. "Who knows what he wants," he said. "It's your baby. Me, I'm staying right here. Another few hours and the infantry comes in—the straight-pants infantry with their armor. They're going to find me holed up here. Just me and Hollister." He grinned and added, "And the little bitch in there."

"All right, Nolan!" Edgerton sounded irritated. "Supposing you show me where those footpaths are. There's nothing to indicate them on this map." Nolan swaggered over, looking back at Mungo with one brief, calculating glance.

Dana lit a cigarette and strolled to the sacristy door, wondering if Hollister felt strong enough to move. He passed Sacco leaning against the baptismal font, his eyes glinting with amusement. Except for Mungo, only Sacco had not donned his equipment.

Reb sat near the door of the sacristy, staring fixedly at the crucifix over the altar. Dana stepped around him and opened the door a careful crack, listening. He did not want to disturb Hollister if the wounded boy was sleeping.

Hollister was saying, in a feeble whisper, "You shouldn't do that, Cadillac. That's the bitch that shot me. She's the enemy."

Dana opened the door wider and peered in. Cadillac was standing with the girl between the cabinets. His Tommy-gun was slung across his shoulder; one of her breasts, jutting through the tattered dress, was cradled like a kitten in his palm. He made no answer to Hollister. His lips were on the girl's, and with his other hand he half-caressed, half-tugged her hair, pulling her head and body down across his arm. His face was composed in concentration and the girl made no protest, sinking back beneath his pressure with a sigh of abandonment.

Dana was surprised to see the fingers of the girl move slowly up Cadillac's back to his neck. Provocatively she caressed his hair, then drew his head downward to her breast. She sighed deeply, with passion this time, not helplessness; her mobile lips lazily teased his ear.

Cadillac heard the door and wheeled on Dana, his hands still occupied with the body of the girl. A slow, contented grin came over his face. "If we're cuttting out," he said, "I got to get what I can. The Quartermaster don't issue this."

Dana grinned. He drew back and closed the door. Edgerton was folding the map. "That's it. Now let's get going, Sergeant Nolan," he said. He addressed the other men. "We'll be gone for an hour or so. You men wait and be ready to move out. While we're gone, you take your orders from—" Edgerton peered around the room. "Cadillac!" he shouted suddenly. "Where in hell is Cadillac?"

There was a little shuffle from inside the sacristy, and Cadillac came out. His face was blank and thoroughly composed. He looked at the lieutenant questioningly.

"What in hell were you doing in there, Cadillac?" Edgerton's face was stormy.

"Looking after Hollister," Cadillac said. "The morphine's wearing off, sir. The kid'll need another shot soon."

"All right, Cadillac. You see to it," Edgerton said sternly. "I'm leaving you in charge while I make this reconnaissance. Keep the men alert and ready to move out." He stared suspiciously at Mungo whose eyes were intent on the tip of a fresh, unlit cigar. "And see that nobody bothers that girl."

"I'll see to that, Lieutenant," Cadillac said. He snapped a brisk salute. Startled, the lieutenant returned it. He left the church with Uhlan close behind him. As Nolan moved out after them he threw a meaningful glance back at Mungo, which did not find its mark. Mungo had decided to light his cigar and was focusing on the flame.

There was a silence when the three men were gone. Sacco was stroking the head of Franklin's pigeon, in its nylon carrier beside his musette bag. Reb still stared at the crucifix. "At ease, men," said Cadillac, retreating rapidly toward the door of the sacristy.

"*Kadillius!*" Mungo's voice boomed like a sunset gun. "*Where the hell do you think you're going?*"

"It's all right, Mungo," Cadillac said smugly. "You heard the lieutenant. I'm in command."

"Okay," Mungo rumbled. "You're in command. Now get your lard-ass up that tower with Sacco's gun and watch the road. And the rest of you—take off your equipment. There ain't any off you going no place. We're all gonna be here for a while."

Their eyes on Mungo, and with tired gestures, the men began to unbuckle their gear.

CHAPTER FOURTEEN
D DAY, 1100 HOURS

Digging was easy in the soft and spongy ground. They had marked out a double foxhole for the two-man gun emplacement, and within thirty minutes, working together, they had gone about three feet down. Dana took a break then, and sat smoking a cigarette. He watched Sacco scoop out the loose wet earth. Sacco worked steadily with easy, fluid motions, and although the sun was high and his sinewy torso gleamed with sweat, he swung his body rhythmically with no sign of fatigue.

They had sited the gun pit on the saddle of the knoll, almost exactly where Mungo had first emplaced the gun. The brass glitter of spent cartridge-cases marked the scene of the fire-fight an hour before. No German who'd come close enough to spot the gun's location had crawled out of there alive to report it. The bodies lay grotesquely in twisted heaps, all along the slope and down through the marshes to the edges of the road. Dana stubbornly refused himself the morbid rite of counting them—the crumpled shapes were men, and not scalps to be numbered. Mungo's fire had been devastating; the carnage was incredible. One man, behind one gun, had worked this slaughter.

Grudgingly, Dana gave voice to his thoughts. "The son-of-a-bitch is a pro, all right."

"Mungo?" There was no pause in Sacco's rhythmic digging.

"Is he a Regular Army soldier?"

Sacco grinned. "Is the Pope a Catholic?"

"Yeah, I figured," Dana said. He stared at the heat-hazed road in the distance, silent and empty in the late-morning sun. "Why don't they come back?" he asked nervously. "What in hell is keeping them?"

Sacco flung a shovelful of earth, then bent to measure out a firing step. "Relax. They'll be back," he said.

"You think that maybe they're moving around us?"

Sacco paused a moment thoughtfully. "They can work a little infantry through the swamps. They have to have the road though, to bring their heavy stuff through."

"What do you figure is taking them so long?"

"They're not sure what we have here. They pulled back to regroup."

Dana stubbed his cigarette into the dirt. "Well, why don't they plaster us with artillery?"

Sacco bent to his work again. "Probably they're bringing it up right now. Field guns—Eighty-eights, I guess. They can't use anything heavier."

"Why the hell not?"

"The bridge. They need it to move up to the beaches.

A One-oh-five barrage would knock it out. Even a couple of Eighty-eight hits might close it down."

"Then why don't we just blow it up? We got enough explosives with us."

Sacco smiled patiently. "Can't do that. Our seaborne's going to need it, to link the two beachheads. We just have to hold it for them, that's all, Dana."

Dana picked up his shovel again, and prodded at the hole in a desultory fashion. "Well, I hope we pull out of here before they get their guns up and lay it in."

Sacco said pointedly, "We're not pulling out."

"Yeah, I know how Mungo feels. All this digging-in crap. But damn it, the lieutenant..."

"The lieutenant should have known better." Sacco's eyes were twinkling. "When you hassle with Mungo, you take second money."

Dana grunted and jumped into the pit again. "All right then—we dig. Take a break," he said. Sacco shook his head. They worked together in silence.

A sudden crackling of rifle fire ripped the drowsy stillness of the morning. Dana dropped the shovel and grabbed for his rifle. Sacco nonchalantly went on digging. The shots had come from the west, where Edgerton had taken his patrol. The firing swelled a little. The hammering of a Thompson was muted by the distance.

Dana said tensely, "That's Nolan's gun. They've run into trouble."

"Bound to," Sacco drawled, flinging up a shovelful of earth.

Dana ran along the knoll toward the church. Looking down, he could see no excitement in the village. Reb was preparing a new spider hole on the other side of the street. Swampy, standing by to haul the earth away, was drinking from a bottle. He offered it to Reb who stopped working long enough to take a ragged gulp.

Cadillac whistled sharply from the tower, and Reb hid the bottle in the hole just as Mungo emerged from the church. The squat form ambled casually through the churchyard and paused to peer in the direction of the now-slackening fire. Then he turned and noticed Dana staring down from the ridge. Impatiently waving his cigar, he motioned Dana back to work. Dana walked slowly back to the gun pit.

Sacco glanced up at his return, but did not slacken the rhythm of his work. The emplacement was almost finished now. The firing had died away and silence lay over the empty marshes, except for the clinking of Sacco's shovel.

"Nothing much," said Dana. "The firing died down. Mungo don't look worried."

"Why should he be worried?" Sacco set his shovel down.

"Well, hell," said Dana, looking at his watch, "they're taking a long time. The lieutenant should be back by now."

Sacco said cryptically, "You think he's coming back?"

The question hung innocently in the air a moment, then Dana reacted, plunging down into the pit and whirling to stare into Sacco's eyes. "What in hell do you mean by that? You think he's going to chicken out and leave us?"

Sacco shook his head. "No. I think that Edgerton wrote himself off when he chose the wrong line of work."

"You mean bucking Mungo, don't you? Mungo don't like officers."

Sacco hauled the gun to the lip of the trench and braced the tripod legs. "That's where you're wrong, Dana. Mungo's not a rebel. Hell, he'd die for Colonel Tighe and thank him for the privilege—or for any of the officers who know their job. Edgerton's no officer. A damned nice guy ... a gentleman maybe ... probably he plays a good game of bridge. But Edge was commissioned by an I.B.M. machine. It riffled through a stack of cards until it found the holes for men with education and an I.Q. number. What's an I.B.M. machine know about battle? It can pick a man for O.C.S., but leading men in combat is not the sort of trade you learn in ninety days."

Dana fit the barrel spindle to the socket of the tripod, and sighted the gun on the road. "Then why in hell don't Mungo get himself a commission? If he's all that Godamned good ..."

"He might, if he was in the C.S.A.—the Army of the Confederacy." Sacco grinned at Dana's look of puzzlement. "That was a good little army, you know. Not much for parading, but they won their battles until they had nothing left to fight with. And the way they got their officers—the men elected them, all the way from Colonel on down. It's the only officer-procurement system that would have satisfied Mungo. The way they got it set up now, he figures that commissions come in Crackerjack boxes.

He paused and patted the gun and laughed. "Mungo would have made a great cavalry colonel. Raiding up the valley behind JEB Stuart—pants all ragged and his beard down to his crotch. He would have died a happy man."

"What in hell's so funny?" Dana asked. In front of them were corpses, rotting in the sun, and a road that would soon be thick with enemy guns, pouring hellfire at the village to take their lives.

Sacco chuckled. "I don't know. It sort of struck me funny … Edgerton leading his funeral parade, like a boy scout in the vanguard of Ghengis Kahn." He vaulted from the pit and lit a cigarette, sitting on the edge with his legs dangling over.

Dana leaned on the firing step, trying to puzzle it out. "You got a screwy sense of humor," he said.

"Yeah," said Sacco, and smoked his cigarette. His face was thoughtful but his eyes still twinkled puckishly. "Always been that way. The wrong things fracture me. When I was a kid, I used to go to see the Marx Brothers. The one that broke me up was Zeppo Marx. Remember him?" His voice was choked with reminiscent laughter.

"The blond one—curly—the one that didn't talk?"

"No. Zeppo was the fourth one; slick, black hair. He was the guy that didn't try to be funny."

Dana, genuinely baffled now, stared at his friend. Sacco grinned and winked at him, and Dana found himself returning the grin.

Up in the tower, Cadillac was bored. Mungo had been up to field-strip the gun and in a matter of minutes had it cleaned and oiled and reassembled. Cadillac, alone again, kept staring down at the bottle passing back and forth between Reb and Swampy. The sun was bright, and along his loins he felt a flood of warmth that was compounded of the sunshine, the memory of battle and the knowledge that the French girl still waited in the sacristy.

Her body had been yielding, her eyes misted over. Cadillac knew about that warm, moist look that women get in their eyes.

He tightened his belt and removed his helmet and smoothed down the sweat matted ducktail of his hair. Alone of all the troopers on the patrol, Cadillac had brought along his overseas cap—the jaunty go-to-hell hat with its parachute insignia and light-blue infantry braid. He unfolded it carefully from his breast pocket and cocked it at a rakish angle on his head. That college-boy lieutenant should be coming back soon; if only that damned Mungo would take a walk before Edgerton returned to the village.

He peered down. Swampy was sitting on the ground now, waving the bottle back and forth. Reb was sprawling in his hole. Mungo must have re-entered the church. He was nowhere in sight.

Cadillac bent his head to the stairway and listened carefully. There was no sound below. That son-of-a-bitch must have gone into the sacristy, trying to muscle what Cadillac could pluck. He took up his Tommy-gun and tiptoed down the stairs, moving as silently as a cat.

The door was partly closed, and from inside the sacristy he heard the murmur of Hollister's voice. Mungo answered gently—he was talking to the kid. Hell, the muscle-brained gorilla wasn't cool enough to munch on a grape when it dropped into his mouth. Cadillac smiled. He would wait a while and make his move when the scene was right.

Soundlessly he stalked out through the churchyard and over to where Reb and Swampy were drinking.

"Caddilac, I-God," Swampy greeted him effusively. "My Tommy-gunnin' buddy. Come and have a little drink of Froggie applejack." He handed up the bottle of Calvados.

Cadillac threw his head back and gulped the acrid brandy. It was fiery in his throat and exploded in his stomach, sending a new flush down to heat his loins. Cadillac felt almost like pawing the ground. "Crazy, man," he said, passing back the bottle. "Where did you get the juice?"

"Out'n that there cellar. There's a whole lot more. Good civilian stock." He paused a moment for another gulp. "Funny how there ain't no civilians left around. Krauts must have drove 'em out."

"There's one civilian they forgot." Reb indicated the church with his head.

"That ain't no civilian," Swampy cackled happily. "That's liberated booty. The spoils of war." His body rocked with laughter. "Hey, Reb ol' buddy-boy—let's go spoil her now." He started drunkenly to his feet.

"Mungo's in there now," said Cadillac, reaching for the bottle again. Swampy sat down and made a broad, expansive gesture. "That's all right," he blurted generously. "Let him lead the outfit in. He earned the right."

Cadillac turned away disdainfully and started back to the church. "Wait a minute, buddy," Swampy called after him. "Have yourself another drink on ol' Swampy. That was sure some shootin' you did. You looked pretty good in there, boy."

"Ah, they walked right into it," Cadillac said, but returned and sat down beside the others. Mungo didn't need him in that cruddy tower. Dana and Sacco could watch the road even better from their gun pit. Anyway, he—Cadillac—was in command. That Mungo, he decided as he took another drink, was getting out of line. "Got to cut that cat to size," he said aloud.

"Cut 'em all to size," Swampy mumbled happily on. "Chop 'em down like cane-stalks. Brrrrr-rat-tat-tat-ta-tat." He swept Germans from the earth with his hands and chortled gleefully.

The alcohol had given Reb a dour, sardonic smile. "You looked inside that armored car?" he asked with sullen pride. "Kee-rist, they're plastered to the walls in there. I squashed 'em all like bugs, with one friggin' round."

The Calvados passed back and forth. The men looked around them, making casual abstraction of the dead that lined the bridge and the banks of the river. Swampy drained the bottle and flung it away. "What's that eager-beaver looey want to pull us out for? Why hell, we can take whatever they send us. Stand 'em off from hell to breakfast—anythin' that comes!"

"Goddamn right," said Reb, and Cadillac nodded. A curious elation had seized the men. They were killers, they were victors, they could never die. The proof of their immortality was spread along the river-bank in field-gray winnows. The Calvados was flaming like a sunburst in their guts.

"Lemme go and get another bottle," Swampy said thickly. "Plenty more in that Froggie cellar." He lurched drunkenly toward the house near the bridge.

The ominous silence had troubled Mungo when he passed the sacristy. He had a gnawing feeling that Hollister was dead, and that the Kraut-loving bitch might have seized his rifle and even now be aiming at another of his men. Coming down from the tower after cleaning the machine gun, he paused by the door with his Springfield in his hand, listening intently. A low sound, sobbing, met his ears, and he threw the door open and looked around with the eyes of a panther crouched to spring.

The kid was unconscious. His bayoneted rifle had slipped from his hands to the floor. His head was cradled in the lap of the girl, she was wiping his forehead with a strip from her dress. The fear in her eyes, as she raised them to Mungo, was veiled with tears of pity and remorse.

"*Si jeune,*" she said. "*Le pauvre gosse—il n'est qu'un petit enfant.*" Her voice was choked with sobs.

Mungo glowered down at her, hard-eyed, scowling. The torn dress left her slim legs bare and Hollister's head was pillowed on her thigh. He groaned and jerked convulsively against the bench, like a child in the throes of a nightmare. She crooned to him softly and stroked his head, like a grief-stricken mother.

Mungo cursed and strode across the room. The bitch had shot the kid to protect the retreat of her rear-echelon Kraut lover. And now she slobbered over him, bawling like she meant it.

He seized her by the arm and dragged her from the bench. Hollister's head rolled onto the folded cassock as Mungo's fist dug harshly into the girl's flesh. *"Non, non,"* she said. *"Il souffre. Sa blessure est douleureuse."*

Hollister's eyes opened wide, glazed with pain. He looked around him in astonishment and terror, and his hands plucked weakly at the bandage on his groin. Recognizing Mungo, he tried to smile. Mungo felt a sudden surge of pity and he turned it instantly into rage.

"Stay away from him, bitch," he snarled, and slapped her hard. Her head rocked back from the vicious blow and her hair fell over her crimsoned cheek. Mungo flung her away from him. She fell to her knees, not daring to look up at him.

"I must have passed out," Hollister said. "I think she was trying to help me." His voice was weak.

"Yeah. She helped you before, kid. She'll do it again if you give her a chance." The words were rasped in a hard, metallic tone that altered strangely as he bent over Hollister. "How's it going, kid? You feel it bad?"

"It feels like I'm turning to jelly inside. Guess I fainted from the pain." The boy tried to swallow. "I'm thirsty, sergeant ..."

"Can't do it, kid," Mungo shook his head sorrowfully. You didn't give them water—not when they were gut-shot. No matter how much they pleaded. "I got something better for you. Kind of ease the pain." Even as he spoke he was preparing a syrette and he slipped the morphine into Hollister's thigh. Hollister shuddered and grimaced again. "It doesn't seem to help," he said.

"Give it a chance kid."

The boy was silent, but his lower lip was caught convulsively between his teeth. His head rolled rigidly from side to side.

Mungo sat on the bench beside him. "Take it easy, Hollister. Just relax. You got yourself the million-dollar wound. As soon as we get back, they'll put you on a plane … hospital in England, and then the States. You'll be bragging to your wife about your Purple Heart." The kid looked too pitifully young to be here; Mungo knew that he didn't have a wife.

"I'm not married, Sergeant," Hollister said. "Never even … never had a girl." He looked up wildly and stifled a groan. "I'm scared," he said.

"Well, your mom and dad then," Mungo said softly. "They'll be glad to see you back so soon."

"Haven't any folks." You could see the ridge on his lower lip, bone-white from the pressure of his teeth.

Mungo talked on softly, casually, with a heavy tenderness in his voice. "Well, who'd you used to live with before the Army?"

"No one. Lots of people—all my age. In the Guardian Angel Orphanage. Ridge and Devon—that's in Chicago."

"That right?" said Mungo. "Funny thing. I grew up in one of them orphan homes myself."

The boy was silent and his eyes were wide with a terrified wonder. "Sergeant," he said. "I'm not going to …"

"How'd you like the Army, kid?" Mungo talked on softly. His huge hands, with surprising deftness, lifted the dressing away from the wound.

"You don't think … ?"

"Take my word for it, you're going to be all right. I asked you how you liked the Army."

"Not too bad," said Hollister, wincing as Mungo raised his body to slip the bandage out from under him. "Except for that chicken lieutenant—Gordon. Everybody bitched a lot, and I did, too. But sometimes … Well, most of it, I liked pretty well."

"Yeah, I know," said Mungo, examining the wound. "The day I drew my uniform—we were wearing the tunics then, with high-button collars—hell, it was the first time I ever felt I didn't have to apologize for being alive. The Army's not a bad place for men like you and me, kid."

Hollister, diverted now, looked up at him and smiled. "Can't imagine you as a kid, Sergeant. Cadillac says you weren't even born—you were issued."

"Yeah? Well I been in ever since I was fifteen. It's the only family I ever had. Maybe when we're out of here—think it over—you could do pretty good in the Regular Army."

The morphine seemed to be taking hold: Hollister's eyes were dulled, the pupils pinned. It gave him a faraway, dreamy look. "When will we get out of here, Sergeant?" he asked.

"Pretty soon now, kid. When the Seventh Corps comes through. You'll be riding out on a Fourth Division tank."

"Cadillac told me the lieutenant said we're pulling out right now. He said they were making a litter for me ..."

"You don't want no litter, kid. That's no way to travel. Go back like a hero, riding on a tank." He was dusting fresh sulfa powder into the wound. The bleeding had stopped, but the flesh was discolored and a nasty fecal odor came from the wound. Mungo laid a fresh field-dressing on, and wrapped it around the torso with expert, practiced hands.

"But the lieutenant said—"

"Screw the lieutenant." Mungo rose. "Do you trust me, kid, or not?" His face was solemn, as though the question had peculiar importance.

"Sure, Sergeant Mungo. Sure I trust you."

"Okay. Then I'll get you back the easiest way. Can't take no chances with a future thirty-year man."

Mungo winked and turned to go. Hollister stopped him. "Sergeant ... please. I got to have some water."

Mungo's face was troubled. He stared around him, not looking at the boy.

"Please! I got to have some. If you knew how it felt."

Mungo hesitated. "Yeah, I know," he said. Then his canteen was out and he knelt beside the boy again. "Got to take a sulfa pill anyway," he said. "It'll screw up your kidneys if you don't have water." He raised Hollister's head and removed a tablet from his infantry first-aid kit. Hollister gulped the pill down and sucked greedily at Mungo's canteen. Mungo permitted him the barest mouthful, then withdrew the canteen and laid the boy's head gently back against the cassock.

"How do you feel now?" Mungo asked.

Hollister sighed gently. "It's better now."

Mungo eyed the girl across the room. She lay, still sprawled where he had thrown her, but this time she looked up at him with anxious eyes.

"Think you can stay awake and watch her?" Mungo's hands were busy with the rifle. Surreptitiously he removed the clip. Hollister could guard her with a bayonet. If the kid passed out again, he didn't want the girl to have a loaded weapon at their backs.

He patted the boy's shoulder awkwardly and turned a baleful glance on the girl. Then he left the room and closed the door behind him.

He stood in the vestry, looking at nothing. A burst of laughter sounded from the street outside. His manner changed abruptly, and his eyes were slitted hard as he strode from the church.

Swampy, Reb and Cadillac were sprawled on the ground with a brace of bottles strewn around them. At Mungo's approach, Swampy and Cadillac lurched drunkenly to their feet, and Reb ducked into his spider hole.

"Mungo," Swampy greeted him effusively, with a just-opened bottle in his hand. "Mungo, ol' buddy, we gotta have a 'lection. Gotta pick a lead-off man to cut the cake. Everybody's gettin' some, exceptin' the lieutenant, because he's a gen'leman and gen'lemen don't..."

"You really need the firewater, don't you, James," Mungo said contemptuously. He snatched the bottle from Swampy's hand. He smelled it and tilted it up to his mouth; his Adam's apple bobbed in a series of long swallows. Swampy watched fascinated, and Cadillac stepped back. Mungo took the bottle from his lips and threw it into the river.

"Got another one right here, if you're still thirsty, Sergeant."

"Had all we're gonna have," said Mungo. "Kadillius!" He wheeled on Cadillac and caught him by the collar. "Thought I posted you up in that tower."

Cadillac swallowed hard but his face was bland. "Now, Mungo—Sacco's watching from the hill. You wouldn't hit a non-com, would you, dad? Remember who's in charge of this detail."

Mungo twisted his wrist a little and Cadillac's toes barely touched the ground. The overseas cap bobbed and slid to his nose. "I had to hit you once, Kadillius," Mungo grated. "If I do it again, they're gonna scratch one Greek."

He released his grip and Cadillac stumbled back and tripped over Reb's bazooka. "Well, hell," he said grinning from the ground. "I was getting pretty bored with those privileges of rank."

They all looked up as Dana shouted. He slid from the knoll, pointing back down the village street. They turned and saw Nolan approaching at a walk, Uhlan trailing after him. Their uniforms and faces were caked with mud, and as they came closer it was evident that Uhlan's hands were trembling on his rifle.

Nolan came up to them and cocked his helmet back. He looked around him with a hard, blank face that broke into a half-smile as his eyes met Mungo's. Mungo's face was wooden. Nobody said anything until Dana joined the group. No one else seemed to want to voice the question.

"Where's the lieutenant?" Dana asked.

"Dead." There was nothing in Nolan's cold, gray eyes.

"How'd it happen?" Dana asked.

"He got shot."

Dana cast a rapid glance at Uhlan. Uhlan turned his eyes away and set his rifle down. He wiped the sweat from his forehead with a mud-caked sleeve.

"How about it, Uhlan?" Dana asked.

Uhlan's lips moved nervously. He ran his tongue over them. "He got shot," he said at last.

The men were silent, shuffling their feet. "All right," Mungo said. "He was a ... pretty nice feller. Now what in hell did you find down the road?"

"Krauts," said Nolan. "A lot of Krauts."

"They moving west? They pushing for the beaches?"

Nolan shook his head. "They're circling around us—building up right here. They got to clean us out before they can get anything heavy through to the beaches."

"Yeah," said Mungo, "they got to clean us out." He looked around him as though measuring his men. "We're going to take a little break for chow," he said at last. "We'll leave Sacco in the gun pit and I want one man to post the village at the other end. Uhlan! Take off down to the wall and watch that road you just came in on."

"Jesus Christ, Sergeant!" Uhlan's face was outraged, sullen indignation bursting through the fear. "I just come back from my second patrol." He took his helmet off and threw it to the ground. He stood staring at it, white-faced, his whole body trembling.

"Take off, Uhlan," Nolan snapped. His voice was like a file.

Uhlan edged away from him, working his lips. "Jesus Christ, can't you ever give me a break? Every crap detail you got—" He shied from Nolan's look.

Mungo sighed patiently and bent for the helmet. He handed it back to Uhlan. "It's the easiest job we got, now, Uhlan. When the Krauts come in, they're coming over the bridge. You won't see any action from behind that wall."

Swampy said thickly, "Why'ncha give him a drink. Feller needs a drink, same as everybody else." He motioned to Reb who handed up a bottle from the spider hole.

"You want a drink, Uhlan?" Mungo asked.

"Goddamned right, I want a drink." Uhlan shot a furtive sideward glance at Nolan. "I need a drink, by God."

As Uhlan gulped the Calvados, Mungo turned to Nolan. "How about you? Want to wash the taste away?"

"I don't get my courage from a bottle," Nolan grated. "I don't need that poison in my system."

He turned away disgustedly and headed for the church. Mungo pried the bottle from Uhlan's nerveless hand. The heavy-jawed, mud-begrimed face was calmer now. "Just take it easy," Mungo said, "and fire if you see them. I'll send a man to relieve you pretty soon." Uhlan nodded and moved off down the road.

Mungo stared after him, shaking his head. He turned back to the men. "Come on in, you Geronimos." He still clutched the bottle. "Let's get out of the sun and get some rest in before the crap hits the fan."

"Gonna get something else in," Swampy said suddenly. He brushed past Mungo, his face indignant, and began running for the church. "Hey, Nolan! Wait your Goddamned turn!" he bellowed. "We're going to do this fair and square."

Mungo's eyes followed him scornfully. "Take it easy, Swampy," he called. "We're going to chow-down first and take a little break. Afterwards you'll have plenty of time to fight over that little bitch."

CHAPTER FIFTEEN
D DAY, 1300 HOURS

Cardboard and cans, the debris of K-ration meals, lay among the pews. Wine bottles rolled in the aisle. The men sprawled heavily, smoking in silence, eyeing each other with the measured distrust of strange dogs.

Swampy was back from foraging another house. Several bottles jutted from the fingers of one hand, and in the other he held a deck of cards. "All right," he said. "We'll cut for her. High card goes first." His voice was thick and he swayed as he walked.

"Swampy, you've had all you need," Mungo said. He removed the bottles from the unresisting fingers. Mungo had consumed more than any of them, but his speech was crisp and his eyes unblurred, and his gait as steady as ever. The big, squat frame seemed impervious to alcohol. The only sign of Mungo's indulgence was a languid softening of his impassive smile.

He strode to the baptismal font where Dana sat, and held out one of the bottles of wine. "How about it, soldier?"

Dana shook his head. "Feel pretty good right now." He stared coldly up into the sergeant's eyes.

Mungo shrugged. "You'll need it maybe. You ain't even crocked."

"Crocked enough, Sergeant."

Mungo turned away unconcernedly.

"I'll take a little juice from you," Cadillac offered.

"*You* would," said Mungo, and threw the bottles onto the heap of packs near the altar.

The Calvados and wine hadn't blunted Dana's mind. If anything, they made him more lucidly aware. It seemed to him that Mungo wanted the men drunk. Did he think they'd kill more readily—face death with greater courage when the Germans hit? Or was it to turn their thoughts away from Edgerton? A dark conjecture about Edgerton's death was turning to certainty in Dana's mind. He smoked and stared at the group near the altar. Well, whatever Mungo's motives, he had the men drunk, all right.

The earlier elation had drained away. Swampy and Reb were both morose and even Cadillac was silent. Their eyes, from time to time, moved with a furtive hunger to the door of the sacristy, and then swept back to meet the eyes of the others with smouldering suspicion. Nolan had his trench knife out. He kept driving it sharply into the dark-stained wooden floor. It would make a chunking sound and quiver until Nolan pulled it out to throw it again. The mounting tension was a tactile presence in the confines of the church.

Reb's eyes flickered sullenly to Mungo and he sprang to his feet. "Damnit all," he said. "I'm goin' to get some! A man got a right before he dies ..." He started for the sacristy.

"Sit down, Reb!" Swampy snarled at him. He threw his deck of cards on the steps to the altar. "We're all goin' to get some—but you ain't first. We play it fair and square."

Nolan snorted disgustedly. He rose and strode to the sacristy door. Mungo watched him stolidly. Nolan, with an angry gesture, flung the door open and stepped inside.

He ignored Hollister, lying flat on the bench near the window, with his eyes wide open but glazed and torpid, his bayoneted rifle weakly clutched in both hands. The girl was crouched across the room, her knees drawn up and her head resting on her arms.

Nolan crossed the room and grasped her by the hair, and threw her head back, staring coldly into her face. The girl was pretty. The tear-streaked cheeks, the eyes that fixed him with terror, made her somehow even more desirable to Nolan.

Her dress had been ripped to the midriff, and although she had tried to pin it together, it opened again as he yanked her to her knees. She raised her arms to shield her breasts from Nolan's hard, appraising gaze, but gasped in pain and dropped them as he tugged her hair again. Beneath the jutting breasts, thrust outward by her posture, her torso curved away to a narrow waist and the tattered folds of her skirt.

Nolan felt a savage need to tear that cloth away. By Christ, he was no whiskey-rotted weakling like the others! He was a man, a warrior, a conqueror, by God! This bitch had tried to kill him, this woman of the enemy who sprawled defeated at his feet. A passion, old as conquest, and more closely linked to killing than to love, tightened the muscles of his massive chest.

He knelt, his mouth screwed up with rage, and bent her body back across his knee, staring into her pleading eyes.

"Window shopping, Nolan?" Mungo stood in the doorway. Nolan threw the girl from him and rose to his feet to face the lazily-smiling sergeant. The girl fell forward on her hands and knees. Her breasts swayed gently as she crawled to the corner of the room.

"Got some objections, Mungo?" Nolan spat the words out from a fury-tightened throat. "Think you got priority? Or maybe you think you're the lieutenant now?"

"Easy, Nolan." Mungo's voice was soft but deep. His eyes above the grin were knife-steel cold. "She don't have your serial number on her yet. The rest of them figure that she's squad equipment. Seems to be some doubt about who gets to use it first."

"Damnit, Nolan!" Swampy's voice echoed from inside the nave. "Play it fair and square." Nolan grunted and strode through the door.

Swampy had his deck of cards spread out on the altar steps. He shuffled them expertly as Nolan approached. "Cut for highest card. Or best poker hand takes it. Any damned thing you like," he said.

Nolan let the fury leak from his muscles, breathing deeply until his chest relaxed. "All right," he said. "We'll play a hand of five-hundred rummy. That okay with you?"

" 'pends who deals," said Reb, eyeing Swampy distrustfully.

"Let ol' Nolan deal." Swampy passed the cards to him. Nolan shook his head. "I ain't playing any card games in front of an altar. Some of you slobs got no respect."

They moved to a pew in the rear of the church, where sunlight flooding through a splintered shutter gleamed golden on the benches. "How about you, Cadillac?" Swampy called out.

Cadillac lit a cigarette and walked slowly out of the church. "I don't gamble," he said insouciantly. "Not without an edge."

"T.S., buddy," Swampy called to his retreating back. "You get it after we're through." He looked across the church to Dana questioningly. Dana shook his head. His mind was busy with other things. He noticed Mungo examining him with slow, appraising eyes.

"What's the matter, Sergeant?" Dana asked. "Don't you like to gamble either?"

Mungo grinned and slipped a fresh cigar into his mouth. "Let them have their fun," he rumbled, and Dana knew that no matter how the card game went, Mungo would take the girl whenever he wanted her, and give her or deny her to the others as he liked.

The other three hunched over the bench, staring at the cards which Swampy was riffling in his hands. "Let me see them cards," Nolan snarled suspiciously. Swampy handed over the deck. "Hell, they're all screwed up," Nolan complained. "There ain't no Jacks—they got these 'V's, and 'D's' instead of Queens. And the Kings are ..."

"It's the same thing," Swampy said. "Look at the pictures. The Froggies write their letters funny. Just look at the pictures."

"Deal 'em," Reb said. "Roll 'em, damnit. Let's get goin'." There was a steady slapping and shuffling of cards, and angry curses as they settled to their game. Their eyes were intent now, on the hands they held. Mungo walked over to watch them play, a faintly sardonic smile on his face.

Dana leaned his back against the baptismal font and shook his head in wonder at these men. They might only have an hour or less to live. Even now the Germans must be circling around them, bringing up their guns to blow them from the earth. And Reb and Swampy and Nolan, with animal intensity, could focus their minds on a game of cards for the privilege of being the first to possess an enemy woman before they died. A privilege, Dana reflected wryly, which Mungo would, by strength alone, reserve for himself.

Dana needed women as much as any man, but not with the shadow of death upon him. And not the sort of woman who would only receive him with fear and hatred. He wondered if he was somehow weaker than the others. Well, Sacco wasn't playing—he was standing by his gun on the hill. And Cadillac had left the scene in disgust. It was only men like Nolan, and Reb and Swampy...

He heard no footsteps, but a shadow brushed his face. Cadillac, with catlike steps, was slipping back into the church. The others, too absorbed in their game, had not heard him enter. A light cotton mattress was rolled under his arm. Dana looked at him questioningly. "For Hollister," Cadillac whispered and noiselessly opened the sacristy door. Dana heard it lock behind him.

Cadillac signaled to Hollister to make no sound. The boy looked at him and nodded vaguely; he seemed dazed and indifferent. Cadillac dropped the mattress behind a cabinet against the farther wall, where Hollister could not watch him. The kid might be zonked right out of his skull, floating on cloud nine, but Cadillac didn't want an audience to catch this sort of scene.

"Been waiting long, baby?" he whispered to the girl. She was on her feet now, cowering against the wall, and her face was completely blank. Her eyes were wide and empty, as though drained of emotion, but she opened her mouth and it seemed for a second that she might be about to scream. Cadillac, kneeling on the mattress, smiled his slow and gentle smile and offered her a D-bar. He extended it coaxingly from his outstretched arm, as he might have offered food to an animal.

"This belonged to my mother." He caressed her with his voice. "I know she would have wanted a girl like you to have it." Her stiffened body seemed to relax a little, reassured by his tone, although the words meant nothing to her. Cadillac unslung his Tommy-gun and laid it quietly behind him.

"Don't like chocolate? Want a cigarette?" he whispered. He proffered her a pack. This time she responded, smiling slightly, as she took a slow step toward him and removed one from the pack. Cadillac patted the mattress beside him. The girl shook her head but bowed her body forward to the lighted match he held out to her. He withdrew it slowly, always just an inch away from the tip of the cigarette between her lips, luring her imperceptibly closer so that she was almost bending over him.

As she lit her cigarette, her torn blouse opened and his eyes traveled slowly over her body from her neck to the line of cotton elastic just below her navel. Gently he raised a hand to her waist and slipped it around to the small of her back, forcing her down to him with gentle pressure. She dropped her cigarette. On her knees beside him now, she flashed Cadillac a quick and calculating look.

Cadillac smiled softly, blew out the match, and picked up her cigarette, drawing on it once and then snubbing it out on the floor. His hand caressed her back, gliding around her waist. The crook of his elbow forced her gently against him. His other hand rose to stroke her cheek, and although her eyes retained that blankly-hostile stare, her body seemed to melt against his own.

He let his fingers play over her mouth, down her arching neck to her firm-fleshed breast. He felt the nipple harden and rise against his palm. His smile was now triumphant. She responded by kissing him with hungry passion. Her moist tongue searched his lips and darted between them. She moaned and pressed herself against him.

Cadillac dropped his hand from her back, across her hips to the hem of her skirt. She wore no stockings and the flesh of her thighs was satin-smooth and warm, almost hot to the touch. Her legs trembled as he touched them, and Cadillac felt the eternal amazement of the male at the softness of a woman's skin along her inner thighs. He returned her kiss and cupped his hand.

Swampy's triumphant cackle sounded through the door. "That's the card I been waiting for. That's her, I—God!" There was the sharp crack of cards slapped onto wood, an instant of silence, with Cadillac tensed, listening—and then Nolan's voice cried out in anger: "No you don't, you hillbilly lush! Those 'V's are jacks and the other one's a King. You don't have nothing but crap in that hand." A murmur of voices, hard accusing; Mungo's heavy rumble, and then Reb's voice crying, "All right, deal them Goddamned cards again!"

Cadillac relaxed and pressed the girl back until her head lay on the mattress.

Hollister saw the toe of Cadillac's boot thrust from behind the cabinet. Next to it, the pointed shoes of that French bitch stiffened for a moment, then one of them withdrew with a slow and indolent motion. Hollister looked up at the ceiling and tried to draw his mind away. There was too much to think about; things were so confused. There wasn't any pain now the morphine had caught hold. He was wrapped in clouds of cotton, floating numbly on a warm and lazy sea. He was going to ride home soon, in the turret of a tank, driven by Sergeant Mungo himself, or was it that Lieutenant Edgerton?

Funny the lieutenant hadn't been in to see him. Only Mungo and Nolan, and Nolan hadn't said much, hadn't even asked him how he was. And that screwball, Cadillac. What in hell was wrong with that guy, necking with that bitch who had wounded him? Sure, she had been nice when he fainted before, but, Christ, she was the enemy, she had tried to kill him, and Cadillac his buddy—well, a member of his squad—was getting mushy with her on that mattress, just as if she was a clean, decent American girl, and not a lousy killer. What was it Mungo called her? A dirty Kraut-loving bitch.

He heard a stifled cry from her—"Non, non!"—a sort of gasp, and Cadillac's soothing whisper. What the hell!

She had held him in her arms before, and stroked his forehead. Exactly like a mother would, exactly as Hollister imagined a mother. He had never known one, but when a guy was wounded, that's what he figured a mother would be like. He had never known a girl friend either, damnit, but he knew pretty well what that would be like, too. Hollister wished he could shut his ears. Damnit all, she was the enemy, the bitch who shot him, and Mungo had put him here to guard her. To drop a bullet through her if she tried to get away.

Again, through the door, he heard the slap of cards and this time Nolan's voice crowing loudly. "All right, there it is! Can you guys match that?"

There was another silence, and then Hollister turned his head abruptly as another, terrible sound stabbed at his ears. Cadillac's voice screamed in sudden, unbelieving terror: *"No, baby, no!"* And the room exploded with the hammering of automatic gunfire.

The girl backed out from behind the cabinet, the Thompson still roaring, bucking in her hand as she emptied it down into the mattress. Cadillac's boots jutted into view again, drummed against the floor and then lay still. Hollister, his rifle up and pointed at the girl, had already swung his feet to the floor and jerked his body erect. He hardly felt the flash of pain in his groin.

The girl ran toward him, toward the window, the Thompson still in her hand. Her face was twisted and her eyes unseeing and she stumbled forward in a mindless panic. Hollister pulled the trigger twice. He had time to wonder vaguely why the rifle did not fire, and then the girl was on him. Her skirt had fallen in tatters to her feet, and it tripped her as she lunged for the window.

It was probably her stumbling more than Hollister that did it. For one strange, timeless instant she was poised above him, clawing for the window; and then she was impaled on his bayonet.

The steel tip slid into her just at the navel, and her body received it with a squelching sound like a ripe fruit bursting. Her weight drove the rifle butt hard against the bench, and then it glanced off to the floor, with the barrel thrusting upwards, still, rigidly supported by Hollister's numb hands. The Tommy-gun clattered to the floor.

Her screams continued endlessly, vibrating in his ears: a piercing shrillness that climbed an octave higher than Hollister imagined the human voice could go. Her writhing torso slid downwards and away, gutting itself on the eight inch blade. He could feel it ripping through until it struck on bone. He released the rifle then, and she rolled against him, still spitted on the steel. As she hit the floor, the screaming sank to a gurgle and abruptly died away. She lay on her side with her face contorted. Her mouth worked frenziedly; no sound came out. She thrashed for a moment and then was still. The tip of the bayonet protruded from her back.

Hollister sank back upon the bench. He began to vomit as the door crashed inward, splintering under the weight of Mungo's shoulder. Mungo burst into the room, the Spring-field in his hand. He glanced at the boy first, and then his eyes swept the room. He lowered the rifle to his side as Nolan rushed in, followed by Dana.

"You all right, kid?" Mungo asked.

Hollister nodded. His eyes were tightly closed.

Mungo bent and picked up the Tommy-gun and handed it to Nolan. Then he worked the bayonet out of the girl's body, twisting it first and then wrenching it free, levering his boot against her breast. He slipped his toe under her and turned the girl's corpse over, concealing the gaping wound.

He turned to Nolan then, his eyes hard. "Okay, you won it," he growled. "Now bury it!"

Nolan turned and strode from the room. His features were expressionless; his skin was deathly white. From the doorway, Swampy mumbled, "Jesus Christ." Nolan thrust him aside.

Dana was staring at Cadillac's body, sprawled out on the mattress with his arms flung up as though to ward off the bullets from his chest. Dana had not realized what a clip of .45 slugs, fired from close range, could do to the body of a man. He felt his stomach heaving and his eyes sought Mungo's, as though appealing for help.

Mungo had bent to retrieve Cadillac's jaunty little go-to-hell cap. The blue-silk parachute insignia was purple now, with blood. Mungo held it in his hands a moment, looking down. "Well, he was a good man," he said.

Dana got his stomach under control. "I thought she liked him. He told me that she wanted him."

"Wanted his Thompson," Mungo said. There was a trace of compassion in his sideways glance at Dana. "You go up on that tower and try to communicate again. I'm going to let those horny gamblers clean up this mess."

Dana mounted the stairs and switched on the radio. He concentrated fiercely, trying to drive the image of his friend's body from his mind. Reception was hopeless: only static and a confused crackling. After a few minutes, he shut the set down. It only increased his growing sense of isolation. They might as well be a hundred miles behind the German lines. Vacantly he stared down the empty causeway, and across the scummy, slate-gray marshes. The scene was bleak and lonely as a foghorn in the mist, but he knew that through the sea-grass of the seemingly deserted swamps, enemy riflemen must be moving closer, stealthily slipping around the village to their rear.

Somewhere in the distance there was small-arms fire. For a moment he listened without reaction. The sound was too far away—it seemed to have no relation to the village or himself. It came from somewhere up the road, grew nearer imperceptibly. He raised his head and peered excitedly across the bridge. It might be the Fifth Corps pushing west from Omaha Beach to effect a link-up with the Utah Beachhead. He saw Sacco running across the knoll and he tore down the tower steps to learn what was happening.

Reb and Swampy were carrying the bodies from the church; someone had wrapped the girl's corpse in a blanket. Mungo stood in the doorway of the church, watching Sacco slide down the knoll.

"It's a jeep," Sacco shouted, running toward the church. "The Krauts are firing at it. Coming this way fast. It might just get through."

Dana followed Mungo out the church door. Reb and Swampy had dropped the bodies behind the embankment. They came racing back. Dana's heart bounded against his ribs. A jeep meant that they were once more a part of the army, not just a little band of hunted men. A swelling volume of small-arms fire came from the east.

"All right, Sacco," Mungo said, "get up in that tower and stand by the machine gun there. Swampy, you take off and work that gun pit on the hill. Hold your fire until we see what's happening."

Far down the causeway, a tiny jeep barreled around the bend toward the village. They could see the huddled figures in the car and hear the popping of a carbine as someone fired back over the spare tire. Spurts of mud and water danced all around the jeep as unseen German infantrymen blazed away at it. Dana expected to see it go hurtling off the causeway, spilling its occupants out into the bullet-agitated swamp. Miraculously, the jeep kept coming on. He could see the tense white faces behind the windshield now, and the long whip of a radio antenna. The jeep's speed faltered when the driver saw the swastika on the overturned armored car across the bridge. Mungo leaped out onto the road, holding his helmet high. "Come on! GI's here!"

The driver gunned it onto the bridge. Tires squealed as is slid to a stop against the solid rubber rear-tire of the German car which blocked the bridge. The occupants came climbing over the windshield. Mungo snatched the slim driver's belt and jerked him off the hood. "Into the church!" he shouted, and the boy took off at a stumbling run. German bullets banged against the armor. A ricochet screamed.

Two more men bounded off the hood. A stocky, helmetless, gray-haired man followed them more slowly. Dana and Mungo lifted him to the ground. He dropped to one knee behind the jeep's radiator. "I hate to leave that radio behind," he told them. Dana saw a bulky unfamiliar set welded to the jeep floor.

"The hell with it, Major," Mungo said. "We already got a radio."

The officer smiled. "Not a Major, Sergeant, I'm a lieutenant-commander." Like the driver, he wore a pair of huge binoculars suspended from his neck. "The radio's important, soldier. We've a Navy fire-control party."

"I'm not risking men to save it," Mungo snapped. "Not yours or mine." His hand closed on the officer's arm. "Come on."

The glass of the windshield exploded and a ricochet whined inches over their heads. They ran for the church then, Mungo and Dana pulling the officer along between them. Wild German shots pocked the street and the church wall. Brick splinters popped into the air.

The officer collapsed into a church pew, winded. "Commander Royal," he said. "What outfit is this, Sergeant?"

"Five-Oh-Goose," Mungo said. He grinned faintly, then explained. "Five Hundredth Parachute Infantry Regiment, sir." He seemed to like Royal. "How did you get way the hell out here?"

"We came in by glider last night with the first wave. Crashed in a swamp about ten miles from here. The pilot's dead." Commander Royal ran a hand over his mouth. "We've been wandering around since dawn, completely lost. Germans all over the roads."

"Any tanks?" Mungo asked.

"Hell, yes," the spindly driver said. "Big bastards."

"What's the name of this place, Sergeant?" Royal asked.

"Sainte Madeleine. That's the Vire River."

"The Vire!" Royal shook his head disgustedly. "That Airedale cut the tow at least twelve miles from our landing field." He smiled pleasantly at Dana and Mungo. "Anyway, it's good to be inside our lines. As soon as we can clear the road for our jeep, we'll get on to your division headquarters. They'll be glad to see us. And to see some Navy gunfire. There's a whole damned task force out there waiting for targets."

"Is the radio working?" Mungo asked hopefully.

"We're not receiving—it got shaken in the crash—and I can't even be sure we're transmitting, but—" Royal indicated his men. "—these are good boys. They'll have it operating as soon as we can do a little repair."

Mungo said wearily, "Look, Commander—you aren't in American lines yet. There's only eight of us. We're cut off here. Surrounded."

Royal sat bolt upright. His smile was gone. The three sailors gaped at Mungo. Dana was perversely pleased by their astonishment. "We can't get to our lines down this road?"

"Maybe we could," Mungo said. "But I ain't going. I need you and your men, Commander."

Royal relaxed slightly and his easy smile returned. He shook his head. "No, Sergeant. They've got more important work to do. Sorry."

"Sorry, hell," Mungo growled. "The only way out is through the marshes, fighting all the way. You can't bring your jeep through. There's no way to move that armored car. The best you can do is wait for dark and try to get your set working then."

Royal ran his thumb over his clean-shaven jaw. In contrast to the battered, grimy men of the patrol, he seemed, in Dana's eyes, obscenely well-groomed. "How about attacking across the bridge, so we'll have cover while we work on the set?"

Mungo shook his head. His sleepy, dark eyes were ironically amused. "Christ, man, they got a whole division out there. We just broke up a battalion-strength attack. They're laying back there now, waiting for more help. Then they'll come pushing through to take this town and get their armor down the road to the coast." He paused to let his words sink in. "And you want me to attack with a chewed-up squad across a mile of open marshland just so you can diddle around with a radio!"

Royal frowned. "But you won't have a chance when they attack."

"We got a damned good chance. This village is a bottleneck—a natural strongpoint—and we're only ten miles from Utah Beach. The Fourth Division may break through here any minute. If we can hand over this bridge, still standing, then we earn our morning's pay."

"That's not likely, Sergeant. With only eight men—"

"I'm staying here and playing for the breaks," Mungo snapped. "I joined the Goddamned Army to fight. If you're scared, just take your frigging swabbies and bug out of here, Commander!"

"I'm not abandoning my radio, Sergeant. And watch your tone of voice!"

Mungo's anger was gone as suddenly as it had come. "Then you and your men just joined the infantry." He turned for a look at the three Navy enlisted men, his black eyes measuring them swiftly. "Their carbines won't do much good at this end of the village, the range is too great. I'll keep one to help with the gun in the tower, and I'll give Hollister's rifle to another." He nodded and turned to Nolan. "You and Dana take the Commander and one man down to the other end. That'll give you five men, counting Uhlan."

Dana led the way down the street, hugging the buildings where he could, and running, bent and dodging, when they crossed the open spaces. As he stepped through the sagging door of the last house, Uhlan spun with his rifle up. The flesh of his round face seemed to sag from his cheekbones. His eyes were round and dull.

"For Christ's sake, man, get hold of yourself," Dana snarled at him. Uhlan's nerves were shot; he had almost pulled the trigger. The realization chilled Dana.

"Where should we go, Dana?" Commander Royal asked, as he and the jeep driver entered.

Dana looked at him mutely. He was doubly surprised that this superior, self-assured officer should have troubled to learn his name, and that he was asking for orders now in such a trusting manner.

Royal smiled. "This isn't exactly our line, you know."

"I'm running this post," Nolan said. "Take your man upstairs." Royal's mouth hardened, and Nolan added grudgingly, "Sir."

Dana stopped them as they headed for the steep stairway. "You'd better look through the house and see if you can find some mattresses," he said. "Throw them across the window sills. They're good to fight behind. They can stop bullets."

The Navy men exchanged a quick look. "Thanks," Royal said. "That sounds like a good idea."

"Wait," Dana said. He handed Royal the two grenades he had taken from Franklin's body. Use them if the Krauts get under the windows." He did not like to give up the grenades, but they would be more effective from the second floor.

Dana crawled to the kitchen through the broken glass and plaster that littered the floor. Two heavy mortar shells crashed outside. "They've brought up a mortar squad through the marsh," Nolan said. He cursed.

"We're probably okay in here. If they're instantaneous fuses like ours, they aren't much good against buildings and fortifications." Dana was surprised to find himself talking almost companionably to Nolan.

"You get your butt out to the barn, and dig in, Okie! I'm keeping my eyes on you, and don't you forget it!"

"Nolan, you're a jerk." Dana felt disgust, not anger. Their lives had depended on each other since the moment they stepped aboard the plane in England, yet Nolan insisted even now, on playing the tough-guy role to the hilt. "If we get out of this, I'll fight you anytime, anywhere you say, but now you need me and I need you. Stop acting like the meanest kid in the playground."

The big man's eyes were unyielding. "Take off, and don't give me any backtalk."

"What an M.P. you would have made, Nolan!"

Dana crawled to the interior door of the adjoining barn and pushed it open. The wide doors at the opposite end hung open, and the segment of sky and barnyard they revealed looked heartbreakingly peaceful. He rose to his feet in the cool dimness of the barn and lit a cigarette. When he had finished it, he unstrapped his entrenching tool and began chopping out a foxhole for himself in the cover of the doorway. When the hole was deep enough to conceal him kneeling, he extended it until he had a field of fire which commanded the wall and the highway.

He nibbled on a hard chocolate D-ration, his eyes raking the field behind the fence and the marsh across the highway. There was no sign of movement from the fold of ground which probably hid the Germans, but every few minutes a mortar shell came crashing into the village. Several landed in the yard in front of the house, and one exploded on its roof, sending a rain of red-tile fragments down into the mud.

Dana knew from the shallow holes they left in the ground that the shells had contact fuses. The only danger to the men in the house was from fragments flying through the windows.

Dana thought of the *feldgrau* German corpses he and the others had sown across the marshes at the eastern end of the village. He wondered what kind of men they had been. Could any of them have told him why they tried to kill him? Could he explain why he had slain them? He knew he could not; he doubted if anyone knew the answer.

And yet they sought each other's death, he and the strangers behind the rise of ground. Well, this much he knew: he was not here to defend his right to boo the umpire or eat his mother's apple pie. He was here because a Federal judge had given him the choice of going to Leavenworth or entering the Army.

The judge was paid by the same government that also paid the marshall who evicted drought-broken families from their farms and hired steel-fisted deputies to bust the heads of men who tried to organize against the fruit growers' associations. And now the government was at war, for reasons too obscure for Dana to credit. It had put him here because he was a working-man, and destined never to be anything else.

To Dana's mind the Germans facing him were only working-men, too. Why fight them anymore? He and Nolan and the rest were hopelessly trapped. Life in a P.W. camp might be hard, but it was better than dying here, and it would come to an end some-time. He remembered Uhlan, at the drop zone, begging Edgerton to surrender. Damn it—Uhlan had been right! Cadillac would still be alive if they had quit then. And Franklin. And Edgerton, himself.

There was a hollow metallic sound, like a firecracker explod-ing in a wash tub. Twenty seconds later a mortar shell burst in the village behind him. Dana knew the first sound came from the firing of the mortar. He thought briefly of trying to get back to the church for Mungo's Springfield and the rifle grenades. Maybe he could knock out the mortar crew from here with the '03.

The thought of crawling a hundred and fifty yards to the church and back with mortar fire exploding all around him chilled Dana. He might do it if he were back with Headquarters Company, First Battalion and the lives of his friends depended on it. But risking his life for men like Nolan and Uhlan and Mungo was asking too much. "The hell with it," he said aloud against the tiny flicker of guilt that rose in him. He rested his back against the wall of the foxhole, munching the chocolate, and waiting fatalistically for whatever would come.

CHAPTER SIXTEEN
D DAY, 1530 HOURS

Reb crouched in the spider hole beside the bridge, staring at the fire-blackened hulk of the armored car. He felt nothing—not the cool breeze that had begun to blow from across the marsh as the afternoon sun waned, not fear, not hope—only a bottomless loathing for himself and for life.

Only hours ago his blood had been singing with elation. He had laid the bazooka shell into the armored car, stopping it right where Mungo wanted it. The Germans had gone fleeing back across the marsh. He had run to the bridge with his M-1 and fired at the running gray figures, blazing away until they were all out of sight, or dead. When he came back to the church, Mungo had grinned at him and punched him jarringly on the shoulder and Reb had felt, then, that he was someone, not just some shack-woman's bastard from the swamps.

But the feeling died abruptly, as it always did. Generally, it came only when he was drunk, and faded with the morning smell of puke and corn liquor, to leave him feeling lower than ever. The feeling had come this time when he stopped the armored car and been lost when he saw the bayoneted girl. Dead, she looked like another sleeping whore.

It would always be this way, as long as he lived. He would never be a man's son—just a poor slut's oversight. No girl would ever give herself to him with love. His women were the kind you took only when you were drunk—bloated and stale-smelling in the hungover morning.

He had gone back to the spider hole and loaded the bazooka after Mungo sent the Navy men with Dana and Nolan. It lay beside him on the ground now, ready for firing. Then he went back for the C-2 and the fuse. Mungo saw him with the gray plastic containers in his hands.

"Where are you going with that?"

"I'm taking it out to the hole with me. I may need it."

Mungo stared at him, long and thoughtfully. "Okay, Reb."

The packs of explosive were at his feet now, lashed into a bundle with the coil of slow-burning wire and a trip fuse.

Far down the causeway, tiny figures emerged from the cover of the trees, moving off to the sides of the road. Reb lit a cigarette and watched them with interest. They were far out of rifle and machine-gun range.

More men appeared from the trees, fanning out into the marsh. A low-slung dark hulk emerged at last, moving into position a few rods ahead of the advancing line of men. The breeze shifted and Reb could hear the rumble of its motors and the clank of its treads on the surface of the road. It was a tank, a big one.

His lips peeled back from his teeth in a terrible smile. "Come on, you big bastard. Come on! I'll stop you, too."

He watched the stand of trees, waiting for more tanks to appear. He wanted the whole German army to come down the road, relentless and overwhelming. There was nothing in this world for Reb, but fire and fury.

The tank halted on the highway, its turret swinging silently around, the poised barrel of the 75 seeking the range. Reb saw the flash of its muzzle. There was a swishing sound and an ear-splitting crash in the churchyard. The ground shook under him. The sound of the cannon reached him two seconds later. *The hell with you. You don't get me that way. You've got to come for me, bastard.*

The tank rolled again, with the waves of infantry plodding on behind it. Every fifty yards or so, it stopped and fired a round. Some of the shells landed on the knoll, seeking Mungo's machine gun, and two ripped huge holes in the wall of the church. Reb wondered how long it would be before the tank commander thought of the church tower. They must not have spotted Sacco's gun there, yet.

He could see a man riding atop the tank now, and knew he must be an officer. Reb watched him waving his arms at the riflemen. *You brave son-of-a-bitch you. You first.* He cuddled the M-1 stock against his cheek. Six or seven hundred yards. A very long range. Reb held his breath and squeezed the trigger.

He missed. The German officer, oblivious, went on bellowing soundlessly at his men. Reb emptied the clip at him. Nothing happened. His eyes could not spot the strike of his bullets; he had no way to adjust his range. Reb slid another clip into the breech. The officer was waving to speed up at the skirmish line. Reb laid the rifle aside and watched. *Later, bastard. Another hundred yards, bastard.*

He put the remaining bandoleers on his lap and thumbed the clips out of the pockets, watching the Germans advance. The cannon was firing every few seconds. Reb ignored the crash of the shells around him, the trembling of the ground. He tapped the ends of the cartridges against the rifle to even them and piled the clips beside his hole. They taught you to tap them on the butt plate so you wouldn't scar the stock. *The hell with that.* The infantry was coming forward faster. Reb laughed at the nervous quickening of their steps. *Don't get yellow, boys. Come and get me. All of you.*

The officer was close enough for another try. He put the rifle to his shoulder, really seeing the enormous tank for the first time. He recognized it from the manuals—a Mark Four, 30 tons, 500 H.P. *Good. Bring the best, the best you've got.*

Reb blazed a full clip of eight shots at the officer. His head jerked up, surprised, and Reb knew a bullet had come close. Neither Sacco or Mungo were firing yet. They were waiting for a shorter range. He banged off a second clip and reloaded, laughing. The officer was ordering a squad onto the halted tank. Reb triggered off the rounds as fast as he could, shooting wildly, impatient to kill.

He fired another clip and another, feeding and emptying the M-1 frenziedly. A man dropped off the tank and lay still. The Germans on the tank were firing blindly now. The infantry began running, lifting their boots high out of the marsh water. Mungo's gun ripped into action and then Sacco's. Gaps appeared suddenly in the neatly-spaced line of Germans. The tanks heavy machine guns sprayed the churchyard and the 75 swung toward the tower, firing steadily.

Reb shot a quick glance backward, saw the bloom of smoke and flame as the cannon shells struck the thick walls of the tower. Ol' Sacco wasn't going to last long, now. Nobody was.

The tank picked up speed. Reb fired into the knot of men atop it, saw some come tumbling down, others leaping to the roadway.

It was almost to the bridge now. Reb saw the cannon swing toward Mungo's knoll. Sacco's gun was silenced. The officer stood along on the tank, a tall redfaced man, waving his Mauser at his men. His mouth worked as he shouted, but his words were swallowed in the din.

Reb searched for another clip for his rifle. *Damn!* He'd used the last of them. *Okay, you bastard! There's still the bazooka.*

Reb snatched the long light tube, and laid it on his shoulder. The tank was on the bridge now, thrusting the jeep and the armored car ahead of it. Reb could see the helmeted heads of the Germans crouched behind it. He waited. He would be absolutely sure when he fired.

The Mark IV almost filled the bridge. Reb got the turret in his sight, and pressed the switch. Flame shot out of the tube behind him. The rocket bounced harmlessly off the thick armor. The German officer still clung to the turret.

The tank's Spandau swung on the spider hole, the slugs kicking up a row of mud spurts. A bullet struck the bazooka tube and spun it high into the air.

"Damn you, bastard!" Reb shouted. He caught up the bundle of C-2 and sprang out of the hole, dodging around the armored car. He thrust the explosive against the tank treads, and tripped the fuse.

A German soldier behind the tank saw him and shouted. The officer spun and fired at Reb. The Mauser bullet struck him in the thick rope of muscle beside his neck. It felt to Reb like a rabbit punch. "Bastard!" he shouted at the officer. He stepped onto the bridge rail and leaped aboard the tank throwing himself on the officer.

The C-2 exploded then. Mungo saw the two bodies fly high in the air.

Tongues of flames licked up the side of the tank. A hatch flew open and a German hoisted himself out. His left leg seemed to be afire. Mungo's burst left him hanging half out of the hatch.

"They're running!" Swampy shouted.

"Keep firing!" Mungo barked. "There's some behind the tank!"

The gray figures had turned as the tank exploded. They were fleeing back up the road now. The Germans in the marsh floundered after them, tripping and falling and rising again.

Mungo pulled the pin from a grenade. Unhurriedly, he lobbed it in a high arc over the tank. It burst fifteen feet off the ground. He saw a German stagger from behind the tank and lurch lifelessly against the bridge rail. The helmet fell from his head and splashed into the Vire.

Mungo crouched behind the gun again and fired steadily until the last of the Germans was out of range.

Swampy and the sailor gaped at the dead men they had strewn across the battlefield. "They ain't going to come this way again," Swampy chortled. "Not with feet soldiers, they ain't!"

"No," Mungo said. Next time it'll be armor."

The attack on the western side of the village began when the tank sent its first shells screaming down the causeway at the men defending the bridge, as if the troops across the meadow had been waiting for that signal. The men crouching at the windows of the house noticed, first: a quickening of the mortar fire.

Shell fragments came through the windows and ripped upwards through the ceilings and roof of the farmhouse. Commander Royal and Rosen, his jeep driver, shrank against the walls in the second-story bedrooms, sheltering themselves from the fragments exploding through the downstairs windows and piercing the floor beneath their feet.

They felt grateful to Dana for suggesting the mattresses they had flung over the window sills. The stout ticking absorbed flying steel as efficiently as earthworks. A steady stream of machine-gun tracers chewed at the brittle tile roof above their heads, and soon they noticed smoke curling from the attic beams.

Dana was crouched in his foxhole at the corner of the barn. High-flung earth pattered down on him from the shell bursts, but he was safe from anything but a direct hit.

The first infantry attack came in a thin reluctant wave. The men in the house saw it first. It was the sound of their weapons that made Dana raise himself to the lip of his fox-hole and begin firing. A small group of Germans came over the far rise of ground, no more than a platoon in strength, and charging straight for the farmhouse. When the answering fire of the Americans tumbled the first few men, the others dropped to the ground. After a moment, they rose and fled back to cover.

Nolan, in the house, had held his fire. He knew his Thompson was not accurate at more than a fifty-yard range. He saw no reason to waste ammunition until the enemy had closed. He tore his eyes away from the charging Germans to look at Uhlan. The rifleman was crouched beneath the window, his arms clasped over his head, his weapon forgotten.

Nolan crawled to him. He kicked him savagely in the ribs. "Man your rifle, you chicken-livered son-of-a-bitch! You were talking mighty tough back in England!"

Uhlan held his side and turned tortured eyes up to Nolan. "They'll kill us, Sarge! They'll kill us all!"

Nolan laughed cruelly. Here's where we separate the men from the boys. Remember, Uhlan? Here's where we find out what soldiering is all about." His own face was white with strain. What was the hardness of his bulging muscles against a steel-jacketed bullet? He hated Uhlan for cracking so quickly.

Nolan thrust the muzzle of his sub-machine gun against Uhlan's nose. "You'll die right now, unless you get up and fight! Man your rifle! Get up and fire!"

Uhlan sat up, shrinking against the wall. Nolan jabbed the gun into his face again, his finger curled around the trigger. "Fire at them!"

Uhlan turned to the window. He tore his eyes from Nolan and pressed his cheek to the rifle stock. He forced the sights on a fleeing German back and jerked the trigger convulsively.

"Squeeze them off, Uhlan," Nolan said, more quietly. "Get hold of yourself, man and you'll be all right." He let out a long breath. Somehow he gained a peculiar kind of reassurance from Uhlan. He was so yellow, and yet he could be made to fight.

Dana reloaded his rifle when the last German disappeared across the meadow. He was sure they would come again. Their officers and non-coms would be threatening and cajoling them right now. In a minute or two they would firm up and charge again. There would be more of them this time.

He wondered how long it would be before the end came. The other end of the village was taking a terrible pasting. He saw the fountains of smoke and flame as the H.E. shells hit the church. He could hear the clanking approach of a tank, and he could tell it was a big one. Even if they managed to stand off the Germans in front, they would be taken from the rear, and soon.

He plucked the clips out of a bandoleer, evened the rows of cartridges, and put them in a neat pile at his knee. The hell with it, he thought. *Everybody dies sometime. If I've got to go*—Dana smiled sardonically and finished the tired old bit of bravado—*they're going to know I was here before I went.*

A burst of cheering rose from the Germans. Then they sprang into view. A long deep line of them, many more than the first charge. They came forward at a dead run, dodging and firing as they raced down on the farmhouse.

Dana caught a broad-shouldered Feld-Webel on the bead of his sight, saw the man swerve as he fired and missed. He swung the rifle to the next man and fired. The starteld German broke his stride and clutched his arm. Dana centered on his chest and fired again, then swung to another target. Two more men fell under his gun, and then the leading Germans were at the wall.

Dana rammed another clip into the rifle. A gray arm swung back to throw a grenade. Dana shot the man and saw the Germans near him dive to the ground. The grenade sent up a shower of dirt. The center and left of the German line withered and broke before it reached the fence. The enemy there turned and ran.

But directly ahead of Dana a mass of men were leaping the wall. He shot the nearest and leaped out of the foxhole, back into the barn. Nolan stood at the kitchen door. He raised his Thompson and fired at someone behind Dana. Then dropped to the ground. Dana threw himself down, and rolled over to face the Germans.

He saw some of them sprinting past the open barn door to surround the house. Then geysers of mud raised up in the barnyard and many of them fell. That would be Sacco, reversing the machine gun in the tower to support this end of the village. A cannon shell burst back by the church and the machine gun was abruptly silenced.

A black egg-shaped grenade hurtled through the door. It landed two yards from Nolan. The noise of its explosion was terrific. Dana saw it lift Nolan in the air.

"*Handen hoch!*" a voice outside shouted. "Come out with the hands high!"

"*Kameraden!*" Nolan shouted. "Don't shoot! We surrender!" Miraculously, he was unhurt. Dana remembered then that Nazi concussion grenades were almost ineffective unless hurled into a tank or a pillbox. "We surrender!" Nolan called again.

A grinning German bounded into the doorway, in bold relief against the daylight. "Come out. *Raus mit!*" He held his MP 40 negligently.

Nolan put a burst of three into him. "Overeager," he laughed, as the German crumpled.

Two of the concussion grenades were flung in at them. Their blast was like a savage blow on the ears.

Two explosions sounded in quick succession outside the barn wall. "I got them! I got them!" The yelp of triumph came thinly to Dana's aching ears, but he recognized Rosen's voice. He dove through the kitchen door and worked himself along the floor to the front room. Uhlan lay on the floor again, trembling uncontrollably.

"Hey Commander!" Dana shouted. "Are there any Germans outside the house?" His voice sounded strange, and he wondered if he was permanently deafened.

"Only dead ones, Corporal," the officer shouted from the upper floor. "Rosen got them with your grenades!" His voice was elated.

"Keep away from the back windows," Dana said. "Some of them got around the barn, I think." His hearing was coming back to normal, but his ears stung painfully.

"How many?"

"No telling. Maybe none. One of our machine guns in the church got most of them."

Rifles were cracking from the woods. A bullet gouged a huge splinter out of the staircase and buried itself in the wall. Dana wondered how long it would be before the Germans came again. "How are you up there?" he called. "How's your ammo?"

"Pretty low, Corporal."

I'm no corporal, Dana thought irrelevantly. What made Royal think he was.

"Do you know this building is on fire?" Royal called down the stairs.

Dana almost laughed. It seemed somehow so absurd that the house could catch fire, as if fate were conspiring with the Nazis to kill them here.

"What?" he asked disbelievingly.

"That's right, son. The beams are smouldering in the attic."

It must have been the tracers, Dana decided. "Well, stay up there as long as you can, will you? The top floor gives us a better field of fire. We won't leave you."

"I know you won't, Corporal."

Why do you trust me? Dana wondered. Why? You've only known me an hour. You never saw me before.

A tremendous explosion rocked the building. "What was that?" Nolan demanded. He had just crawled through the kitchen door.

"It came from the bridge," Uhlan said.

The three of them lay listening for a long time. The sounds of battle from the eastern end of the village had somehow altered. It took Dana a while to isolate the change—he no longer heard the clatter of the tank or the roar of a 75. "Do you think they got the tank?" he asked Nolan.

A flicker of hope danced in the big man's eyes. "How could they?"

They lay on the floor, their heads raised a few inches, dreading the resumption of the tank's firing. The single American machine gun was still pounding away. There did not seem to be as much counter-fire from the Germans.

The gun stopped firing after a few bursts, and then there was silence from that end of Sainte Madeleine. Had Mungo somehow stopped the assault across the marsh again? It was impossible, Dana thought. He had resigned himself to death just a few minutes ago. Yet he was still alive, the Germans beaten off.

"Hey!" Uhlan breathed. "The Germans are waving a white flag!"

Nolan and Dana raised themselves cautiously, disbelief in their eyes. They peered obliquely through the windows. There was a flutter of white cloth at the edge of the trees. It moved back and forth in a metronomic arc. The Germans had stopped firing.

Nolan turned stunned eyes on him. His voice was hollow. "Is it a trick? Do you think they really want to quit?"

Dana shrugged. "I ain't going to walk out there to find out, *Sergeant.*"

Uhlan crawled hurriedly back into the room. He had found a dish towel in the ruins of the kitchen. He draped it over the front sights of his M-1 and thrust it gingerly through the window. Nolan eyed him sullenly, indecisively. After a moment he seized Uhlan by the collar and hurled him back from the window. "What the hell do you think you're doing, Uhlan? We're not giving up!" he snarled.

"What's the good of going on, Sergeant Nolan?" His voice was quavering; he seemed about to cry. "We'll only get killed. They'll kill us all!"

"Put it down you yellow bastard!"

Uhlan plucked the towel from his rifle. He stared sadly at the floor.

"Here comes a German," Dana said. He felt light-headed, almost gay. For the first time he could see the hollowness in Nolan. The man was huge; he was strong as a bear. But his courage depended on the eyes of others—it was nervous, thin, a bluff. It was not an inexhaustible glandular secretion like Mungo's courage. Nolan's kind was borrowed; his nerve was brittle. He was almost as frightened as Uhlan.

A solitary German was walking slowly across the meadow toward the house. His head was bare and he held it high. He walked with proud military precision, holding a fluttering white cloth on a stick high above his head.

Nolan worked the bolt of the Thompson, ramming a cartridge into the chamber. He was kneeling at the window with slitted eyes. "I'll dump the bastard when he steps across the fence."

"You're going to kill him?" Dana asked him, outraged.

"What do you think?"

"I won't let you do it!" Dana jumped recklessly to his feet. "You ain't in charge here, Nolan. Mungo is."

Nolan shot him a scornful look. "Get down! Do you think Mungo wouldn't shoot him?"

"I don't know." Dana spread his feet angrily, gripping the rifle, wanting to smash the butt into Nolan's face. "I don't know what you or Mungo or any of you crazy Regulars would do. But we got some wounded—at least one man, and maybe more after that last attack. I ain't letting you shoot that Kraut until we talk to him!"

Nolan laughed contemptuously. "I'm going to shoot that Kraut, Okie," he said, in his cold, deliberate tough-deputy manner.

Dana looked into his narrowed eyes and believed him. He shot a glance at the window. The German was coming steadily on. He was almost in range.

If he let Nolan kill the man this way, what mercy could they expect when the Germans overwhelmed the village? Nolan's compulsion for heroics was insane, but Dana could no more cope with him now than he could back in garrison. "Commander Royal!" he shouted. "Come down here!"

The Navy officer appeared on the stairway. "What's all the argument about, boys?"

"This crazy bastard wants to shoot that German with the white flag," Dana told him.

Royal's smile vanished. "You can't do that."

"This is an Army deal," Nolan said, without turning his head. "You're not in charge of anything but your little radio, Commander."

"Sergeant's Mungo's in charge," Royal said, coldly angry.

"How do you know Mungo's still alive? You hear what they've been dropping on the other end of town?"

"Put that gun up, damnit!" Royal snapped. "I won't let you shoot a man carrying a flag of truce."

Nolan laughed, still watching the German. "Who's going after Mungo?"

Dana had been considering that question, long before Nolan asked it. Bringing Mungo back meant a hazardous round trip. Across the marsh, a 57 mm gun was firing intermittently into the village. The road to the church was doubly exposed, for the intervening houses might be German-occupied. He had seen a group of Germans run past the barn; he could not be sure that Sacco's gun had stopped them all. If any had infiltrated into the houses, their rifles would be trained along the street for the first American to show his head.

Royal turned to him. "What do you think, Dana?" His eyes were earnest, and Dana knew the man was not patronizing him. He was honestly seeking his advice.

"I'll go get Mungo." Dana said angrily. "I'll go meet this German, too."

Royal's face showed his relief. "Good man," he said, and turned to Nolan. "If you shoot that Nazi, Nolan, I can promise you a general court martial." He paused deliberately, his eyes locked on Nolan's. "You'd better put that gun up, son. You're not talking to any Army shavetail now."

Nolan snorted and lowered the Thompson. "All right," he growled, "go bring him in here, Okie. But get it through your head that nobody's surrendering."

Dana stood on the window sill and jumped to the ground outside. He remembered an earlier moment, when he had considered making the dangerous trip to the church for Mungo's rifle grenades. He had decided against it then—it had seemed an unnecessary risk of his life. Why in hell was he being so brave now?

He stepped only a few paces forward, wanting the house at his back. The German was big and handsome, with the trim, athletic look of a ski instructor. He wore the silver-braided epaulets of a captain. He leaped the fence and crossed the yard toward Dana, smiling. Dana brought up the muzzle of his rifle.

The German stopped and nodded; his smile was polite. "Good afternoon, sir. You are in command here?"

Dana ran his eyes over the narrow-waisted tunic, the neatly-fitting jackboots which showed a trace of polish beneath the swamp mud clinging to them. Dana said, "You talk pretty good English."

"I studied in your country before the war." He brought his heels together and extended his hand. "Hauptmann von Ritter. A pleasure to meet you, er … lieutenant?"

Dana scowled and gripped the M-1 harder, the muzzle pointed carefully at Von Ritter's groin. "I ain't no lieutenant. Get your ass in the house." The man was Edgerton's and Royal's type, not his.

The German stiffened and stepped angrily past him. He leaned his improvised flag staff against the scarred plaster wall of the house before he stepped up through the window. Dana followed him.

Von Ritter's eyes found the bronze oak leaf on Royal's collar. His heels clicked and his arm came up in the Wehrmacht salute. "Good afternoon, Major. Hauptmann Von Ritter."

Royal's eyes were cold. "Stand over in that corner and keep your mouth shut. There'll be a man along to talk to you directly."

Von Ritter's chin lifted. "I expect to parley with the officer commanding here."

"Is that a flag of truce you were carrying?" Royal asked him curtly.

"It is."

"Then why in hell are your guns still firing?"

Von Ritter shrugged. "We are in the field. Communications are difficult. I have sent a runner to them. Are you in charge here?"

"No," said Royal. "Get over in that corner."

The German stepped punctiliously over to the corner of the room. "If I may speak to the man in—"

"You will," Royal snapped. He nodded to Dana.

Two 57 mm shells burst in rapid succession along the street outside the house. Uhlan winced. Dana found the eyes of the other Americans on him. Nolan's were coldly curious, the others regarded him with sympathy and awe. He sucked in a deep breath and wished someone else were going, longing to keep his vulnerable flesh here between the solid walls. The enemy captain was nonchalantly lighting a cigarette—it would be nice to take him along to the church and back. No German rifleman would fire on him if he walked with Von Ritter at his side. Loyalty to the others made him discard the idea—it would not do to let the German see how few men defended the village.

The hell with it. Dana pulled the front door inward and slid on his belly down the two steps to the farmer's yard. Holding the M-1 ahead of him, he crawled on all fours to where the hedge met the corner of the house. He paused there and scanned the upper windows of the houses that lay ahead of him. He was certain now, with superstitious dread, that one of them must hold Germans.

The disintegration of the village awed him. The street was strewn with rubble. Gaping holes had been smashed in the walls and the red-tile roofs, and Dana could see orange flame licking away the interior of one house.

He gathered his legs under him and sprinted to the next house, dropping down beside its wall. His heart was hammering wildly. Far up the street a shell roared in and hurled brick-dust and cobblestones high in the air. He pressed his face against the earth.

One more house separated him from the church. One more yard to leap across, and then one final sprint to the church. Dana crawled along the front of the house, his stomach muscles tightened in expectation of a bullet that might pierce him at any moment.

He lifted his head and saw that a corner of the church tower had been torn away by shellfire. Terror turned his intestines to water. Was anyone left alive back here? He raised himself and sprinted for the intervening house. He dropped to the ground, crawled again—panting, trying not to think of rifles zeroed on his back—came to the corner of a house again, leaped to his feet, and charged to the church.

The door was choked with rubble. The top of the rude stairway that climbed the inner wall of the tower was burning with a crackling sound. Dana stumbled over the stones into the church. The rear wall was almost completely gone. The crucifix had fallen across the crumbling altar.

A paratrooper lay in the tiny arched doorway that led up to the tower. Dana knelt beside him and gently brushed the grime and mortar dust from the strangely peaceful face. The skin was still warm to his touch.

The facial muscles twitched beneath his fingertips. The mortar-whitened eyelids fluttered, opened wide, and Sacco once again, but dimly, grinned at him. "Hey, Dana ... you okay, kid?"

"Yeah, I'm okay." Dana's voice was choked. "Where did they get you? Where're you hit?"

"Chest," said Sacco. His voice was soft but without a tremor. Incredibly, the oddly tilted eyes could twinkle still. "I caught the big one, Dana."

"You're going to be okay." Dana said, aware that he was lying, struggling to believe the lie. "We'll get you out of here."

"No you won't." Sacco grinned again and coughed. Blood welled slowly from the corner of his mouth and trickled over his chin. "I like it here. A good place to be leaving from. Always wanted to do it in a church." He winced a little, then his face relaxed.

Dana's throat constricted. His hand shook slightly as he laid it on the shoulder of his friend. "Where'd you put the morphine? You'll need it for the pain."

Sacco's eyes were bright as his eyelids widened. "You kidding, Dana? Morphine ... for the ultimate experience?" His voice was fainter and although he kept on grinning, the words came slowly and with difficulty now. "Don't want to doze at the main event. This is ... what I paid my money for."

Dana was silent with a fearful understanding. For the first time there was insight into Sacco's mind, and there were no words for the shattering awareness. Looking into Sacco's face, he tried to smile. After a while, he said, very slowly, "Sacco—Fortunato—is there anything you want?"

Sacco winked. He gestured with his eyes to the corner of the church. "The pigeon. On my webbing. Let him go."

"Back to First Army? You got a message for them?"

Sacco feebly shook his head. "Let him go. No message. Let's muster him out. He's just another pigeon now." His eyes were growing duller.

Dana squeezed his shoulder and rose to his feet. He crossed to the corner near the sacristy and found the pigeon, still hooded in its carrier, among the litter of packs and equipment, untouched by the fallen debris. He heard a groan from the sacristy.

The door was sagging and he pushed it open and entered with the pigeon in his hand. Mungo was bent over one of the Navy men, winding a glaringly-white bandage around his dirt-blackened, bloody head.

A huge hole had been ripped in the sacristy wall. Smashed stone and woodwork littered the floor. Hollister still lay on the bench, miraculously alive.

A 57 mm shell crashed outside. Dana threw himself on the floor and felt the pigeon tremble in his hand. "Goddamn them!" he wept. Mungo turned his head stolidly and then went back to bandaging the sailor. The man seemed lifeless.

"Ain't he dead?" Dana asked.

"No, but he's got a bad one in the head. You seen Sacco?"

Dana nodded.

Mungo shook his head. "After they took the first shell in the tower, Sacco carried this man down with a fragment in his own chest." He finished with the bandage and knelt beside Dana. "How was it up at your end?" he asked. "Anybody get it?"

"No."

Mungo nodded, chewing on the cold cigar stub. "Good. We took a pasting here."

Dana forced the firmness in his voice. "Anybody else alive?"

"Swampie and the other swabbie. How did Royal do?"

What the hell difference did it make how Royal had conducted himself. They weren't talking about a baseball game. But Royal had guts; he was fighting well. "He did okay," Dana said, grudgingly.

"I figured he would."

"What happened to Reb?" Dana didn't know why he went on talking. Sacco was bleeding his life away outside, and the crawl back to the house still lay ahead of them.

"He threw a charge of C-two under a tank. Then he jumped on top of the frigging thing and slugged the officer."

"Jesus!" Dana breathed.

"He was looking for it, Dana. Couldn't you tell? Some guys got to get themselves killed."

"He ought to get the Medal of Honor."

"The C.M.H.? If he wanted that, he should have waited for a couple of officers eyewitnesses. Enlisted men ain't good enough." Mungo threw away the cigar butt. "What did you come back for?"

There's a German captain in the house with a white flag. He wants us to surrender, I guess."

"Yeah?" Mungo's thick eyebrows went up. "Well, let's go back and talk to him. He rose and winked at Hollister. "Take care of things, kid." Hollister nodded weakly.

Dana followed Mungo out of the sacristy, still with the pigeon in his hand. Mungo moved through the rubble of the church in a crouching trot. They stopped beside Sacco, and Mungo knelt over him. "How's it going, soldier?" he asked very gently.

Sacco made no answer, but he opened his eyes, all the brightness gone now, the pupils glazed over. He lifted one hand slowly and with the fingers close together, wriggled it feebly through the air in a gesture Dana remembered from the airstrip. *Move right through it, leaving no more trail than a goldfish going through the water.*

Sacco's hand fell limply to his side.

Dana turned his eyes away; the room seemed misted over, his sight was blurred. When he looked again, Mungo was removing the two grenades that hung from Sacco's belt. "Let's go," he said gruffly, and moved, crouching, to the door.

Dana followed with the pigeon in his hand. He stopped and knelt in the open doorway. He removed the bird from the khaki fold of nylon and it quivered a moment against his palm, the little feet still curled under it. He released it with a gentle toss and looked back at Sacco, at the calmly composed face among the battered blocks of stone. The bird fluttered upward and circled for a moment, as though reluctant to leave that place. Even Mungo threw back his head and watched it. The pigeon rose and curved away toward the sea, soaring up until it was a speck against the clouds.

Mungo turned his head to look back into the church. "Well," he said. "He was …"

"*Damnit! Shut your mouth! Don't say it, you coldblooded bastard!*" The words were hot in Dana's fury-tightened throat. Tears ran down his cheek as he shook his rifle under Mungo's chin.

"You said it over Cadillac, you glory-hunting son-of-a-bitch! You said it over Franklin and Carr and the lieutenant. You'll watch all of us die here, and you'll never feel a thing! Fortunato followed you from Africa to here. He stood beside you, soldiered with you, saved your frigging life. And now he's lying back there, with his chest caved in, because you wouldn't pull us out of this death-trap. And all you can say about it, now you got him killed …."

The words spilled over in a choking torrent. "… All you can say is—'*He was a good man.*' Goddamn you Mungo! Goddamn you to hell! Goddamn your stinking stupid GI hide." Dana was sobbing. " '*He was a good man,*' " he repeated, with bitter irony.

Mungo stared directly at him. There was something baffled in the big man's eyes—something reproachful, and even hurt. "What else is there to say?" Mungo asked him softly. "When a damned good man goes down. What else is there to say?"

Dana dropped his eyes and caught his breath again. He stared back down the village street.

CHAPTER SEVENTEEN
D DAY, 1630 HOURS

Mungo kneeled beside him, watching the street. "Okay. Let's get down there, Dana."

Dana checked him. "There's Germans in those houses, maybe. Keep your eyes open."

"Okay," Mungo growled. "Just follow me and do what I do."

Dana started to rise, but Mungo pressed him down again. "Keep your ass down. There's a fifty-seven coming in any second."

Dana stared at him in astonishment. It was impossible to hear the shells coming—the gun fired at such a velocity that the projectiles outsped the sound of their passage. The gun was hidden somewhere up the road, around the bend; Mungo couldn't possibly see the muzzle-blast. An instant later a shell crashed in and crumpled the wall of a house beside the bridge.

"Let's go!" Mungo shouted. He was up and running, moving with his startling speed. Dana followed him across the churchyard. Mungo sprinted heedlessly past the first house and, without taking cover, started across the gap between it and the next house. Midway he shouted, "Down!" They dove to earth and rolled to cover. A shell sent tiles flying from the roof of a building across the road.

Dana looked at him open-mouthed. "That gunner can't see us," Mungo said. "He's just firing into the town at random."

"But how can you tell when he's going to fire?" Dana demanded. The cannonading followed no set pattern. There was no rhythm to the firing, no precisely timed intervals between the shots. It was impossible for Mungo to predict the shells, and yet he seemed to be doing it.

Mungo shrugged. His eyes were probing the houses ahead of them. "I don't know," he said. "I just can tell."

"You're guessing," Dana said angrily. That was the only explanation.

Mungo produced a cigar from his pocket. He slipped it in his mouth while his eyes went drifting over the windows of the houses. "Ever see an outfielder turn around at the crack of the bat and tear off maybe fifty yards, his back to the plate, and then stick up his hand and catch the ball?"

"No."

"Well, I have. Seen Joe Di Maggio do it lots of times."

"What's that got to do with it?"

Mungo chewed on his cold cigar. His eyes were narrowed on the house in front of them. "Do you know how Di Maggio does it?"

"No."

"Neither does Di Maggio. He can't explain it. It's the same way with me. I just know when that gunner is going to lay one in here."

"You're lying, Mungo." *He's crazier than Nolan,* Dana thought. *And everybody's letting him run the show.* "Let's get going."

"Wait." Mungo took a grenade from his pocket. "If there's any Germans in this town, they're in this house right here."

"Why?"

"Because they ain't in any of the others. Cover the doors." Mungo pulled the pin of his grenade, and held the handle down. With his right hand, he grasped the pistol grip of his Springfield. He pointed the heavy rifle at the window, as easily as if it were a stick. *"Raus mit! Handen hoch!"* he boomed. "Come out with your hands up! *Schnell, God-*damnit, *schnell!"*

A frightened boy ran out the door, his hands over his head. He wore the spotted green, knee-length camouflage coat of a German paratrooper. "Comrade. *Kamerad!*" he babbled.

Mungo turned the Springfield muzzle on him negligently. *"Wo sind kameraden?"*

The boy jerked his head at the door. "One," he said. "One man. *Ich habe kleine Englische.*"

"Call him!" Mungo barked at the terrified youth. "Dam-nit, get him out here!"

His tone registered, if not his words. *"Karl,"* the boy called. *"Los, Karl. Raus."*

A second youth came through the door. He clutched the bicep of one arm in a bloody hand. Like the first, he looked no more than seventeen.

"Any more?" Mungo demanded. *"Das ist alles?"*

The boys were bobbing their heads. *"Ja, alles,"* the first one said. Mungo released the handle of the grenade. He waited a few seconds, then he stepped to the door and flung the grenade into the house. The Germans flung themselves on the ground.

"Cover them," Mungo snapped. He charged into the house a split second after the explosion. In a moment he was back, crouching in the doorway, grinning at Dana. "Better keep down. Here comes another shell."

No shells fell. "You bluffing bastard," Dana said.

Then a shell burst opposite the last house. Dana's jaw dropped. They would have been fatally close to the spot if he had started the prisoners forward a moment ago.

Mungo prodded the Germans to their feet. He made them lie down again at the door of the next house. Nolan met them there. His eyes bulged with fury. "Mungo! Are you going to surrender?"

Mungo's eyes swept over the swampy meadows beyond the house. "No," he said quietly. "Now get your butt out here."

Nolan crawled across the tiny yard. Mungo demanded in an angry whisper, "Why didn't you put anyone in that house across the road?"

Nolan's eyes surveyed it, puzzled. "This one has the best field of fire," he said. "The other one sits low, and that rise of ground cuts off most of the view."

Dana hesitated at the door, as baffled as Nolan. The house they had defended held the most commanding view of the meadows. Nolan had been right to post them there.

Mungo shook his head disgustedly. "You should have put men in both houses, you frigging knucklehead." His voice was pitched too low to carry into the house. "If they'd had enough sense to hit you on that flank, too, they could have run right around you."

Dana stared at the meadow, seeing it now in Mungo's perspective. A determined charge would have carried the Germans easily into the other side of the village.

"Well, they didn't hit us there," Nolan mumbled sullenly.

"They didn't, but they will," Mungo snarled at him. "Now get your ass over there and wait for me."

He turned from Nolan and dug his toes into the armpit of the unwounded German prisoner. "In you go," he said.

Von Ritter's eyes blazed as the two boys followed Dana through the door. The tall Hauptmann looked pointedly at Mungo's chevrons and asked Royal, "Where is the American commander, Major?"

The Naval officer nodded at Mungo. "Do your talking to this man."

"But he is only a sergeant!"

"I'm all you get, bud," Mungo said. He was staring at Von Ritter with frank curiosity. He struck a match to his cigar and grinned at the German. "Are you a Prussian?"

Von Ritter ostentatiously relaxed his position of attention. "I am. And I want to speak to your commanding officer."

"Are you a *Junker?*" Mungo pronounced the word the way it looked in print to his American eyes. Von Ritter nodded. "*Wehrmacht?* Regular Army?"

"Yes, Sergeant."

Mungo looked him up and down and grinned. "Just what was it you wanted to see me about?"

Von Ritter forced a smile in response. "I offer you a chance to surrender."

Mungo nodded. "Why?"

Von Ritter drew in a deep breath. "Your troops have performed commendably in defending this little place today. It was an admirable stand. We Germans—" he smiled broadly at Mungo, "—particularly we Prussians, respect gallantry in a foe. Therefore, we offer you your lives."

"Why?" Mungo asked.

He really is crazy, Dana decided. What right has he got to make us go on fighting, just because he's in love with war. Sacco and Reb dead in the last half hour, and maybe the sailor, too. How much longer did Mungo think eight men could hold the Germans off?

"You see," Von Ritter said into the waiting silence, "we know that you are just an isolated platoon—"

"That's your guess," Mungo said.

"From the Five-hundredth Parachute Infantry Regiment. The Five-Oh-Goose you call it, don't you?"

"We took prisoner those who were wise enough to give themselves up." The German shook his head sadly. "Most of your comrades are already dead. Your commanders sacrificed them stupidly."

Mungo spread his hands. "That's the way it goes, eh, Captain?"

"Precisely. Fortunes of war. Brave men, but in an impossible situation. Your regiment was scattered terribly last night. As a unit, it has been annihilated." His smile swept the room.

"Gentlemen, save yourselves. Lay down your weapons. You've done everything that duty demands. As prisoners you'll be treated well. Now come out with me, with your hands up."

Mungo flicked the ash from his cigar. "Why?"

Von Ritter retained his smile with an effort. "Because we are going to take this place today. With tanks and artillery. You cannot stop us. When we take it you will all die. Your deaths will gain nothing."

Mungo stared deliberately out the window behind the German's shoulder. Two German medics were moving among the dead and wounded in the meadow. "You think it's going to be easy?" Mungo asked.

Von Ritter refused to let his gaze be turned toward the window. "You can not stop us," he said firmly.

"You ought to see the other end of town," Mungo said. "I'll bet we dumped more than a full company there. We got us a Mark Four, too."

"Will you or will you not surrender?" Von Ritter's face was flushed.

Mungo smiled at the captain blandly. "Give me your Luger," he drawled.

"I will not! I am here under a flag of truce. I will not give up my sidearm."

Mungo, with the Springfield still held in one hand, jammed in into the German's belly. "Hand it over," he said coldly. "If you're as tough as you say you are, I'm going to need it more than you."

Von Ritter whirled on Royal. "Do you let American enlisted men treat officers in this manner?" The prodding muzzle of the Springfield cut off the rest of his protest. Von Ritter slowly unfastened his pistol belt and let the Luger drop to the floor in its holster. He was livid with rage.

"I will give you one half-hour to reconsider," he said.

"Tell your story walking, bud," Royal answered.

The *Hauptmann* stepped through the window and snatched up his white flag. "If you make us fight any longer for this village, all of you will be killed." He spat on the floor at Mungo's feet.

"Any time you think you can take this town, you come ahead and try it," Mungo said. "Until you do, stop spitting on my floors."

Von Ritter shot one last glance at the cowering prisoners in the corner. "You have one half-hour to think it over."

Dana watched his anger-stiffened back as he stalked away across the meadow. "There goes our last chance," he said, and looked to Mungo. He was down on one knee, watching the German captain's retreat. His lips moved silently.

Dana could feel the iron grip of fear in his throat. Royal's expression was abstracted, vaguely melancholy. Someone had to talk up—they couldn't let Mungo throw their lives this way.

"Commander," Dana said, his voice too loud, "there's only two men left at the other end of the village. Two troopers got it, and one of your own men is hit in the head, pretty bad. He may be dead now."

Rosen and Royal exchanged a look of sudden dismay. "Which one?" asked Rosen. "Burke or Hansen?"

"I don't know their names. The dark one."

The sailors nodded. "Burke," Rosen said.

"I know you ain't no infantryman," Dana pleaded, "but we don't have a chance in hell anymore. And this guy, Mungo, is crazy. He wouldn't quit if he was here all by himself!"

Dana waited for response. He could hear the faint cracking of burning timbers from the roof above their heads. The smell of wood smoke was stronger.

Royal looked lost in thought. "You're an officer," Dana said with mounting anger. "You got the say about giving up, not Mungo."

"We've got a job to do son. This is a war we're in."

"Yeah. But nobody said we got to get ourselves killed when it don't do any good at all." What was wrong with Royal? Was he supid—in a trance?

"You don't understand how lucky we been so far, sir," Dana said. "They ain't fired nothing but light stuff at us, so far—tree-burst stuff that goes off on contact. They got shells that burrow into concrete before they go off. Just one of them can wreck a concrete pillbox. I've seen it on maneuvers. Ten direct hits would flatten out this whole village."

Royal nodded, giving him his full attention. Dana spoke more urgently. "They ain't thrown it at us yet. Infantry outfits don't carry that kind of mortar ammo with them unless they know they're going up against fortifications. But they'll get it. They probably got it already. All they have to do is drop a few rounds and then walk over here and plunk their bayonets into whatever part of us is sticking out from under the ruins."

"Well, son, Sergeant Mungo is an infantryman, too, and a lot more experienced than you are. If he thinks—"

"I already told you," Dana shouted. "Mungo's nuts! Don't you see we've had a solid-gold horseshoe in our pocket? Yeah, we knocked out an armored car and a tank. We got the car with a bazooka, and that's gone now. We got the tank because a man threw a mess of explosives under it, and blew himself to hell! We got no more explosives left. All we got is rifles now, and light machine guns. How's Mungo going to stop the next tank that comes across the bridge? With experience?"

Royal turned to Mungo. "Is that true, Sergeant?" For the first time, his calm seemed to be cracking.

Mungo's lips continued to move silently. His eyes were on the back of the distant Von Ritter, strutting back across the meadow as if it were the parade-ground at Potsdam.

"I can't order him to surrender," Royal told Dana. "You know that, don't you?"

"That's right," Mungo said. "He ain't in charge, Dana." He was adjusting the leaf sight of the Springfield. He cast one look out at the quiet, breezeless meadow. Von Ritter had vanished.

"If you give the word, sir, all the rest of the men will quit." Dana ran silently over the roster of survivors. Only he, Swampy, Uhlan, Hollister, Nolan and Mungo were still alive, out of the eleven men who had jumped with Lieutenant Edgerton the night before. Not even Nolan would fight on alone beside Mungo.

"Christ, Commander," Rosen said. "This ain't our fight. If that bridge hadn't been blocked, we'd have gone barreling right through here with the jeep. We'd been all right by now."

Royal squatted, frowning, in the center of the room, an unlit cigarette forgotten between his lips. The hand on which he wore his class ring clenched and unclenched.

"Kamerad! Kamerad!" The shouts came from outside. The four pairs of eyes in the room swept to the windows. *"Kamerad! I surrender! Wait for me!"* Uhlan, helmetless and unarmed, leaped the wall and ran heavily across the meadow toward the Germans in the trees. He cast a fearful look back over his shoulder. Then he ran on, waving his arms. *"Kamerad!"*

A burst of automatic firing threw up dirt twenty yards behind him. Uhlan stopped, rooted to the spot. He cast a pleading look back to the farmhouse.

"That was Nolan," Mungo said. "He can't stop him—the range is too great for a Thompson. If Uhlan had any brains at all, he'd realize it." Mungo sat on the floor, crossed his legs, and laboriously tucked his ankles under his thighs. Only Dana realized he was getting into the Army's "cavalry position"—a favorite of sharpshooters. Mungo raised the butt of his Springfield to his shoulder.

"Sergeant Mungo!" Royal said sharply. "Don't fire at that man!"

"I'm not going to waste any bullets on Uhlan," Mungo answered equably. "I need them all for Germans." Mungo took the cigar from his mouth and rested it on a piece of bric-a-brac lying at his feet. "This is the Army, Commander," he said. "We don't shoot Americans." Dana remembered Sacco's story of the Navy shooting down the planeloads of 82nd paratroopers on the Sicily jump.

Uhlan still stood where Nolan's wild burst had halted him. His feet danced a pitiful shuffle of indecision. Beyond him, a German soldier leaped out from the trees and waved him on.

Mungo laid his cheek against the stock of the Springfield and took a long breath. Dana kept his eyes on the cheering German soldier, fascinated. Then Mungo sighed and lowered the rifle. Dana shot him a startled glance. Did this mean Mungo was going to surrender?

Uhlan took a few hesitant steps toward the trees, looking back over his shoulder. Then he broke into a shambling run. Mungo cursed. Uhlan was scarcely a hundred yards from the trees now.

Mungo raised the rifle and fired suddenly, ejected the spent shell and rammed another into the chamber.

Uhlan looked back at them and stopped abruptly, his hands at his sides as if at attention. He seemed braced for a bullet in his back. Dana felt a wave of pity for him, knowing the terror he felt.

The German soldier waved at him violently. Then he made coaxing motions with his hands. Uhlan took a few steps toward the trees and stopped.

A second German appeared from the trees and waved to Uhlan. He stood behind and to the side of the first. He looked like Hauptmann Von Ritter.

Mungo sucked in his breath, and then let part of it out—the sharpshooters trick they taught you on Army firing ranges.

The Springfield roared. The tall, blond German flew off his feet and did not rise. Mungo worked his bolt and sighted again. The first Nazi soldier still stood in the open, waving to Uhlan, unaware of his captain's fate. Mungo fired again. The German fell to a sitting position. Mungo reloaded, aimed and squeezed the trigger. The man went flat.

Dana looked back to Uhlan in time to see him turn and race desperately back toward the farmhouse. He twisted in the air and fell heavily and writhed a moment, cut down by a prolonged burst of fire from the outraged Nazis. Dana could see Uhlan's body jerk as the machine pistols cut it up.

"My God!" Royal cried. "What shooting!" He pounded Mungo's back. "That must have been over four hundred yards." Dana wondered if he had seen what happened to Uhlan.

Mungo put his cigar back in his mouth. "Five hundred and twenty," he said. "The *Hauptmann* paced it off for me, walking back to the trees." He shook his head amiably. "And that Kraut thought he was a soldier!"

"Well," Dana said heavily, "we ain't getting no half-hour to surrender now, are we Mungo?"

"Hell, no, Dana." Mungo picked up Von Ritter's pistol belt and slung it over his shoulder. "Commander, how do you feel about taking orders from Dana?"

Royal sent a brief, approving glance at Dana, and nodded. "He's a good man, Sergeant."

"Okay. He's in charge here. I'm going over to the house across the road and help Nolan out. You know what to do, Dana. Good luck."

"Do you think you're snowing some rookie?" Dana snarled at him. "I'm supposed to feel like a big deal, now, is that it?"

Mungo shook his head. His gaze was direct and there was no mockery in his smile. "No, Dana. I'm putting you in charge because you're soldiering good. You didn't think I was going to pack in, did you? As long as I'm alive, we're going to hold this village." He paused a moment. "And it ain't for glory, Dana. We're protecting the outfit. It's our job to go on fighting."

"You fixed it so we got no other choice, Mungo." Dana turned his back on him and crawled to Uhlan's rifle. It was empty. He found no clips in the olive-drab bandoleers Uhlan had dropped among the thick sowing of spent cartridges. He heard Mungo growling at the two German prisoners, and turned to watch the three of them crawl to the door.

"You better get up those stairs while you still got a chance," Dana told Royal. He could barely force himself to look at the man. If Royal had shown a little guts, this hopeless fight would be over now, and Uhlan would still be alive.

"Those roof timbers in the attic are burning pretty bad now, Corporal," Royal said. "When they get weak enough, the whole roof is going to fall in on us."

"I ain't no corporal," Dana said. He ached with tiredness. Why in hell was he being asked to make decisions? "That attic has no ventilation. It'll be a slow fire. Stay up there as long as you think it's safe. It gives us a better field of fire across the meadow, with men on the second floor."

"Okay," Rosen said. He crawled to the staircase and worked his way up it, staying as flat as he could. Royal, creeping along behind him, turned to smile encouragingly at Dana.

Looking up, Dana could see the smoke curling down the walls of the upper floor. Why in hell did they trust his judgement on what ought to be done? Did the whole damned Navy think an infantryman's badge made you a general? Couldn't they think for themselves?

He remembered then, the clips of rifle ammunition he had left in his foxhole when the waves of German infantry had swept across the wall. Might as well get them, he thought doggedly.

He crawled out to the hole, past the sprawled body of the German that Nolan had tricked into entering the barn. He recovered the clips; there were six of them. Eight rounds to a clip, and precious little left beside that. Mungo had taken the *Hauptmann's* Luger. Did he want to fight on with German weapons when their ammo was exhausted?

Dana crawled back to the house again, heavy with fatigue.

Mungo was still crouched in the doorway, holding the prisoners under the Springfield's muzzle, poised for a dash across the road. The wounded German's arm was bandaged now. Dana wondered if Mungo had done that. Just like the crazy bastard: cruel one minute, gentle the next. "If you're going over to Nolan, go on!" he spat. "Take off before I put a bullet in your battle-happy butt!"

Mungo smiled. "Right after this next Fifty-seven shell. There's one due any second."

"Those noises you hear are in your head, Mungo!"

A shell-burst drowned out his words. Mungo prodded the Germans with his Springfield. *"Raus!"* he barked, and the three of them vanished through the door, sprinting across the street.

CHAPTER EIGHTEEN
D DAY, 2300 HOURS

A thump and clatter sounded on the stairs. Dana turned and watched Rosen come sliding down the steps on his belly. He could see the orange flicker of firelight on the wall behind the staircase, and he knew the fire must be opening wide gaps in the ceiling of the floor above. The smoke and heat and the crackling noise of the fire had been growing steadily in the four hours he had lain here on the floor, waiting for the Germans to attack.

Night had fallen without the Germans charging across the meadow again. An intermittent hosing of their tracers fell on Sainte Madeleine. Dana could tell from the direction of some of the fire that they had extended their line all the way to the marshes on the right, cutting off any exit.

Their failure to attack neither puzzled nor cheered him. He knew the Germans were in sufficient strength to sweep over the remainder of the patrol at will. They must be waiting to do it in the most economical manner.

They would get artillery from their forces in Carentan, or else the heavy mortar shells which would be equally as effective in smashing the buildings from which the Americans fought, or they could come across the meadow in relative safety as soon as the moon set. It made little difference, Dana knew. He and the others were doomed.

The 57 mm cannon across the river had not interrupted its steady firing. Dana had little more to do than lie on the floor of the house, watching the meadow and listening to the explosion of the shells. At first they had reminded him angrily of Mungo's assertion that he could tell beforehand when they were about to strike the village.

Then an odd thing had begun to happen. Gradually, he noticed that seconds before some of the shells fell, he would feel a tightening of his diaphragm against the hard floor on which he lay. His gut would tighten and then the shell would fall. The unconscious calculation in the depths of his mind did not warn him unfailingly, but the throbbing tension preceded the shell-bursts so frequently, that he came to believe it possible, against his will, that Mungo had not been lying to him.

"Commander Royal sent me down," Rosen said. His voice was apologetic, as if he were ashamed of being the first down the stairs. His eyes were tearing from the smoke. "That roof's going to fall in any minute."

"Yeah," Dana said. "You done good to stay up there so long." The slim jeep-driver deserved the praise, but uttering it was an effort for Dana. He did not want to think of others and what must be done for them. He wanted to have only himself to think about, to find some way he could live through this night. His mind and body ached with fatigue.

Rosen turned his eyes to where the flames were reflected on the upper wall of the staircase. "I hope Commander Royal comes down from there, before it caves in on him."

"You like him, don't you?" Dana asked.

"He's a good officer."

"I wish he'd had the guts to stand up to Mungo," Dana said. "We'd be out of here now, rolled up in a blanket with a German guarding us."

"We haven't got much chance, have we, Dana?" Rosen asked.

"We got less than that." Couldn't these Navy men use their eyes and ears?

Rosen was silent for a moment. "Royal's got guts," he said. "If there's anyway to get that radio through to your division headquarters, he wants to keep trying."

"Didn't you hear that German captain? There ain't no division headquarters. There ain't no frigging division." What was the use of trying to make him understand?

"A Shore Fire Control Party is a damned important job," Rosen said, as though anxious to convince himself. "That's why the Commander won't give up trying. We call down fire from the battlewagons lying off the beaches. Hell, a sixteen-inch gun throws a half-ton shell. A battleship salvo can do more damage than the whole damned Air Corps—smash up everything inside a square mile."

Dana interrupted him impatiently. "Is that radio you got in the jeep working?"

"The rectifier tube maybe got smashed when the glider nosed over," Rosen said. "We can't receive anything at all, so we can't be sure we're transmitting." He rubbed his jaw. "But the transmitter's separate. Maybe it's okay."

Dana wondered disgustedly why Royal thought he had to lose his life in defense of a ruined radio. He held his silence. It would be pointless to criticize Royal—Rosen so obviously had all his faith in him.

A loud crash above them jerked their heads around. A shower of sparks fell on the stairway, and they heard another rumble of beams and masonry hitting the floor above. A burning timber fell through the stairwell and bounced crazily into the room. Royal came down the steps in two bounds and threw himself on the floor between them. A third and louder crash came from the floor above. The whole building shook. "My back!" Royal shouted. "It's burning!"

His jump-jacket was smouldering in half a dozen different places. Dana and Rosen beat the sparks out with their hands. "Thanks," Royal said. "Thanks a lot." He was breathing heavily.

"I tried to stick it out too long. That damned roof nearly fell on me."

The room had grown noticeably brighter. They could see the orange glow of firelight on the wall of the stairwell and the air was growing thick with smoke. "Are we going to stay here?" Rosen asked nervously.

Royal looked at Dana. "What do you say, Corporal?"

Dana looked grimly out at the dark meadow. When he abandoned this post, he gave up the patrol's last hope of survival. "I'd like to stick with it as long as we can," he found himself saying. "This is the only house that really commands the west side of the village. Once we pull back to the church, the Krauts can come right up on us, under cover all the way." He noticed the uncertainty in Rosen's eyes and added, "We'll get out of here before the walls cave in. These French farmers really build a house."

Royal nodded. "You're the boss, son."

"Go ahead and see if you can grab some sleep," Dana said. "Both of you. I'll stay awake."

He gave the word to leave the house shortly after midnight. The smoke was thick in the room and it had grown unbearably hot, even when they pressed close to the windows. The plaster had cracked and fallen from the ceiling in huge chunks. They could see the flames through the widening interstices of the floorboards above their heads. The weight of debris would come crashing down in a matter of minutes. The fire had begun in a sealed attic. The stout old house had withstood it for six hours.

Dana led the way to the door. "Nolan! Mungo!" he bawled into the night. "I'm getting out of here now!" Mungo's bellowed "Okay!" reached them from the house across the road. Four dark figures, Mungo in the lead, sprinted through the firelit patch of the cobblestone street and dove into the shadows. A stream of German tracers lanced after them.

Rosen braced himself to plunge through the door. Dana caught the pistol belt around his waist and stopped him, instinctively, "Wait!" he shouted. A 57 mm shell burst down the street. Dana slapped the boy's thin buttocks. "Okay, go!" Rosen charged for the shadows in a head-down lunge. He drew no fire.

Dana wondered how fast Royal would be on his feet. For the first time he saw a trace of fear on the older man's face. "Go ahead," he said. "I'll be right behind you." He slung the M-1 across his back, and, as they hit the street, he pushed the officer so forcibly that Royal almost stumbled and fell. A burst of machine-gun fire struck the bricks beside them, the dancing line of bullets missing them by inches. Then they tripped over the prostrate Rosen and fell face forward in the little ditch in front of the second house.

"Thanks, Dana," Royal said.

"Okay, okay." He had shielded Royal's back with his own vulnerable body. He did not know why he had done it, and Royal's gratitude embarassed him. "Start crawling to the church," he ordered gruffly.

He found Swampy sprawled on the floor of the ruined church, his back against the wall. He recognized him with a sense of shock. Under the grime and the sweat-streaked camouflage, Swampy's face was long with fatigue and tension. The sailor, Hansen, was beside him. The two German prisoners were curled on the floor beside the confessional, trying to sleep.

Swampy tried to smile at him—the grin was grotesque. Dana limped over to him. He had noticed an annoying stiffness in his left leg when he rose to his feet after the long crawl back down the road.

"How's Burke?" Rosen asked the other Navy man.

"He ain't come to yet," Hansen said. His voice was husky with strain. "He's hurt bad, Billy."

"Jeez," Rosen said numbly.

Dana leaned against the wall and let his back slide down it until he was sitting on the floor beside Swampy. He could see Nolan at the ruined wall behind the altar, peering out at the ground beyond the river.

Moonlight streaming through the gaping masonry gave a macabre, nightmare quality to the scene.

"What's wrong with your leg, ol' buddy?" Swampy asked.

"Charley horse," Dana mumbled and felt his calf. His trouser leg was damp to the touch. "I'll be Goddamned," he muttered to himself. He undid the laces of his jump-boot and slipped it off his foot. Then he drew his knife from the zippered pocket at his throat. His fingers encountered the Donald Duck-emblazoned cricket, and he flung it angrily away. He slit the elastic binding at his ankle, and drew the jump-pants up to his knee. There were two tiny holes in the flesh of his leg, just below the bulge of calf muscle.

Dana shook his head wonderingly. He felt nothing but astonishment. "Well, what do you know? I've been shot, Swampy. I wonder when that happened."

Swampy stirred himself to peer at the wound. He shook his head. "This sad-assed outfit's had it. He hung his head dejectedly. "Eight men dead, and that poor swabbie, too."

"Hollister's dead?"

"He sure looks dead." Swampy shook his head ruefully. "And we been in France just twenty-four hours."

Dana felt almost light-headed. "Wait until things really get rough," he said. The two sailors looked at him sharply. He ignored them and began bandaging his leg.

A series of muffled booms sounded at the west end of the village. "What's that?" Hansen whispered hoarsely. His eyes were wide.

"That's German," Dana told him stolidly. "Tossing grenades into the houses we left. They got plenty of time. They got all night to work their way down here." He slid the boot back on his feet.

The three faces were turned attentively to him. Out of the depths of his own despair, he found a perverse relief in frightening them. "Come morning, they'll be in the houses right across the street. When the tanks come over the bridge and we stick our heads up, they'll pop us off like turkeys looking over a log."

"Oh, Christ," Swampy growled. "Why don't that dumb Commander quit. We ain't got one chance."

"He's letting Mungo make the decisions," Dana said. He put the helmet on the floor and lowered himself until his face was hidden in the liner. He struck a match, and when he sat up again, a lit cigarette was concealed in his hand.

"We could try slipping out of here, through those marshes," Hansen said tentatively.

"The moon is awful bright..." Rosen's objections trailed off. It was plain he wanted to be convinced that escape was possible.

Swampy cursed softly. "Christ, I don't care if we try sneakin' out of here, or give up to those Krauts. I just don't want to sit here, waitin' to get killed like a rat in a friggin' trap." A muscle twitched angrily at his jaw line. "What do you say, Dana?"

The sailors turned their glances to him raptly. Dana drew on his cigarette and did not answer them. *Why ask me? Why in hell don't you make up your own minds?* From inside the sacristy, someone was moaning feebly.

After a long silence, Hansen said, "That moon will go down later. It'll be good and dark, then." The three of them were watching Dana.

"What about the wounded man?" Dana asked. He knew that what he meant was, *what about Mungo? He'll shoot you if you try to stop fighting.*

"We can't take him along," Swampy said, and turned his hands up. "That's all she wrote."

"If the Germans are going to kill him," Hansen said, "they'll kill him all the same whether we surrender or slip out of here."

"Mungo won't let you go," Dana said. *Why argue with them?*

"The hell with Mungo," Swampy said sullenly. "Tell him we're taking off."

"Tell him yourself," Dana said flatly. "Here he comes."

Mungo was striding toward them from the sacristy, Cadillac's Thompson in his hand. The broad, hard-fleshed face betrayed no sign of fatigue. "Tell me what?" he asked them quietly.

Swampy glanced at Dana and then turned angrily to Mungo. "We're givin' up, Mungo. We're all through fightin'. We ain't lettin' you get us all killed off like the others."

Mungo nodded at his words, the heavy-lidded eyes impassive. "You got more sense than I thought, Swampy. At least you aren't going to try sneaking off through those marshes."

"I ain't crazy. We wouldn't get a hundred yards." Swampy got to his feet with an air of finality. "We're gettin' us a white flag and we're goin' out and givin' ourselves up.

"You can stay here if you want, Mungo," Swampy said. He slid the musette bag and rifle belt from his body and dropped it to the floor with his M-1. "But we're gettin' out of here. We're packin' it in."

Mungo shook his head. "No, you're not, Swampy. We ain't surrendering. None of us."

Swampy bent swiftly and straightened with the M-1 in his hands. He backed from Mungo, his eyes blazing wildly, ready to swing the muzzle on the other men. "How about it?" he demanded of the sailors. "Are you goin' to stay here and get killed?"

Hansen and Rosen moved to his side. "How about it, Dana?" Swampy did not take his eyes from Mungo. Dana remained seated on the floor. It was useless—Mungo's will was iron.

"How about it, Nolan?" Swampy's voice was shrill. Dana watched Nolan's face working in the moonlight. He crossed the church to stand behind Mungo. The lump in his columnar neck bobbed several times before he could say, "I'm backing Mungo."

Swampy snapped the rifle to cover them both. "You're going to have to shoot me to stop me."

Mungo said easily, "I wouldn't shoot an American soldier, Swampy. But you're going to have to shoot me to get out of here."

Swampy backed another step, the M-1 muzzle fixed unwaveringly on Mungo's broad chest. "Sailor, get somethin' white to wave!"

"Wait a minute," Dana said. "How's Hollister doing, Mungo?"

"He's going to be okay. I been taking care of him."

Dana shot furiously to his feet. "Don't give me that crap! Swampy says he's dead. If he's dead, say so!"

"He's still alive. He can still pull through."

"You're lying! You don't give a damn about the kid!"

Mungo's veiled eyes flinched for an instant, then hardened again. "I care about that kid, all right. I want to see him live."

"Yeah, I've got you figured out now, you bastard," Dana snarled. "You been feeding us that 'don't leave a wounded man behind' crap all day long. You been using Hollister to cover your real reason. You just want to stay here and fight until we're all dead. You're blood-crazy, Mungo. You're off your friggin' head." He turned to Swampy and the Navy men. "Okay, I'm going, too."

"You surprise me, Dana," Mungo said. "You been soldiering pretty good today."

"Soldiering!" Dana snarled. "Is that your whole Goddamn life?"

Mungo nodded. "Yeah. It's always been my life. I got no family, no woman. Just a uniform and a rifle and a serial number. I don't know where I was born or who my folks were. I might as well have come from Mars. I wasn't nothing but an empty suit of clothes walking around until I got sworn in. I wasn't nothing—I didn't exist."

"Well, we did, Mungo," Dana said. "We ain't Regulars, Goddamnit—we're civilians...people, human beings! We had lives before we got into the Army. And so did Cadillac and Sacco and Uhlan and the rest of them you've gotten killed. We want lives after the Army, too. So we're quitting, Mungo!"

Mungo turned away from him. His broad shoulders slumped, and he dropped his head. His face was suddenly tired and worn, the jaw muscles slack.

"Okay," Mungo mumbled. "I'll go with you." He shuffled over to the two German prisoners and wearily prodded them to their feet. "We'll send them out first. Get your white flag, Swampy."

Swampy ripped a long splinter from a shattered pew, and prowled around the church for a piece of white cloth. Silently, Commander Royal handed him a handkerchief. In a moment Swampy was back, knotting the cloth to the improvised standard, thrusting it into the hands of the unwounded German. Dana gaped at him drunkenly. He'd won! Somehow he'd backed Mungo down. The big non-com was going to give up. They would live.

Mungo and Swampy were pushing the two bewildered Germans through the door. The sailors dropped their carbines and followed. Dana laid his M-1 on the floor. Nolan shook his head disgustedly, he could not disguise the relief on his face. He propped his Thompson against the wall and crowded through the door with Dana.

The others were crouched in the dark angle of the church and the tower. Mungo seized the first German by the arm and pointed to the road, now brightly lit by a burning farmhouse. *"Vorwart!"* he commanded. *"Handen hoch!* We surrender, *verstehen sie?"*

An incredulous look shot between the two youths. Then they began an animated conversation in German. Mungo prodded their spines with his Thompson. The two began moving hesitantly toward the road, away from the cover of the church. The Americans watched breathlessly as they stepped into the flickering orange light, shouting fearfully in German. It seemed a long time before an unseen German hailed them. *"Was gib'st? Wer sind sie?"*

The youths answered excitedly, pointing at their captors and waving the white flag. Another German voice shot questions at them. The boys moved toward it, both of them talking at once. *"Halten sie!"* Mungo barked. He gestured threatingly with the Thompson. "Can't let them try any tricks," he said casually to the men.

The boys stopped. After a prolonged conversation, the unseen German officer shouted a reply which was obviously acquiescent. They could hear him issuing admonitory orders to his men. The Germans in the road turned and waved them forward, grinning.

"Hot damn!" Swampy shouted hysterically. "It's okay! They're goin' to take us!" He started forward with his hands held high, followed by Dana, Nolan and the Navy men. The two German prisoners, silhouetted in the firelight, were cheerfully waving them on.

A sudden dreadful hammering exploded behind them. The Thompson bucked in Mungo's hand. The German with the flag was lifted from his feet and hurtled to the ground. His wounded companion ran, his hobnailed boots clattering against the cobblestones. Mungo triggered off another burst. The German fell dead.

CHAPTER NINETEEN

D PLUS ONE,
0100 HOURS

They dived headlong back into the church, crouching, as machine-gun bullets ripped against the walls and whistled overhead through the gaps in the masonry. They found the white-faced Royal confronting Mungo. "What happened out there, Sergeant?"

"He shot them," Hansen stammered. "He killed the two Germans!"

Royal looked Mungo in horror. "They were prisoners! That's murder."

"Murder, hell—that's war!" Mungo spat. His face was hard and his voice as firm as it had ever been. "Nolan! Get back to your post! Swampy! Guard the door! Rosen and Hansen! On the windows, both of you!" The futile bursts of German gunfire died away. He swung on Dana. "All right, go take a look at Hollister. See for yourself, *civilian.*"

"Sergeant Mungo," Royal said heavily, "I'm going to report this. If we live through the night, so help me God, I won't stop until you're court-martialed. You're going to pay for this!"

"Yeah, yeah," Mungo said impatiently.

Dana picked up his rifle and walked to the sacristy. He told himself angrily that he should have known that Mungo would never give up. How the hell had he been fooled by the bastard? He remembered the sag of Mungo's shoulders and his dragging steps as he crossed the church to the German boys. *Oh, you dramatic, double-crossing son-of-a-bitch, you.*

He knelt beside Hollister and heard with astonishment the labored, ragged breathing. Then Mungo hadn't been lying about that! The boy was still alive!

"Can you talk, kid?" Dana asked him quietly. "How do you feel?"

"Don't worry," Hollister said feebly. "I'm okay. The seaborne get here yet? The Fourth Division tanks?"

"Soon, kid, soon," Dana said to him, and turned his head away.

A step sounded behind him. "Commander?" a voice asked from the corner of the room. "Yes, it's me," Royal's voice answered. Dana saw the seaman still lying on the mattress where Mungo had bandaged him that afternoon. The bandage on his head and eyes was ghostly white in the dimness of the room. Dana patted Hollister's shoulder and joined the Navy officer at the wounded sailor's side.

"Where are we, Commander?"

"We're still in the village," Royal answered gently. "In the church."

"I'm blind," the boy said matter-of-factly. There was no tinge of hysteria in his voice.

"They'll fix you up in sick bay, when we get you back," Royal said.

"Are the Germans going to get us?"

"We'll stand them off; don't worry about them. You just take it easy, Burke."

"I can't see them, sir, but I can hear them," Burke said. "Let me have my carbine, Commander. I'll get anybody who comes in the door."

Royal and Dana exchanged a stricken look. The commander nodded briefly. Dana took the carbine from where it lay against the wall. He removed a magazine from the boy's belt and inserted it, working the bolt to drive a shell in the chamber. He clicked off the safety and put the weapon in Burke's hands.

"Okay," Burke said. "Tell the other guys to sound off in English before they come in here. I'll get any Kraut who tries to come through that door."

"Commander Royal." It was Mungo's voice from the sacristy door. "Do you think there's any good in fiddling with that radio of yours?"

Royal stood slowly. His voice was tired. "We should make another effort to see if we can raise something. We're too far east for U Group, but there might be something along this part of the coast."

"Okay. Pick who you want for the job, and let's get going. I'll go along as a guard in case any Krauts have snuck across that marsh to the bridge."

"I'll take Rosen with me. He's a good man. We'll try a feed-in from the jeep battery." Royal patted Burke's shoulder before he left. "You're going to be all right, son."

"You're in charge while I'm gone, Dana," Mungo's voice rumbled. "Let the men take what sleep they can get, two at a time. But keep an eye out, all around."

"Nolan's your assistant squad leader. Let him do it," Dana said angrily.

"I'm putting *you* in charge. Nolan's shot his bolt." He turned away then. A moment later, he led the two Navy men out over the rubble of the collapsed wall to where the jeep still stood, dwarfed by the bulk of the tank on the bridge.

Dana spent the next hours prowling through the dark ruin of the church, peering through the shuttered windows at the street and the churchyard. The grenading of the houses had stopped, but he was sure the Germans had not left the village. He let the three other men sleep. Nolan showed no reluctance at surrendering his authority. He seemed almost happy to take Dana's orders.

Fatigue lay on his shoulers like a weight, and his leg had stiffened so that every step was an effort. He felt no desire to sleep. He wondered once during the night if this was the way Sacco had felt about death. The 57 mm. fire stopped an hour after Mungo crawled out to the jeep with Royal. The German commander must have gotten a runner back across the river with the intelligence that his company was in the village.

The eastern sky was just losing its pitch-blackness when he heard Mungo's hoarse bellow from the bridge. The Spring-field cracked and a Schmeisser-burst answered it.

Dana sprinted to the rear wall. Swampy and the others raised their heads, bleary-eyed. Rosen came tumbling in over the rubble as Dana poked the M-1 out, searching for a target. He could see only the pin-prick flashes of German weapons on the far river-bank. "Kraut patrol," Royal panted as he stumbled into the church.

"Where's Mungo?" Dana demanded. Grenades were flashing and booming at the bridge.

"He's hit," Rosen said. "I saw him go down."

The Schmeisser ripped again and then Dana saw Mungo running drunkenly toward them, his helmet gone. He held his hand pressed against his neck as he came. Dana sprayed the river-bank with his rifle. Mungo clambered laboriously over the rubble and fell at his feet.

There were no answering flashes from the river-bank. "All right!" Dana shouted. "Cease firing! Save your ammo!" One by one, the guns silenced.

Dana bent and caught Mungo's armpits and dragged his heavy body farther into the shelter of the church. He laid him beside the altar. Royal knelt beside him. Dana touched the hand Mungo held to his neck and it fell limply away. Blood coursed feebly from three neat holes spaced an inch apart. It would take a Schmeisser to do that.

Dana dug his thumb into the pressure point at the hollow of Mungo's collarbone, and the flow of blood slackened and became an ooze. The non-com's hillock of a chest moved faintly, but the eyelids did not flutter. A cold cigar butt still hung from the corner of his mouth.

"I saw them shoot the rifle right out of his hands," Royal said. He was sprinkling sulfa powder into the wounds.

Dana looked down at Mungo. *You wanted to stay and fight and get everyone killed, he thought. And your number just came up.* "He told me Reb wanted to get himself killed," Dana said. "Maybe that's what this big bastard wanted for himself, too."

Royal placed the pad against the wounds and wound the bandage around Mungo's throat and tied it in place. "He was a good soldier, though." He looked up at Dana. "I guess you're in charge, now."

The far-off whine of a powerful starter came to their ears, and a huge motor coughed into life. Another followed it, and another. Soon a chorus of motors rumbled at them from across the river.

"Those are Tigers," Dana said, his voice awed.

"There must be a regiment of them," Nolan said. "Jesus!"

"That's why they sent that patrol out," Dana told Royal. "To see if we had anything at the bridge that would stop them. Did you raise the ships on your radio?"

Royal shrugged. "We still can't receive, so there's no way of telling."

"That patrol's probably gone back to report by now," Dana said. "I'll take you out there again if you want to send out the co-ordinates on that tank concentration."

Royal swallowed hard and reached for his map case. "Okay, Dana."

Dana nodded at him. "Wait until I get out there and give you the word that it's all clear." He thrust a fresh clip into the M-1. He didn't want to think why he was doing this last piece of insanity.

He saw no hope in trying the radio again. He was simply doing the things he was supposed to do, playing out the string.

He stood abruptly and ran limping through the graveyard to the bridge. No one fired at him from the other side of the river. He dove to earth in the protection of the burned-out tank and crawled between it and the jeep. Cautiously, he poked his head up. Nothing moved on the other side, and he heard no sound. He turned his head and whistled softly back to the church. In a moment, Royal was beside him, flicking the switches of the radio.

Dana crawled out to the far end of the bridge, hearing Royal say softly into the microphone, "Boulder Dam! Boulder Dam! Urgent! This is Shore Fire Control Six…" He waited fifteen minutes before crawling back to Royal. "Okay. If we haven't raised them yet, we never will. Let's get back." The Navy man nodded.

Dana covered him while he ran, dodging among the grave markers, back to the church. Then he rose and hobbled after him.

Swampy and Nolan huddled beside a window, arguing busily in hushed tones instead of watching the road outside. Rosen knelt at Mungo's head, staring down at the big sergeant. The non-com's eye's were closed. He breathed laboriously through his mouth.

Dana sank onto his haunches, his back against the wall, listening to the thunder of the tank motors. He shuddered, thinking of the damage the Panzers would do when they struck the Allied beachhead. He could imagine the enormous confusion on Utah Beach today, ships unloading men and vehicles and supplies, the shoreline stacked with every imaginable sort of impedimenta until there was scarcely room to maneuver a jeep, let alone the armor that would be neccessary to counter this massive German penetration.

No, they couldn't stop the Panzers here. Not with seven men, not with a regiment. But they could slow them down and that meant something to the dogfaces slogging up from the beaches. It was easy to bug out, to turn tail and run—and Dana remembered that, for over thirty hours, that was exactly what he had wanted to do—but something was different, now.

Something was very different. Being in command was the smallest part of it. He had not wanted command. Mungo had thrust it on him. Now he wasn't just a lonesome Okie, a would-be draft-dodger aching to be safe. He was a soldier, and a soldier by choice, responsible to all the men around him, to Colonel Tighe and the Five-Oh-Goose, to the seaborne troops fighting up from the beach, and responsible, finally, to himself.

It was more than just responsibility. It had to do with not letting your people down. It was poor blinded Burke, sitting with a carbine in his hands, still ready to do his part. It was Sacco, lying dead amongst the debris, dying only when his job was done, after turning his gun to cover Dana at a moment when Dana would have died but for him. It was Commander Royal, product of money, position and rank, willing to take orders from an Okie private.

He had thought at first that Royal was patronizing him. But the officer was man enough to forget his rank and follow Dana because Dana knew his job and did it well. Royal had said as much. Dana raised his eyes to the bridge. Royal had gone out again. He was crouched beside the jeep with the radio mike in his hand. Hansen knelt beside him, carbine ready. It was something to be proud of—a man like Royal willingly taking orders from you.

That was what Mungo had tried to show him. Mungo had known what the job was from the first. He was Army, and he knew the Army's job: to fight—to take and hold its ground, to protect its own against anything that came.

All right, to hell with the reasons. There wasn't any sense left to it any longer but he was going to go on fighting. Sacco had said there wasn't any sense to be found in this world.

There was not much left to fight with, but what there was, he was going to use, just as Mungo would. He wondered if it was worth the risk of climbing the knoll to get the machine gun from the pit. The darkness was beginning to give way to dimly filtering light of false dawn. He might be spotted, silhouetted against the skyline. He would need some cover—Nolan's sub-machine gun.

Nolan and Swampy were still huddled together, speaking in whispers.

"Nolan," Dana called. "Let's get out on the hill. I'm going to get that machine gun and I want you to cover me."

Nolan shook his head and walked slowly over to him. "Listen, Dana. We've got to get out of here, before it gets light enough for them to see us. We've got to get moving right away."

Dana noticed for the first time that Nolan and Swampy had their webbing on, their musettes slung across their backs.

"What the hell are you talking about? We've got wounded here. We've got a job to do."

Nolan's voice no longer had that domineering harshness. His voice was a plaintive wheedle now, much like Uhlan's. "Hell, you can hear those Panzer motors. You don't stop Tiger tanks with LMG's. If we take off right away, head straight for the marshes ..."

"I ain't goin' no place," Dana said.

"Look, we need you."

"How come you need *me*, Nolan? I'm just an Okie screw-up. You were going to bust my head for giving you your lumps, remember?"

"That's forgotten about. That was garrison stuff. This is for real—we're in a jam. We've got to stick together, or none of us will get through."

"What about you, Swampy?"

Swampy shrugged. "Them that fights and runs away lives to fight another day, Dana."

Dana looked around him helplessly. If there were only someone to back him up. Mungo lay stiffly on his back, his dark eyes squinting at them, his hands crossed on his laboring chest. Blood was soaking the bandage at his throat.

"We're the only ones left who can still take care of themselves," Nolan said earnestly. "Let these sailors stay if they want to, but get your equipment on, Dana."

He had to stop them. He wished he had his rifle in his hands. He had never felt so naked and alone. "You ain't going no place," he said.

Nolan pointed the Thompson at his belly. "Get out of the way, Okie," he said. "Come on, Swampy."

"Listen," Dana said desperately. "What about the wounded? Hollister and Mungo and the swabby. We can't leave them for the Krauts. You know what they'll do to them now. Maybe if we hold out just a little while ..."

Nolan cut him short with an impatient jab of the Thompson's muzzle, and Dana remembered vividly what Cadillac had looked like when the French girl was through with him. "I've got no time to argue with you, Okie." Nolan's voice was tight and angry now, the sullenness undercut with something like hysteria. "You try to stop me, and I'll drop you where you stand."

"You won't do it, Nolan. You ain't got the guts to gun me down. Mungo was right when he said you'd shot your bolt. You're big and mean, but you're never any good unless you've got a poor slob like Uhlan around to remind you how tough you are. Or a man like Mungo for you to try to measure up to. But they're both of them gone and now you need *me*, Nolan." Nolan's mouth jerked. The Thompson trembled slightly as he pointed it at Dana's face. "I'll give you just three seconds to step aside, you feeble little Okie bastard. Then I'm going to blast you over on your back."

Dana saw then that he had been wrong. He couldn't face Nolan down with words alone, no matter how keenly they struck home. He looked into Nolan's eyes and saw he was going to shoot.

A gun spat sharply behind them. Nolan's head snapped back. He stumbled forward with a look of incredulous surprise. The gun spat again and again and each time Nolan stumbled forward as though a giant hand had shoved him. The Tommy-gun hit the floor and his knees buckled. His head fell forward until his forehead struck the ground. He died kneeling, with his body curved at the waist and his head against the floor.

Dana's unbelieving eyes jumped to Mungo. The big sergeant was lowering his head painfully back to the floor. *Hauptmann* von Ritter's Luger jutted from the huge fist, looking toylike and absurdly harmless despite the smoke curling out of its barrel.

"Jesus Christ," Swampy breathed. "I thought he wouldn't shoot an American soldier."

"Nolan was—hell, he was no soldier," Dana said numbly. He stared down at Mungo. "Thanks," he said. The big man's lips did not move, but the black, impassive eyes were open now, and he seemed to nod his head.

"Swampy, we're going for that gun." Dana snatched up the Thompson where it had fallen from Nolan's lifeless fingers and led the southerner out the door. It was getting lighter. The eastern sky was shot with gray. He dashed to the gun pit on the knoll, careful even in his haste to keep his head below the skyline. Swampy followed him, robotlike.

He set the machine gun up in the rubble of the wall where he could cover Royal and Hansen out at the jeep. He sent Rosen back with his carbine to guard the windows.

When he had threaded a fresh belt into the gun and wormed a hollow for his body behind it, there was light enough to see the first Mark Three poke its delicate 50 mm snout out of the trees beyond the bend of the causeway. Behind it, the noise of those which were to follow rose in a crescendo.

Dana and Swampy could see the wave of grenadiers fanning out into the gray water of the marsh on each side of the lead tank.

"Royal," Dana shouted. "Get back in here!"

Royal shook his head and waved his hand impatiently.

"Royal! Damn it, they can see you! Get your ass back here!"

Already German guns were barking, and masonry exploded at the wall of the house just beyond the bridge. Hansen screamed back at him, "I think we've raised the *Quincy!*"

"Screw the *Quincy,*" Dana shouted. "Damn it, take cover."

He could see the ugly snout of the leading tank wheel directly towards the church. The 50 mm flashed and bucked in recoil, and a shell went shrieking overhead. Dana swiveled the machine gun on the leading waves of infantry and triggered off a burst. The infantry went down, but the tank came rolling massively forward.

Before his finger tensed for a second burst, a curious, low-pitched fluttering sound swelled and filled the air. Beyond the grove of trees there was a glaring flash and he found himself aiming through trembling sights at a world that rocked and bucked insanely. Even the ground beneath him heaved, as a thunderous concussion roared against his eardrums. A section of the road belched upward, just beyond the trees, and twisted shapes that might have been men or metal rose and spun and dropped to earth again.

Swampy was shouting something in his ears. The ground continued to shake beneath him as the salvoes poured in. Royal still knelt at the jeep, his huge binoculars raised to his eyes, calling in fire corrections.

Hansen rose and hurled himself across the heaving church-yard to throw himself down beside Dana. "We got them!" he shrieked into Dana's ears. The words were faint and muffled in the roar. "We got the *Quincy*. Those are nine-inch guns. They're going to plaster the road right up to Isigny."

Dana swung his machine gun silently across a now deserted field of fire. The German infantry was down and even the tanks were straggling away, blundering heavily off the road to bog down in the marshes.

When the barrage lifted the silence was intense and the haze rolled peacefully across the marshes. A Mark Four, its stubby

75 barrel pointed downward to the swamp, disgorged its crew through the turret hatch. Dana aimed carefully and raked the fleeing figures with a prolonged burst of fire. Two fell and the others disappeared behind the marsh grass. Nothing further moved along the road.

Hansen was pounding him on the back. "We broke them up," he shouted in near-hysteria. "We broke them up before they could get near the bridge."

Dana lifted his head from the gun. "They'll be coming back," he said.

He wanted terribly to drop his head and sleep. There was something to be done yet before the next attack. He tried to remember, as his leaden eyelids dropped. There were Krauts still waiting in the nearby houses. Probably they wouldn't show themselves. They would wait for the next attack.

He called out to Swampy, "Damnit—stay at that window. They might be creeping up on us. Keep yours eyes on those houses." Then he remembered nothing more.

CHAPTER TWENTY
D PLUS ONE, 0900 HOURS

Dana might have been asleep for ten minutes or an hour. He awoke to Royal's hand shaking his shoulder, to the sound of tank motors blended with the rattle of small arms and the blast of artillery. He rolled over wordlessly. His hands fell mechanically on the machine gun. He peered through the mist anxiously, across the clumps of sea grass and the scattered heaps of dead. Nothing was moving in the swamp.

"They're coming in from the west this time!" Royal shouted.

He caught up the machine gun, tripod and all. The west—the other side of town. The gun would have to be emplaced in the tower, or what remained of it. Swampy and the two Navy enlisted men were at the windows, blazing away.

"The Krauts are runnin'!" Swampy shouted. "They're headin' for the swamps. Give it to the bastards!"

Dana started up the steps to the tower, the gun cradled in his arms, the belt dangling behind him. "Get a box of ammo," he barked at Royal. He straddled a fire-blackened beam and stared down at the street. Below him were helmetless, unarmed Germans, waving their hands in supplication.

He brushed loose bricks and mortar dust from the ragged-edged wall that was the top of the tower now, and emplaced the gun. The Germans scattered back into the houses when he swung the muzzle toward them. The meaning did not sink into Dana's fatigue-numbed mind. He was thinking wearily that he would need an assistant up there with him, to hold the legs of the gun while he fired.

A shell shrieked over his head. Dana turned his head and saw a flash of fire raise a geyser of swamp water behind a Tiger tank wheeling to concealment in the clump of trees across the river. "Hey!" Hansen screamed in the church below him, "those tanks got orange panels on them!"

Dana squinted back down the road to the west. He saw the high silhouette of a Sherman tank lumbering slowly toward the village. Behind it was another, and a third, and two half-tracks from which jutted the familiar round helmets of American infantry. He could see the Germans fleeing in every direction. Some stopped and waited with their hands high for the arrival of the armor.

The Shermans spurted 50-caliber machine-gun fire at the running figures in the marshes. Dana lit a cigarette and stared at the scene, almost distinterested. When the tanks rolled to the edge of the village, Dana started wearily down the tower.

Swampy was standing at the door, mumbling to himself. He turned his head to Dana. "They're our own," he croaked. "The seaborne. They're our own damned tanks."

Rosen was repeating thickly, "Beautiful, oh, the beautiful tanks."

Dana stumbled heavily across the church and found the orange-smoke identification grenade in Mungo's pack. He lobbed it through the doorway, out into the street, and watched the smoke billow brightly upward. He heard the motors roar again at the end of the village, and the treads clattering on the cobblestones.

He remembered that there was still something more to do. He entered the sacristy where Royal was bending over Burke, speaking softly as he tendered the blinded boy a cigarette. Dana turned to Hollister; the kid was awake and smiling weakly. "They're here," Dana said. "Our tanks are here."

Hollister nodded calmly. "I know," he whispered. "Sergeant Mungo told me they would get here today."

Dana turned and shuffled back through the church. He stood in the doorway as the first rumbling Sherman lumbered up almost to the bridge and stopped. The turret opened and a grimy head shot out—a grease-splattered tanker with his eyes almost as tired and worn as Dana's. The two weary men faced each other for a moment. "Who the hell are you?" the tanker asked him.

"Five-Oh-Goose," said Dana. "You from the Fourth?"

"Five-Oh-Goose!" He ducked and yelled something to tthe others in his tank, and then his head shot out again. "Christ, you people get around!" he said. "Yeah, Seventieth Tank Battalion. We're with the Fourth. Come up from the beaches. Run into your people all the way."

"Medics," Dana said. "You got any medics with you?"

The tanker pointed back to the half-tracks, which had stopped in the village now, spilling men in fieldjackets and leggings, wearing infantry packs. They were racing through the houses, rounding up the Germans who remained in the village.

Dana limped up the village street. At the second halftrack he found a young lieutenant with a red cross on his helmet. Dana led him and a pair of aid-men into the church.

He motioned toward the sacristy where Hollister and Burke were lying. Dana stopped one of the aid-men, a sergeant. He pointed to where Mungo lay, the Luger still jutting from his fist. The cigar had dropped to the floor beside him.

The aid-man bent over him. Gently he propped up Mungo's eyelid and touched the eyeball with his finger. It was as cold and lustreless as a marble.

"This one's dead," the aid-man said.

Dana nodded and turned his face away.

The aid-man started toward the sacristy, hesitated a moment. "Buddy of yours?" he asked.

Dana dropped his cigarette and ground it out. "No, not a buddy." He leaned against the wall. "He was a good man, though," Dana said.

THE END

www.ingramcontent.com/pod-product-compliance
Lightning Source LLC
Chambersburg PA
CBHW021437020726
47499CB00006BA/2034

This time, torn by fear for the life of the "hares", I swam under the hole. Admittedly, the breaststroke, so as not to swallow the water in which the deceased had been staying.

I quickly made two loops and climbed up as before. Leaning over the edge, below I saw hands extended towards me.

I threw the water bottle and calmly, not sure if I was understood, said:

"We will help you right away. Hold on a little longer, we'll reach you from the top. Here," I pointed to the top of the tank, lighting it with the flashlight.

The black figure of the woman picked up the water bottle and swam into a darkness that the beam of my flashlight couldn't dispel.

I quickly went back up, where Bronek had already begun to burn a hole in the deck of "Berta".

"Ladder and stretcher. We need a stretcher. Preferably two pairs. And a harness for children. There are children there," I said to the Third. "I heard a child's cry."

"Oh, shit!" He blurted out.

The stretcher is included in the standard equipment of "Berta" and the fire ship, and so is the ladder. It's five meters long, that's enough. We put everything next to the burned hole, above the main deck, on the other side of the ship, so that the waves wouldn't reach there.

Then we dragged the deceased from the hatch[1] to the fireboat so that he couldn't be seen.

"How much longer?" I asked Bronek.

---

[1] Hatch - an opening that allows entering the tank, closed with a cover fixed with screws.

"You can see, it can't be faster."

"Sure I can, but it is because of my nervousness that I urge you so."

He burned two holes in the center of the circle, or rather an ellipse. We poured water over everything to make it cool faster. I pulled the rope through the holes to keep the damn thing from falling down. Bronek finished the burning.

A beam of light illuminated the interior of the empty tank - there was no water there. There was nothing but empty rusty space.

The Third quickly put the ladder in and we went all the way down. In the corner of the tank loomed some figures.

"Be careful with the light, it was dark for a couple of days," he called to me.

We walked closer, lighting the bottom. In front of us, some boards lying on the frames made a makeshift floor. A woman with a small child was lying on top of them, and the other, standing over her, was holding the bottle of water that I had brought. There were some lights - probably there was no fuel in them anymore, that's why it was dark there. There were cups, aluminum bowls, some things in bundles and three hammocks. It was pretty nice equipment but something had gone wrong.

"Do you speak English?" Asked the Third.

"Yes," one of the women replied. "Thank you for saving us. We already gave up hope when Booaba didn't come back and gave no sign of life. Did you find him?" She asked.

The Third didn't answer, just asked the next question:

"How is the child?"

"Weak. There was no water."

"We're leaving. Cover your eyes with the handkerchiefs, child's too," he said, tearing his T-shirt to pieces and giving it to the woman. We did all this in twilight.

Taking first one woman and then another, we helped them get on the deck. The second time we went down to the tank with the stretcher on which we put the little girl. She was maybe eight or ten.

Bronek, standing under the hatch on the lower rungs of the ladder, illuminated our way so that we safely pulled the stretcher onto the deck.

The Third reported everything to "Neptun".

"In a few days we'll take them to our place, if the weather allows it," the old man informed us.

"Please, give me a hint on what I can and can't give them to eat. They haven't drunk and eaten for couple of days."

"Pap, like that for child - in small portions."

"And where to get it?"

"Do you have rice?"

"We do."

"Then make pap out of it."

"I looked at the bottle held by the older woman - probably the mother of that little girl. It was almost full, so she knew she couldn't drink everything at once. That's good. I took water from her and poured over the girl's face and her entire body. The water will be absorbed faster. I gave the child two more sips from the bottle. Her eyes were blindfolded and she didn't quite know what was happening, but her mother seemed to be reassuring her by saying something in their language.

"It's dusk. They still have to be transported to the prow of "Berta", which won't be easy," said the Third with fear in his voice.

"We have to wait here until it gets darker. We won't be able to lead them to the front of "Berta" blindfolded," I replied.

I took the girl on my back and we went. The women, with the help of Bronek and the Third, followed us. After a long time, we were already in the mess. It got dark.

"And what now?" Bronek asked.

"There's a big cabin[2] at the end of the hall. Take two mattresses and blankets to that room and let the women and child stay there. We still have an unpleasant duty. A funeral," said the Third sadly. "Before that, let's consider whether to tell women about everything."

Just in case, we reported the problem to the captain. The answer was short: no.

"I'm not going. Go alone with Bronek. It's enough that I got him out of the water."

Reluctantly, but they went. After that, I never asked how it went, and neither did they themselves. During this time, I took all three of them to the cabin and showed where the bathroom and kitchen were.

"Rest," I said.

"Where's Booaba, my husband?" The old woman asked again. This is how I judged her based on the fact that she had such a big daughter, but I asked:

"How old are you?"

"I'm twenty-seven," she replied in a puzzled voice, looking at me suspiciously.

"Where is Booaba?" She asked again.

"I don't know," I lied.

The Third with Bronek returned, tired and depressed.

---

[2] Cabin - a seaman's "apartment" on a ship.

"It's a tough day," said the Third. "Could it be even worse?"

"Yes, it could. But it better not be," replied Bronek.

I went to sleep. I was tired not so much physically, but mentally from all these events.

"Richie, Richie, get up," I heard Bronek's voice.

"I'm coming," I replied sleepily. "So it's morning already." Memories vanished like a glass bubble.

"Alright, I'm getting up now, after all today I'm not leaving anywhere," I told him as I walked downstairs to the mess.

It was time for coffee and waiting breakfast, made by Bronek.

The women and the little girl recovered surprisingly quickly. The older one sad, was crying in hiding. She already knew she had lost her husband - she thought the wave had washed him into the sea as he had tried to save them.

They didn't talk much about themselves, but their English was pretty good. When they stopped being afraid in general, and of us in particular, they slowly revealed their history to us.

Banal, but with tragic effect. Some of their distant relative worked in Durban, on "Berta". They found out that the barge was going to Europe and decided to get there. In the Netherlands, where they wanted to get, they had kin. The local shaman for a solid fee guaranteed them a safe and successful journey. They were only to beware of "green figures". Funnily enough, this is how Dutch customs officers are dressed, so maybe there is something to this magic. It was true that the barge would go to Rotterdam, but not directly - first it had to be unloaded in Gabon, and the Old Man would probably deport them from there. Sad but we couldn't help it.

Having a lot of time and free access to the barge, their distant relative cut a hole during some renovation works so that they could go inside and hide.

The night before the ships were loaded, they boarded the barge, bribing whoever it was necessary. Something, however, went wrong. The hatch was supposed to be open, but it wasn't. The first few days they were waiting quietly for the barge to get far enough away so that it was impossible to return to the port.

But when the storm came, Booaba went through the hole to the second tank, wanting to get outside and open the hatch. But he didn't come back anymore. They didn't know what and why happened. They thought that the other hatch they were supposed to leave through was open, but it wasn't, and no one had the courage to tell it them. This would have meant that they were sentenced to death on purpose.

Then, while discussing, we concluded that Booaba had tried to get out onto the upper deck of the barge by a tear in the hull and then he probably had fallen, hit his head and, losing consciousness, drowned. In the darkness there, it was very possible.

It was time for my watch. I walked reluctantly to the wheelhouse. Before my eyes there were various indicators of detectors, energy cabinets arranged in a row against the wall, levers of hydraulic devices and other useful instruments showing the operation of devices on the barge. At the other wall there were devices with the use of which the barge was flooded for the loading and unloading. But that was not my domain. At the moment, I was only interested in the chair and tank sensors which were to be dry.

The weather outside hadn't changed much. The wind was still raging, and splashes of water were entering the deck of "Berta". I checked everything in the bow, and wet, I returned to the wheelhouse. Now I had a little free time, I was supposed to do my next rounds after an hour. This hour was the time for further memories - sitting in the armchair, I came back in my mind to the beginning.

To the day I had met Kinga.

Chapter 2

Kinga

I looked at the phone. "Maybe it will finally ring, I've been waiting for over three months. How much longer?"

From the kitchen, Kinga called out:

"Come to me, you will help me. I didn't like it, although it was just an excuse on her part. I looked into her blue eyes - they reminded me of my last cruise. The sea there also had that hue. When leaning overboard, I looked at the pile of blue water foaming by the bow, rising with the nervous movements of the ship, I could see that his pear[3] was not pushing the water forward, but cutting it with the blunt part of the bow.

That's why the dolphins disappeared.

---

[3] Pear - the end of the pear-shaped bow reduces water resistance, which saves fuel.

They love to swim under the bow and romp, pushed by its force. They used its movement to play like a windsurfer.

I was looking at the young dolphins who stayed close to the female thanks to their neat tail moves. Every now and then - more often than adults - jumped out of the water to get air. These rhythmic movements of the entire herd caused that the eye couldn't rest on one individual. They swam in flocks, but each of them had or was looking for a partner.

Suddenly, I noticed two specimens, one slightly larger than the other. The smaller one had lighter skin. It was moving forward in spirals. It could seem that it was escaping, but no - it was just encouraging the other dolphin to romp. Having swam up to her, because it was a female, he turned sideways, rubbing against her belly.

Suddenly, the larger male broke away and circled around the female, rotating around his own axis. Making sure she didn't get too far away, he shot up to get air. When jumping out of the water, dolphins take on their characteristic appearance. First, the blunt nose goes up, followed by the whole body, to bend into a semicircle in a second and softly slide into the water. One, two, three jump to a meter height, swimming next to each other in a sequence known only to them.

Is there any hierarchy there, who can jump to take a breath and when? They don't seem to leap to breathe, we know it, but it looks as if they were having fun and enjoying the fact that they can emerge from the water even for a second.

Right after they slip into the water, they straighten the whole body. They don't fall into the water unknowingly like flying fish, which nature has provided with the possibility of spreading thin membranes adjacent to the sides of the quasi-wings.

In panic, while escaping from the attacker, they jump out of the water and spread these wings. They fly carried by the force of the wind and their own momentum, but unknowingly they don't direct them or themselves, which is why they can be found on board so often in the morning. They can't get out of it anymore.

I watched the dolphins glide through the water one by one.

Behind the larger dolphin a smaller female jumped out and suddenly both of them, slightly wagging their tails, turned sideways and got closer to each other until their abdomen touched.

We were sailing at a speed of about fifteen knots, and they used the movement of the water that the ship was pushing ahead. Their tails, facing the bow about ten meters away, were moving sideways to catch balance.

The dorsal fins were set horizontally to the waterline, and they kept them in the same, slightly unnatural position.

Suddenly I noticed that this pair of dolphins were having sex. It was clearly visible that the large dolphin stuck together with the smaller female. "Right. They are mammals. How human it is," I thought. "Do they know I'm watching them?"

The water was clear and the visibility was ten or twenty meters deep, allowing me to watch this spectacle of nature. I, old sailor, still believe in their intelligence. I whistled in a short, high-pitched tone - they heard this whistle perfectly, and curious, approaching the side, every now and then diving under the surface of the water, they drew an ellipse, foaming the water with a wave of their tail. Several of them, having swam under the side, dived sharply, disappearing quickly from my sight. They would swim under the hull and emerge on the other side of the ship.

"Will I have sex with Kinga today? We've rarely gotten close to each other lately."

I detached myself from those memories when I heard Kinga approaching me.

I felt her hug me from behind with her whole body and whispering in my ear - her warm breath caused an impulse of desire.

"What are you thinking about, beloved?"

"About you," I lied.

She wouldn't have understood what the strength I was slave of, was in me. It's not that I wanted to get away from her and all that we call home here.

"Come on." She took my hand and walked from the kitchen, up the stairs to the living room.

I walked, knowing what would happen right away.

"Dinner's ready," she went off-topic, taking off her blouse at the same time. Every time I looked at her full breasts, I felt a rush of warmth in my whole body.

"Slowly…" she whispered, with her whole body snuggling up against me. I hugged her with one hand and unfastened the stubborn bra with the other.

"Ring, ring," … The sound of a telephone broke between us.

"Damn it. Why now?"

Kinga tilted her head back. Her wavy hair fell back over the orange color of the sofa. She fell on it with her whole body, lifting her legs up. The sofa groaned under her weight, and I noticed out of the corner of my eye that she was without a thong.

"She prepared for this, she will wait for me to finish the conversation," ran through my mind.

"Good afternoon," I said to the receiver.

"Good afternoon. This is Karolina from Petronafta speaking," I heard.

I knew that voice, I had waited for it so long.

"Are you ready to leave, Mr. Richard?"

"Always on the alert for you!" It sounded ambiguous, but it was supposed to be that way too.

A short laugh answered me.

"That's good. You are flying to Frankfurt the day after tomorrow, and from there to Nigeria. Departure from Gdansk at 2 p.m., in Frankfurt a three-hour break at the airport, and then a flight to Lagos at 5:30 p.m.

At 1:50 p.m. local time. An agent will pick you up and take you to the helipad. You have the helicopter in three hours, five o'clock in the morning Nigerian time," she sang standard phrases into my earpiece. "The Fitter is flying with you. You'll meet him in Frankfurt," she added.

"I understood. I will manage to pick up my contract and clothes in Gdansk before," I replied.

"That's great. All your documents are legit," she continued. "Only the health certificate expires in six months."

"By then, I think I'll be back home," I said.

"Yeah, yeah. So I'm waiting for you in the company."

"Thank you, goodbye," I said.

"See you later," Karolina replied.

"She has learned a lot," I thought. I remember when she started to work in the company. She was such a docile mouse, but professionally well-prepared - three languages, internship in the US in an oil company, first-class appearance. That's probably why the boss hired her - he had someone to go with for business talks. I think there was nothing between them and there will be nothing, because Karolina knows how to keep men at bay.

"Who called, honey?" came from the sofa.

"I'm leaving the day after tomorrow because I've gotten a contract," I replied, approaching Kinga.

She held her hands out towards me.

"Come here," I heard her slightly hoarse voice. The timbre of her voice changed probably because she was surprised that after two days I would be gone.

I lay down beside her, cuddling against her breasts. She started to undress me. Her slender fingers gently brushed my shoulders as she removed my shirt. I felt the desire again. "Which cruise is it?" my thoughts were in completely different climates.

Kinga pledged to drive me to the airport in Gdansk. She was very excited about my first contract trip. The first since we moved in together. This was the third month of adapting to each other. Before leaving, she was very impulsive, she tried not to show how much she was troubled by our breakup.

"Take care of yourself," she said in a concerned voice. "You know how much I love you. I will wait and miss you."

Yes, I knew she loved me. The nights before my departure were very passionate and crazy, as if we had wanted to make love for days, and yet it cannot be accumulated. Only memories of them can be kept. And I have a lot to remember...

Kinga, right after the phone call from the company announcing my departure, started to celebrate the last three days, including two nights.

"Darling," she said in a passionate voice in which I could feel a great promise to fulfill all my whims, as Kinga always announced her wishes in a sweet, captivating voice, with an expression as innocent as if she had been to make a coffee for breakfast.

"I'm going to prepare a bath."

It was already late in the evening. She locked herself in the bathroom, prepared something there, and after a while she exclaimed:

"Richie! Come here to me finally, everything is ready."

I went inside. The bathroom was spacious, covered here and there with orange and white tiles with a mosaic trail.

We had a large hot tub which we gladly used.

High-gloss furniture was fully harmonized with the decor. The large mirror opposite the tub reflected everything that was going on inside it.

I also have to add that everything was created out of Kinga's invention. As expected, she prepared another surprise.

She always surprised me with something new. This time it was lit candles placed around the bathtub, light turned off and a stick of incense smoldering somewhere in the corner, from which a thread of white smoke was maundering. Out of spite, I said:

"What is that smell?"

"How can you, darling? This is the scent of jasmine!" Kinga said in a high voice.

I didn't want to spoil the mood by saying that the smell of incense reminds me of slums in India, where to kill the stench of a street gutter, such incense is burned.

On a shelf next to the tub, in a container of ice, there was a bottle of champagne and my favorite snacks, fresh strawberries.

Kinga, completely naked, was sitting in the water. When I entered the bathroom, she turned on the hydro massage. First level so that the water gurgled calmly and didn't make a lot of noise. It was enough, however, for its depth to be interrupted by air bubbles emerging from the holes on the bottom and the sides of the bathtub.

It covered Kinga's body with a mysterious glow in the light of flashing candles.

Beautiful view.

With the speed of a Pershing, I undressed and got into the tub. I smelled the pleasant, delicate, slightly irritating scent of rose oil that Kinga poured into the water. I sat down behind her, jostling with my knees, and wrapped my arms around her, whispering in her ear:

"Honey, you are amazing ... I adore you."

"I know," she replied. "Pour the champagne," she said, tilting her head back and kissing me passionately on the lips. She knew how much I liked it.

"Oh no," I said after a moment.

Not out of laziness or shame, but out of curiosity.

I had always been curious about Kinga and this time I wanted her to get up so that I could watch her get out of the tub naked and pour champagne into our glasses.

"You know," I said. "I'd like to look at you in the light of those candles," I said in a low voice with a hint of a request.

She looked at me out of the corner of her eye as she turned in the tub.

"Alright. But it will cost you 'a little something'..."

"What?" I pretended I didn't know what she meant.

She handed me a bottle of champagne, which she opened in one neat movement.

"You got what you wanted," she said in a sexy voice.

I didn't ask what she meant - champagne or caresses from a moment ago, but I think the latter. I was looking at her beautiful body

27

and perfect figure. Her hair, loose, a little long, and soaked at the ends, was plastered over her neck and shoulders. The breasts, slightly tilted outwards, were so firm that she boldly used these qualities, pissing the guys around - walking without a bra and swaying them to the rhythm of the steps taken. Her delicate waistline harmonized with the smooth, velvety skin of light brown color, the remnants of a summer tan. The back with slightly protruding shoulder blades beautifully flowed down to the buttocks.

She picked up two glasses and slipped softly into the water.

This time she sat facing me. I poured champagne into glasses.

A concerned voice escaped from her lips:

"To your happy return, darling."

"To your patience while waiting for this return," I replied.

We drank up. I poured again. This time she took a long sip of champagne and clung to my mouth. I parted my lips a little and she shared the champagne with me, the excess of which ran down my chin.

She sat down next to me. Her breasts protruded halfway from the water that flooded her nipples again and again, as if caressing them with bubbles of air coming from the bathtub nozzles. I envied the water this pleasure. I clung to them. She bent like a string of a taut bow and lifted a little. I was ready to fuse with her in the love act, but Kinga liked the longer foreplay. We caressed for a long time. Kinga prolonged her caresses, making me boil. I was like a volcano which is about to erupt. Kinga seemed to be waiting for it. She turned her back to me.

I clung to her, looking in the mirror at her waving breasts and half-closed eyes, and then I led us to the land of delight that Kinga announced with loud sighs, drawing air into her lungs. After a long moment, we fell to the bottom of the bathtub, panting at the same time as if after a 100-meter dash. Satisfied and happy, I started smearing Kinga's whole body with aromatic oils that were numerous in our bathroom. She gave in to it lying with her eyes closed.

That night we slept clung to each other like two magnets, hugging.

Chapter 3

Departure

In the morning there was a big mess - checking the packed luggage with a piece of paper on which we had written down what to take.

After we dealt with the large suitcase, we started to complete hand luggage that could be brought on the plane. I paid special attention to this to avoid any unpleasantness when checking in. I calmly explained to Kinga:

"Honey, leave these bottles of cologne and put them in the large luggage with the other shaving utensils.

"And this, can I put it in?" She stood over me, showing my sailor's knife.

"You probably want them to take me straight to Guadeloupe," - it was right after the tragedy at the World Trade Center.

The most important thing was the laptop - I can't imagine a contract trip without it.

It is a piece of home locked in a computer memory. When I want to recall some fragments of the past, I turn it on and watch the moments gone by. I see Kinga, I hear her voice.

The two days until our departure passed very quickly. We discussed all matters. Kinga was left alone for so long for the first time.

"Honey," I told her, "I'll be calling from the airport and then from the ship when I get there. "You will see. When you have to deal with everything yourself, these three months will fly by."

I signed the contract for three months, I didn't want for longer, although Karolina said:

"Mr. Richie, I can't propose three-month contract, but four-month one at most, and that's only with a plus!"

And I was firmly in my reply:

"No, I can't. I really ask for three-month contract for the first time, and without a plus. I left my young wife," I explained to her, "for the first time for so long, let her get used to it and toughen, then we will return to the standards."

"Alright, but it's only for you that I'm making an exception because of your young wife."

She said so. But she knew that Kinga had a different name and wasn't my wife. In the contract, I always gave all the data so that it was impossible to hide anything from her.

That day finally came. We spent the last night before my departure like an old married couple, without going crazy.

In the morning we got into the car and went first to Gdansk, to the company, then to the warehouse for work clothes and to the airport.

We got there an hour and a half before departure. Finding a place to park the car was a bit of a problem. Having toured the terminal area twice, I finally managed to park my car in an unguarded parking lot.

"Have I parked in a good place? Will you have any trouble while leaving?" I asked Kinga.

She had to back up while taking a sharp left turn to find herself on a road that was narrow and one-way. I was hoping no one would block the car during this time.

I jawed on as I pulled the suitcase out of the trunk, and over my shoulder, I already had slung a carry-on bag.

"Give me that, I'll carry it," Kinga offered.

"I can handle it. The suitcase has wheels and the hand luggage is not heavy. There is only a laptop and newspapers," - I always took some newspapers with me, sometimes a book.

Now from the books I only had a Polish-Russian dictionary. I knew from Karolina that some of the ship's crew were Russian-speaking sailors.

We walked to the terminal entrance, it was quite a long way. It seemed very close as we drove, but, dragging a stubborn suitcase, it wasn't like that anymore. Kinga was chattering all the time, trying to hide her nervousness.

"Richie, did you take everything? Did you forget something? I put the pills in your cosmetics which are in your suitcase, and the laptop cables are in your hand luggage, in the side pocket."

"I'll be fine, don't worry, darling," I replied a little louder every now and then, as the wheels of the suitcase rattled, dragged along the cobblestones of the paved sidewalk leading to the terminal entrance.

"I know, but it's better to be prepared for everything and know where a given thing is, so as not to look for it later," she said. "You fly so far ... Aren't you afraid?"

"I'm not afraid of the flight," I replied, "I'm just afraid that the luggage won't come with me."

"Sometimes it happens that the luggage gets missing somewhere and flies to another place. Most often when you have a connecting flight, just like I do now."

"And what will happen when it gets missing?" She asked.

"It rarely gets missing and is not found. Although an average tourist will have his missing luggage brought to the hotel on the same day or after a few days, I don't have such a possibility," I explained. "My luggage won't catch up with me. The ship won't be waiting.

"So what would you do then?" She got worried.

"I would get some money and buy the most necessary things, if I have anywhere to buy them.

And then I would call you and you would bring me the rest," I joked.

"Alright, Richie," she replied seriously.

We went inside. We were welcomed by a little spacious hall. I looked at the departures board, searching for Frankfurt - "there it is." I was a bit afraid that there would be no flight or that there would be some replacement. I didn't tell Kinga about it so as not to worry her.

In the office I was informed that some of the aviation personnel were on strike in Germany, but they didn't know who and where. They had, however, information that the flight should have taken place as planned. Despite that, a certain amount of uncertainty was sown in me. We approached the baggage check-in.

"I have a reservation," I said, giving my name.

"Yes, that's right. Your passport, please," answered the young girl sitting behind the counter.

After a while my luggage was taken, and I collected my ticket.

"Please be at customs in half an hour at the latest," she added.

Kinga stood by my side the whole time, holding my arm.

"We still have half an hour, come upstairs, let's have a drink," I said in a slightly hoarse voice.

We went up the wide stairs. There was a bar just to the left. We went in and sat at a table.

"Kinga, drive carefully back home. I can see you're a little distracted," I said, looking into her eyes, which got hazy and sad.

"Yeah, yeah, I will drive slowly," she assured me, nodding her head.

She hugged me.

"I don't like goodbyes."

"Neither do I." I said, kissing her cheek. "I'll call you as soon as I arrive in Frankfurt. Then from Lagos. I'll be there early in the morning. I may wake you up," I added.

"I don't know if I will be able to fall asleep at all ... It's the first night without you."

"It's time for me to go," I said, seeing that the line of people for customs clearance had decreased to a few people.

"Take care of yourself," Kinga said. "I love you very much," she assured me.

"I love you too. I will call as often as possible."

We got up. Kinga threw her arms around my neck and kissed me on the lips.

"Remember. I love you," she added again. "I'll wait."

"Just don't cry," I said, seeing the corners of her mouth twitch.

"No, I won't," she assured me.

I took my things and went to the customs without looking back.

Standard check-in. I placed my shoes, phone, belt and keys in the basket. I put my bag on the table and walked through the gate - silence, so everything was OK.

The customs officer was checking my laptop for a long time, but finally gave it back to me. I got dressed and looked at the hall. Kinga was still standing in the same place and watching. I waved to her and went to the plane. I was flying with Lufthansa, so I knew the standard would be European. The flight took less than two hours. At Frankfurt airport, I walked about half a kilometer to another terminal, using the moving walkway every time it was available. I sat down at the bar. "I have to take good care of my luggage," I thought and called Kinga.

"Hello," I heard her voice.

"Honey, I already arrived. Are you home yet?"

"Yes, I'm just sitting with Natka and talking. She is trying to cheer me up because I'm very sad."

In fact, it was only after returning from the cruise that I found out that Kinga had felt bad and Natka had treated her. My first contract trip was a lot of stress for her. Natka is Kinga's colleague. Nice girl, it's good that she is with Kinga now. They both liked each other from the very first moment when fate brought them together. And I have a lot of sentiment for her, counted in good relations.

I had two more hours until my departure. I sat down, ordered coffee and mineral water, and thought:

"How long has it been?"

Chapter 4

Meeting

Christopher called me.

"Richard? He asked, "Are you home? We have to meet. I'd like to talk to you. I have a matter to discuss, and besides we haven't seen each other for a long time.

"Hello, I'm glad you've called," I replied. "I'm home now, wondering what to do with myself."

"When did you arrive?"

"A week ago," I said. "I had a tough, very tough cruise. You know, damn it, how it is sometimes at sea," I said rhetorically.

He didn't know. Christopher is a typical landman. He saw the sea only from the beach and from the deck of a cruise ship, and sometimes from his yacht, although he mostly sailed it on the lakes.

I once asked him:

"Christopher? Why don't you go on the yacht somewhere further, for example to Kolobrzeg?"

"I don't like the sea. I have a yacht because it adds splendor, but I prefer our lakes. And immediately he countered:

"And what do you get out of this sea?"

Sometimes I too wondered what I really got out of this sea.

We met the next day in Sopot.

Then I met Kinga. Christopher always, when he was in our house, said:

"You see, if not for me, you wouldn't have met."

It was already summer, and not only on a calendar. Outside, the sun was shining mercilessly. I went with Christopher for an early dinner at such a nice pub at Heroes of Monte Cassino street.

Somewhere in the center of the promenade, on the right, just behind the clothing store, there was a small stylish restaurant. You entered it by walking between the tables and umbrellas, as in the case of almost all pubs on the promenade.

There was a cozy twilight inside. The light brown wood tables were solidly constructed, and next to them were chairs that matched the style of the interior.

The paintings hung on the walls showed maritime views, and the whole was complemented by typical sea lighting - ship lamps and a tastefully made lantern with light rotating inside. Some real greenery filled the corner of the restaurant. I liked this place not because it had such a maritime decor, but because of the dishes they served there.

I liked squid in batter and shrimp salad. In those days, it was not possible to eat such a meal everywhere. Fresh fish was always served there as well.

I knew if I ordered flounder fillets it would have been flounder caught by local fishermen a previous night, not frozen one, from a local store. I remember today that I ordered whitened fish soup, cod fillet, fries and a set of salads, plus a beer.

Christopher and I sat outside, under an umbrella, right next to the promenade. I liked to watch this rippling human flow pouring from top to bottom and bottom to top. Diversity, cool style, you could see it all there. It was for such views that the elite from all over the country - and not only the country - came to Sopot.

We had been sitting like that for half an hour. Christopher told me about his affairs of the heart. He met one girl at a disco and was wondering whether to deepen this relationship. He was afraid that the shawty had the hots for him because he was the head of a gastronomic company.

"Excuse me," I heard suddenly. I turned my head in the direction the voice was coming from. Two girls were standing over us.

"Is there a free seat here? Can we join you? One of the girls said, the taller one.

The shorter, blonde, was silent.

I scanned the surrounding tables, indeed they were all occupied.

"Of course!" Christopher crowed like a rooster, getting up from his seat to let the girls pass.

Right. Now he will mate like a peacock. He's good at it.

We had actually eaten dinner already. Christopher, without asking me, ordered coffee and a portion of ice cream with fruit and whipped cream. Probably just so as not to get up too early. And the mating began.

"Is ice cream good here?" Asked the deity with black hair.

"It depends on what kind of ice cream[4] a person likes," Christopher replied.

I thought that he would scare them off with such a talk, but they didn't get it, or pretended that they didn't understand the allusion - if there was one in Christopher's response.

"The best is dairy and chocolate ice cream," I replied, because Christopher had ordered me such, although I wasn't particularly fond of chocolate ice cream.

"Indeed - the ice cream there was delicious. Wasn't made from powder in an ice cream machine, but was traditional, made out of milk and eggs. There were no lumps of ice or powdered milk, like in that from vending machine, when in a hurry the staff chooses wrong proportions.

Hardly anyone knew how it was made, but the guests appreciated its taste, so the place was always full of people. The ice cream was characterized by a delicate, cool aftertaste of cream and a slightly bitter taste of chocolate, plus real fresh fruit with whipped cream, made of fresh egg whites. It wasn't cheap, but it was worth paying a little extra to savor its taste.

The girls exchanged glances.

"Excuse me!" the tall girl with black hair turned to the waitress, "we are asking for two portions of dairy and chocolate ice cream with whipped cream and fruit as well as two white coffees from the espresso machine.

The blonde was casting glances at Chris. She was sitting across from him.

Chris started the conversation banally:

---

[4] An ice cream means also a blowjob in Polish.

"It can be seen that you are not from here."

"Really? And how do you know that? Is something sticking out of me, or what? The blonde said in an aggressive tone. "Except for her breasts, nothing else is sticking out," I thought.

"No, no, I just thought that if you didn't know that here is the best ice cream in Sopot, you are not from the Tri-City," Christopher replied.

"Is it bad?" This time the tall girl with black hair spoke.

She was actually a bit more than of average height. She was only tall compared to her blonde friend.

"No, no, it's great! Let more such beautiful girls come to Sopot," Christopher continued. "It makes Sopot more beautiful and interesting."

"Are you coming back from the beach?" I asked.

"Yes," the taller, black-haired girl replied. "We have been baking in the sun since morning. And what you guys are doing here?"

"I'm Chris, and this is Richard," he introduced us.

"Kinga," the black-haired tall girl replied.

"And my name is Ula," added the blonde.

"That's great, the first pancake is always spoiled," said Christopher not very resolutely. "I live and work in Gdynia, and Richard is a sailor."

And why did he blurt it out? I was angry that he said it so early.

"It's interesting occupation," said Kinga.

"But very demanding and difficult, and it also makes a freak out of a man," I said.

"Why?" Kinga asked, looking at me with a smile. "I don't see any weirdo in front of me.

"I meant the mental side, not the appearance."

"Really?" She was surprised. "Why is that?" She said, staring at me with blue eyes until I felt weak. If I wasn't sitting, I would definitely have had to sit down. The look was knocking me off my feet.

"A sailor becomes distrustful after several years of sailing."

"Distrustful of who?" She asked. She looked at me with such innocent eyes that I thought she was making fun of me.

"Of women," I said aggressively.

"Of all?"

"No. Only of the ones that are beautiful, cute and have blue eyes," I smiled at her.

Christopher entertained Ula very well. The time had passed quickly. The ice cream was eaten, the coffee was drunk, and we didn't feel like getting up. We arranged to meet the next day in the afternoon in Gdynia, at the Square. Christopher promised to show them Gdynia and Kosciuszko Square, because they hadn't been there yet. I waited for this time impatiently. I was curious if they would come. Back then, I didn't know that they didn't live in the Tri-City, but in Tczew, in their aunt's house. It is quite far, you have to travel an hour by train. Christopher drove his Merc up and parked right next to the fountain.

I came from Sopot by electric train. I assumed that we would to go have some fun and maybe drink good wine. I could always come back by taxi. Chris looked nervously at his watch and towards Swietojanska Street. It was obvious that he had made a hit with Ula.

We made an appointment at the fountain, where everyone can get, even if he doesn't know Gdynia and the Square. They came on time. They came from the sea. As it turned out later, they had been next to the beach since the morning.

Kinga - a revelation. Dressed modestly but tastefully. The white tight dress emphasized her beautiful body, slim figure and tan. Without a bra, her breasts and protruding nipples were eye-catching. Long legs in white high heels and a short dress that barely covered her shapely buttocks made her breasts ripple as she walked, barely keeping them in check. The see-through dress showed more than it covered. The sight caught my imagination, but I calmly said to her:

"You look beautiful."

"Thank you, you too," she replied.

"Can a guy look beautiful?" I was surprised.

"That's not what I meant," she teased, looking at me with a mysterious smirk.

"Then what?" I dwelled on the subject.

"You are dressed so… unconventionally."

Indeed, that day I went to the store and bought myself a summer sports cream jacket with delicate longitudinal stripes. It fit me perfectly, highlighting the tan I had acquired that summer. Under my jacket, I wore a black T-shirt with a stand-up collar that I spotted on my previous voyage in Spain. In addition to it, plain white denim pants and Italian moccasins. Branded sunglasses, then fashionable mirror shades, completed my image. I wanted to make the best possible impression on Kinga. We were walking along the square, and I was telling her the story of the warship ORP Blyskawica, which now serves as a museum for tourists. I also talked about its twin ship, ORP Grom, which sank in the Norwegian fjords, fighting Germany there during the Second World War. I told about the fate of the sailors who sank there, and now rest at the bottom of the cold waters.

She swallowed everything like a hungry pelican. With her mouth wide open, she stared at me with those captivating blue eyes, every now and then asking:

"Really? Was it really like that?"

When we were passing by the "Dar Pomorza" I took her hand and pulled her behind myself. The first contact with her body was a shock to me. An impulse ran through me, my blood pressure shot up, and my heart pounded like crazy.

She must have felt my hand tremble. She didn't say anything - she just looked at me with a spark of a smile in her eyes, but she didn't withdraw her hand.

"Come on, let me show you the real ship where real sailors worked."

"There are no real sailors anymore?" She asked.

"There are," I replied. "But then the ships were wooden and the sailors were of steel. And now there are steel ships, and the seamen of wood," I said.

"Why?"

"It's a longer story. I'll tell you another time."

"Do you think you'll have the opportunity?"

I was confused. The more that I was holding her hand the whole time. I felt the warmth of her palm. Her slender, delicate fingers hold my arm and didn't seem to want to let go of it.

"It depends on you."

This time she was silent.

Maybe that was because we were just climbing the gangplank to the deck of a sailing ship. I didn't use the guide. I myself showed Kinga around the sailing ship, briefly telling its story.

It was already late. We were the last tourists to leave the deck of the "Dar Pomorza".

Christopher and Ula got lost somewhere - they weren't with us on the frigate.

"What now? How do we find them?" I felt the concern in her voice. She looked around, seeking for the silhouettes of Ula and Christopher.

"I think they're here in the restaurant. In The Rose of the Winds," I told her soothingly.

"Come on, let's check it," she urged me.

I knew Christopher, I knew that he didn't like walking and sightseeing. He had already visited everything. He knew every object worth seeing in the square. He didn't use to go to fast food bars, and since it was the closest to the "Rose of the Winds", he probably dragged Ula there. It was a large restaurant almost at the very end of Kosciuszko Square. The only one of this type.

It was situated in a building on the first floor of which there was a large passage hall, leading from the middle of the alley to the right wharf. In the hall, there were offices, White Sailing counters, and a few souvenir stands. A crowd of colorfully dressed people was flowing constantly. Children screamed as they ran up the stairs to the other side of the square. The entrance to the "Rose of the Winds" was outside of the building, in the middle of the promenade. You walked quite high up the steep stairs leading to the building. As we walked up those stairs, Kinga took my hand.

"Hold me so I don't fall," she pleaded, turning to face me.

I took the opportunity and put my other hand around her waist. It wasn't necessary at all, because she was good at wearing high heels. "What does it mean?" I thought.

The hall upstairs was full.

"All tables are full," the manager of the room informed us, and the bouncer standing next to us clearly wanted to translate his words by hand, when Kinga tried to go inside anyway.

"They're not here," she said, surveying the interior with her eyes.

"Are Christopher with "LUCY" here?" I asked the manager.

I knew that almost all restaurateurs in the Tri-City knew Christopher.

"Oh! Mr. Christopher is here. Why didn't you say so?"

I shoved into his hand the money for the pass.

"Please follow me." He led us inside with a servile smile on his face.

He guided us to the end of the room. Christopher was sitting at the best table that was always reserved for VIPs, and he definitely was one.

"Where were you?" He asked. It was evident that he was having a great time with Ula. "Stay for the dancing," he asked, "you are my guests."

The girls exchanged knowing glances.

"We're going to the toilet," said Ula.

"What is Kinga like?" He asked as the girls disappeared from sight.

"You know ... something amazing. She makes a huge impression on me," I replied.

"Just don't fall in love," Christopher knew my love experiences.

"Vice versa. And what's Ula like?" I asked.

"She's a very nice girl. Cool, casual, and she knows what she wants."

"And what does she want?"

"Have fun and get the best out of life," he replied.

"How do you know that?"

"She told me," he replied with his gaze wandering around the room.

The girls were back.

"We can stay until 11:00 pm or 5:00 in the morning," Kinga said as they sat down at the table.

"We live in Tczew and we have to get there somehow," added Ula.

"Alright. We will arrange for you a return to your house in Tczew at the time you want," I declared.

"We don't live permanently in Tczew, we stay there temporarily with our family, but it is quite troublesome," said Ula in a melancholy voice. She was sitting next to Christopher, leaning on his shoulder.

The waiter brought us a menu card. Kinga leaned over so that I could read with her, even though the second menu card was on the table. I looked at her cleavage involuntarily. She noticed my gaze and smiled confusedly but she didn't back away. Startled, I stared at the menu, even though I didn't really need it to place my order.

I noticed Kinga didn't know what to order. She hesitated, looking at the prices. It wasn't cheap there.

"Go ahead," I said.

"Help me."

"What do you like?"

"I don't go to restaurants… often," she added. "I leave it to you."

She probably didn't want to decide because of the prices that could shock ordinary people.

"You're at the seaside. We'll start with an appetizer."

"Alright," she agreed meekly.

I assumed the girls were hungry, and I wanted a good meal myself, so I ordered smoked eel, salmon with lemon, and eggs with caviar, and then a plate of Pomeranian cooked meats. When we moved on to the second course, Kinga asked:

"Order the borscht with dumplings."

There was terror in her voice.

"And what about broccoli cream soup with croutons?" I asked.

"You can order," she replied.

For the main course, a battered halibut with a set of salads, and a glass of white semi-dry wine. Vodka and snacks were already ordered by Christopher.

Kashubian herring, which he liked very much, an eel in jelly, some shrimp salads and Provencal mussels in curry sauce, arrived on the table at a rapid pace. He wouldn't have been himself if he didn't fool around and order a portion of snails. After the order was fulfilled, the waiter discreetly stood next to us and kept our table in order. Christopher signalized him with his finger when he wanted the waiter to pour alcohol into our glasses.

At the suggestion of Ula, they ordered for the second course roast wild boar with beetroot, buckwheat and red cabbage. Christopher was telling something Ula, who burst out laughing every now and then. She had such a contagious laugh that when you heard it, you wanted to laugh too.

I talked with Kinga about the beach, such a loose topic.

I listened to her voice. She told that she enjoyed to lie on the sand and sunbathe. Her voice was slightly raised, she shouted over the playing orchestra.

Suddenly her question reached me:

"How old are you?"

"I'm thirty and a bit," I replied. I didn't give her the exact age.

"You don't look that old," she said. "I would say twenty-six or twenty-eight at most."

"Wow," I thought, "does she really think so, or want to justify the fact that she is here with me? I'm probably old for her generation."

Kinga was no more than twenty-two. I didn't ask her about her age because earlier, when talking about the beach, she said that she had graduated last year. I didn't know what school, and I didn't care.

"Does that bother you?" just in case, I wanted to get her acceptance of the situation.

"No, it doesn't at all," she said too eagerly to hide her disappointment. Maybe she thought I was younger, but destroyed by the sea?

"And you must be twenty," I said sweetly.

"Something like that."

This time Kinga didn't want to say how old she was. Probably so as not to reveal the age difference that separated us.

Christopher hold court on the dance floor with Ula. They interrupted their meal to dance. They were doing quite well. I waited for Kinga to finish eating. I enjoyed too much watching her do it. Gently, with a certain amount of uncertainty, she put the caviar on a teaspoon and put it in her mouth. Her pink lips leaned back to reveal white gleaming teeth. There could be seen a grimace. She mechanically crumpled the napkin, fearing that if she didn't like it, she would have spat it out into the napkin, but her face suddenly brightened. She must have felt the delicate taste of crushed by teeth roe balls, and the fishy aftertaste melting like ambrosia on the tongue and palate, too delicate to set the tone, but distinctive enough to feel it. I already knew that it was the first time she was eating it.

"Do you like it?" I asked.

"Yes," she replied, nodding her head.

"Be careful, it has a strong libido effect."

"Are you kidding? For women too? I thought it was only for guys," she added after a short pause.

"Check it out for yourself," I teased, but she didn't take it up.

The orchestra played "Captain's Tango".

"Would you like to dance?" I asked.

"I thought you would never make up your mind," she replied, standing up.

I was a bit scared, because I wasn't good at "this stuff", but I couldn't resist - I was too anxious to dance with her.

We went to the dance floor. There I gallantly kissed her hand and embraced her.

I tried to lead the dance lightly and calmly. She danced freely, without the tension which was in me. I tried to hide it, but she probably sensed that I was tense and hugged me with her whole body.

"Don't be afraid, I don't bite," she said.

"It's a pity, it could be nice too, as long as it doesn't hurt," I said.

Suddenly I felt a slight bite of her teeth on my neck and the warmth of her lips.

"Was it pleasant and not painful?" She asked, looking at me with an innocent smirk as if nothing had happened.

Slightly shocked, I replied:

"It tasted, I'm asking for more ..."

"Maybe, maybe someday," she said with her body clinging to me.

We had danced to the standard three orchestral pieces before it took a break.

We returned to the table, and I watched with pleasure as Christopher openly adored Ula. It was evident that she succumbed to his charm with pleasure. We drank alcohol. Christopher and I had vodka, and the girls had drinks.

Kinga, looking with a surprised gaze at the waiter bustling beside us, asked:

"Why is this waiter still standing next to us? There's nobody at the other tables?" - It was obvious to me, because Christopher was sitting at it.

"That's his job," Christopher replied.

The truth was, however, that the waiters knew Christopher and were aware that it would have benefited them if he remembered them, because if they had to change jobs, they could have applied at his company. Besides, he always left them a generous tip.

The orchestra started playing some cuddly melodies.

"Come on, Richie," Kinga said and took my hand. On the dance floor, she snuggled up to me quite comfortably, resting her head lightly on my shoulder.

Her breasts pressed against me. She took my hand and slid it from her back onto her waist so that I could hug her tighter. I felt the heat flooding me.

"Love me, love me," she hummed together with the soloist, looking at me significantly, or maybe that's just what it seemed to me?

As we walked back to the table, she didn't release my hand from hers until we sat down at it. I tried to be gallant and held her chair as she sat down, but I really used it with pleasure to look down from above her head at her cleavage - at her shapely breasts. I knew that she knew I was looking there because every time I handed her a chair, I leaned forward and brushed her cheek with my lips saying: "thank you for the dance."

"Pervert," her eyes said as I sat down next to her.

"At midnight, the summer hit of 'Rose of the Winds', striptease," Christopher said in a deep, slightly mysterious whisper.

We were all in good spirits and we were waiting with interest for the performance. Two scantily clad girls and one guy in a fiery orange leotard ran onto the dance floor.

"Fireman, or what?" Ula asked.

As they undressed to the music, he breathed fire and juggled flaming torches. Christopher loudly commented:

"The one with the red fake hair has nice breasts and long legs. The latter sucks."

Ula bravely echoed him to suddenly blurt out:

"Mine are bigger," she turned to Christopher.

"Really?" He became interested as if he hadn't seen what was hidden under Ula's blouse.

I thought I was going to hear "check it" but I didn't. Keeping in mind Christopher's character, I knew that he would do it anyway, it was only a matter of time.

Kinga took my hand.

"Why are they doing this?" She asked.

"Probably for money," I said. "They can have three or four performances in one evening."

"I couldn't do it, but don't think that I condemn them."

We danced and had fun until four in the morning. With considerable effort so as not to fall over, we went downstairs, where taxis were already waiting for customers like us. There, after a few minutes, I agreed with Kinga that we would meet in Sopot in front of the pier after a few days and we would go to the beach.

Christopher called a taxi. He arranged a course with the driver to Tczew, paid in advance and when the girls were getting in, he said to the driver:

"I have your number, please drive them home politely."

"Of course!" replied the driver, glad that he had such a windfall. "You can be completely calm."

As I was bidding farewell to Kinga, she rested her hands on my shoulders and kissed me lightly on the lips, saying:

"Thank you for a beautiful evening."

"I thank you, I haven't felt like this for a long time."

"How?" She asked.

"As in the good old days," I blurted out. "Holy shit," I thought, "what are you talking about?!"

At the same time, I slipped my phone number into her hand, which I had written on a napkin.

"Let me know when you get there, I'll be waiting."

I already knew from Ula that the girls were looking for a job and a dwelling in the Tricity. Christopher promised them that he would look for something for them.

We stood with Christopher for a moment, exchanging our observations about the girls and the chances for further closer relations.

It seemed that Ula would be happy to stay with Christopher, but it was not appropriate for Kinga to return to Tczew alone - because of her family, of course. It was well past five when Kinga called.

"Richie? Were you sleeping?"

"No. I've been waiting for a call from you."

"I'm already on the spot. Do you have something to write?" She asked.

"Yes."

"Then write down my aunt's phone number," she said and gave me the number. "Call me when you want," she added in a sleepy voice. "Good night, I need to sleep," I heard.

All morning and afternoon she slept away the dance evening.

Christopher called after two days. We hadn't seen each other since the dancing.

"I hired Ula at my company," he said at the outset, as if he had been afraid that I would ask him about it. I learned from him that he hooked up with Ula. "For Kinga, there is also a place in my restaurant," he added.

"No thanks," I said. "I'm already seeking something for her."

At that time, I was intensively looking for a job for Kinga. I met her after a few days.

It was probably Wednesday. Kinga called me at home and we made an appointment for the morning in Sopot. I was waiting for her at the entrance to the pier. She came on time. I was curious how she would behave and if the charm of dancing at "The Rose of the Winds" hadn't disappeared together with the morning mist blowing from the bay side, which was enveloping us at that time.

"Hello," she said fondly with a hint of stage fright in her voice.

It was obvious she didn't know how to act, but she bravely approached me and kissed my cheek.

"I'm glad to see you, I missed you," I said calmly. "All the time I thought you wouldn't want to see me anymore."

"Why did you think so?"

"You know why. You are beautiful, young, and I'm already getting on in years."

"It's nothing, years don't matter, but feelings," she replied and took my hand.

We walked on the alley along the beach until we passed a Chinese restaurant. Right after, we turned left, between the dunes. Kinga was wearing an airy summer dress, and on her feet, she had some sandals.

In her hand she was holding a large purse, quite tasteful, matching the color of the outfit. I had a blanket with me which I had taken from the car. I put it on the edge of the beach, under the dunes, so that no one could lie down behind us. She pulled out a large towel and quickly took off her dress. She was in a one-piece swimsuit with a string wrapped around her neck from behind, holding the bra. She lay down beside me and asked:

"You're not working now?"

"No," I replied, "I have dog days until the next contract."

"How long?" She asked.

"Usually three or four months," I explained to her.

"And what are these contracts?" she continued the topic.

"See, I don't really have a permanent job. A contract is an agreement I sign before I go to the ship. An agreement between me and the company that owns the ship, i.e. the shipowner or the shareholders representing it. In short, it says for how long, for what money and in what position I will work there, as well as the shipowner's commitment that after the end of the contract it will send me home at its own expense."

"You know, Richard, in our town there is no vacancy. I mean, where I live, there is no way of finding anything. Unless you have friends or a family that will hire you," she took up the topic. "That is why Ula and I decided to look for something in the Tri-City. Anything, even just for the season."

"And you don't want a permanent job?" I asked. It was difficult for me to ask what she could do. But Kinga is smart, she sensed immediately what I meant.

"I graduated an economic high school and I study part-time."

"Well ... Maybe I will be able to help you. I promise I will do my best, and soon," I said, looking into her eyes.

I figured girls were having a hard time.

"Ula already has a job in the restaurant. Christopher got her it. She began Monday as a waitress," she commented my words with a hint of jealousy in the voice. "But I don't want to work as a waitress."

"I guess you don't," I replied. We considered the topic completed. She took my hand and, laughing, screamed:

"First come, first served!"

We ran and, holding hands, we fell into the water. We ran on, but slower, as if in slow motion, overcoming the resistance of the waves pouring through our bodies. When we were half-submerged, ridiculously bouncing in front of each frothy breaker approaching, I felt like a teenager again.

"Do I have the right to be with her?" the thought tugged at me, but I quickly dismissed my doubts, justifying myself with the slogan: 'everyone has the right to happiness.' I felt happy again.

Kinga crouched in the water, sinking herself up to the neck. Her hair was in a bun, which made her swan neck seem longer than it really was. The water ran down her body, marking every recess of her body, and remaining in water droplets on her shoulders and décolleté. Laughing, she took my hand and, jumping up, dragged me into the sea.

"How well are you swimming?" I asked.

"I can swim a little bit," she replied, "but I have a sailor with me, so I'm not afraid."

"Did you know that it would be better for a sailor not to know how to swim?"

"Why?" She wondered, looking at me suspiciously. "Are you kidding me?"

"Because when the wave washes him into the sea, and he is several dozen or several hundred miles away from the shore, he will not tire, but will sink quickly," I replied.

"Don't make fun of me. I'll be afraid for you."

"What does it mean?" I thought again.

"But I swim a little bit!" I calmed her, because she was already pulling me towards the shore.

In fact, I swam very well. In my youth, I earned some extra money working as a lifeguard on the beach.

"Lie on the water and hold on to my arms," I said, and showing off, I towed her into the sea. After several dozen meters, she got scared and let go of me, saying:

"We're going back to the shore. You snooze, you lose!"

"I'll give you a head start - swim."

When she was close to the shore and she felt the ground under her feet, I moved towards her. I crawled like the good old days, taking a sip of air from under my arm every other arm stroke. I was approaching her quickly. She didn't manage to reach the shore when, just before the second reef, I caught up with her and pulled her legs. She fell into the water. I grabbed her arms and yanked her up. She hung on me, wrapping her arms around me, hugged me and kissed me on the lips, lengthening the kiss so that there was no doubt that it wasn't just a momentary peck.

We walked back to shore embraced like a couple. Kinga dried herself with a towel and lay down on her stomach. In a moment, when her skin was dry, she reached into her bag and pulled out the sunscreen.

"With sun protection," she said. "Please smear my back."

I put some cream on my hand and began to lubricate her back with circular motions. Much of the body didn't have to be smeared because most of it was covered by the bathing suit.

"You have delicate hands. Now it's my turn."

I was lying on my stomach, feeling her hand overcome the resistance of my skin, which was getting slippery with cream. It was quite a nice feeling. We lay a little longer, baking in the sun. Kinga was rubbing against me every now and then as she turned towards the sun, and when she settled down, she took my hand and held it, pressing lightly with her fingers. She told me where she come from and where she lives.

It was evident that she was waiting for a returning and confessions from me, but I was not ready for it yet. I sat down on the blanket and said to Kinga, looking into her eyes, which I couldn't see because they were covered with large, dark sunglasses:

"Let's go eat and drink something."

I knew, however, that Kinga saw me perfectly.

I myself had my famous mirror shades on my nose so that I could look at her without embarrassment. We were walking barefoot with shoes in our hands. I had the blanket thrown over my hand. My car was parked nearby. It was maybe fifty yards from the alley we had come out of. Surprisingly, I was able to find a free parking space when I arrived there that morning. I had the large car then, just right for me. I have liked such cars. I have never gone nuts for any luxury brands. I threw Kinga's blanket and bag inside and we went to the pier.

Kinga stood in line for tickets. I let her buy them. Maybe it would make her feel better. We walked on the pier, but it was hot and there was no breeze from the sea, so we quickly returned onto Heroes of Monte Cassino street.

"I'm hungry. What would you like to eat?"

"Pizza," she replied.

"Okay, then come on," I said, taking her hand. We walked up the promenade to the pizzeria. After we ate and slaked our thirst, we went down. I took Kinga to House Center, where you could drink great coffee under an umbrella.

"How do you like this mime?" I asked after we sat under the umbrella. The artist was giving a performance in front of us.

"He's funny, but it probably have cost him a lot of work. And isn't he too hot in this outfit sometimes?"

He was dressed in a black tuxedo and matching pants, and his entire face was covered with white cosmetic paint. Large exaggerated lips completed his appearance.

"I suppose so," I said, "but it's a good school. At once he can see if he can get people's attention by what he does."

It was already afternoon. On the beach, Kinga told me that she had to come back to Tczew earlier that day and help her aunt with some work at home.

"I have to go now," she said. "Soon I have a train to Tczew."

"Do you want me to drop you off?" I offered.

"No, it's not necessary. I can handle it."

I walked her to the SKM station, and when her train came, I hugged her and kissed her cheek.

"I'll be waiting here for you until tomorrow."

"Don't talk nonsense, you don't miss me that much. You have known me for a short time."

"But intensely," I replied, when she was already getting on the train.

I dated Kinga regularly. We were at a cinema and on several walks. I already knew how to help her.

After a week, I called Kinga in the evening.

"Take all the documents tomorrow and come to Sopot at nine o'clock in the morning. You will go to a job interview.

I'll meet you at the station."

Chapter 5

Job

At nine in the morning I waited for Kinga in Sopot, on the platform, where long-distance trains arrive directly from Tczew. She left, wearing a white blouse, a black knee-length pleated skirt, and black pumps as appropriate.

"Hello!" She greeted in a cordial tone.

"I'm glad you're here. You look pretty, like a fresh high school graduate," I joked.

"Don't be silly, I want to do well."

"Yeah, yeah I know. If there is a guy in the personnel, you will sweep him off his knees, and looking at you, he will sign whatever you want," I laughed.

"Where are we going? She asked.

"To a bank," I said, wondering how it had happened that Kinga was going for this job interview.

I had a good friend, whom I met in Christopher's house during one of his famous parties with a roasted boar. He was one of the directors of the bank in Gdansk.

I called and made an appointment with him and his wife for dinner, which was, incidentally, quite nice. When I presented my request to him over the vodka, he immediately said:

"I'll get your girlfriend a job at any bank you want. Take your pick."

"That's what I told him about Kinga, but is she my girlfriend? I think not yet.

I chose the bank in Sopot to have Kinga at hand. And, secondly, it was a large state-owned company, where it is easier to hire someone. I gave him Kinga's surname. Two days later he called me.

"Let your girlfriend report directly to the human resources manager. They already know everything there. The manager was ordered to employ her."

I thanked him saying that I would pay him back accordingly.

"You already did. You're welcome. I'm glad I could help."

We drove to the bank in a car about five minutes. I stopped at the parking lot in front of a tall building and, walking along a wide passage under it, we entered its second part. In the car, I had calmed down Kinga.

"Don't worry, everything will be OK," I assured her.

"But what am I going to say there?" she was nervous.

"You will come in, greet the workers, introduce yourself and say: 'I'm here about a job interview in the personnel.' You can handle the rest. Right?" I asked.

"Yes, yes," she assured me.

"You will talk and we'll see what turns up," I said.

I was ninety-nine percent sure they would hire Kinga, but I didn't want to tell her that. I wanted her believe in herself when she got this job.

Various offices were housed in the building's spacious hall, but the first three or four floors were occupied by a bank. There was a bar to the left of the entrance.

"Come on," I said, embracing her with one arm. "Let's go in there. We still have time to ten o'clock.

It was the first time I saw that the girl at the information desk looked at me strangely. "What does she want?" ran through my mind.

"I'll order a coffee. Did you eat breakfast?" I asked Kinga, which with her head in the clouds, was sliding around the room with her gaze.

"Yes," she replied, "but I wouldn't be able to eat anything now," she told me in a slightly nervous voice.

"Listen," I told her, "don't be nervous. Imagine that your friends are working there and treat so those with whom you will talk to. They will sense it."

"Okay, okay," she replied, but I could see she was already inside with her thoughts.

I didn't realize then how hard experience it was for her and what stress she was undergoing at that time.

"I'll be waiting for you at the bar down here," I told her.

At ten o'clock punctually, we approached the personnel door, and I, without giving Kinga time for dilemma, knocked, opened the door and lightly pushed her towards the entrance.

She closed the door, but I could still hear her say:

"Good morning!"

Strangely, her voice was calm. After about ten minutes she came. I saw her happy face and a wide smile. She was holding some papers in her hand.

As she sat down, in a happy voice, with the speed of a machine gun, she chattered in one stroke:

"They hired me, they hired! I just have to fill out this questionnaire and give it back in the room next to the Human Resources."

"Take it easy," I said.

"I'm happy!" She continued in a high, happy voice.

"So when do you start?"

"August 1st."

"So we have two more weeks of vacation left," I thought.

"Tell me," I asked, looking into her laughing eyes.

"I went in," she reported very emotionally, "there were about five people sitting there, each behind a desk." I greeted them, introduced myself and said that I was here about the job. 'Wait a minute, please' said a woman at the first table, got up and went to the other room.

She came back in a moment and said:

'Please see the manager.' I walked in. There was only one desk in the room and some middle-aged woman who said to me:

'Please sit down. Do you have documents?'

'Yes,' I said, handing over my document folder.

She opened it, read the documents, and after a while she asked:

'You don't live here?'

'No, but it's not a problem. I will rent an apartment with my friend. She is from my hometown and she already has a job.'

"Yeah, yeah," she continued, leafing through the documents. You had an apprenticeship in a dairy after the graduation. What did you do there?'

'I helped with accounting,' I replied.

'Okay, okay,' she continued.

'When can you start working?' She asked.

My throat was dry due to nervousness. I could barely speak. 'It's so easy to get a job?' flashed through my mind. Oh, Richie, you must have had a hand in it. Fess up."

"Me? Nothing of the kind!" I denied it eagerly.

'So I tell her that right away.'

'That's good,' replied the manager. 'You'll start on August 1st. You will work as a cashier in the consumer department. Right over here, a friend will give you a circular. Please fill it in and leave it in room three hundred and twenty-one. All the necessary information will be provided to you by the boss of the department in which you will work. She got up, so did I, and we went into the other room. The manager said to the women working there:

'This is Ms. Kinga, she will work with us from August 1st. Please provide her with the relevant documents.'

I thanked her. She said goodbye and went to her room. The girls gave me the questionnaire and the circular, and said that when I filled them in, I should have returned them in the next room, where I would be told what to do next," she said in an excited voice, sipping a cool cola I had ordered earlier.

"I'm glad," I assured her.

"You don't even know how happy I am," she said, fidgeting in the chair.

"I see, I see."

"I have time until Tuesday to give back the questionnaire," she continued the interrupted thread, "Now we can go. I have to call home and tell them about it."

She put both hands around my face, approached me and asked:

"You got it for me?"

"Of course not," I lied again.

"Thank you anyway. You're loved," she replied, kissing me on the lips. She called from the payphone in the lobby. A moment later we were already in the car.

"What do we do?" I asked. "Why don't we go to the beach? I have the blanket in the car," I told her, driving through lower Sopot from the Sopot Wyscigi railway station.

"I've never been here," Kinga said, looking at the charming houses by the beach. "I don't have a swimming suit," she added after a moment.

"It's not a problem."

"No way. I won't bathe naked, and what I'm wearing is not suitable for the beach."

"I was driving along Mickiewicz Street towards Heroes of Monte Cassino street, looking for a free parking space. You only found it when you encountered a car that was just leaving.

Near the Grand Hotel I turned left into a side street, then left again - towards the promenade. A Jeep was leaving on my left. I parked in its place.

We took a bag with the blanket and went to Heroes of Monte Cassino street. Kinga immediately took my hand and held it tightly, as if being afraid that I might have run away from her.

"Richie, come on, let's buy newspapers," she asked. "I want to look for a place to live. There is not much time, and it is high season," she said in a voice full of excitement and joy.

"Yes, it will be difficult," I said. Suddenly, one thought struck me.

We bought newspapers and walked down Heroes of Monte Cassino street. It was interesting sight. Swift streams of people were mingling with each other. Everywhere were gardens with umbrellas, which, by shading the tables underneath them, gave illusory hope for a bit of coolness.

The heat was pouring down from the sky, and it was not yet noon. The whole body cried out, "coolness, I want coolness!" I put my arm around Kinga's waist saying:

"Come here," and I dragged her with me.

"What for?" She asked, but didn't resist.

"You will see."

We went inside. It was one of those exclusive boutiques at Heroes of Monte Cassino street, stocked with that year's hits. The saleswoman approached us.

"How can I help you?"

Kinga was silent, looking at me suspiciously.

"Some swimwear for this lady, please," I said to the saleswoman, pointing at Kinga.

"I don't want it," Kinga said softly. "Don't be silly."

But I persisted and, picking over the clothes on hangers, I twirled them, looking for something suitable for Kinga and asking every now and then:

"Maybe this one?"

"I don't want any swimsuit," she replied, but I kept fumbling. Finally she overcame her reluctance and started looking through the clothes with me.

I noticed that for a long time she was looking at a lovely set of a two-piece swimsuit in a beautiful reddish color - just right for her.

"Do you like it?" I asked.

She glanced at the price.

"No," she replied. "It's too expensive for me."

"Nothing that is for you is too expensive," I whispered in her ear.

"They don't have my size ..." she tried again.

"Ma'am, choose the right size for this lovely girl," I said to the saleswoman.

She went to Kinga, they talked and after a moment Kinga was walking to the changing room.

I pretended I wanted to go in with her.

"I'll help you fasten the bra."

"Stay where you are," she replied, lightly pushing me away with her hand. "Maybe later," she added after a moment.

"Will you call me after you get dressed?"

"Yes," she replied, already behind the curtain.

After a while I heard:

"Come on, see how it fits."

I went inside. Kinga looked beautiful. In my opinion, the swimsuit was just right. The underwired bra lifted the bust a little, pulled the full breasts towards themselves and clang to them, preventing them from jumping out. The slightly cut lower part accentuated and lengthened the waist, giving Kinga the appearance of a professional model. She looked as if she had been about to go out onto a catwalk. The color of the swimming suit harmonized with her tan.

"I like it," I said.

"Me too," she replied.

"Then don't take it off."

And before she knew it, I tore the tag off the bra.

"It's too expensive for me!" She bridled.

"Expensive, because it's branded," I replied. "This is a gift from me for looking so pretty in it, for getting a job and for agreeing to go to the beach with me," I whispered in her ear. She hugged me for a moment.

"Thank you!"

I went inside the boutique and before Kinga got dressed, I paid for the swimsuit, talking to the girl at the cash desk so that Kinga would hear it:

"The swimming suit stays on the lady."

"Please pass it, it's lady's," she replied, handing me a small plastic bag with the symbol of the bathing suit company.

I handed it to Kinga, who was just coming out of the dressing room, stuffing her clothes into her purse. After less than ten minutes, we were lying on the beach, browsing the advertisements in the newspaper.

"It would be good to find an apartment close to the workplace," said Kinga, leafing through the newspaper we had bought earlier at the kiosk. "Ula works in shifts, but it is also difficult for her to commute from Tczew.

There were a couple of ads that we marked, but they came from brokers.

After about three hours of baking in the sunshine, interrupted by repeated cooling of the heated body in sea water, we decided to go to the office intermediating in the renting of apartments.

"General Anders Street," I read in one of the ads. I know where it is. Let's go there.

On the spot, it turned out that in order to receive the necessary addresses, a so-called fee must have been paid. Quite a lot for providing information with no guarantee that it will be useful.

"It's weird," I said. You really paid sight unseen, knowing nothing.

"And what if we don't take advantage of the offers?" I asked the lady who served us.

"We will keep looking," was the practiced answer. "You cannot count on the return of the money paid, this is our cost."

We agreed with Kinga that they would look for a small two-room apartment or something similar as close to the workplace as possible.

Kinga made up her mind and paid for this dubious piece of information.

I looked through the offers proposed by the office, because Kinga relied entirely on me, knowing that I know Sopot. I chose two offers.

"We'd like to see these apartments," I said, giving the addresses we were interested in.

"When?" Asked the lady from the brokerage office.

"If it's possible, even right now," Kinga replied.

"It's not far, I can give you a lift," I interrupted.

"There's no such need, my friend will go."

She called a young girl.

"Show our clients the apartments."

The first one was in lower Sopot, near the medical clinic.

After ten minutes we were there. It was a "teacher's" skyscraper. That was what the inhabitants called it, probably because it was a Teacher Housing Cooperative. Fifth floor, neat staircase and intercom. The apartment was a bit neglected and it should have been be repainted. There was a small stove, a larger room and a smaller one. The bathroom only had a shower and a washbasin, but it was covered with light pink tiles almost to the ceiling. Beside there was a small toilet and a little corridor with a closet. The shelves above the ceiling crowned "a product of real communism" with the slogan: "all for the people."

The furniture was modest but quite neat. There was a corner sofa bed in the large room. It was evident that it was a set you could sleep on.

There were also a little sideboard, a table and four chairs in the corner, and a nice wicker rocking chair. By the window there was a small table with a vase, probably for the TV set, I thought, looking at the cables hanging nearby. In the smaller room there was a chair-bed, a table and two small armchairs. There was a small space by the wall, next to the window, which was filled with a fairly tall, glass-enclosed mini-bar with shelves and drawers. The furniture was in good condition - you can see that it had been recently bought.

"I'll repaint it, clean it up and it will be alright," Kinga rejoiced.

"One advantage, and a great one," I said to Kinga, "is that it takes ten minutes to get to your workplace on foot."

"Really? Then we take it," declared Kinga.

"And you don't want to see the other apartment?"

"Where is it?" She asked.

At the other end of Sopot - Kamienny Potok. From there you will have to commute a few stops to work.

"I take it," she said again.

"Ula will have to commute to work by bus or trolleybus, but it is very close to the stop," I assured Kinga.

"I talked to Ula and she relies entirely on me. I mean on you," she corrected herself.

"Did you make up your mind?" the girl from the agency struck while the iron was hot.

Kinga looked at me for confirmation. I nodded.

"Yes," she replied.

"Since when?"

"Since now, if it's possible."

"Then we will sign a contract, write down the meter readings and, after the owner's approval, you will be able to move in."

Kinga didn't correct her statements about future tenants. We went back to the office. There Kinga went into shock. The kind lady forgot to inform us that we needed to pay a deposit in the amount of three months' rent, and the rent for the apartment was payable in advance. Four-month fee in total. I was looking at Kinga thinking she was about to cry.

"Wait outside," I said, pulling Kinga aside. I'll talk to the manager, maybe something can be done.

She came out sad.

"I will pay for everything," I told the manager. "But please don't tell the girl anything and give me the confirmation of the payment separately. Is it possible?"

"No problem, sir," she replied.

I took money out of my wallet and paid for everything in one go. I got a receipt and went to Kinga saying:

"You got it. You only have to pay monthly rent and utilities from mid-September. Satisfied?"

She threw herself on my neck, kissing me, or rather pecking me, and thanking me every now and then.

"Come on, sign the contract and get the keys."

She handled the paperwork quickly, while I was sitting on the couch, innocently watching her leaning over the desk and sticking out her ass while signing the documents. "She is lovely," I thought. "Ah, if only I could pull that dress up," I was obscene in my mind.

She took the keys and wanted to go to the apartment right away.

"Relax, we'll go there soon, let's just eat something, because I'm hungry," I objected, knowing that she probably hadn't eaten anything since that morning. "You probably too, sweetheart?" I blurted out.

"Seriously?" She asked.

"What: 'seriously'?" I pretended to be a fool.

"You said 'sweetheart', don't deny it."

"You don't even know how much," I replied, smiling at her. She knew I was serious.

"Why don't you tell me about this?"

"I didn't want to scare you."

"Silly ..." she said and hugged me.

We went to the International Cultural Center. I, unlike Christopher, liked to come there, but only for breaded chicken with fries and salad. We ate quite quickly, because Kinga really wanted to come back to the apartment to see it again calmly.

It was on my way, so I pulled up to the bank to show Kinga how to get back to the rented apartment. From the bank, we went straight down the main street, almost to the end, then we turned left, right, and we got there.

"It's very close indeed," Kinga said.

We went inside, and she immediately began to look around the apartment, poking around wherever she could and saying loudly:

"This will be painted, that will be cleaned up, the stove must be scrubbed because it is a bit run-down, and the oven has probably not been washed for ages."

I didn't want to spoil her mood, so I nodded meekly: "yeah, yeah, it can be done."

She finally sat down on the couch across from me. I moved closer to her, embraced her, and kissed her passionately. She kissed me back, hugging me gently.

"This is a good start," I prophesied.

"It's not enough for a start," she whispered, pressing against me. We kissed again.

My hand began to wander over her body. "Over safe terrain for now, but what will happen in a minute if we don't stop?" I thought and took my hand from her back. She stopped kissing me, sensing my dilemma.

"What's wrong?" She asked.

"Nothing," I replied, "one thought just has come to my mind."

"What?"

"Since when do you want to live here with Ula?"

"Preferably since now," she replied. "As soon as I arrange a transport to get all my stuff here. Ula probably too, but she works and won't have much time. It's high season and they have a lot of guests."

"I can go with you to Tczew right away and bring what will fit in the car."

"I have nothing there in Tczew, only the most necessary personal items. I have to go home."

"Then take my car and go." I knew she had a driver's license. She told me on the beach that she had been driving her father's minibus and the brakes had broken down.

She looked at me in that particular way, with the gaze of an incredulous child who has just been offered a toy.

"Are you kidding?"

"No, I'm not kidding at all."

"Go with me," she said.

"I would go gladly," I said, holding her hand and gently stroking it, "but I can't. I have to see a doctor in Gdynia tomorrow. I'm getting a new health certificate and I already have an appointment. It will take me half a day," I added. "It's well past six o'clock, it's getting late. If you need to go, it's time for you to leave," I was afraid to be alone with her for fear that we would end up in bed. I didn't want that - for now, I had to tell her about myself and my past first.

"Now I will go to Tczew, spend the night there, and in the morning, when Ula is free, we will go home to get all the things."

"OK, do what you think is right."

We went downstairs, holding hands. We walked over to the car. It was parked near the gate from which we came. Kinga pushed herself into the passenger seat.

"Where have you sat? Sit down here and drive."

"Okay," she replied and settled herself in the driver's seat. I showed her how to shift into reverse, where to press to turn on the lights. She moved.

She was doing pretty well, and I got rid of the fear that she wouldn't be able to handle it.

"We'll drive to the gas station, and then you'll give me a lift."

"Where do you live?" She asked.

"In Karwiny, at the exit to the bypass. From there, the way to Tczew is very easy, all the time straight to Lodz. We will refuel in Karwiny, there is a gas station next to my house.

She drove on.

"Do you see the figurine over there at the intersection? You will reach the stop lights and then turn left towards the cemetery."

She kept to the right lane. She was driving slowly but securely.

In Brodwino, on the serpentines, she strained the car a little while going uphill, but she quickly sensed the gears and continued to go smoothly.

We got to Karwiny, to a Shell gas station.

"Go and buy a map, I don't have one."

"What do I need a map for? I know the way."

I filled up the car. Paying for fuel, I bought Kinga a map, bars, and drinking water.

"You see, we are here," I showed the place on the map, "and half a kilometer from here is the entrance to the Tricity beltway. You should drive on it all the time to the end, and then turn slightly right, towards Tczew."

"I know," she replied, "I've taken this road a couple of times." Recently, by taxi," she reminded me. "I can handle it."

"I live here," I showed her a skyscraper that could be seen from the station, it was on the other side of the street.

"Won't you invite me?" She asked.

"Of course, I'm inviting you. Let's drive to the house."

"No, no," she withdrew, "I'd like to get home before dark. I'll come in another time," she added.

I didn't insist - for obvious reasons. We said goodbye somehow so quickly.

"Call me as soon as you get there," I said, hugging her. With one hand pushing back her hair, I kissed her gently on the neck. I gave her the car papers. She drove away, waving her hand at me. When I got home, I immediately took the phone and called Christopher, who was at work as usual.

"Is Ula there?" I asked.

"She is" he replied, "but in the second bar."

"When you see her, say that Kinga just rented an apartment for them in Sopot. A moment ago she went to Tczew by car.

"Mine," I added after a moment.

"Wow," I heard, "you fell for her.

But she's worth it," he assured me.

I briefly described him the situation.

"Alright, I will give Ula a day off and let her go with Kinga tomorrow. She'll be glad you when I tell her it."

"And how is it going with Ula?" I asked.

"Dude ... You don't ask such questions," he replied, joking. "He knows I'm married and separated," he added.

"Oh. And?"

"Nothing. It doesn't bother her. For now," after a second delay I heard his assurances.

"Don't believe the women. When they say that, it may be just the opposite," I said to him.

"Yeah, yeah, Richie. You are a disbeliever after your last ordeal, but you are right, it may be."

We also talked about nonsense and the fact that the dance party was worth repeating.

"Christopher! In that case, I invite you and Ula to "Niedzwiadek" in Kashubia this weekend. Will you be able to go?

I will book two rooms there. Just in case," I added.

"Hope we don't sleep together," I heard him laugh.

"Go without us, because it's hard for me to set a specific time at the moment. We'll get to you," he assured me.

"Great, so I'm waiting in Bear Cub."

I hung up. Well, everything was easy for Christopher, he didn't even say if he would ask Ula if she would go with him. But I had to ask Kinga. There were three days left until Saturday. I was lying and watching TV when the phone rang.

"I'm on the spot," I heard Kinga's voice. "Have you been nervous?"

"Yes," I said, "but only about you." I spoke with Christopher. Ula has a day off tomorrow so she can come home with you.

"Really? That's great!" she rejoiced.

"Kinga?" I asked. "Would you like to come with me to Kashubia this weekend? We would go with Christopher and Ula."

"Great, I'd love to go! And is there an occasion coming up that I don't know about? You haven't told me anything before."

"Yes, an occasion to be with you. How did you get there?" to change the subject, I kept asking.

She briefly told me how she had been going to Tczew.

"When I stopped in the parking lot in front of my aunt's house," she was singing, "she saw me through the window as I was getting out of the car. When I went upstairs, she asked:

'What car is it?'

'My friend's,' I said.

'Since when do friends give cars?'

'You know, auntie?' I said to her. 'That's not all. I got a job in a bank in Sopot, I start on August 1. I also rented a flat, I already have the keys,' I continued. "My aunt looked at me suspiciously with her eyes widening in surprise." 'When did you get all of this?' she asked, "and I told her that in one day," Kinga babbled to the receiver.

'Tomorrow I will go home with Ula to get things. You'll get out of our hair,' I told her. "My aunt was very happy that I found such a job. She immediately took the phone and called my mother, she's her sister," continued Kinga.

I listened to her voice with pleasure, it was still trembling with the excess of sensations.

"Richie," she said softly, I felt warmth in my soul, no one had talked to me like that for a long time. "I will be back the day after tomorrow at noon, you know, it will take me all day to pack, and at the night I'm afraid to go," she continued in the same tone.

"Okay, no problem. I can handle it, I will wait for you."

"I have to go. I'll call you tomorrow night from home," I heard.

"I'm kissing you strongly," she added after a moment. It was the first time she had said that to me.

"I'm also kissing you on those lovely lips," I replied, deliberately taking the same pause as her. After a while I added:

"And not only there ..."

"And where else?" I heard a soft whisper. I was stunned.

"Wherever you enjoy it," I continued to play those word games.

"Fine words butter no parsnips," she replied.

"Could it be an allusion to today's situation in the new apartment?" ran through my mind.

"I take your word for it," I heard Kinga's voice and her soft giggle.

"Good night," she said.

"Good night," I replied. "Take care of yourself," I added and hung up.

This conversation was very promising. I spent the next day visiting many doctors for the necessary examinations.

I didn't have time to visit all the doctors at once, so the next day I went to the dentist and ophthalmologist for a certificate. When tired, I dragged myself home from Gdynia, I immediately fell into my armchair. After a while the phone rang. It was Kinga calling from a gas station with the news that she was on her way and would be in Sopot after an hour. She asked if I would help her because she was alone. Ula had to leave home earlier, and the previous day she returned to her aunt in Tczew to be on time at work, at seven o'clock.

"Then drive to the gas station in front of the house, I'll be waiting."

I had an hour for myself. I freshened up quickly by taking a shower, then I got dressed and went downstairs. Kinga was already waiting. She was standing next to the car. She looked lovely in denim shorts and a skimpy tank top. The station guy almost flattened his nose as he clung to the windowpane while watching Kinga. I felt proud, I don't know why - after all, he wasn't staring at me. We greeted each other affectionately.

"Will you drive, Richie?" She asked, "I'm tired."

I got into the car, which was completely stocked with things and bags. The rear seats were unfolded, so probably everything the girls wanted to take could fit in the car.

We went to the apartment rented by Kinga. There I started unloading the car. Carrying the washing machine was the worst job, but some guy helped me to bring it inside. Good thing the elevator was working. I filled the whole elevator with the bags and clothes, and somehow carried it all inside.

Kinga immediately started unpacking the things. First, she pulled out some dishes to make us tea.

"You know what?" I said to her, "you keep fighting here, and I will pop out to the store. I'll buy something to eat and you'll make some tea before I get back."

In the store, I bought the most necessary products. I went back to the block and pressed the button on the intercom.

"Who's there?" I heard Kinga's voice.

"It's me, Richard."

There was Ula in the apartment, who had come back from work earlier. The spell was broken. We drank tea and talked about next day's trip to Kashubia.

"I won't bother you during the furnishing of the apartment. I will connect the washing machine and I'm off," I said to the girls. Kinga, who escorted me to the car, justified herself with disappointment:

"Ula was supposed to arrive late at night ..."

"It's okay," I said, "get some sleep and call me in the morning when you're ready to go. We have to leave by nine in the morning at the latest.

We will stay there until Sunday," I added after a while.

The next day around nine in the morning I started to get nervous. Kinga didn't come, she didn't call, and it was high time to go. It was difficult for me to book rooms in "Bear Cub". It was high season, and in addition weekend. I mentioned the name Chris, and I got two apartments - only such rooms were available. As it turned out later, they were apartments in name only.

I agreed with the boss of "Bear Cub" that he would keep the reservation of the rooms until noon, and then, if we didn't arrive, he would rent them to other guests. The phone rang at ten minutes past nine. Kinga told me that she was ready, that she was standing with a bag somewhere near a house next to a taxi stand, but she didn't know where it was, because she was looking for an active telephone and got lost.

"Don't be nervous, take a taxi to the gas station, it will be faster that way. Tell the driver to go to Karwiny, to Shell. I will be waiting there already.

After fifteen minutes the taxi arrived. First got out of it the long legs in high heels, then the denim shorts and finally Kinga with huge sunglasses, smiling. From the door of the taxi, she called out:

"I'm not late, am I?

"Of course not," I replied.

We got into the car and set off. I told her about myself all the way. I told her briefly about my failed relationship. I had been already divorced. We had broken up because of my job. The ex-girlfriend hadn't stood the test of time, and while I had been at sea, she had found other man. When I had gotten back, my suitcases had been already packed. I had experienced it calmly, because I had suspected something for a long time and had been basically prepared for it.

It was a monologue. Kinga didn't ask about anything.

When I finished, we were already entering Koscierzyna. She only spoke once:

"It's all sad."

We didn't come back to this topic for a long time. Only before my first voyage, when we were already living together in our new nest, she unexpectedly said to me:

"I will not betray you, Richie, don't be afraid. I can be faithful and I will wait for you."

In "Bear Cub" we were greeted by beautiful weather and a nice receptionist. There was a lot of laughter during a check-in.

The receptionist said to us:

"Here are the keys to your room upstairs. Will you also take the second keys for Mr. Chris?"

"Of course," I said, and with no intention of explaining who would sleep with whom, and in what room, we went upstairs.

We entered the apartment. First, we saw a simple corridor with a large closet, small cabinets with shelves and a mirror with a small chest of drawers. It didn't make a special impression. From there you entered a spacious living room with an imposing sofa and two large armchairs by the wall, with a rectangular table between them. A large TV screen with speakers standing next to it looked at us from the opposite direction. In a word: standard. We entered the next room, where we were greeted by a Kashubian bedroom decor with a wooden bed. On either side of it were bedside tables and a beautiful fluffy rugs on the floor. To the left of the entrance, in the bedroom, was a second door. I looked inside.

"Bathroom," I informed Kinga.

We went back to the living room. Kinga looked at the porch.

"It's beautiful here!" She exclaimed.

We were hungry, slightly sweaty and most of all nervous. This was the first time we had found ourselves in such a situation. I started unpacking things. I pulled out my clothes from the bag. I put a large towel over my shoulder and said to Kinga:

"I'm going to take a shower."

"Alright," she replied.

Before entering the bathroom, I approached her and gave her the keys to the second apartment, saying:

"You have a choice."

"I won't use it," she replied and hugged me, tossing the keys on the table.

The bathroom was large for a guesthouse of this class. It had a bathtub, separate shower and interesting decor. It was very clean, everything glistened.

"It's probably especially for tourists from Germany who come here often. For them, everything has to be polished to a high gloss," I thought as I stepped into the shower. I soaped my entire body and hair. I didn't hear Kinga enter the bathroom.

"Move over," I heard her voice behind me.

It wasn't confused at all, just warm and inviting. I tried to open my eyes, but there was foam on them and they pricked quite badly.

After I washed them, I felt Kinga spreading a gel on my back in smooth, circular movements, to, after a while, sliding her hands on my stomach, lower and lower, at the last moment move them to my thighs.

"Is she ashamed, or she's doing it on purpose?" I thought. My hands were against the wall. I succumbed to these caresses with the lascivious thought: "What will happen next?" When I felt that I was already excited in a way that was obvious to her, I turned to face Kinga. She hugged me. We started kissing each other passionately and greedily, as if it had been a reward for our restraint.

I stood behind her. I started to spread the gel all over her body. However, I didn't withdraw my hands. They reached every recess of her body. I didn't want this first time to be in the shower, so I took Kinga in my arms and carried her to the bedroom. Water dripping off us made marks on the floor.

I gently laid her on the bed. It was large and had a soft, comfortable mattress. The sheets smelled nice of lavender. Kinga's eyes were slightly closed.

"Are you ashamed?" I asked.

"A bit, you look at me so greedily." She raised her hands and put them on the pillow behind her head. Her breasts rose first, then lazily sank, flattening slightly. We made love nervously - I didn't know anything about her body and needs. Back then, she didn't tell me what she liked. We finished quickly. Lying naked on the bed, cuddled to each other, we were silent for a long moment. Eventually, without dressing up, Kinga got up and went to the porch, grabbing a towel and wrapping herself up in it on the way.

"How lovely it is!" She exclaimed. "Come see it!"

I stood behind her, putting my arms around her waist. In front of us there was a slightly sparse wood. From our balcony, we could see a lake among the trees. Its surface was covered with fast-moving reflections of the sun, which, lying low above the horizon, stroked its depths, and bouncing off the water, it gave the illusion that it was about to sink into its abyss. The sound of the wind liltingly breaking through the spruce branches and jasmine bushes as well as the scent of wild roses growing nearby made Kinga not want to return to the room.

"Come on, let's go for a walk," I asked.

We dressed quickly and left the guesthouse. We spent the afternoon strolling, and then we went down to the restaurant to feed our hungry bodies. The dinner we had was delicious, and we also drank a whole bottle of wine. Warmed up by the walk, wanting to rest before the dancing, we went back to our room and lay down on the bed. Now it was me who started the mating spectacle.

I courted to Kinga like the capercaillie to his female. I tried to excite her and prepare her with words, describing my impressions. We didn't speak then about emotions, but only about sensations.

"I like you ..." I whispered passionately in her ear, teasing it with the tip of my tongue, only to move it gently over the skin behind the ear. "Close your eyes," I asked, and as she did, I picked up her T-shirt, whispering:

"Do I see well? Or maybe I'm just dreaming about it? Do these wonders belong to me?" I asked, kissing her protruding nipples. Taking them in my mouth, I teased them with my tongue.

"No, it's impossible ..." I said, and I paused to, having heard the soft: "yes, they are yours, only yours," start all over again.

Kinga was clearly enjoying this game. I continued sliding my mouth down. I asked:

"Do I have a clear path? There is no barrier here?

Or maybe I need a pass?"

"You already have it!" She replied, tensing her body and lifting her belly up. I moved my lips even lower. I stopped at the navel: "Is this what you are waiting for? No, probably not," I answered to myself, kissing and caressing this beginning of everything. I moved my lips lower and lower, running the tip of my tongue over her delicate, fragrant skin. I sensed her excitement. At the last minute, however, I skipped what she was waiting for and kissed the inside of her thighs. They were wonderfully velvety and soft like Indian silk. I told her what I felt:

"You are beautiful, wonderful, I'm crazy about you!" and going all the way down to her feet, I kissed her toes, starting with the smallest one. She couldn't stand it.

She tucked her legs up, grabbed me with them and drawing me to her, she said in a passionate whisper, as she had done then on the dance floor in the Rose of the Winds:

"Love me, love me!"

We still made love greedily, but without the sense of shame that Kinga hid in the deepest recess of her soul.

It gave us great joy and satisfaction discovering our needs and sensations. We tried to synchronize so that the ending was simultaneous and profound, although Kinga said:

"Take your time, take your time ..."

To some extent, we succeeded.

Relaxed, with devils in her eyes, she dressed for the dance in a low-cut dress, under which she didn't wear a bra, and whose end of the neckline, or perhaps the beginning, almost reached the navel.

Kinga's breasts were covered only on the left and right sides, all the rest was jostling, trying to free itself from the material covering them. The dress flowed down, tightly hugging the waist, to take the shape of a wine glass upside down at the bottom. The bare back was cut up to the middle of the waist by two narrow ribbons crossed in the middle, flowing from the shoulders to the neckline.

"Look," she showed me the dress, turning around quickly. The flared bottom of the dress lifted strongly, revealing her almost bare buttocks and a skimpy piece of fabric at the front.

"If you're going to dance dressed like this, I think I'll call security, because I won't be able to drive the guys away from you, and I want to dance the evening away with you!

"But you like me?"

"Of course! You are beautiful and all the guys in the room will envy me."

She liked that answer because she came up to me saying:

"Now we can go."

It was high time to go downstairs and take up some booth.

The dance hall in "Bear Cub" was divided into booths and free-standing tables. Opposite the entrance was a dance floor and a place for an orchestra. The booths were separated from each other by a high wall covered with purple fabric. A solid wooden table and two benches could comfortably accommodate four people. To the right of the entrance was a stylish bar, well stocked with a variety of drinks.

Kinga and I were sitting in a booth by the window, near the orchestra that was just setting up the instruments.

"There is a soloist," I said to Kinga. "I don't know why, but for me an orchestra without a soloist isn't very interesting. I like when a woman sings.

"What would you like to drink?" I asked, as a waitress dressed in a folk Kashubian costume was approaching us.

"I want champagne," I added. Only champagne can complete such a successful beginning of the afternoon," I said, smiling at Kinga.

The dance floor was still empty when the band started playing "Summer, Summer" - the hit of the season.

I poured the champagne into glasses and, handing it to Kinga, I said:

"To the days we have spent together."

"To the wonderful moments during these days," she replied. I didn't know yet how prophetic these words were.

We drank up. I could feel the taste of champagne. Decently cool, it brushed my palate with bubbles, driving my taste buds to ecstasy.

"Do you like it?" I asked Kinga, nibbling on my favorite champagne side dishes, fresh strawberries, and at the same time putting the fruit to Kinga's mouth, saying:

"Try it."

We were so occupied with each other that we didn't notice when Christopher approached us.

"Are you in office already? Do you have the keys to our room?"

I went with him to the reception where Ula was standing. Giving him the keys to their room, I whispered:

"Kinga is in my room."

"No problem," he replied. He took the keys and they left.

After about half an hour he came with Ula. They joined us.

"What took so long? We have been waiting for you for an hour."

Christopher was elegantly dressed as usual - in that year's hit of the season, a cream sports jacket without a lining, as well as linen pants and leather shoes. Under his jacket he wore a short T-shirt whose color stood out from the rest.

Ula was beautifully dressed as well, and talkative as usual.

She barely sat down, and she began to tell how fast Christopher had driven his Merc.

"She squealed at every major bend," added Christopher.

I imagined it. I knew how Christopher could drive a car. I was always afraid to go with him on a longer trip, because he was racing as if he had been taking part in some kind of rally. It must have made a great impression on Ula. She was sitting next to Christopher, leaning against his side and whispering something in his ear.

"Hey," said Kinga, "what are the secrets at the shared table?"

"Nothing, nothing, we're just discussing if I can have a day off tomorrow."

The orchestra began to play. I asked Kinga to dance. We had a great time, dancing in circles together every now and then. Christopher quite often danced with Kinga. Hugging her, he waved his hand at me so that she wouldn't see it. But it was seen by Ula, with whom I danced then, willy-nilly. Ula in the dance was very predatory. I didn't dance as well as Christopher and it was hard to tame her. We had fun until dawn. Not feeling our legs, we collapsed into bed, after taking a quick shower together. In the morning we were greeted by the sun shining from under the lowered blinds.

While still having fun, Christopher said that he had to go back to work in the morning.

Ula had a day off, so we agreed that she would stay and come back with us. We got up around noon. I put on white pants with an equally white short T-shirt. I looked out the window, but Christopher's car wasn't there anymore.

"He's gone," I said to Kinga.

"So I'm going to Ula. Order breakfast, we will come soon."

Sipping coffee alternating with blackcurrant juice, I waited in the restaurant for half an hour before the girls showed up, but it was worth it.

Both refreshed, made-up, dressed like twins - in shorts and identical T-shirts - looked great. We ate the breakfast we had ordered quickly, because the buffet had already been cleared. None of us had a hangover. Me, Kinga and Ula only had drunk champagne, and Chris had drunk hardly at all. He had needed only one drink for the whole night.

From "Bear Cub", from the dining room, one could go directly outside through a doorway overlooking a beautifully arranged lawn. Down to the lake, led large and wide stairs, which gently sloped down to the road crossing the space between the guesthouse and the lake. We went down the stairs and, crossing the street, we walked to the lake, to the small pier, where there was also a marina for kayaks and other water equipment.

"Girls, what do we do? Do you want to swim, sunbathe or go for a walk?" I asked.

They chose to walk. Wdzydze Kiszewskie, where we were, is a typical summer village. There are a lot of guesthouses, seasonal cottages and dachas in that locality. We walked lazily on the road along the lake, passing the bus terminus. The girls wanted ice cream, so I had to wait in line for five minutes to satisfy their whims.

I took both Sunday tourists to the open-air museum, which Wdzydze are famous for. I went there mainly to show them a beautiful, old, stylish wooden church.

"It was moved from the village of Swornegacie[5] and is about ninety years old," I said.

"Is this village really called like that?" they asked surprised.

"Yes. It was dismantled beam by beam and taken here to the open-air museum, where it was put back together. That little church was one of the main attractions of the open-air museum. It often happened that young couples from the Tri-City or the surrounding area came here to get married. It was not easy to realize, but it was possible."

We entered the open-air museum. There were people everywhere, which put us off sightseeing a bit. We decided to see only the church and what could be seen from the outside, i.e. windmills, stylish peasant and fishing huts. We bypassed a small museum full of people, and continued walking. Kinga and Ula kept telling each other something, not paying attention to me at all.

"Can't you talk with each other at home?" I asked.

They took me by the arm, each on one side, and I led them to the church.

"Does the church function like a real church?" Ula asked.

"Of course! Services are held here every Sunday."

---

[5] Swornegacie is associated with fractious pants.

We went inside. Paintings immediately caught our attention. Beautiful, brightly colored, folk-style religious scenes adorned its ceiling. The pulpit, made entirely of wood, seethed with gold, and beautifully carved ornaments, various wooden figures of angels and saints, as well as wooden benches completed the work.

Kinga sat down on the bench, and I sat next to her. She was praying. I was wondering for what. I prayed for her. I already knew that she was the only one. I felt it with my whole being.

We left the church as if purified, enchanted by its sight. On the way back, I told the girls the history of the open-air museum founded in 1969 and the fate of its founders, Teodor and Izydora Gulgowski. I told about the difficult life of the local Kashubians, who were to be forcefully Germanized not so long ago. And yet they have had their own culture, language and writing for centuries.

"How do you know all this, Richie?" Kinga asked, curious.

"I'm a Kashubian myself," I joked, adding after a moment: "I wasn't always a sailor."

"Really?" said Kinga. "And what did you do? Tell me."

"Maybe another time," I said to Kinga, looking significantly at Ula.

She let go of the topic.

"Yesterday you had an example of the folk tradition," I laughed remembering the previous evening. The girls then experienced a bit of this Kashubian "otherness", when at midnight the hosts of "Bear Cub" offered their guests snuff in accordance with the old Kashubian custom.

Knowing this practice, I got a very little of it on my hand and carefully snuffed. Kinga and Ula bravely snorted quite a large portion of snuff and immediately their eyes almost popped out. They started sneezing, and from that sneezing, tears ran down their cheeks, smearing their carefully prepared makeup. Christopher and I had a lot of fun. They swore later that they would never be persuaded to such pleasure anymore.

We spent the whole afternoon idyllically and feeling as if we had been on vacation. I didn't want to leave with Kinga from "Bear Cub". We came back only because of Ula. If it weren't for her, we would probably have stayed a little longer. All the way back, she told us about work.

"I work in a hotel restaurant," she said, "this job is even nice. What kind of guests come there! The entire elite of singers, actors and musicians from famous bands. There are various events at the Summer Opera in Sopot," she chirped excitedly, as if I hadn't known about it. But Kinga probably didn't know.

"Most of the artists performing there stay at the hotel and then come over for meals. Yesterday I saw ..." and she mentioned half a dozen names from the front pages of newspapers and TV news.

We returned to Sopot. It was a warm, pleasant evening.

"Shopping done, we're going to the seaside," I said.

I went from Pilsudski Avenue and stopped in the parking lot of the Sailor's House. "For hotel guests only," said the sign in front of me, but I didn't mind it.

Kinga was here for the first time. She had already seen the boulevard, but from the other side, when she had been with Ula on the beach in Gdynia on that famous evening, when we had been dancing in the "Rose of Winds".

"It's been over a month since we met," I noted.

"Yes, Richie. How this time passes quickly."

"Let it pass even faster when I'm on the contract trip," I unnecessarily blurted out.

"When will you go on the cruise?"

"I asked the company to extend my time off a bit, so I think that at the beginning of October."

We walked along the breakwater towards Orlow.

"Give me a boost," Kinga called, and began to scramble to the top of the concrete cover.

"Aren't you scared?" I asked.

"No, no, it's so beautiful here!"

I looked at the bay through her eyes. Indeed - it was a beautiful sight. The waters of the bay were covered with boats - little Optimists. Their sails of different colors against the shimmering water reflecting the sun, looked like butterflies sitting on a greenish meadow.

"Probably a regatta is taking place now," I told Kinga.

There were ships at anchor in the distance.

"Do you see these ships?"

"Yes, but I have no idea of what types they are. The white one is probably a passenger ship," she replied, pointing to the white vessel sailing to Hel.

"Yes. This one is going to Hel. We have to go there sometime."

"And the one on the right?" I asked.

"I don't know."

"It's a bulk carrier and there's a tanker next to it, then a reefer, the one painted white with four taps … cranes," I corrected myself.

"How do you know from so far what kind of ships they are?"

"Get off now," I asked, holding out my hands.

She jumped down, leaning on my shoulders.

"That's easy. Each ship has its intended use, that's why it's built differently from others," I explained. "That one," I said, pointing, "is a tanker." It carries all kinds of fuel, so it doesn't need any big cranes," I was on my high horse. "The other one is a bulk carrier, because it has a number of holds to carry various types of bulk cargo. May have cranes, but it doesn't have to."

"And the white one is a floating fridge-freezer. It carries frozen products or fruit and vegetables."

Kinga, proud to learn the secrets of the seafaring school, said:

"Now no one will surprise me!"

We came to the end of the boulevard. There was a woman with flowers standing there. Kinga sat down on the bench. I bought one rose, returned to Kinga and said:

"I love you. Come live with me."

"Alright, Richie," she said simply. "I love you too."

She hugged me and kissed me longly, ignoring the passing people, but no one was interested in it anyway. It was a common sight on the boulevard. The sea and the summer made people show their feelings.

Kinga's first day of work in the bank came. I took her to work first thing in the morning. We agreed that I would come pick her up and we would go to the stores to look for furniture.

"I keep my fingers crossed," I said on parting.

Kinga was at work and I went to the store to do some shopping. This cottage had to be furnished finally. But I bought nothing. I couldn't decide on anything. I thought I would wait for Kinga. I picked her up from work. Madly excited, she told me how it was there.

"This bank is so big. I had to go with the circular to many rooms. Then they assigned me to one girl. She is called Natka and she also lives in Sopot. I went with her to her cash register and she taught me, or actually I was watching her work and I didn't even notice when the day was over.

Nice girls work there," she added.

Ula quickly found a tenant to replace Kinga, and it was her colleague who was looking for a room at the moment. Kinga and I agreed that we would live in a house.

We would do shopping in the afternoons and on Saturdays and Sundays, when Kinga was free. We went straight to the store and bought a king-size bed and a large closet. Kinga liked the closet very much.

"Yes, honey, if you like it, we take it," I said and laughed out loud.

"Why are you laughing, I don't understand?" Kinga was nervous.

"Nothing, it's nothing."

"The closet is covered with mirrors, we will have a lark," I thought.

The next morning, when they dumped it all into my cottage, only thanks to my neighbor's help I was able to put it all together by the evening, luckily not breaking anything. Kinga came back from work by bus.

"And what do you think?" I asked. "Do you like the bedroom?"

"It's lovely!" She said and jumped onto the bed. "How soft it is, come on!" She exclaimed.

We lived in Karwiny for two more weeks.

After a month, the living room with kitchenette, bathroom and bedroom was ready. Kinga struggled with the curtains, and I ordered window blinds. The color was chosen by Kinga. We let go of the top for now. The following Sunday, while walking around Kosciuszko Square in Gdynia, Kinga and I stopped at one of the places where the brand new "AB" beer was sold. Soon after, this brand disappeared from our brewing market, but now it reappeared. To this day, I have a fondness for this beer. Then, curious about the brand, I ordered two, for Kinga with raspberry juice. We met then by chance the owner, or in fact the president and shareholder. He bought a brewing plant in Elbląg and started the production of this beer there.

Some guy came up to us. You could tell by the clothes that he was from far away. He asked in excellent English:

"Do you like this beer?"

"I don't know," Kinga replied. "I haven't tasted it yet," she said with that smile of hers that knocked guys off their feet.

"It's good," I interrupted, "and cool, too," which wasn't always the case back then.

You could see that it was nice for him to talk to someone who knew the local customs and the city.

Andre could speak a little Polish, but his wife Julianna couldn't. We walked around the square, talking about the local habits. Andre and Julianna invited us for coffee, and that is how our relationship began. We made an appointment for next Sunday. This time in Sopot - he ran an advertising campaign there. I told Christopher about this meeting.

"Maybe this acquaintance will prove useful to you," I told him. "Give me your yacht for three or four hours," I asked. "I'll show them the bay."

"Okay, no problem, but you know what? Maybe I'll make it and go with you."

He didn't make it. Calling earlier he said:

"You know, Richie, I can't make it, but maybe you will come with them to my pub for dinner."

"We'll see. And how is your mini-bar on the 'Phantom'?" I asked. That was the name of his yacht.

"Full," he replied. "Maybe you want a steersman? I know you can handle it, but you'll have more freedom with the helmsman. I have such a young boy who is eager to sail. I will send him and the yacht to Sopot."

"OK let it be. At two o'clock, at the left pier."

I also agreed with Christopher a few more details about the sails and fuel.

Andre and Julianna were on time.

From the church at the top of Heroes of Monte Cassino street we went down towards the pier. I don't know if Andre was impressed by the promenade, but Julianna was delighted. They quickly got along with Kinga and from time to time they jumped away from us, stopping at clothing stores. They watched and picked over clothes. While waiting for them, I bought two beers.

"Try this beer," I said to Andre, choosing the best beer in my opinion.

"It's good, but mine is different because has a specific taste. You don't have such one here yet."

Kinga and Julianna bought a huge portion of ice cream.

"How do they get along?" I thought. Kinga barely knew English, as much as she had learned at school.

We entered the pier, walking slowly towards the yacht.

"You know, Andre, if your beer is as good as you say, it will be popular. We like the new here."

"I'm counting on it, but good advertising is half the battle," he replied. "In Sydney, where I live, this beer is highly appreciated."

"I suppose so," I agreed with him. "When I was in Sydney I didn't see that beer."

"You were in Sydney?" he was surprised. "When?"

"About two years ago."

But he didn't ask what I had been doing there. He just said:

"In Australia, it has a different name than in Poland."

"Too bad," I said, "maybe it would have been better to keep the Australian name of the beer."

When we got to the "Phantom", I invited them aboard. A little surprised, they entered and sat down on the side seats.

Karol, the helmsman sent by Chris, quickly left the pier and headed towards the Orlowo Cliff. The view of the Orlowo Cliff from the bay is a beautiful picture. The sea in this place shows its strength, breaking off a piece of the hill every year, which, in spite of the waves, suddenly rises again at its shore. The leaning trees at the top of the cliff cry desperately for help, but no one and nothing can help them. Sooner or later the water will wash out the soil, and they will fall into the sea as another victim of the insatiable element.

Andre started the conversation about women.

Looking at Kinga, he asked:

"Where can you meet such beautiful girls?"

"In Sopot," I replied. "And is it possible to meet such beauties everywhere in Australia?" Now I asked, looking at Julianne.

"No, just on the beach."

We burst out laughing.

Kinga and Julianna joined us bringing drinks.

"You have a different sea, shallow and with small waves. You cannot swim on the board," Julianna began.

"But it has one advantage that your sea does not."

"What?" She looked at me surprised, doubting my words. After all, their oceans are the most beautiful in the world.

"There are no sharks here and the sea sometimes becomes covered with an icy shell," I revealed the charm of the Baltic Sea.

"Ha, ha," she laughed. "Sharks aren't that dangerous. It is rare for them to attack a human."

"But the fear of sharks is always there."

"No. Believe me, it reminds of cars. Accidents happens, but people are still driving."

"It's not the same," I insisted.

For Kinga, this conversation was too fast.

"I'll make some coffee," she said and went downstairs. She came back without coffee, but in a bathing suit. She lay down on the deck. "What's wrong with her?" ran through my mind.

Julianna got up.

"So I will make the coffee," she said and stepped inside.

"I will help you," I said and followed her.

The cockpit[6] was uncovered and from below you could hear and see everything that happened on the deck ahead of the stern of the yacht.

"Where are you from?" I asked, pouring coffee into cups.

"From Geelong. Do you know where it is?"

"Yes, although I've never been there."

"And you?"

"I'm from Gdynia."

"What do you do?"

"I'm a sailor. And what do you do?"

I heard Kinga ask Andre in a slightly low-key voice:

"Will you smear my back?"

---

[6] Cockpit - a cavity in the exposed deck of a watercraft in which the crew can stay.

"He will have fun," I thought. Julianna continued:

"I'm an architect, but I have been traveling with my husband for a year and I haven't worked."

I saw Julianna glance out of the corner of her eye at Andre as he was smearing Kinga's back. "She's still jealous," I thought. "That's good."

"How do you like it here?"

"It's fun," was the casual reply.

Andre called out to me:

"Can I steer?"

"Of course!" I didn't have to tell Karol anything, because he was fluent in English.

After a while I noticed that Andre excellently sensed the wind, making the turns. We went back upstairs with coffees on trays.

"He is familiar with sailing," I told Kinga.

"Can they all sail?" She asked.

"Probably yes. In their country, a sailboat is like a bicycle for us. All of Australia is surrounded by the waters of the oceans."

Andre and Julianna had fun, steering by turns. When Karol didn't steer, he told Julianna some nautical stories. It was evident that she was very pleased to be adored by such a young boy.

We sailed along half the bay and dropped them off in Gdynia, in the sailing pool, which looked great at this time of the year.

As we sailed into the pool, the greenish panes of the aquarium glistened in front of us.

"What is there?" Julianna asked.

"This is a small sea aquarium, not what you have in Australia," I said. Beside is the Maritime College - now the Maritime Academy.

Saying goodbye, we invited them to a party on Saturday at our home. They took a taxi to Elbląg and we took the second one home.

Kinga, as soon as we got into the taxi, asked aggressively:

"Do you like such women?"

"What?" I replied surprised.

"Don't pretend. You simpered at Julianna!"

"How do you like it here?" She mocked me.

"It was just a polite phrase," I justified myself, though I was actually pleased, "really, sweetheart. I only see you, no one else. I love you and no one else matters to me."

"And that's how it has to be," she said reassuredly.

At home, we sat down to a supper hastily prepared by Kinga.

"You know, honey, we've been living here so long that we have to celebrate it to make our life here remain so good."

"Then let's throw a housewarming party," she said, pleased with the idea.

"Invite guests," I replied.

"Whom?"

"Anyone you want. I will invite Chris with Ula, our neighbor, and Tadek and Zenek with their wives."

We already invited Andre and Julianna.

"But here I know only my colleagues, not counting Ula ... Can I invite them? They are very curious who you are."

"Of course you can. Invite whoever you want. Kinga invited four colleagues. It was then that I met Natka, Braszka, Genia and Ala.

We agreed that the event would take place next Saturday. I stocked the bar, bought a cake, and the good was brought to me by Christopher.

"Take one waitress from me," he suggested during the phone call.

But I gave up - because of Ula.

"We can handle it. Thanks, but I'll pass."

Saturday came. I was a bit nervous about how Kinga's friends would react to me - after all, I was older than her. Around six o'clock, the guests started arriving. Kinga's colleagues came first.

"This is my Richie," Kinga introduced us, "and these are Natka, Braszka and Genia. Ala will arrive later."

The girls looked at me with curiosity - they probably thought that Kinga's guy was a dinosaur.

"We welcome, please come in," I invited them.

However, I didn't have time to take care of them, because Christopher came with Ula. It immediately got merry and loud. Ula, as direct as ever with her contagious laugh, immediately juiced up the whole company.

"Where is a music system?!" She exclaimed.

After a while, when Kinga showed her where the audio equipment was, we heard:

"Kinga! How do you turn this on?"

The girls rushed to help her, and Kinga and I went to open the door. Andre with Julianna arrived. In greeting, they gave us a bottle of red wine.

"Come in, please," Kinga said, shouting over the music.

Seeing their uncertain expression, she reassured them - "Half of the company speaks English." They entered the living room. Kinga turned the music down and announced:

"It's Andre and Julianna from Sydney. They only speak English, so girls - beat out your brains and fight!" She laughed.

"Hey, hello," they said. Christopher approached them and started a conversation. He knew I was busy with Kinga as more guests were just coming in. I heard him set the ball rolling:

"Do you know what we are celebrating tonight?"

"Yes," replied Julianna, "living in a new place ... home," she corrected.

"How do you say 'urządzamy parapetówkę' in English?" Christopher asked the girls, but they didn't know.

"We housewarming," someone called.

Christopher interpreted, there was a lot of laughter. Everyone interfered with the conversation, and finally Ula pointed to the window sill.

"Oh, yes," Andrew confirmed.

However, I was convinced that he didn't fully understand what the sill was about.

Finally all the guests arrived so we sat down to the table. The girls efficiently helped Kinga bring warm dishes, and Christopher and I poured alcohol.

Everything that was on the table was the work of Christopher's chefs. He had also brought the tables earlier. Lovely boy.

The alcohol was poured out profusely. The girls danced to the music that drowned out all conversations.

Chapter 6

Casino

"Richie! I've never been to a casino," Kinga said right after she came home from work.

"Come on, let's go there on Saturday, please, please," she played up to me. "Together with Chris and Ula," she added, standing on her tiptoes and brushing her lips against my neck. She had the voice of a little girl asking for a new doll.

Kinga never said, unlike me, "Christopher" but "Chris".

"And how much money do you want to lose there?" I asked.

"Me?" She asked surprised. "Nothing, we'll just watch."

"You go to the casino to play, not watch," I made her realize it.

"And what would you play? Roulette, cards or one-armed bandits?"

"Only slot machines, I promise, Richie."

I called Christopher.

"Have you heard about this collusion of the girls? They want us to go to the casino."

"Yes, I know, Ula told me. And you know what? It's a good idea, I need to de-stress."

"We will not go to the hard hall, we will just have fun, playing the slot machines. Maybe on Saturday?"

"Okay, then see you Saturday. We'll be in front of the casino at nine p.m."

I hung up. Kinga kept her head to mine the whole time, eavesdropping on our conversation.

Ula called me at work today and asked: "persuade Richie to go with us to the casino. I've already talked with Chris, I think he will agree," she chattered into the receiver. "Once, during a walk, Christopher told her that he had had a great time in the casino. Will we go?"

"He just didn't say how much it had cost him," I added. Christopher wasn't a gambler, but he sometimes liked the glitter and light emanating from places where you could taste the "big world."

"Okay, let's go. She deserves it," I thought about leaving for three months soon.

"Sweetheart! Come to the table, I have everything ready," I called to Kinga.

"Where did you learn to cook?" She asked, sitting down at the set table.

"I learned to fix while sailing on different ships and with different cooks."

During this dinner, I was telling Kinga about my culinary experiences. My worst memories were related to the Filipino. What he cooked and how he cooked could be used to create the "Anti-cuisine.

Thai edition" book. And yet Thai cuisine is acceptable even to Europeans - well, maybe not all of it would be suitable for them to eat. I remember we called him a shrimp - because of his small height. The cook took it up himself. AB Edward once spoke to me in Polish in front of the cook in the mess.

"Cook! This shrimp doesn't know how to cook at all, how did he get here?"

"I'm a shrimp?" The cook asked, standing next to him.

"Yes! Shrimp," confirmed Edzio. "I'll teach him how to cook," he said firmly, and polished the Filipino all morning.

"Look, potatoes shouldn't be peeled into a cube, but as thin as an apple, got it?"

"Yes! Yes!" he said and continued to cut into a cube.

"A difficult case, but I will cause that he will be like a European clumsy cook," added Ed, not broken by the failure.

The shrimp served us potatoes on the table like some forbidden fruit. Three cubes per person and he sprinkled them with sugar.

"Boil the water with the meat and the bones, then add the tomatoes - do you get it?"

"Yes! Yes!"

"Then add the vegetables to the water, because the soup must be cooked with vegetables," he continued.

"Yes! Yes!" was only heard.

We came for dinner. There was a tomato soup with rice.

"Rice is good," said Edek and began to pour the soup into the plate. "Fuck!" I heard. "What are the pickled cucumbers doing in this soup?! he said and ran to the shrimp with that plate.

He quickly shut himself in the locker and cried out:

"Ed! Ed! I wanted it to be tastier!"

The next time he served us a fish, a red one, it was a sea bass, if I remember correctly. The shrimp served us a fish wrapped in foil.

He roasted it in the foil in the oven," commented Edzio.

"That's probably a good thing?" I said, not entirely convinced.

We unwrapped the foil and there was - indeed - the fish, but whole, with the head and not gutted. It smelled like hell.

"Do you want it?" I asked the other Filipino who was sitting across from me, and handed him my fish. After a while, I heard him suck that head and I saw him pick out the eyes and some remnants, and eat it, smacking. I couldn't stand it and left.

"Your dinner was delicious," Kinga praised me.

"Thank you sweetie."

It was Saturday night, it was dark and cloudy outside, and we were supposed to go to the casino.

"How should I dress, Richie?" Kinga called from the other room.

"Preferably as for the evening. We're going to the casino at the Grand Hotel."

"I'm putting on a suit, the dark one. I don't feel very special in it, but it's the casino and there must be evening clothes," I called to her, sipping coffee in the lounge.

Suddenly I heard:

"Sweetheart! Come and help me fasten my dress."

I walked into the bedroom and I goggled. Kinga was dressed in a long black dress with a cut on the back to the buttocks. At the front, the dress was tight-fitting, with a small neckline extending from the back to the front, to the middle of the breasts, so that then, slightly expanding with a piece of hourglass-shaped material, glide up, and like a collar, cling to her neck. The material was as if runny and shiny like silver. Black high heels and a neat silver handbag. Revelation.

"What am I supposed to fasten here?" I asked. "Everything is bare."

"Oh, here." She turned her back and pointed at her neck.

"When did you buy this wonder?"

"Recently, when Natalka and I were wandering around the shopping center in Gdynia.

To the Grand Hotel, we got by a taxi. The entrance to the casino was from the side of the building, from the alley of trees leading to the beach.

Christopher and Ula were waiting for us. We went up the winding stairs to the Grand, where a porter dressed in an appropriate livery stood like a statue.

"There will be a lark when they ask you to show them your ID," I said to Kinga.

"No! It's impossible, I don't look so young."

"But they don't let you in until you're twenty-one, and you don't look that much."

"Oh Jesus! And I didn't take the ID!" she got scared.

"Don't worry, I will stand security for you," said Christopher in a very serious tone. "You look so beautiful that you will crush their fears."

"Thank you! And you look as if you wanted to break the bank at the casino."

"Oh! It would be useful, there is never too much money. Come on, I'll buy you a drink for good luck."

"Richie," Christopher told me, "take care of Ula."

He took Kinga by the arm and they went to the bar.

I saw Kinga wave her hand at me without turning around.

I took Ula's hand:

"Take my arm, you look so pretty. Let everyone envy me going with such a beautiful girl."

"Thank you," Ula said, blushing. After a while she recovered and called out:

"It's fun here, where are the slot machines?"

"Come on, we'll go to exchange the money for chips first."

We went to the bar where Christopher and Kinga were sipping drinks.

"See, Richie! I have a tricolor drink!"

Using a different density of the liquid, the bartender poured alcohol and juices into a glass so that they didn't mix.

"Do you know its name?"

"No."

"It's the Third Foot. If you drink too much of it, you'll have to prop yourself up with a third leg."

"So a double drink for me!" Ula, who was listening to us, exclaimed.

I took Kinga's hand and we went to the slot machines. We were gliding on soft, fluffy red carpets. It is no coincidence that they are red, this color causes aggression and raises adrenaline. And all this is needed to play, play and play again.

The various slot machines were lined up, some back to back, other against the wall. Lights flashed in them. The characteristic sound of handles being pulled and pictures spinning was heard. It excited us, we fell into a trance and, as if enchanted, we stared at the reflection of flashing lights. "Crash, crash, crash" - and so all the time you could hear the freezing pictures. Everything merged into a melody to which we were to lose everything we had - at least that was the rule of the casino. We chose two free slot machines standing next to each other.

"Take it," I said to Kinga, handing her the multi-colored tokens arranged in a special box - half of her monthly salary.

"Maybe you can multiply them?"

She stood in front of the machine.

"Richie! What is it about?"

I didn't know well myself, but the fun was great. Christopher served as an instructor.

"If you press here, you increase the stake. This button - you play for the entire displayed amount, and here - the slot machine plays for you."

"Okay, I won't remember it anyway!" She screamed.

Kinga stood by the machine next to me, on the left was Ula, and beside her was Christopher.

The game started.

We were pulling the handles like crazy, staring at the spinning pictures.

"So once again. This time also nothing," Ula loudly commented on her actions. "Bloody thief!" She cried.

The guy next to her turned in surprise, and she gave him "smile number six" and leaned forward so that her breasts almost popped out. In a little angel's voice she said:

"This is what I meant," she said and gestured to the one-armed bandit.

"Have you lost?" The guy asked.

"And do you have a recipe for winning?"

"You have to keep trying until you succeed," he prompted.

"Gambler," I thought. By doing it you could only get broke.

Kinga played with concentration. She got three cherries, but made a small bet, so the win wasn't high. The slot machine spat out a handful of chips. She was glad and laughed out loud.

"Richie! Is it a lot? Come to me, I don't know what to do! Look," she said and showed me a large handful of chips. "Should I play or stop?" She wondered.

"And can you stop and walk away?"

"Yes, come on," she said and wanted to leave.

"Then play on."

"Why?"

"You don't have the makings of a gambler, so keep playing."

Kinga and I played with a variable luck. But we lost everything anyway.

Broke, we went to the bar to drown. After a while, Christopher and Ula returned.

"I'm a little better off," he said.

"I feel better too, but I won't waste any more money on those guys there," said Ula and pointed at the camera's eye.

"Chris? Can you hang out here somewhere?"

"Good idea, we're all going," Christopher decided and led us to the entrance for hotel guests.

We were dressed appropriately, so we entered the hotel without a hitch. Heading down, we decided to go to the ballroom. It was packed with people, and all the tables were full. It was obvious - the high season. We sat down at the bar. I went to dance with Kinga. A great band, known in Poland, was playing.

Christopher and Ula were sipping drinks. And so by turns, they danced while we sat, occupying the only two free seats at the bar. We kept ordering drinks with weirder and weirder names, trying to guess what was in them. It wasn't good for me. I was getting increasingly drunk.

Drinks are treacherous beasts. They hit you by surprise. You sip such tasty wonders, thinking that there is hardly any alcohol there, until you suddenly realize that you are already done. The legs are not the same, they go where they want, not where you want.

"I've had enough," I said to Kinga, "take us home."

Kinga took my arm and we left. Christopher and Ula stayed, but he hold his drink. In the hall I mumbled to the porter:

"Taxi, please."

What happened next? I don't remember much.

Kinga told me in the morning:

"You slept in the taxi, snoring mercilessly."

"I must have dreamed of slot machines."

"Then you barely got out of the cab and crawled home on all fours. I hope the neighbors were asleep and didn't see us. You barked at the dog on the way.

At home, you went straight to the bathroom and tested the strength of the tiles on the floor with your teeth.

I undressed you and covered you with a blanket because you didn't want to go to bed, saying that you were in your berth. After three hours, you crawled up to me terribly exhausted. "How are your teeth? Are they intact?" She asked.

"Kinga ... Honey, I'm so ashamed, I can't drink much, no more than three or four drinks. Watch me the next time. Now give me something for a hangover."

Chapter 7

Flight

"Hi, Richie," I heard. It was Bronek, we were supposed to go to the ship together. We had known each other for a long time, we were on a few contract trips together. It was with him that, on one of those trips, we survived the attack of Somali pirates. Bronek, who lived in Szczecin, flew to Frankfurt from Berlin, where Karolina booked his ticket. After checking in, we got on the plane to Lagos quickly and efficiently. It was a big Boeing. We had seats in class "E". I sat down in the middle row consisting of four seats. Air conditioning was on. Muffled roar of engines before take-off, taxiing ... and after a while I felt we were climbing steeply up. We were flying. Next to me, on the left, was Bronek.

"We have eight hours of flight," he said, looking around curiously.

The width of the seats was small, but sufficient for me. Only the distance to the seat in front of me was too little in my opinion. My knees were bent and I couldn't easily straighten my legs.

On my right there were two women, probably Nigerians. The younger girl, with a dark brown face had black, ebony hair. She had elongated bun consisting of oddly braided tiny wisps. Each braid was made of three strands, and they formed one thicker braid. These connected braids stretched from the neck to the top of the head.

"Who wanted to bother so much?" I thought.

Ornaments were woven into her hair. Dull balls and little shiny tubes looked like twisted shells of a crustacean. Everything was arranged from the bottom to the top so that you could see the black skin separating each braid. At the base of the head, all the hair was put together tightly with a buckle made of bone with beautifully carved Arabic ornaments. The buckle had a series of holes of various shapes, from under which a red ribbon of shiny material was visible, wrapping the braids. The bun fell down like a cascade of willow twigs and hung without touching the neck, so that with a more violent turn of the head, trying to keep up with it, it thrashed, swinging from side to side. Her attire was regional, stylized as European, which is often seen in young African girls lately. She was reading The Times.

"Probably a student," I thought.

I pulled out the newspaper and, reading, waited for the flight attendants who had already started delivering drinks somewhere at the beginning of the compartment. A small lamp at the top gave a dim light. It was too dark to read for a longer time, so I put the paper down and turned on the monitor. The screen was mounted in the passenger seat in front of me. I set the satellite view option and followed the route the plane was taking. We were just flying over the

Alps. Thinking about Kinga, I must have taken a nap, because Bronek woke me up, poking me on the shoulder.

"What would you like to drink?" He asked.

"White coffee."

I also got a cookie and a glass of red wine.

I looked at the monitor screen. We were over the Mediterranean Sea and we were approaching the Sahara Desert, flying a little from the side, from the Atlantic. "Probably such is the air corridor," I thought, looking at my watch. Almost half of the route had been covered. I was trying to sleep. It was dark on the plane, and somewhere in the distance, in front of me there was a glistening white light. Probably a passenger was reading something.

Not far behind me, I heard a loud baby cry. Suddenly, to my surprise, I heard the raised voice of a woman speaking Polish:

"If you don't calm down right now, I'll hit you in the ass."

It stunned me. I resisted the urge to turn and see who it was. I know that Bronek heard it too, because he looked at me.

"What a company we have," he said and turned, searching for the voice with his eyes. "It's dark, I can't see anything," he added after a moment.

The baby cried even louder. This time it was heard:

"Hush, hush, baby, sleep."

When we were served a meal, I ate it with great relish. In Frankfurt, I only had consumed a sandwich prepared for me by Kinga. "If only I could fall asleep," I managed to think. The voice of a flight attendant woke me up:

"Buckle up," she said.

"So we are already landing," I thought.

Carefully straightening my numb legs, I tried to revive the frozen muscles. Eight hours of sitting is no joke. Finally, with a loud screech of tires, we landed.

Getting up from my seat, I was looking for the owner of the previous day's voice. There she was. I hear her say to children in Polish: "faster, faster". A fat white woman with blond hair, steadied by a tall black man, was pushing with two chocolate boys. Sometimes the fates of Polish women are strangely twisted. We got off the plane. The terminal was just like any other terminal, but only somewhat empty. Although Lagos isn't the capital, it is a large port city with a population of ten million.

We checked quickly. In the middle of the hall, next to various souvenir shops, next to a Swarovski display window with products made of crystal and gold, we were greeted by an agent holding the inscription "NEPTUN" in his hand - that was the name of our tugboat.

"How are you?" He asked.

"We're fine," Bronek used the standard formula.

The agent led us to the place where the luggage was sliding down the baggage belt. I quickly spotted my suitcase. We went outside, and there we were hit by a hot, humid breeze.

Our guardian spoke on the phone and a Jeep picked us up right away. Inside, next to the driver, sat a guy armed with a machine gun - our security. There were frequent kidnappings of foreigners in Nigeria and the company was hiring security constantly, of course the company we worked for, which was based somewhere outside Lagos.

It was about thirty kilometers from the terminal to the center. There was a two-lane road leading there. Then it took us half an hour to fight our way to the company's headquarters, inside of which there was a helipad.

The driver drove like crazy, honking again and again. The sight of the security guard with a rifle influenced the drivers who, seeing such an arsenal, meekly drove out of our way.

"The ship is by the platform," the agent informed us. "Twelve of you will fly, five to the ship. You were the last to come, the Russians reached us at noon yesterday. We are almost on the spot."

We were greeted by a wall, about three and a half meters high. At the top there were barbed wire and broken glass embedded in concrete. We drove along this wall for half a kilometer. One gate, second, third - we finally drove inside. We entered the building because we had about an hour left. We went to the office for coffee. We were welcomed by the proud sign "Shell Company". Inside, the building was spacious and it was cold there, and in a special part of it, a separate area for guests, you could relax, drink coffee and eat something. Of course, all at the expense of the company. We met three Russian men there, or rather one, because the other was Latvian and the third was Ukrainian. This was a complete team.

Sitting in comfortable armchairs, we started a conversation - first in English, but seeing that not everyone was fluent in it, we switched to Russian. I spoke Russian as well as I spoke English. I know English only from textbooks and conversations with other people who have learned it as I did. I learned Russian being in Russia, and spent a total of about three years there. I knew the two seamen sitting with us from earlier contract trips - Sasha and engineer Sergey. I didn't know Andrei, a young Russian from Kaliningrad. We speculated what we would experience upon arrival on the ship. Where would we sail? Or maybe we would stay the entire contract under the platform? "Neptun", our tugboat, was an auxiliary vessel for servicing and securing the work of oil rigs. A powerful engine with more than one hundred tons of bollard pull was capable of almost any job.

Chartered by the Shell Company from Petronafta, it swung everywhere they sent it. Mostly to the dirty work, where the Americans didn't want to send their people.

"I tell you, we will be projecting for two months under the cap - that's what we called standing under the platform. "It's getting more and more anxious here, see? Even security guards came to pick us up at the airport, which hadn't happened before," said Sasha.

"Come on. The guerrillas don't go that far," said Sergey, "and if they do, not to us."

"Take it easy," I said, "After all, we have no control over where and when we go."

Andrei didn't say anything.

"First time in our company?" I asked.

"No. I've already been on one contract trip lasting four months, but it was in Ghana."

"On what tug?"

"On Empire," he replied. "It was even interesting."

A female voice came from the loudspeaker, inviting us to go to the exit.

Our luggage was already brought to the helicopter, which was standing near the entrance.

Obeying the regulations in force, we went inside, putting on vests and fastening seat belts. There were twelve of us, not counting the pilots and one lifeguard, but only five of us were going to the ship. We barely put on the headphones when the helicopter took off. The flight was smooth. From above, I looked at the views passing below us. In less than twenty minutes, the platform was visible. It rose majestically out of the water, and our tug swayed on the wave beside it.

Circling, the helicopter approached the landing area on the platform. The round area, placed on the side of the platform directly above the water, was painted with two yellow, round rims with a large dot in the center and lured us with the gestures of the guide standing on it. We landed softly on the pad. The platform staff quickly unloaded our luggage and placed it in the basket. Here we went our separate ways. Bending down, we said goodbye to them and entered the basket.

Chapter 8

"Neptun"

The crane quietly lowered us to the stern of the tug. There were colleagues who had already finished their contract trip and were returning home. "Here I am," I thought, "this is my second home for the next three months."

I took over Tadek's duties, thanking him.

"Tadek, you are a nice guy, thanks for agreeing to stay a month longer."

"It's nothing Richie. You actually did me a favor. I really wanted to be at home for Christmas and New Year, and thanks to that I will be now. Otherwise I wouldn't be. "And I won't be. I will be back only in January," flashed through my mind. I went to the cabin, picking up the luggage on the way. After a while, dressed in overalls, I reported to the Old Man with my documents.

Grzesiek had been the captain there for years. A bit nervous, but a brick. He had arrived four days earlier.

"You are here already? Report to the Chief, we have a problem with one of the elevators.

"Neptun" was a large tugboat. The superstructure was shifted far forward and concealed at the rear, at the base, two huge hauling winches. Each of them looked straight at the stern. The stern deck, low-mounted, almost flush with the water surface, and was stocked with some pipes and other equipment. My watch had begun.

In the evening I sat down to the computer in the office. As usual, it wasn't working when we stood under the platform. I reached for the satellite phone, punched in my code and called Kinga.

It was 7 pm Polish time. Kinga should have been home by then.

"Hello," I heard her voice.

"It's me, honey. Do you remember me?"

"Richie! I can hear you well. Where are you?" It was known from her voice that she was surprised that it is possible to be heard well from such a distance.

"And what do you think? My thoughts are with you and my body is on the ship."

"Yes I know. Is everything all right? How are you?" She peppered me with questions. "Do you have luggage?"

How well she remembered my story about luggage!

"Yes, I have. I have everything, only you are not here."

"I'm not really there, but with my heart I am with you. I am, I'm waiting, I love and I miss you already."

"Kinga, sweetheart, how was your journey from the airport?"

"Good. On the way, I met Natka. She spent the night at my dwelling. I was a bit afraid to be alone on that first night. But now I have to overcome my fear," she said. "I put your photos wherever I could and when I walk around the apartment, I see you everywhere."

"Only you could have come up with such an idea," I said, surprised. But I felt very nice. "How are things going at your workplace?" I asked.

"I'm still training, but I'm doing quite well. At the beginning of the month, I will sit alone at the counter."

"Then take care of yourself and no necklines or skimpy skirts."

"Richie ... You know very well that one can't dress like that for work."

"And have I said for work?"

"Don't worry, I keep these qualities only for you. You know, I already called home and said that I would spend Christmas and New Year's Eve with them. They wanted to meet you very much and wish you could come."

"Another time, honey. When I come back, we'll go there for sure. I have to go. Kisses, bye, bye."

"Take care of yourself, Richie. I love you."

I hung up.

Mid-December came. We were swinging at the platform for a long time. Time passed quickly. There was a lot of work, we traveled several times between several platforms and we were at the port twice to pick up the delivery of equipment.

The third time it was before Christmas, on December 21st - this date is engraved in my memory and I will not forget it for a long time. I was on watch with Stas. "Dog watch" as we call it here: midnight to four in the morning. We waited to enter the port.

"Tomorrow," we heard every morning. This time it seemed that we would get in in the morning, so the Old Man sailed to the harbor roadstead. The deadline was changed every three hours, then in the evening he heard: "tomorrow at six in the morning will come the pilot." We dropped the anchor, waiting for the morning.

I looked around. There were only ships, so out of curiosity, I began to count them.

"Don't bother, I've already counted. There are about eighty of them," Bronek informed me.

The captain ordered double watches. Whenever he could, he stayed away from the mainland. This is because of the black freedom fighters, the "Niger Deltas" as they called themselves. You heard about robberies and kidnappings all the time.

Stas and I mounted guard in the stern under the superstructure, making a round every half an hour. Stasio was sitting on a bench on the right side, and I was fishing for squids on the left one. I put a large lamp overboard to illuminate the water. This attracted the squids that swam in whole flocks.

I had a metal bait attached to the line, and spinning it quickly, I threw it far from the side.

It was around four in the morning.

"Soon will be the end of the watch," I told Stas. "I'm going to see the bow.

I went alone. We had double watches and there was also a third officer on the bridge. He must have been napping or reading something because he didn't notice anything.

I was coming back from bow to stern. I was already on the lower deck when a black figure rose in front of me.

"Alarm! Alarm!" I shouted as I pressed the switch of the cellular radio. "Where's Stasio? - flashed through my mind and that's why I didn't follow the instructions, which orders to run as far as possible in such situations, simultaneously setting off the alarm. Anyway I had nowhere to run away. We stood there for maybe five seconds, and I alternately shouted: "alarm" and: "Stas, where are you?"

The tall black man with a bare chest stood at a distance safe for me and didn't move. Me too, but he knew why he wasn't moving and I wasn't. I felt a blow to my head and I fell. I saw as if through a mist that one of them was reaching with his hand for the cellular radio I was still holding, and the other was going through my pockets. I heard the alarm buzzers howl. I got up, pushing the attacker away with my hand. Out of the corner of my eye, I saw the other individual's sudden hand movement and a flash. Instinctively, I parried the blow with my right hand. The blade of a long knife hit my right hand above my wrist and, knocked out of the blow line, slid down my stomach, hitting the wide navy belt I was wearing with my jeans. It lost momentum by cutting it, but it still slit my pants down to the middle of my thigh.

I heard Stas' screams. The attackers escaped by jumping into the water.

They left on the fast motorboat.

I sat up with shock. Only now did I understand that I was close to death.

"Richard, I'm going to the top," said the Third, seeing blood trickling down my hand and stomach.

I looked at myself.

"I'm fine," I thought.

The wound on my arm was a few centimeters long and was bleeding a lot. The skin was cut quite deeply, but nothing was damaged. I moved my hand and fingers.

There was a blade mark on my stomach, quite long but superficial. My head hurt, it was from the impact.

Everyone came running, hearing the alarm. The Old Man in pants and barefoot, very nervous, looked at me carefully.

He gave commands:

"Take Richie to the bridge and dress his wound."

We went, you don't discuss with a nervous captain.

The third officer bandaged my arm and grabbed the instruments, wanting to sew it. Then he pulled out the appropriate tools and searched for an anti-tetanus injection. I was giving myself up to it. The captain, already dressed, stepped onto the bridge. He checked the radar and called the port.

Meanwhile, only at the sight of Chief's shaking hand, I asked:

"Gentlemen, no sewing." And said to the Chief:

"Give me this injection, and the skin on my wrist will be tightened with clamps, bandaged, and it will be OK." The Old Man, though he wasn't standing by us, could hear everything.

"Okay, it can be done that way too," he confirmed.

It took maybe five minutes. Meanwhile, the captain reported the incident to the port authority, agent and company management in Lagos. He also sent a fax to Petronaft in Gdansk and made an appropriate entry in the ship's log.

"Richie, go and lie down. Take a break."

Please - I had time off anyway. My watch was over, it was already half past five in the morning.

"I've already notified the agent, and when we arrive at the port, you'll go to the doctor."

"I don't want any doctor. I'm fine."

"That's what I was instructed to do, and I also think that the doctor should see you."

I couldn't argue further. Everyone discussed the incident at breakfast.

"It's good that it ended like that," Bronek said.

The third officer suffered the greatest consequences. The Old Man called him on the carpet. The Third came back worried.

"What could I do? I didn't sleep on the bridge," he explained. I looked at the radar from time to time. The alarm mode was active, but it showed nothing anyway. And it couldn't because as you saw for yourself, they had a rubber boat, which can't be captured by the radar."

"But your eyes are probably better than radar," the Chief gibed at him.

"Unless they are closed," added Stasio.

"It's good that Richie was vigilant, otherwise we could all end up miserable."

"Stas, where were you?" I asked.

"When you went to the bow, I went inside, to the toilet. I closed the door. That's why they didn't go inside. Do you remember the boats getting closer to the ship before? Maybe then they found out how to get on board."

"As far as I know, no one bought anything from them," the Chief assured us.

"The devil knows, maybe one of the Negroes had been on board earlier."

It was true that they came by boat offering beer, vodka or whiskey. There were also boats in which the girls sat. Waving their hands in a peculiar way, they encouraged the sailors, hoping that some man would take one of them into the cabin. They didn't sniff at money, but most often they wanted to take a shower. Water is a treasure. A real rarity, unavailable to them. When one of the sailors waved at them graciously, they sailed to the side. He looked at them, picking one or two like horses in a runway, and said:

"Come."

There was no fear that they would steal something or leave his cabin themselves, no matter what happened. He chose them and they were his. They got into the cabin, gladly ate when you brought something to them, drank a cola, and tried to sell some trinkets, bracelets or pendants. They went to the shower. If you wanted to, you could go with them. That was the price of water. What they did there was another story.

"No, no one bought alcohol for sure," said Stasio in an irritated voice. "I got out of the toilet and was walking aft when I heard your screams, so I ran towards you. The Negro jumped out from behind the containers and dashed towards the stern end, then leaped into the water. By then all the buzzers were howling.

"Maybe it's good that we weren't going together. They saw me, but they didn't know where you were.

"Which way did they board the ship?" The mechanic asked.

"If I knew, they wouldn't come in," Stasio retorted.

"That's fine. I have nothing against you, I just think aloud."

"They most likely climbed onto the side between the containers and attacked from there," I said.

"We made a tour of the entire ship. They didn't go between the containers." On the port side, below the bulwarks, which were half covered with pipes, Andrei noticed something.

"Check it out here!" He exclaimed.

He found an anchor hooked over the projecting part of the aft deck reinforcement. The hook was wrapped in rags. You couldn't hear the impact when it fell onto the deck. At the end, a cut line with two knots dangled.

"They were barefoot, now I remember," said Stasio. "When the black guy was escaping, he was barefoot, so nobody could hear them. They can climb such knots very high," he added.

"Not only knots, but also the anchor chain," confirmed Sergey, who was with us.

Ending the discussion in the mess, over coffee, we came to the conclusion that they weren't partisans from the "Niger Delta" who kidnapped people for ransom, or common thieves who steal everything they could get their hands on. Everything indicated that it was a specialized gang of "cash-thieves," as the local police called them.

They are bandits who steal money and some other valuables. But what they want most is the captain's safe. Everyone knew that the captain always had a few thousand dollars in the safe, because without it, nothing could be done here. You have to pay for everything in cash.

They act perfidiously and are very dangerous. First they overpower watch keepers on board. Then they put the watchman to sleep on the bridge. If they manage to do so, the ship is practically theirs. They go inside and if by chance they don't come across a forayer who raises the alarm, they walk from cabin to cabin and release the sleeping gas. When they check each of the cabins, they break into the captain's one, and steal money and anything of value.

"They wouldn't come in mine," Andrei said.

"You talk nonsense! If you were sleeping under anesthesia, they would enter whatever way they wanted, through the doorway or porthole. You wouldn't wake up anyway," Stasio chided him.

The Chief called me:

"Richie, the pilot will come at eight. As soon as we moor and the agent arrives on the ship, you will go with him to the doctor. Get ready. I will go out for maneuvers."

We docked at nine. An hour later I was on my way to the doctor with the agent. How did he call that?

To the first aid point. The doctor would decide what to do next, would tell me if I needed to go to the hospital or maybe do some tests.

Before leaving, the Old Man called me over. "Probably to pick up the papers," I thought. It turned out that not only because of that.

"Sit down, Richie. Here you have fifty five-dollar bills from the firm. If you need to give someone a baksheesh, do it."

Also take these three cartons of cigarettes. For security at the gate, the customs officers, and for the doctor. Also go to the cook, he will give you water for the journey. "Oh! How generous he is," I thought.

I felt a little bad that the guys were going to drudge and I was going for a ride.

I was sitting next to the agent in his air-conditioned Toyota and I was thinking about Kinga. How was the girl coping with the whole house? In addition, I left her my dog. It was the second half of December, soon would be Christmas. I didn't like Christmas, maybe because I spent so much of them alone, away from everything that is close to me and what I love. It would be also so now.

We left the port. There was a brief check in at the gate, but only the agent came out of the car, taking my papers. After a while I saw the head of the guard in the cap. He asked the standard question how I felt, then he looked at my bandaged arm.

"I'm still alive," I replied.

He laughed. I handed him two cartons of cigarettes, so he returned to the building from which the agent left shortly after. The barrier went up and we drove on.

After fifteen minutes of driving, the asphalt road ended. We drove onto red compacted sand. A cloud of dust trailed behind us, obstructing our view. "Where the hell is he taking me?" I thought.

He must have noticed my nervousness because he said:

"We're taking shortcuts, it will be faster."

"OK," I replied, "drive carefully."

After half an hour we approached some buildings. Around the corner, we were stopped by people armed with rifles. They were young. One of them, in a dirty undershirt and jeans, had short hair and was waving his gun menacingly. I saw the agent laughing out of the other side of his mouth.

"You're a Russian fisherman, you don't speak English, and we're going to the doctor," he said, stopping the car. He got out and they were talking.

The slob waved his rifle at me. After a while, he came up with a menacing expression emphasizing how important he was, and he spoke:

"Zdrastvuy," - that was probably all he knew. I answered him in Russian:

"Zdrastvuy, what a cool rifle you have! What are you doing here?"

Further, in English, the slob asked:

"Are you a fisherman, do you fish?"

"Yes, yes, fish," I said and I showed with my hands how big fish I caught.

"Are you going to the doctor?" He asked, looking at the bandaged hand.

"Yes, yes. Go, go," I replied.

Seeing that my English was just as hopeless as his Russian, he waved his hand and walked away, allowing us to keep going.

The agent returned and we headed off.

"This is some local guerrilla, a fraction of the fighters of the 'Niger Delta'," he said. "They cause us trouble all the time."

I'm not even surprised. As we passed some pipelines, two huge columns of fire shot up from the ground about two hundred meters away, reaching high into the sky. The fire was yellow, torn, almost without smoke. Seeing what I was looking at, the agent said:

"It's gas, it's burning all the time. It's never night here. And so for twenty years.

"Terrible," I thought. "How can they live here?"

The ground there is no longer red, but dirty, gray, without any vegetation or even a bush. Full degradation. "Am I contributing to this?" I was wondering.

We drove into the sprawl. The half-naked children waved their hands at me, clinging to the door of the car, and the girls were standing, leaning against the walls of a shack made of everything they had, and smiling at us.

We stopped in front of a shack that turned out to be a local shop. The agent got out of the car and stepped inside. I also got off. The children immediately clung to me, stretching out their hands and shouting for a baksheesh.

I entered the small shop. I looked at what was on the counter made of boards and on the shelves. Surprisingly - there was quite a lot. I noticed candies and cola. I said to the young girl:

"Give me a full packet of cola and a carton of these cookies."

The girl in the local dialect called out to someone. A woman emerged from behind the screen.

"What will it be?" said an older, fat woman wearing a long colored skirt and having her head wrapped in a turban. I repeated. She snarled something at the girl. The latter quickly handed me cola and cookies.

"What's your name?" I asked the girl.

"Asulu," she replied. That's probably how it should be written.

The agent looked at me in surprise.

"Lovely name," I told her, although I had no idea what that meant. Later, the agent explained to me that in the Ogoni dialect - of the local inhabitants - it means "Morning".

"How much do I pay? In dollars?" I asked Asulu. She looked at the old black woman. She growled something again, but in a more friendly tone.

"Twenty dollars," Asulu told me.

I didn't bargain. Let the old woman think she could have asked for more. I pulled out twenty dollars and handed it to Asulu, though the old woman held out her hand sooner. Asulu, however, quickly gave her the money.

"And this is for you," I said, "for being so pretty," and I gave her ten bucks.

A smile lit up her face. I took the cookies and cola, and on the doorstep I distributed everything to the children. Fate was kind to me today, let me also be like that," I thought.

"The old woman will take her that money anyway," the agent told me as we got into the car.

Well, life doesn't spoil the girls here.

Finally, after about twenty minutes, we drove into the town. It was obvious that the agent knew the way very well. Driving along side streets, we rolled into a square enclosed by a large mesh fence. We stopped at the gate. "There are gates everywhere," I thought.

The old Negro, the doorman of this inn, apparently knew our car, because he opened the gate immediately. In front of me there was a small brick building, and next to it some kind of fence, behind which two goats grazed, and roaming chickens pecked something out of the ground. We entered the building where a young girl greeted us on the threshold. The agent talked to her and said to me:

"I'll leave you here, I'll be back in three hours."

"Why so long?" I asked.

"The doctor has to get to you here," he said and disappeared.

It didn't look like a medical clinic. But there nothing compares to what you know. It all depends on the money you have. For the poor, there are different ones, and for the very poor, there is nothing. There are also clinics for the rich. "I'm not one of them," I thought, looking at the shabby walls. But I know that's how it works there. You don't spend your money in vain. I also knew that if the need arose, there would have been a place for me in the best hospital in the town. At least I thought so. "Better not," I thought, sitting in a comfortable armchair.

"Will you eat dinner?" The young girl asked.

"And what do you have?"

"Chicken and rice."

"No thanks," I replied. I was afraid of an ameba.

"You're safe here," she laughed, but she knew I was serious and I wouldn't eat.

"Then I will call your friend," she said and disappeared behind the door.

"What friend? I have no friend here. Or maybe her friend? Who is she talking about?" I thought.

After a while, I saw a young boy coming from the other doorway.

"Zdrastvuy," he greeted.

After a while, I already found out that he was a motorist on a Russian fishing trawler. He fell ill and had a high fever. The doctor on his ship, unable to deal with it, handed him over to the agent - the same one who brought me there.

"My ship has already left for the fishery, and I've been here for the third day. I will probably come home," he said, worried. "I don't know if and when my ship will come here again," he nagged. We talked a little and he went to dinner. He has no choice but to eat.

Maybe an hour passed when a young woman in late pregnancy entered the hall.

I looked at her curiously. You don't see a face like this often there. Beautiful European features, bloodless eyes without a red rim, shapely nose, as well as prominent lips and dazzlingly white teeth. Also black hair, but short and surprisingly straight. "Probably one of the parents or grandparents was white," I thought.

She came up to me saying:

"I'm a doctor, I will examine you in a moment."

Then she called out to one of the girls:

"Turn on the electricity!"

Did I misunderstand? After a while, however, I clearly heard the rattle of the generator. The domestic power plant works only on request. Well - it's Africa, no wonder. We entered the office.

Horror of horrors! In better ones I had been with my dog. An office is an exaggerated term. It was quite a large room, and under the window there was an iron, shabby bed from the days of the foreign legion. On the other side, there were a couple of low, white cabinets where paint peeled off from old age. In the center of the room, there was a large wooden desk and a faded executive chair.

The woman sat down behind the desk and started filling out the questionnaire, asking me where I was from, what had happened, what my name is. Her assistant was running around me, if you could call the girl that, because she didn't even have a kittel. "She must have come straight from the kitchen," I thought, "or from the goats that can be seen outside the office window."

The doctor moved from behind the desk. "She's having a hard time," I thought, looking at her body and unsteady gait. She inspected my wound and gave the command:

"Don't remove the buckle for a week."

She changed my dressing efficiently. Before putting on a sterile bandage, she sprinkled yellow powder on the wound. She touched my head, sensed a large lump, pressed it, and asked:

"Does it hurt?"

Sure it hurt, but for fear of staying here, I said quickly:

"No. It doesn't hurt at all."

The doctor jabbered something to her quasi-nurse and she pulled a can from a drawer. From this can, with her bare fingers, she took out, counting out eighteen white-and-blue oblong capsules, and put them in a plastic bag.

The doctor, writing out the "report" of the visit, read aloud:

"Three times a day, every eight hours."

"I'll throw it into the water right away," I thought. I think it's needless to say why.

She added a tube of ointment. I watched it. "Made in Switzerland," I read. "It will be useful," I thought and put it in the plastic bag.

I asked the doctor:

"Will you give me a leave of absence from work?"

"And how much do you want?" It sounded like "and how much will you give?"

I pulled out a carton of cigarettes, but seeing her disappointed expression, I added twenty dollars. She wrote me seven days.

"OK," I said, "call the agent."

After a while the agent drove me to the ship. I napped all the way, because I was after watch, I had been awake, and besides, only now I was just getting stressed.

The Old Man wouldn't be delighted with the sick leave. I got it for myself as a security for the future, should anything happened following this event. The seven days of sick leave, the old man had to record in his journal and send it to the company. I didn't intend to coast, but I had to think about myself. On the ship, they waited only for me. After unberthing, I received the order - go to sleep. I quickly ate a late dinner. After the meal, I went to the Old Man with my papers and informed him:

"I have a sick leave," I put the document on his desk, "but I'll go to work." I spent all my money on baksheesh - I didn't care if the agent told him what I had spent thirty dollars on. He didn't say anything.

In the mess, at lunch, the Third Officer announced:

"We're sailing to Durban - South Africa. We will take a barge from there and tow it to Gabon."

There was an uproar. Everyone was happy with the news, it's better than standing under the platform. If we did the job, the contract would end. I went to sleep. I was tired of all the events. In the morning I called Kinga who answered the phone and in a breathless voice informed me:

"You know, I was in town with Ula. I went to the bookstore and bought a large map for the wall. I hung it in the living room, and I marked the place where you are with the thumbtacks. It's very far. How are you? You're healthy?"

"Yes, my dear. I'm fine." It's terribly hard to talk on the phone from the ship - what should I have said to her? After all, I wouldn't talk about work. And all these: "I miss you, I would like to be with you, I can't wait" sound artificial and dry. And what had happened, I wouldn't tell her anyway, because what for? She would have only gotten nervous. So I told her the latest news:

"We are sailing now to South Africa, to Durban, it's from the Pacific side. When we get back from there, the contract will end."

"How is that? You will be sailing all Christmas and New Year's Eve?" she realized only now.

"Yes. That is why I express my good wishes for Christmas and New Year now. On this occasion, also give my best to the parents and all my friends."

"Thank you ... I also wish you all the best, Richie, Merry Christmas and Happy New Year. You know, honey, I've gotten three days off. The manager told me that since I'm from far away, I will be given three days off for Christmas. So I'll be home all the week. Right after Christmas I go back to work, and for the New Year's Eve celebration, I go to Natalka. Together with the colleagues, we agreed to spend New Year's Eve on the pier in Sopot.

"I'm glad," I replied, although I wasn't. I preferred to spend the New Year's Eve with Kinga.

There are a few days left until Christmas ... I'll be sad without you.

"Then I'll call you home on Christmas Eve, when you get there. Kisses. Bye, bye," I said and hung up.

We sailed to Durban for ten days, swallowing about five degrees a day. At the entrance to the port, we received a helicopter pilot. It was faster and probably safer that way, because the large Atlantic wave made it difficult to reach us by motorboat.

It was already the New Year, the fourth of January. In the port, we stood by the barge. It was modern, self-submersible. On board, there were carried out preparations for the cruise. The teams were loading and securing the cargo. This part of the work didn't belong to our obligations, but the captain told me to go and observe everything, especially how the cargo was stowed[7]. After all, it was the captain's responsibility to bring the cargo safely and securely to the port of destination. On the barge, I learned that loading and fastening would take a minimum of a week. I had to organize my time somehow. We don't always have the opportunity to visit the city in which we stop, and now there was an opportunity to get to know the local attractions.

The next day, a heated discussion took place over breakfast in the mess. Chief began:

"Listen, the company gave the welfare money, quite a lot."

"How much?" Asked the third officer.

"As many as it takes. It depends on what we decide to do."

"Who was here?" I said.

"I was, but five years ago," Yuri replied.

---

[7] Stowed - mounted, attached rigidly.

"What's interesting to see here?"

"I don't know. I didn't go far. I was only in the dolphinarium and on the Golden Mile."

"The city is large, has over a million inhabitants," showed off the mechanic. "Get that Indian over here. There is one man who sell everything and take care of everything, girls too," he added.

The Indian came, glad to be able to earn some money.

"We have the world's largest oceanarium," he praised.

"Yes, yes, everything is the greatest," Bronek said sarcastically.

"You can also go on a photo safari. I'll get it for you," he offered. "There is also a diamond mine with a grindery, you can visit it and buy a diamond right away. It is much cheaper than in a store, but you still have to spend no less than a thousand dollars."

"Interesting, but not for us," shouted Bronek.

"You shorty. You wouldn't even buy an old cubic zirconia," Stasio teased him.

Bronek was known for his avarice. But as he claimed, he had had a difficult childhood which taught him to respect money.

"I prefer to go on the safari," I said.

"Are you crazy?! Stasio said, "It would take about three days!"

"How long would it take to travel, quickly explore and return?" I asked the Indian.

"I know you don't have time, ten to twelve hours is enough. The park is close, just outside the city."

"I'm all for it!" Andrei called.

"Bake in the sun and drive in a car? It's not for me. I prefer to go to the aquarium," the Chief expressed his opinion on the photo-safari.

"Then we'll do both. And that's it," the first mechanic interrupted. That's where we were at.

"I'm going to the Old Man. He will tell the agent to get the papers."

And to the Indian I said:

"Come tomorrow with an itinerary for the photo safari and oceanarium for several people and with costs. We'll see what you're worth."

The captain accepted our plans with one reservation: they couldn't interfere with our duties. We established who was going where and how to set up watches so that everything worked fine. There were four of us on the photo safari. To the oceanarium and for a city tour were going eight people, in two rounds.

The next day, the agent informed us:

"It's OK, you can go on safari for about fourteen hours. The cost is one hundred and eighty dollars per person. The Indian wants two hundred and twenty dollars per head, but this will include two meals and the rental of a telephoto camera."

The Old Man chose the first, cheaper version - scrooge, he'll probably put the rest in his pocket," the boys said. In turn, the Indian will drive people around the city and to the aquarium. He wanted ten bucks a person, but the captain was supposed to hire a minibus with a driver and buy tickets. The Old Man agreed to it, probably because he was going himself. I followed the Indian. "Listen," I said to him, "I have a day off now, take me to a jewelry store." I knew he would get a baksheesh there if the customer he brought to the store, bought something in it. "It have to be cheap and fair," I added.

"Are you Russian?" He asked.

"No. Pole."

"That's good because nearby, in the center, a Pole has a shop. You will probably find something interesting," he assured me.

"Wait a minute, I need to get dressed."

"OK, I'm waiting," he replied with a smile.

Yuri shouted to me:

"Where are you going?"

"To the center."

I'll take you there."

"Just be quick. Hurry up," I agreed with a hint of dissatisfaction in my voice. I preferred to go alone for such purchases, but Yuri is a nice guy, so I couldn't refuse him.

The Indian drove us to some uninteresting place, but it was indeed a shopping center near the port. We entered the building from the yard, then went up the stairs to the first floor where we were greeted by a solid steel gate. We were expected there, as a young white woman stood behind it, asking what ship we were from.

"There are discounts for seafarers," she informed us. "Where are you from?" She asked curiously.

"From Poland and Russia," Yuri replied. The blonde took us further, to a large room full of jewelry showcases. I was breathless when I saw the diamond ware there.

"What would you like to drink? Coffee, water, wine?"

"Maybe wine." Yuri replied, with his nose stuck to the diamond rings.

After a while, the boss came with two girls. A tall, aged man, elegantly dressed, shone a diamond ring on his finger for starters.

He greeted us with broken Polish with a Ukrainian accent. He waved his hand at the two girls who stood politely behind him. One spoke Russian, the other spoke Polish. "This is the right approach to the client," I thought, and in Polish I turned to the blonde:

"Do you serve in all languages here?"

"No, but we also speak Hindu, Japanese, Chinese, Ukrainian and the local dialect.

"Great," I praised her.

There was a short conversation with the boss, who assured us in Polish-Ukrainian that everything there were real diamonds, which he had been trading for over twenty years.

"I only sell diamonds," he explained to us, "and the gold in which they are framed is given to the client for free. Prices are in dollars and there is a twenty percent discount for seafarers. We issue a certificate and a guarantee for each diamond," he said, wished us a nice shopping experience and discreetly disappeared, leaving us with a bottle of delicious red wine of local production at our disposal.

The Indian was right - prices started at a thousand dollars upwards. At large diamonds, instead of the price, there was information - negotiable. I asked the blonde girl to help me choose an engagement ring - "a small one," I added.

"What size?" She asked.

I didn't know it, but I remembered that I once put on Kinga's silver ring on the beach and it only fit the little finger of my left hand. The blonde girl brought the patterns, took measurements, and after a while she showed me four small, delicate rings. I liked one of them right away, not the cheapest one, but also not the most expensive. One brilliant mounted on a golden heart with a ring made of white gold. Wonder! Sitting at the table and sipping wine, I listened to the blonde girl explaining me how to distinguish a real diamond from cubic zirconia or quartz. She showed me four loose stones and asked if I could tell the difference between two rhinestones and two diamonds. I took a magnifying glass, and nothing - I couldn't see any difference between them.

"And you will recognize?" I asked.

"These yes, but others not always," she assured me. "Look," she said, taking the electronic gadget and touching the pebbles in turn, "the diamonds cause a clear signal of the device, and the rhinestones don't."

The only thing left for me was to hope that what she said was true, because I don't know anything about it anyway.

I got a certificate written out with a detailed description of the diamond, a guarantee for the fixation and the bill. I paid and we were all satisfied, as Yuri bought a signet ring. We just go to the center to buy a Durban souvenir. I bought a wooden sculpture of a Zulu warrior at a souvenir stand. We wandered around the shops a little more and returned to the ship.

The next day, the agent informed us:

"Departure for the safari the day after tomorrow."

Two days passed quickly. In the morning a small bus came to pick us up. A little shabby. Four of us were supposed to go, but unfortunately the mechanic had to stay, as there was some urgent work to be done on the machine. So we drove alone to the outskirts of Durban. Several passengers who lived outside the city got in the bus there. We drove about ninety kilometers and only on the spot it turned out that we didn't reach the park, but its edge. There we changed to a large Jeep with an open roof. The further road led through the African bush for about a hundred kilometers. We were all the time in the car. There was a security guard with us, or it would be better to call him a hunter - just in case.

It was quiet, nobody attacked us. Lions looked at us as intruders, not as food.

You could see everything and take pictures. However, you had to be well prepared for it. Other travelers had good brand name telephoto cameras and spotting scopes. We only had binoculars from the ship and ordinary digital cameras. I didn't even have a satellite phone, but I saw a Japanese talking quietly as if he had been in the center of Tokyo. The views were beautiful, the car stopped every now and then and we looked at the lions that the guides showed us first. They were lying not far away, about ten meters from us. But when they heard the click of camera shutters, two of them got up and lazily jogged to the nearest bushes.

We looked at them with curiosity, and they looked at us with boredom. Seamen from a Japanese container ship sat next to us. They had two or three cameras each and were happy to share them, allowing us to see everything through telephoto lenses that make the views perceived as if they were right in front of us.

I saw elephants quite up close, antelopes too. Giraffes from afar, and yet their large swinging necks gave the impression of palm trees swaying in the wind.

The most important thing, however, was this space and how quickly the guides knew where the animals were. I suspect that they communicated with each other via satellite, or maybe they knew it from experience and many years of observation.

We drove to a river where hippos were puddling. Their mouths wide open above the water looked like toothy flowers with bulging eyes above them. The constant yawning made them seem terribly bored. Maybe it was some peculiar advances characteristic of those fat bodies. Over the water, there were birds flying everywhere. Species of varying size, shape and color covered all places, from sandbanks to muddy shallows and tall grasses, creating a mosaic of different colors and a cascade of sounds carried by the water, interrupted time and time again by the sounds of roaring elephants taking a mud bath. The bush, wind and smell were unique. There is no such stench as in a zoo. The animals were used to humans, but still wary.

We looked from a small hill towards the valley with the antelopes. You could see the warm air moving over the green grass, scratched here and there by worn down hooves. Among them rose, like a marshal's mace, a mighty Baobab, on which a leopard was lazily basking, not giving a toss about some intruders watching it. You could hear the sounds of roaring elephants, the belching of antelopes, and the short clatter of hyenas, and among it all, and the crackling of camera shutters. And only this made you feel that you were not at home, but among these animals - in their territory. Here we were in the cage, and they, being in the wild, watched us. It was clear how this patch of land was divided. Where lions walked, and where did elephants and antelopes. Whose kingdom was by the water, and who ruled there. The hippies in the water are like lions in the savannah. They are not afraid of anyone and are quite noisy and aggressive at this time.

Whole flocks of birds were visible, their flashy hues and colors were unlike anything we have here. Even at this distance, we could hear their varied singing and screaming gibberish. Suddenly we got breathless at the sight of a startled flock of pink flamingos with long necks pointing straight at the sun. Their simultaneous start from the water in which they stood knee-deep, and then the form of a wide-spread carpet, undulating with rhythmic movements and rising upwards. Their wings spread wide, beating air, sparkled in the sun with all shades of purple. Behind them, everything that had wings and could fly took flight.

The view, when the horizon in front of us is blocked by numerous flocks of birds soaring into the air, can only be compared to an exodus. Taking off from the water, they first quickly move their feet on the surface, and when they gain speed, they take flight. Then they fly up in a circle and make a lot of noise and scream that is probably meant to warn other animals that something is lurking down there and it's dangerous. They fly so for a few minutes only to land in the same place after a while. The bravest ones land first and glide to the ground, ready to go up again at any second. When they land, the next ones go down in waves, making a lot of noise to get the best feeding place. "From where there is so much food for this mass of birds?" I wondered.

If you watch antelopes eat grass, you might think they are our good cows in the pasture. But it is a deceptive sight, because if you look closely you will see that not all of them feed. There are also advanced specimens that watch carefully and, above all, smell the air to sense the danger. If they see something, there is a short burp, and everything that lives move forward. You can hear the pounding of hooves on the ground and the movement of the air as the mass of bodies runs forward, not being sure if it's not a trap set by lions and if there are no lionesses lurking in the bushes in the front. Because it is lionesses that hunt. The males are lazy and, as befits the king of beasts and the ruler of these lands, they wait for the females to catch something. However, it is the lions who start tearing the prey first and choose the best bites. I saw an interesting sight when I looked up, where scavengers soar high against the sun: large, strong vultures waiting their turn. But not only they want to sit at this table - lots of other animals too, everyone will find a piece of their cake here.

Hyenas wait closest to the lions. You can't see all of them, just the protruding ears with the wisps of hair sticking out on their tips. You hear short, angry barking, as if they warned the lions that they will no longer tolerate eating their food. However, they don't dare to approach them closer, because then a lioness moves towards them as if from a catapult, which, even when fed, will not share food with them. When a lioness attacks, a female hyena, because it is her that is in charge of a herd, leaps aside and, running away, snaps back. She doesn't fight because she knows that she has no chance and may not survive the moment when the lioness catches her. After that, everything happens as in a movie that is projected from the end. The lioness returns to the victim, and the hyenas again come closer. When the herd of lions devours for today, tomorrow, and maybe for a few days, then with a gentle jog, it goes away to rest - preferably where there is some shade. The lioness climbs the branch, and the lazy lion lays down in the grass so that he cannot be seen at all. The sun is bending down to the ground, turning red and illuminating the hot, undulating air rising up with our sensations.

We came back tired but satisfied - with a lot of new experiences and many photos.

Chapter 9

Barge

It was already after African attractions. It was time to go back to Earth.

We sailed out on January 12th. At the briefing, the Old Man ordered:

To the barge are going:

Richie, the Third Mechanic Sergey and Fitter Bronek. You're taking the barge. We will sail when they finish loading. Get everything ready for about three weeks.

It will take us two weeks to go to Gabon, and we got another week for any surprises. After such an announcement, we spent more and more time on the barge. Everything was already prepared so that it could be drowned, or rather partially drowned, so that a load could be placed on it.

Most difficulties were posed by precise placing on it one of the elements of the platform, which was quietly moored at the quay. It was a floating rectangular support base of the oil rig, about thirty by fifty meters in size, with four poles seventy meters high. Each was in the shape of a square with sides less than three meters, with tabs protruding like a giant thread, spaced a meter and a half apart. At the base of each pole there was a clamping ring with hydraulic devices. When the hydraulics was turned on, the poles began to slide down.

The small port tug that secured the barge looked like a toy that was added only to emphasize how different it was from the actual size of the barge.

After two days, the water was already pouring over its deck. Three or four meters more and it would be possible to place this gigantic element towering over ships on the deck of the barge.

The Shell dockmen quickly dealt with this part of the work, pulling the sunken stern part of the barge under the platform. Of the entire barge, only the beak was visible, which placed high, was protruding above the water. Only then did they begin pumping out the water from the barge's tanks until its deck rested against the bottom of the platform.

"It's enough for today," the head of the operation told us. "We are waiting for the river boats, they will arrive tomorrow."

The loading of the six flat-bottomed river boats and three patrol boats took three more days. The barges were loaded across. The river boats didn't fit in this way and protruded a few meters above each side. And yet the barge was huge - like a small soccer field.

The Old Man sail out from the current berth. We set the stern under the bow of the barge and handed over a tow line. As the remaining water was pumped out of the barge, I started getting ready to get on it. We loaded all the devices, accessories, provisions and rescue equipment. Back-up generators, portable pumps, welding machine, cables and other things needed for a two to three week stay were the highlights.

The barge was specialized, so it already had everything needed for towing. There was a short briefing in the captain's room, during which we agreed on all possible options - including leaving the barge.

The prognosis is good, but here, at the very bottom, we might come across a storm. This area is famous for short, very strong winds. Take this into account," he warned us against the effects of bad weather. "Let's go," he added.

We went to our object, where the captain checked the fastening, devices as well as rescue and communications equipment, and only then decided:

"We can sail."

Before towing, we ate the last meal on the ship in the mess, during which I thought about fixing meals on the barge. Anyway - I liked it. The cook gave us ice cream on parting:

"Here you are, fill your boots."

Stasio, who was watching it, couldn't stand it:

"Wait a minute, what about me, I'm a dog? I would eat it too!"

"You already had your portion of ice cream," the cook answered him, "when you were on land and you picked up an Asian girl."

"And he has what he wanted," I thought. "What for did he tell everyone that he had met an Asian girl and dated her for a few days?"

"Ah, guys, how sweet she is," he boasted, "and what tits she has!"

"And how much did that sweetness cost you?" Bronek's curiosity was reaching its zenith.

You only have money in front of your nose, and you haven't spent even a single rand[8]!"

"It was worth it!" Stasio said and disappeared, fearing further questions.

We didn't say goodbye so as not to tempt fate. And he was already preparing a surprise for us.

Before entering "Berta" I called Kinga:

"Honey, I'm getting on the barge and I won't be able to call you."

"Why, there's no phone there?" I heard.

I was stunned, but I calmly explained:

"No, there is nothing."

"So what are you going to do if there's nothing there?"

"I'm going to sit and think about you."

---

[8] Rand - local currency.

"Alright, alright ... And when will you call me again?"

"In about eighteen days."

"So much time?!" She exclaimed.

"Yes, unfortunately. I can't do anything about it."

"So be it, I'll wait."

"I love you!" I added.

"I love you too, take care."

"When we talk again, I'll be home a week or two later," I reminded Kinga.

"I know, I cross off every day on my calendar."

"Bye-bye, I have to go."

"Bye, dear," I heard.

We passed a quick security check on "Neptun" and a longer one on the barge, where border guards scoured the entire ship, looking for stowaways. It was clear so we could sail.

A small port tug helped us when leaving the port. It was attached to the stern of the barge and served us as the helm.

We had a lot of work to do on the barge as they pulled us with short reins[9] to make it easier to maneuver. After leaving the port, we dropped the chains into the water and we could relax. "Neptun" gave a tug line. "It is about six hundred meters long," I thought.

Once again, we checked if the loads were fastened properly. It seemed to us that they had it done reliably and professionally. Everything was fine. How illusory these hopes were, we saw after a few days.

---

[9] Reins (harness) - ropes used to tow a floating object.

The first days were peaceful, the time on the barge was passing quickly. We adapted to the new reality, and days and nights, we spent working and chatting.

"We've already passed Elizabeth," the Chief reported to us on the radio.

We marked our position on the map that the first officer had given us on parting. It was already worn out, but very useful for us.

"We have a bad forecast for tomorrow, it will be a little windy," he added. "We have nowhere to hide, so we will storm."

The Old Man was moving away from the mainland. Tomorrow he would change the course and we would go up, more north.

"We have passed Cap Down," "Neptun" reported to us. We saw that it was blowing more and more. There was a sudden break in the weather. It was the cold air masses from Antarctica that caused these severe storms. We fastened everything rigidly. The wind began to change direction rapidly to the southeast, still gaining strength.

"If only nothing else happened," cawed Bronek.

This time we didn't go to the cabins, but spread out in the mess. We brought mattresses and blankets inside and, lying on the floor, we tried to take a nap.

"Berta" began to sway unnaturally to the beat of the gusts of wind and the waves breaking onto the deck. "Neptun" tried to set its bow towards the wave, but carried by the wind, it began to slowly approach "Neptun's" leeward. "If it goes on like this, it will overtake it and start towing it," I thought anxiously.

With great reluctance, the beak of "Berta" climbed the wave, then sharply left it sideways, tilting dangerously.

"I don't think we will sway," said the third mechanic.

"Theoretically not. The barge is wide and long, but the water will come aboard," I told him.

"Neptun" faced the wave.

"It seems that already the eight is blowing," I said, looking at the wind gauge.

Our living quarters were in the bow and we were shaken terribly. I sensed there was something wrong with the barge.

"You can't see anything," said the Third, returning from his round of the barge, "but what we are supposed to see, if it's freezing cold," he replied to himself.

I called "Neptun".

"Neptun, this is Berta" - that's what we used to call the barge, because who would like to say "three hundred and ninety-three" which was its number.

"Berta," replied the captain who was on the bridge of "Neptun".

"He's still on the bridge," I thought. I knew he wouldn't descend until the wind calmed down.

"Could you decrease the speed a little?" I asked. "We are being shaken mercilessly."

"We're sailing slowly, it can't be slower," he replied. "Is something going on?"

"No, nothing," I said. I didn't want to talk about my hunches, but my instinct said: "check everything you can."

As the enormous waves hit the barge's blunt beak, it seemed to stop for a moment, then twitch and move forward with leaps, overcoming the resistance of the waves crashing against it. With each such jump, you could see the tow line jerking upwards, wanting to leap out of the water. It couldn't. It wouldn't pop out. It would rather break.

The straps of the chains to which the tow was attached, gnashing horribly at the chock, were swinging from top to bottom in time with these strokes. But the chains are attached to the tow line to absorb with their weight the stresses caused by the waves.

"We have to grease the chocks more," I called to Sergey.

With special grease, using large brushes, we smeared the chains in the chock - the grinding stopped.

After a few hours, "Berta" shook even more. We called a huddle.

"Something's wrong," I said. "We shouldn't be shaken like that."

"Maybe it's because of the poles? They are so high," the Third speculated. "The center of gravity is high up there," he added.

"I don't think that's it. They are stable. It's something different."

"But what?" we all wondered. I called "Neptun" again:

"Yes, "Berta", we hear you," I heard the Old Man.

"Captain, I want to go outside and see if everything is okay."

The captain asked again:

"Is something going on?"

"I don't know," I replied this time, "I have a feeling that something is not right because we are being shaken terribly, and we shouldn't be."

The captain knew that I had a lot of experience and I was the only one in the crew that had sailed on wrecks while they are being towed.

There was a moment of silence.

"Alright, but take care of yourselves," he agreed. "Communications every five minutes," he added.

I hadn't finished talking about my hunch yet when the alarm in the control room started howling. The detector showed the water in the tank amidships. The water level was rapidly increasing. We turned on the pumps, which were powerful, but the water wasn't diminishing.

"We need to find out what could be the cause of this," The third set up the plan of "Berta".

We leaned over the drawings.

"It's strange," said the third mechanic, "water flooded the center of the tank in front of the stern, but the bottom of the barge is dry."

We conveyed the message to the ship.

"Check what is happening, from where this water gets into the tank," commanded the Captain.

"You'll come with me to the deck, under the platform," I told the third mechanic. He was younger and more agile than Bronek.

"Fitter stays in the control room, tapped. We will try to check everything," I distributed tasks. We went, wearing only shorts, life jackets and safety belts. We wrapped the cellular radios in foil to prevent them from getting wet, and put them in shorts pockets. I put on sneakers. "I won't slide on the wet deck," I thought.

"So let's go. Bronek, prepare coffee, we'll be back in half an hour," asked Sergey. He was wrong - we came back only after two hours.

The worst situation was on the bow of the barge. Water flooded us with each wave, and gusts of wind didn't allow us to straighten. Needless to say, we were like a "drowned rat" - soaked from head to toe. The water was twenty-eight degrees, so those compulsory water jets weren't bothersome. As we walked, we shouted to each other.

"It's OK here," called the Third, pointing to the spare tow line on the bow deck.

We checked everything thoroughly and went down to the main deck of the "Berta". We hid behind one of the little ships mounted on the upper deck. I reported to "Neptun":

"On the bow, everything is alright, we are moving on."

Wind-blown splashes reached everywhere. Salt water flooded my eyes, I had to rub them with my hand every now and then to see well.

"Damn it!" The Third shouted to me. "Will it calm down?"

"It's not in full swing yet," I thought.

"It'll be quiet until tomorrow," I shouted to him. And it would probably be so, because there the storms, though violent, are short.

To go further, we had to get on the river boats and, across their decks, go to the other side to descend to "Berta's" deck - and so six times.

We rested every now and then to connect with "Neptun".

The patrol ships were flat-bottomed, so we passed under their bow from the leeward.

I was going first, two meters away followed by the Third. I came out from behind the bow of the patrol ship, heading towards the center of "Berta's" deck, when suddenly I heard a terrible creak of metal sheet being torn. Despite the howling wind, it was clearly audible.

I stopped, signaling the Third to stop too.

"Be careful. We're not going any further."

We got on board the patrol ship to see everything from there carefully. My hunch - or maybe the experience I had gained - didn't let me down. When the wave descended from the deck of the "Berta", pouring back into the sea, it momentarily exposed a strip of torn deck metal, about twenty meters long. The tear was half a meter wide in some places, or even more. Water raging across the deck poured in there. With each stronger impact of the wave, the metal sheet either was torn further or the opening got slightly sealed. "It probably depends on whether we are high on the wave, then stress occurs and the deck breaks, and when we are at the bottom of the wave, it gets sealed," I speculated. We wanted to enter the patrol ship's wheelhouse, but unfortunately it was closed.

"Where's the key? It has to be here somewhere!" The Third called to me.

"It is here for sure! This is what we agreed with the loading manager!" I yelled back to him.

"I got it!" He cried, "There it is." It was attached with wire to a door bolt on the other side of the wheelhouse. We went inside.

"It's really cool," the Third was still shouting.

"Keep it down, you don't have to yell like that anymore."

I connected with "Neptun" and described what we saw. The Old Man told us to wait there. He would probably talk to the company about what to do with it.

"Captain," I said, "I will go aboard the river boat and see if the sides of "Berta" are also torn."

"Alright, go, but be careful."

We boarded the river boat. First I went to the bow. I looked at starboard - nothing. Everything was fine there, the starboard of "Berta" was intact. The tear on board the "Berta" stopped about fifteen meters ahead of the starboard. Then we went to the stern of the little ship, it was not so good there.

The tear on the port side was quite wide. It didn't reach the waterline, but the water was still breaking in there.

I lay flattened like a frog on the stern of the boat, tilting my head outward. I was afraid that the wind would take me away and throw me into the ocean. Admittedly, I was attached, but the devil knows what could have happened. The wave didn't reach the little ships, only splashes of water hitting the side of the "Berta", carried by strong gusts of wind, and flooded me again and again. I looked closely. No - the water wasn't breaking in anymore. It had already flooded the entire tank to the line of the breach in the side of the "Berta". When a wave glides from the bow in such a mounting bank, flooding the deck, it pours into the center of the tank, but when it passes this place, it pours out. So the tank was full now.

The Third held my legs so tightly that they got numb. We returned to the wheelhouse of the patrol ship.

I described the situation to the Old Man.

"How's the platform?" He asked.

"It stands," said the Third. "He knows that much," I thought, "he sees that it stands."

"The pillars are stable, they aren't swaying. They are tilting back and forth, but with the barge, so I guess it's okay," I reported.

It started to get dark. The captain asked again where the tear was and how wide the holes were.

"Between the penultimate and last patrol ship, from the stern side of the "Berta"," I repeated. "From the port side, it starts two meters above the waterline and extends twenty meters to starboard," I clarified.

There was a constant feverish exchange of views. Probably in the company they determined what tank was flooded and what we were exposed to. After a while the captain said: "Go back to the wheelhouse[10], to the bow of the "Berta". When you get there, report."

The wind grew stronger.

---

[10] Wheelhouse (bridge) - a navigation room on a ship with a high degree of integration of the functions necessary to maintain efficient internal and external communication, determining the position and safe guidance of the ship.

"How hard is the wind blowing?" I asked.

"Ten," answered the Chief.

"We went back to the bow. Standing in the doorway, the third mechanic shouted:

"Coffee, coffee! I want coffee!"

"And do you want to eat chocolate?" Bronek asked.

"Yes, but with coffee."

"Well, here you are," Bronek replied and pointed at the sheet[11]. There was a calendar with a naked black girl on it.

None of us knew then how prophetic the words were. "It's good that we are still in fine spirits," I thought.

We drank coffee, having wiped ourselves thoroughly with a towel before. The Chief called us:

"Where the hell are you?! You were supposed to report!"

"We're just going into the mess[12]," I told him.

"Okay. Look, nothing can be done yet. Night is falling, and you shouldn't wander there at night."

"And what if the crack gets longer?"

"What's meant to be, will be. We have a forecast which shows that the wind will die down tomorrow, at most the day after tomorrow evening. Until then, one of you must be awake. Keep watch by turns. Check the raft. Sleep in the belts. Set the main headlamp on the poles. Our people will also watch what happens," he gave orders. "If the barge breaks, maybe you'll hear it. Don't leave it hastily. It has watertight bulkheads, and even if the stern breaks off, the bow should swim."

---

[11] Sheet - on a ship: an interior wall of a room.

[12] Mess - a dining room on a ship.

"And what will happen," I said, "if the poles collapse on us?"

"The company concluded that it is rather impossible. Being heavier and higher than the rest of the cargo, they will fly aft, into the water. They calculated that they wouldn't reach you in the bow."

"It must be really bad, since they are already analyzing such variants," I thought looking at them.

"OK," I replied.

"Communications every half hour."

"Take care," I heard before they hung up.

We checked the raft, we put the belts on and I went to take a nap, because I didn't think I would be able to sleep. However, I fell asleep. I felt someone prodding my shoulder. I was immediately awake.

"Are you alright? Is something going on?"

"You can't see or hear anything," Bronek replied to me. "Get up for watch."

I had a "dog watch". In the morning the wind raged even more. "Berta" was still shaking, and the water flowed over its deck. I shone the floodlight on the entire barge, piece by piece. Nothing. It looked like everything was fine. Then I set the spotlight so that it illuminated the poles. It was for "Neptun", they would be able to see them well through binoculars. "Is the worst over?" I thought, waking the Third for watch.

I decided to sleep more until eight o'clock. When it got lighter, we would see what was going on there.

They woke me up before seven.

"Get up, go to the control room. The Old Man is waiting."

A quick conference. We with the captain, he with the company, and then with us.

We got the orders.

"You have to go into the tank where the skin is torn and open two valves. One of them is at the bulkhead, from the stern side, and the other, from the bow side. Both on the left side. If you succeed, you will pump out the water from the torn tank, and then from the bottom ballast one."

"For what?" I thought, but I figured there were smarter people there and they knew what they were doing.

We looked at the plan of the barge.

"They are," said the third mechanic, "here," and he pointed.

"And where's the hatch? When we were there, I didn't see it," I was surprised.

"It must be amidships between the little ships. It's here," the Third pointed at the place on the layout. "Damn it. Who will go? We?" He asked, looking at me.

"Is there gas or not?" Bronek wondered aloud.

"There shouldn't be," replied the Third.

"And this is supposed to be enough for me to get in?" Bronek wasn't convinced.

The Third was very intense and wanted information from the Old Man:

"A written order from the company? With a log entry?"

"Yes. Of course," the Old Man replied.

We had no choice - we went. We were wearing life jackets, safety belts, and the Third took the keys and a safety line. We didn't get dressed, there was no need - we would be dripping with water anyway. We put on the helmets and I taped a small waterproof flashlight to mine. I picked up the other large one. The Third took one more, just in case.

It took us half an hour to reach the hatch which turned out to be locked with screws so tightened that it was impossible to unscrew them with a wrench.

"We are going back to the little ship, we have to find some pipe or crowbar," said the Third. "But where to get it? We'll look around here."

We split up both ways.

"Here it is," I called to the Third. On the sheet by the companionway, there was a fire ax and a crowbar in a display case. I broke the glass and took the crowbar. Sergey grabbed the ax.

"What do you need this damn thing for?"

"Maybe it'll come in handy," I heard him lugging it into the hatch.

We swiftly opened the hatch, which was quite low above the deck, so from time to time it was flooded with a larger wave pouring across the deck. Splashes of water carried by the wind whipped our bodies dressed only in T-shirts and shorts. Water gurgled in the sneakers but I didn't pay attention to it anymore.

"Fasten the rope latch," shouted the Third.

OK - I fastened and we were already connected with a safety rope. We knew the communication procedures by heart. Sergey, however, repeated:

"One jerk: OK, two jerks: ease it, three or more jerks: pull me out."

"Okay, okay," I said, then added:

"Under no circumstances go down, no matter what happens."

I took off my life vest. I had a modern roll on my chest, put over my neck, but I was afraid it would open up in the tank and make a mess.

"Are you doing the right thing?" He asked.

"I don't know."

I was slowly going down the metal clasps. The ladder led straight down into the darkness.

After a while, darkness enveloped also me. The flashlight on the helmet wasn't too useful, it only illuminated the clamps in front of me. Holding on with one hand, with the other one I reached for the other large flashlight strapped to my belt. I turned it on, and a beam of strong light brightened the darkness a little. I directed it down. Two meters below me, raved the water, flowing to the rhythm of the rocking of the "Berta". "How deep is it there?" I thought as I went slowly down. I felt that I was submerging my feet in the water. I was going down. Sergey was still letting go of the safety line with sensitivity.

The eyes were adjusting to the darkness, and from above, a faint glow shone as far as the water. Only now did I begin to hear the sounds "Berta" was making as it struggled against the waves. Those dull grunts of steel frames gripping with hundreds of tons of water, compounded by the empty space of the tank, penetrated through me, each time causing a shiver of my whole body and an instinctive urge to curl up as if before an unexpected blow struck from an unknown direction.

Suddenly I heard the creaking of the sheet metal pieces overlapping, and the waves hitting the side. The echo intensified this cascade of intermingling sounds that, mixed with the roar of the wind, made the warning signal sound in my head - run away, quickly.

I suppressed this self-preservation and continued to go down carefully. I was already submerged up to the waist. Every now and then I was touching the space with my foot, checking if I could already stand on the bottom of the tank. One more buckle, and this time my leg caught on the frame[13]. I stood on it, but I couldn't stand like that for a long time. Holding the buckle above the head with one hand, and standing with one foot on the frame, I lowered the other leg.

"Will it reach the bottom of the tank? It should, the frames aren't high," I speculated. I felt the bottom, but up to my chest, I was submerged in the water, which, to the rhythm of "Berta's" jumps, reached up to my chin, flooding my mouth. I stood on the bottom on my both legs. OK. What a relief. I could go on. I remembered about the third mechanic and tugged the rope once - it was OK. Sergey returned the jerk, so everything was alright.

It was dark, I was trying to figure out where that goddamn valve was. I heard a monstrous, rumbling with a resonance grind that made a shock pass through me. "It's from the cold," I told myself.

I looked up and saw a glow, a point little brighter than everything else.

"This is my only hope of return," the thought flew through my head like lightning.

I kept walking, looking at the side of the "Berta" lit by the flashlight. Suddenly I felt water flooding me. My eyes and mouth were shielded by the helmet, but I felt its salty taste breaking into my nose and throat anyway. I leaned forward sharply to hide my face and eyes. It was only after a while that I realized that I was standing under the torn deck plating. This is where the ocean waves from above were breaking into the tank, showing their strength and anger.

I had to find that shitty valve. How far had I gone? It seemed like I had walked all the way around the stadium, but it probably wasn't more than twenty-some meters.

I was sweeping everything around me with light.

---

[13] Frame - the basic transverse element of a ship's carcass.

"Fuck!" I swore, cheering myself. "How am I supposed to find that shitty valve?!"

I tried to remember the diagram I had watched.

"It must be here somewhere! Two meters from this bulkhead," I thought, having the diagram in front of my eyes, "here I'm standing!"

Suddenly it dawned on me - "it's under the water, that's why I can't see it!"

As a rule, the valves are located less than a meter from the bottom of the tank. I put the flashlight in the water trying to see something. Nothing. The light shining from the helmet gave a reflection on the water and it bothered me. I turned it off. I put the flashlight in the water again, this time better. Suddenly something dark appeared to the side. I stepped closer and felt around with my foot again and again. Finally, I found something. There it is. Now it was only necessary to unscrew it. "Damn it! Do I have to do so many things the hard way?!" I continued cursing when my hands didn't reach the valve. I had to submerge. I turned on the headlamp and attached the large flashlight to my belt. The beam of light swept around everything but not what was needed. I stood astride over the valve. Taking a gulp of air, I bent down, plunging my head into the water, and I grabbed the valve wheel. The flashlight on my helmet went off, but I kept turning. Dear fitters! It's good that they didn't tighten this valve completely, because I would have to go back for the crowbar. I turned the wheel until it stopped. Panting heavily, I wiped my eyes stinging from salt water with my hand.

"The valve is open, now I have to go to the other side of the tank, that's a lot for these conditions," I thought.

I was walking carefully and slowly, every few meters lifting my leg and standing on the frame - then the water was above my waist. I descended from it to the bottom of the tank, and the water reached my chest. It was with this rhythm that I moved on. Each time I swept the water in front of me with the use of the big flashlight, trying to keep the correct direction of March. One time my foot slipped and I fell facedown in the water, extending my hands in a flash. However, I didn't let go of the flashlight.

I felt the lifeline tighten and hold me. I swam face down, and opened my eyes - a strong beam of light illuminated the rusty bottom of the tank. "It's nothing that my thoughts play a trick on me, and my imagination shows shadows, some floating corpses, and slimy creatures with long tentacles - it's the subconscious," I told myself. "This is the effect of the recently watched movie about the pirates," I was calming myself down.

But I was wrong - it wasn't a movie, but a real corpse. A dead man whom I took for dreams and hallucinations. It was hard for me to get to my feet because the third mechanic kept the line taut and didn't let it go. He didn't know what was going on - he felt a tug, so he held the line down. But how could I give him a signal when I couldn't get to my feet? Finally, I pulled my knees up to my chin and, crouching down, I put my feet on the bottom. I was completely submerged. I straightened up and stood on the frame. I jerked the line once, he answered in a moment, I jerked twice, he loosened the line and I moved on. I lost my helmet somewhere but I kept going. Now I was walking over the frames, lifting first my right leg, then the left one. Later the Third told me:

"I felt a tug. I had my heart in my mouth. 'What's going on there?' I thought. I decided to wait half a minute and pull. I felt the line twitch like a fish on a hook.

"I tried to get to my feet," I explained.

"Yeah. Now I know. Next you gave the signal and I loosened the line. Then you walked on."

I knew that the second valve was in the same place as the first, just on the other side of the tank. I walked and walked, lighting the way with the flashlight. Now, however, I shone not on the water, but on the top of the tank - then I knew better which way to go.

Something black loomed in the water again. Overcoming my fear, I directed the light there. The black stain was jiggling in the light.

"What is this?" I asked myself.

I stepped closer and suddenly I got hit by consciousness - it was a corpse. Dead body - but black. He was a Negro. I could see his extended hands clearly, he was swimming with his face turned to the bottom. I turned back quickly to the exit. Like a madman, I climbed up and yelled to the Third:

"I saw a dead man!"

"Bullshit! Where's a dead man here?"

"I'm sure! I didn't hallucinate!"

"If you are sure, report it to "Neptun". Ask them what to do with it?"

"Neptun, Neptun. This is Berta."

"I hear you, Richie," answered the Old Man.

"There's a black corpse in the tank."

"Richie, how much did you drink?" the Chief asked.

"Damn it, I drank nothing! I'm telling you the truth! Anyway, if you don't believe it, see for yourself!" pissed off, I answered in a nervous voice.

Moment of silence - consternation.

"What have you already done?" asked the Old Man.

"I turned on one valve."

"Stop the work. We have to pull him out and search the tank."

"And wouldn't it be better to pump out the water first?" I asked, hoping the Old Man would agree to this suggestion.

"No," he answered firmly. "And you want to look for the second valve while he's floating there?" he added.

"Sure not."

"It'll be easier to get him out, you don't know how long he's in the water," he continued.

"Alright, I have no choice. Nobody's going to do it for me," I agreed and headed back to the tank.

Chapter 10

Gabon

"Richie, Richie! Are you sleeping?" I heard Bronek's voice.

"No, I remember. Has it been four hours? Good thing time passes so fast," I told him.

The Old Man gave a *prikaz*, you have to finish the tank work and pump out the water. Will you get in?" He asked.

"And do I have other option?"

I went with the Third again. Under that goddamn hatch and into that shitty water.

I entered the tank as if into a familiar bathtub. "Nothing can surprise me here anymore," I thought. This time I walked calmly towards the valve, knowing more or less where to find it. I found it quickly, but this hatch was bolted harder. I got tired of unscrewing it. Dipping my head in the water, I stood astride next to it and, holding my breath, I turned the wheel over and over until I finally opened it. I made it. Now I could go out. I tugged twice and felt the Third take out the line slowly. I moved towards the glow. I reached the hatch and, completely exhausted, I slowly climbed the ladder. Finally, I was on the deck. With my last efforts, I got onto the little ship and fell on its steel deck.

"How long have I been there?"

"Half an hour," answered the Third, looking at the watch.

"Oh God. How quickly the time has passed."

The Third reported to the "Neptun":

"The valves are turned on!"

"The pumps can be activated," they answered. "That's it?" I thought. "Not even 'kiss my ass'?"

Bronek turned on the pumps from the wheelhouse.

"Let's go for coffee," he shouted.

"Why does he talk about coffee so often?" I thought. I needed to rest more, a long way against the wind awaited me. We would go back, being whipped with gusts of white squall[14] blowing from the bow side.

"The wind isn't blowing so hard now!" I cried out.

Now probably there was no risk of breaking the tug line, which I had feared the most.

We returned to the "Berta's" bow. Bronek was still pumping out the water from the tank.

"See if the water level is decreasing."

"The gauge shows that it's decreasing." After an hour the tank was empty. On "Neptun" the situation was calm.

---

[14] White squall - a wind that breaks in all directions, creating a ring of swirls with a speed of over 100 knots.

"Report, if something happens."

Little Chi-Chi found a way to spend the time. She flipped our map, and on its blank side, she drew her village. She probably was talented because it looked quite interesting.

Our idyll in the mess was interrupted by the Chief's call:

"Berta, Berta, the tug line has broken!"

But we already knew about it. We noticed that "Berta" slowly turned sideways to the wave. We quickly put on seat belts and life jackets, and ran to the bow of the barge. We told our girls to put on life belts and wait for us in the mess.

We immediately fell into the whirl of raging wind. We heard the deafening roar of water slapping against the hull and gusts of wind. The whips of water carried by these gusts knocked us off our feet. It was some temporary squall, extremely strong, that tugged "Berta". The tug line couldn't stand it and we were now at the mercy of the raging element. Leaning heavily, clinging to the bulwarks[15], we went to the bow to see what was happening.

I saw "Neptun" make a turn. However, it didn't make an arc to reach us, but being almost in the same place, it turned towards "Berta". I watched the waves get it, and one by one furiously slam into its side. The force of the advancing wind caused the tug to lie down on the side. "It is tilted so strongly," I thought as I watched it lie on the starboard side, and the onrushing waves were further increasing its tilt, bursting onto the deck with foamy breakers. But it slowly rose and, with its whole power, flowing with the wind, it moved towards us to give us a heaving line.

I hooked the safety line to the protruding part of the hauling winch becket and fell to my knees. Now I was able to see what was

---

[15] Bulwark - a protective railing.

going on with the tug line. I was like a dog on a leash that limited my movements to two meters around the point of attachment. But it was enough to notice that the reins' chains were hanging loosely from "Berta's" bow chock. Bronek has already started the windlass aggregates. Now I had to release the chains as quickly as possible so that they could be hauled onto the bow deck of the barge. Of the harness with a piece of broken towline, we would take care later. Now it was necessary to give a spare chain, to which on the "Neptun", they would attach the tug line from the second hauling winch.

I buckled myself briefly at the winch and stood on my feet. Out of the corner of my eye, I saw the Third shouting something to me. He stood at the winch levers and loosened the chain. It's good that we had everything prepared for this variant of events. I reached for the previously prepared pipe and with its help I unscrewed the chain attachment on the hauling winch. I was standing on my legs wide apart and the wind was hitting my face, but the line endured and allowed me to keep my balance.

Unscrewing the chain security took me about two minutes. The Third saw that he could pull the chain back and started the hauling winch. I unhooked the safety line, fell to my knees, and on all fours, holding on to the winch, I slowly approached him.

"Berta" was already positioned sideways to the wave. One could feel its resistance towards the wave blows. I turned anxiously, looking at the towers to find out whether they still stood or if they had already broken. They stood - their broad base and good security had worked well for the time being.

Hiding behind the winch, we watched "Neptun" which, working hard on the wave, were approaching us.

"We are ready!" I screamed into the phone, shouting over the roar of the wind and the bang of the waves.

We had to prepare. Ten minutes more and they would shoot the heaving line from Neptun. The ship would come to us from the windward direction, and the line flying with the wind must have arrived to the bow.

"Berta", "Berta," I heard the Chief calling.

"Yes, we hear you," I called back to the phone, holding it close to my face.

"Are you ready?"

"Yes, we are waiting for the heaving line, everything is OK here. The hauling winch is working, we can take the line," I reported.

"Neptune" was close, I saw sailors dressed in storm jackets bustling on its stern. I knew that the Bosun would shoot the heaving line. He must have taken into consideration the wind strength, the sway of "Neptun" and the drift of "Berta". Only the experienced Bosun could handle this task relatively quickly.

The Third and I got into position and waited. Splashes of water made it difficult for us to see, but the Old Man got "Neptun" very close to "Berta". It was about fifty meters from us. The Bosun shot from the hip. We saw the heaving line fly towards us, but unfortunately the first shot was a miss, the line fell into the water about five meters from the bow.

"Damn it!" The Third swore.

Now was to be a second try. I knew the Bosun would hit this time. He already knew how to make allowance for the wind strength correctly. It would have seemed simple, but "Neptune" wasn't motionless, but was thrown by the waves. The deck swayed underfoot and the blows of the wind made it difficult to shoot.

I watched as the second line raced towards us, passed over our heads, and fell into the water on the other side of the "Berta's" bow.

I grabbed the line and ran to the bow chock. I fell on the deck and dragged it through the chock[16]. Out of the corner of my eye, I saw the Third lean over me. I gave him the weight of the line.

"Pull it!" I shouted to Neptun.

They started pulling when we loosened. First they took out the weight, then a steelon line went into the water, followed by a steel one, which was attached to the chain with a shackle.

"Neptune" efficiently maneuvered the speed so that the distance between it and "Berta" was relatively constant. I cut off the securing of the chain with my sailor's knife. It fell into the water with a thud, pulled by the steel line that was being taken out by Neptun. The Third and I shook hands.

[16] Chock - an opening leading from a deck to a side, through which an anchor chain and shaft pass.

But that's not all: "Neptun" was slowly moving away from us, releasing the tug line from the hauling winch. When it was about seven or eight hundred meters away from us, it began to face the wave, slowly turning us as well. We checked the towing chain attachments.

I greased the chocks while the Third finished the attachment of the winch. Satisfied, we returned to the "Berta" wheelhouse, where Bronek and the frightened girls were waiting for us with coffee.

"Hello, Berta," I heard the Old Man's voice, "thanks. Good job. Check everything on board," he gave the order. But we had already done it without waiting for him to tell it us.

The next day the storm began to subside. The wind was clearly weakening, the waves were still big, but they weren't hitting "Berta's" prow so much. At the bottom there were chocolates waiting for us - the real and the sweet ones in a box. It was little Chi-Chi who had located somewhere boxes with candies that we hadn't remembered about and, cheerfully playing up, she was chowing down on them in excess.

"They can make her sick," Bronek worried, staring greedily as the pieces disappeared from the box.

"And have you seen the child who got sick from eating chocolates?" Asked the Third rhetorically.

He would have eaten them himself, and so would have I, but whatever, we wanted her to have a little fun - she had been through so much. The Old Man warned us in a stern voice two days ago:

"Do you know the procedures for the "hares"?

"Not really," I told him.

"Don't hire for any work, feed them what you eat, and if they don't want to eat it, give them what they want, let them cook for themselves. Give those blankets, sheets, towels, cleaning products, soap. Treat them right and make sure they are okay. Give them water to drink and wash, toothpaste." He paused, realizing he had overshot the mark.

"And a toothbrush," the Third mocked him.

"And what about sex?" impudently asked Bronek, insolent because of the taunts of the Third.

"Forget it!" The Old Man was upset. "You want to catch Aids?" he added already in a calm voice, realizing that he had been caught out by Bronek.

But it wasn't that easy. When we were out, the women did the laundry. They took our scattered towels, sheets, and whatever else was waiting for the Neptune's washing machine, and held a cleanliness festival. We felt stupid when, having returned inside, we saw very clean clothes hanging all over the place. The women liked to come to the mess in the evening to poke around and talk. They always asked when we would reach the Netherlands.

Nobody told them the truth, as there was no need.

In the morning, as soon as it got light, we went to check the torn deck. Nothing had changed there. However, we were able to safely go down to the tear and inspect it. It didn't look very good, there was some residual water at the bottom of the tank. "My helmet is out there somewhere," I thought, but didn't go for it. This is a tribute to "Berta". Let it stay there.

The deck plate was strangely torn, twisted and overlapped in some places. I checked the port side - the water didn't reach the torn cover and didn't pour inside. I measured the level from the deck to the surface of the water, and the Third wrote everything down.

Two more days passed this way. We checked whether "Berta" was taking on water. It had sensors everywhere, but we didn't know if they were all working after such a storm.

"It's dry everywhere," the third mechanic reported to Neptun - that was his job."

We were worried that they would take us the company. It was nice talking to the women, and little Chi-Chi, living silver, stuck her nose everywhere. She followed us like a shadow every now and then saying: "Bos, Bos - I will also go."

On the third night, after rescuing the women from the closed tank, while napping in my bunk[17], I felt that someone was slipping under my blanket. Frightened, I turned on the little lamp over my head and saw Kiri lie completely naked beside me and smile pleasantly, trying to put her arms around my neck.

I jumped out of my bunk like from a catapult.

"Go to your cabin!" I said to her.

I took her hand, gave her the armband that was lying under the bunk with my other hand, and so as not to offend her even more, I gently led her out of the cabin. I was still awake when I heard the door open. "What the hell?" I thought. In the glow of the lamp I turned on, I saw her older sister coming up to me and throwing off her mantle. What a circus. Apparently they thought that I like older women and therefore her sister came.

I led also her gently out of the cabin, but the surprise on her face hurt my male ego. "This time I will lock the cabin - maybe they both want to come," I joked in my mind. Apart from the incident with pretty young Kiri and her older sister, nothing special happened to me that night.

I was amused by this event, but for both women it was a dishonor. How is that? They are no longer attractive even to white guys? Are they not quite young and pretty? All morning they were angry with

[17] Bunk - a sailor's bed

me. They showed it, turning to me officially: "Bos this, Bos that", whereas before they had used the English name Richard. I, not discouraged by this and in order to improve my and their mood, complimented them from time to time saying: "Your hair is so beautiful" or "your bow is nice" - and embracing them with my arm, I hugged them for a little while. It made them feel that I didn't despise them, but for reasons unknown to them I couldn't have sex with them.

When I told the boys about it at breakfast, silly teases began. "What happens if I get back onto Neptun?" I dreaded to think. I began to regret my honesty.

"How nice and beautiful you are," the Third made fun of them, but only when he was with us. When no one saw, he fawned on Kiri:

"Maybe you want milk or juice? Take it, it's tasty," he said, handing her a fried quarter of a chicken.

Did she visit him at night? I don't really know, I didn't spy on them and I didn't care. I thought the world of Kinga and no other girls were on my mind, even if they were pretty black women. Strange, right? But true.

"The older one was in my cabin, but I chased her out," said Bronek.

I didn't believe him too much, but I wouldn't ask.

"And what about you?" Bronek asked the Third.

"Why do you care about my nighttime sleep?" The latter replied and with this statement, he closed the topic.

The next day the captain ordered the barge landing. They launched a raft. The First Officer from the deck, the Chief from the machine and the Second Mechanic were brought by Andrei which himself didn't get on board, but stayed on the raft. We lowered a pilot ladder[18] for them, they climbed up, and immediately we went to see everything again.

"Nothing can be done," said the Chief, mechanic, guy with a lot of experience. "We can only strengthen the deck by welding metal sheets to the part that was torn apart."

"We'll see if we have enough of this sheet, it will be difficult to get it on board," I said.

"Right," the Chief agreed with me, "only that one from "Neptun" we can place here.

They reported everything to the Old Man who passed it on to the company in Lagos. The company decided:

"You're not going to strengthen the deck. It would take you a few days and the result would be questionable. Go to the port," they replied.

The case of "the hares" was also resolved. The Chief told the Old Man about their situation on "Berta", how the women had installed themselves and whether they were treated well. They were very scared when they saw the raft going to "Berta".

"Is this for us?" they asked.

"I don't know," answered the Third.

The company, however, decided that the women would stay on "Berta". It made sense from the point of view of the shipowner and "Neptun". "Berta" stayed to be unloaded in Gabon, and "Neptun" was returning to Lagos which was the last place anyone would have wanted to stay in. The women were also very afraid of being left there. Its gloomy and bad reputation as a bandit city was known all over Africa and beyond. Why cause "Neptun" trouble regarding

---

[18] Pilot ladder - a rope ladder used on a ship, among others to receive a pilot.

deportation, and the shipowner related costs? The decision was made - they would stay.

The women probably thought they stayed because of us. The night visits to the cabins began again. This was the only way in which they wanted and could repay us for treating them well and saving their lives. This time, however, they found the door locked, at least in my cabin.

In the evening, we moved ahead with full power. The weather forecast was good. It seemed that we would manage to cross the Gulf of Guinea calmly. Only now did we breathe a sigh of relief. The storm was over - the weather was good so we could go on. For the rest of the way the sun put us through the wringer. There was no air-conditioning on "Berta", so it was stuffy and hot during the day, and cold and muggy at night. Standard - the tropics. As always, when taking the equipment onto the barge, we had forgotten something.

"Damn it," said the Third, "you should have taken at least one fan."

"Be glad that you have a fridge, even that lacked in the past and they managed somehow," Bronek persuaded him.

"Or maybe you would like a TV and a video recorder?" I said.

"Why not? So much of it knocks around the ship."

"The Old Man would give you a TV, or maybe you would like also an inflatable girl? Because these here are dangerous, you can catch something," Bronek teased him.

"Shut up," said the Third. Time passed quickly. In the evenings, when dusk fell, we had nothing to do, only talks. But the topics also got exhausted quickly and we went to bed early. Watches at night diversified this monotonous mode. I liked to go out onto the deck of "Berta" after midnight and look at the sky or the fast moving water.

I got used to the fact that there are no familiar stars in the sky, only constellations with strange names that are completely invisible in our sky. I thought about Kinga then and that I would be home soon.

I began to remember the days spent together.

Chapter 11

Return

Three guys and two women is an explosive mix. The Old Man preferred to leave them on "Berta", because on "Neptune" the risk of unpredictable situations would have been greater. Here, both women treated us as their kin. On the day when the sun was the most bothersome, they came out onto deck, wearing only bands around their hips and showing their bare breasts in all their glory.

When young Kiri, jokingly, teased Bronek about ice cream, or how much she could eat at once, she was touching him with her breasts, pretending that she was wrestling with him. Bronek hated that.

"Cover up!" He said excitedly, pointing to Kiri's protruding, young breasts.

"Why? It's warm and I'm not going to church."

"Words fail me."

The next day, I called both girls to come to my cabin. They came in, surprised, wondering what I wanted from them.

"Listen," I began, "what I say is to stay between us."

"Okay, Richard," they assured me.

"We are approaching the port of Gabon. There we will have customs."

"Is there any solution to that?"

"The barge you are on is Dutch owned. When we reach the roadstead, employees of the American Shell Company will get onto it. You must then demand asylum from them. You understand? Make up something, a tribal persecution or something similar. Firmly demand asylum and protection, invoking US and Dutch law. It's the only way to prevent them from taking you off the barge. I don't think they would do it by force. Say that your relatives in the Netherlands know everything and have already notified the embassy, the police, the press and whomever it is needed.

"Thank you, Richard," they said, and a little encouraged they went to discuss the matter.

Ten days passed.

One morning, the Third called out:

"You can see Gabon!"

I dragged myself out of the hammock and went out to the bow. The land was visible in front of Neptune. "Finally," I sighed under my breath. We were already tired of this trip. We were approaching the port of Gentil. There would be unloading, but that was not our concern anymore. In the roadstead of Gentil, we dropped two anchors in the water just in case.

We said goodbye to the girls who, crying, hung around our necks, not wanting to let us go. Kiri and her older sister had already given me a piece of paper with a phone number and address, asking:

"Richard, call our relatives and tell them everything, okay? Will you do that?"

"Yes, of course, already today, I promise. I will definitely call," I assured.

The brigade, sent here from the company, got onto "Berta". We gave them the barge and in the evening we were on the "Neptune". On the occasion of the successful towing, the Old Man ordered a barbecue.

Time passed quickly from Gentil to the Lagos roadstead. First of all, a decent bath and sleeping in our own bunks - that's all we had been missing. On "Berta", the food wasn't bad, we didn't complain, everyone prepared something that they knew how to do, and as we were not too picky, we were satisfied with what was available.

I called Kinga.

"In four days, at 2 p.m. Polish time, I will be in Gdansk," I informed her. I fly to Paris and from there via Warsaw to Gdansk," I said and gave her the flight number. "Are you happy?"

"Of course, Richie! I'll be waiting at the airport! Now I can tell you, I have a surprise for you," Kinga informed me in a mysterious voice.

"What?"

"Oh no. I won't say on the phone."

We said goodbye, happy that we would meet soon.

Another call I made was to the Netherlands. I told people I didn't know in detail what had happened to Kiri and her sister. I also had to talk about Booaba, which wasn't easy. On that side, they asked me to let the girls know that they would start acting in their case.

Then I called the barge manager and filled him in, asking him to pass everything to the girls.

Six months later, out of curiosity, I called the Dutch phone number again. I was happy to hear that Kiri and her sister with little Chi-Chi finally reached the Netherlands and they cordially invited me to their dwelling.

In the evening, away from the port, while drifting, the captain threw a party. He also gave a short goodbye speech. We would go home the next day.

Andrei prepared a spit and the Cook the food. There was a chine and chicken, all seasoned well, plus some red sausages and fish. The meat was juicy and I liked it. Hardly anyone drank the non-alcoholic beer that the Old Man gave, but there was no alcoholic beverages.

We mainly discussed the events on "Berta". We argued over how real the possibility for the barge to break in half was. Everyone agreed on one thing - the platform with the pillars would have collapsed. Then we argued further: in what direction would it have collapsed?

Those who returned home had one leg already on the plane so the Barbecue ended quickly. In the morning we dropped anchor on the roadstead of Lagos. The entrance to the port was visible.

"There are so many ships here!" Bronek was surprised. "I will count them!" he said but stopped at one hundred and fifty. "Damn, I haven't seen so many ships in one place."

"A third of them are floating warehouses," I informed him.

We had our things already packed and we waited for the motorboat, which would bring friends for a substitution and take us home. Two hours later it arrived. We handed over our duties quickly and waited for the Old Man, but he was in no hurry, our flight was only at midnight. The captain didn't want to wait at the airport that long. I was substituted by Tadzio.

Finally we set off, waving to our mates from the deck of the motorboat.

"Will I be back here in three months?" I was wondering.

Before entering the port, awaited us a check-in on the motorboat and an obligatory baksheesh, but the captain was prepared for it - he gave cigarettes and we sailed on.

On the left side, I saw a half-sunken ship and some boats milling around it. We asked the agent what happened.

Its rudder failed and it's stranded. Now they are looting it because the shipowner abandoned the ship.

A bit further along the shore stretched the slums. You could see the huts made of different things, some metal sheets used as a shelter, a lot of debris, waste, bottles and God knows what else. A sad sight, especially when you look at children playing like all the others in the world, but at this dumping site.

On the right, we passed ships at the unloading quay as well as military patrol ships. We were sailing under the road, a four-lane wide viaduct crossing a branch of the river, overhanging it high enough for ships to pass freely underneath it. The motorboat turned towards the shore. We docked at a tiny piece of broken concrete.

"Should we go this way?" The Old Man asked.

"It'll be closer," the agent replied.

We walked on, carting our luggage. Two cars were standing right by the water, next to the ending concrete. They came for us. Bodyguards armed to the teeth in some brown uniforms stylized as the US Army ones got out of them. They grabbed the Old Man's luggage and carried it, and we had to carry our baggage ourselves.

It took fifty meters to walk. After a while children stuck to us. There was a small market beside. I was looking at colorful stalls and booths with various goods. There were a lot of people here and even more children running barefoot and kicking soda cans.

It wasn't very clean there. The ground was compacted, and there were some puddles here and there. A typical African gutter. Everything that was unnecessary was spilled right on the ground. There was no sewage system and electricity. We got to Lagos. "This part of the port isn't very representative," I thought.

Finally we drove to the customs office. The cars crossed the gate, which closed right behind us.

"Water under the bridge, they have caught us," cawed Bronek. "We won't get out soon."

"Don't talk nonsense," I told him.

But the agent took the papers, telling us to stay. The Captain got out of the second car and they both disappeared inside.

We were sitting happy all the more that it was feverish outside, and the car was air-conditioned. Music made our time pleasant, African rhythms, but it's still music.

"I'm going to smoke," Bronek announced.

"Sit," I said, "do you want to pay the fine? You can't smoke here." For Bronek, the financial argument is the best argument. Ten minutes later the agent and the captain returned and we drove to the airport under the escort of a security guard.

We lined up for customs clearance. There was a long line of people standing there, almost all of them were Africans. Customs officers rummaged in their luggage. "Will they," ran through my mind, "rifle also through our bags?"

My luggage was locked with a thin plastic clamp - such one they sometimes show in the movies, where they put it on hands instead of handcuffs. It can't be broken by hand, it must be cut with a knife. Bronek was standing in front of me, he also had a bag closed in this way. It was his idea anyway.

"It can't be opened, and I don't think they use knives there," he argued.

He was right. The customs officer tugged at the clamp for a long time, but it didn't yield. Resigned, he waved his hand. Seeing this, I didn't put my bag on the counter, but with my foot I was sliding it across the floor, and on the top, I put only my hand luggage. The customs officer looked inside, saw the laptop and said:

"Move on."

We gave our luggage and headed to the gate. From there we quickly and efficiently moved to the departure zone. They just took all our cola cans and tried the old money trick.

I stood behind Bronek and heard the officer say:

"You have money, so put it on the table - we will count it."

"What money?" Bronek replied and, turning sideways, turned out his empty pockets in front of him. "I spent everything I had on baksheesh," he added with a disarming smile.

"I don't have anything either," I assured the customs officer, who nodded his head, but wasn't entirely convinced.

Whoever gets fooled and puts money on the table will no longer see the same amount. The officer, counting it, will skillfully bleed such a person, taking at least half of it. And to whom will you complain if the complaints are admitted by the one who plucked you, and the plane is about to depart?

Finally we walked over to the free zone and strolled around the lobby looking at the shops and boutiques. I wanted to buy African wood products for my home. After long haggling, I bought a head of a shaman and an African beauty as well as two wooden masks. I took Bronek with me for shopping. I can't haggle, and he is a well-known specialist in this field.

It was like this: we went inside, Bronek asked what I liked and added:

"Just don't show the fat seller what it is."

I could speak, so I spoke Polish to him:

"You see that big shaman head with these ornaments stuck in the tree? Buy it."

"We'll try," he said with a twinkle in his eye, and entered the boutique.

The spectacle began. Bronek took a completely different figurine.

"How much?" He asked the seller.

"One hundred and fifty dollars."

"What?! I'll give twenty."

The outraged salesman gurgled some epithets.

"One hundred and twenty," he dropped the price.

"Twenty-five dollars," answered Bronek.

"No, no," the fat man yelled, sweating more and more.

Bronek grabbed my hand and we left the store. The fat man ran after us and pulled us back.

"A hundred dollars," he said indignantly, and almost broke down because of asking so little.

"No, no," Bronek insisted.

We keep watching and he casually nudged with his foot the head of the shaman who stood on the floor. He asked:

"And for that?"

The distraught fat man answered softly:

"Eighty dollars."

We waved our hand and started to leave, saying:

"We're going to your friend."

The fat man shouted behind us:

"Sixty!"

"Will you pay fifty?" Bronek asked me.

"Yes," I replied.

"I'll give you fifty bucks, that's the last word."

The resigned fat man said:

"OK."

And yet the shaman was bigger and prettier, I liked it, but I overpaid anyway, because in the bazaar I would probably have bought it for half the price. I bought the rest in the shop beside, with the same repeating scenery. Finally, we got on the plane and flew. I slept all the way, only a voice woke me up:

"Please fasten your seatbelts. We're landing in Paris."

A transit bus drove us to the terminal, where we had a flight to Warsaw. I had a change in Warsaw. Then I was flying to Gdansk alone, because Bronek was waiting for a flight to Szczecin. Time dragged on mercilessly, I was already tired of this flying. Finally, Rebiechowo, I took my luggage quickly and went out into the hall.

There she was! Kinga was standing there beautiful and smiling, holding one rose in her hand. "Is this an allusion to the rose from the boulevard?" I was wondering.

We greeted each other with kissing and hugging. Kinga whispered in my ear:

"We will have a baby."

Chapter 12

M/T "Anna Broere"

The rumble of the rotor blades couldn't drown out my thoughts. I was sitting in the middle of a naval rescue helicopter with my three friends. There were pilots and one lifeguard from the rescue elevator.

Everything happened so fast that only now I was able to calmly analyze the situation.

In the morning Kinga, rejoicing, said to me:

"Richie! Maybe I will manage to buy you a new shirt today for this pinstripe suit, after all you won't wear the old one."

"Yes, yes," I replied, "but where? The whole city is covered in snow and it's freezing. And in addition this wind.

"Not far here," Kinga replied, "there's a little boutique. We'll go over there and I'll find you something."

Hela, Kinga's mother, had gotten up earlier than we did and just came downstairs for breakfast.

"Good morning, sweethearts," she greeted. She was a woman of medium height, kind and very obliging, and since she was also an excellent cook, she wanted to make us something for breakfast. But the kitchen was the kingdom of Kinga.

"Mom! Sit down at the table, I'll make breakfast myself."

"Okay, I'll just make some coffee," she replied, pacing around the kitchen.

"Pour yourself from the coffee machine."

"No. I prefer an ordinary one, brewed in a glass."

"How is Olenka, were you in her room?" Kinga asked.

"Olenka is sleeping well. Her diaper is dry, I checked it, don't worry."

Then the doorbell rang.

"I will open," Kinga declared. "Who is it at such an early hour?" She wondered.

I was just sitting at the table, trifling with a remote control. I was changing the channels. After a moment I heard Kinga exclaim in an upset voice:

"Richard, someone to see you!"

I went to the door, in the corridor stood a military police, a lieutenant and a mat.

"Mr. Richard?" here was my name.

"Yes, what is it?" I replied.

"We are gathering the crew for a rescue operation. In the Baltic Sea, near Rozewie, a Dutch merchant ship drifts ashore. It has to be manned by a Polish crew, and you were selected from your company.

"And what about the crew on that ship?" now I asked the question.

A rescue operation is underway and they are being brought ashore by helicopter. You have five minutes to get ready, we're waiting downstairs. Our helicopter will be waiting for you next to the school playground," he said to me in a dry military tone that sounded like a report.

"Please hurry up," added the lieutenant. "They didn't even ask if I agree," I thought.

Without asking any more questions, I rushed to the garage for my work stuff, shouting to Kinga:

"Make me quickly two sandwiches and a coffee."

It's good that my things are always arranged and ready to use after a contract trip. I quickly threw a warm Norwegian jumpsuit into the bag. I would put on a jacket and my warm shoes.

"Where are the warm socks?!" I shouted to Kinga, who, pale, burst into the garage behind me, asking:

"You gotta go?"

"I gotta," I replied shortly.

I quickly jogged back into the kitchen. I took a sip of the coffee Kinga had made for her mother, but it was too hot, so I poured some cold milk from the fridge. I grabbed the sandwiches and stuffed them into the spacious pocket of the jacket I threw over me.

"It's been five minutes?" I asked Kinga.

"I don't know," she replied tearfully.

"Come on, darling," I added, trying to cover up the unpleasant taunt from a moment ago. I hugged Kinga. "I'm sorry," I whispered in her ear, "but I have to go, this is my job. I'll call you as soon as I can. All the best in the New Year," - that day was New Year's Eve, we were supposed to party together.

I kissed her and ran to Olenka's room. I saw that she was sleeping sweetly. I leaned over, gave her two kisses on the cheeks, and ran outside. I waved to Kinga, who was standing in the doorway with tears in her eyes.

The off-roader stood with the engine running, and started as soon as I got in. It was two hundred meters to the school, but the gate was open and the area was secured by gendarmerie sailors, so we drove onto the field. The lieutenant reported on the phone that we were ready.

"Wait for the helicopter," we received the order from the naval base, which was in constant communication with the Maritime Rescue Center that was in charge of all services.

"What's happening?" I asked the lieutenant.

"I only know that the Dutch sent an SOS signal[19] - it is carried ashore and the crew is evacuated.

Polish Ship Rescue at all costs wanted to save the ship. I didn't know why at the time, and probably neither did the lieutenant.

You could hear the helicopter, which landed smoothly on the field after a moment. The Maltese cross proudly displayed on the carcass announced that it was a rescue helicopter. I jumped in. I saw two familiar faces - of Motorcycle and the bosun with whom I had been on the Poseidon recently. Raising our hands, we greeted silently. I sat down next to them, fastened seat belts, put on headphones and heard the pilot's voice:

We are taking off. We are flying for one officer to Wejherowo. He's ready and waiting for us in the square of the local military unit.

I ate sandwiches in silence - I didn't know when I would have the opportunity to eat again. There was noise, so I couldn't talk anyway.

Less than ten minutes later, we landed for him. It was Alek K., First Officer. I knew that guy, we had been once together in Kolobrzeg on the rescue ship called "Storm". Alek was talking to me, but I didn't hear him. I showed him with my hand that I could hear nothing. Finally, he waved with resignation and fell silent. I was pleased with their presence, at least I knew with whom I would work.

We were approaching Rozewie and after a while we saw a lighthouse. A tall circular structure with a white base shot up with a tower of red brick, at the end of which gleamed a white, glazed porch with a light flashing in a certain way. It rose straight out of the sand dune by the beach, surrounded by stunted pines and birch trees

---

[19] SOS - an international signal in Morse code for a call for help. Save Our Ship or Save Our Souls.

leaning in the direction of the wind. I glanced down at the beach, with foamy waves breaking onto the shore, now covered with snow. Long and high, for this part of the Baltic Sea, white breakers flooded the shore to the edge of the dunes. You could see that there had been a storm recently raging there. The wind had already eased, but the sea was still rough. The ship was visible nearby, and a little further there were the buildings of Karwia. We were approaching quickly. The pilot set the helicopter sideways to the starboard side of the ship. I could clearly see the entire ship covered with a mass of ice. The entire bow and its mast were completely coated with a thick white shroud of frozen water. Only the tip of the thin antenna were protruding, whose tip was wobbling in the wind. The entire cargo deck, as far as the stern, was strewn with a glistening snow. The right side of the superstructure was also icy, from the deck to the top. The lifeboat hooked up to the davits[20] was one large chunk of ice with icy ropes hanging down that made it look like a scenography for a glacier climbing movie. Only the stern was partially free of ice. From above, there was visible the aft deck covered in a thick layer of snow, that reached the top of the bollards. On the other hand, there was no ice at the top of the wheelhouse, from which a black chimney rose in the middle of the base. It was the only part of the ship free of ice and snow. That's because it was warm from the exhaust fumes of a running engine escaping there.

There was no one in sight. There were no position lights on the ship, only on the upper mast of the wheelhouse, there were two red lights arranged one below the other, at the sight of which a warning signal sounds in every sailor - "a ship not responsible for its

[20] Davits - a lifting device on board a vessel, most often used for lowering and lifting a lifeboat.

movements" - I remembered their meaning. "Has the entire crew been evacuated yet?" I was wondering.

The ship was drifting toward the shore that was three or four hundred meters away. "We won't make it, it will run aground," the thought flashed through my head.

"We will drop you off at the wheelhouse next to the chimney, on the most advanced part of the wing," I heard the pilot's voice. "Get ready." The helicopter arrived from the stern side, over the starboard.

I fastened my harness, put on my life jacket, took off my headphones, and took position beside the elevator. I was second in line. The first to leave was the boatswain, Jozef R. He was a tall, well-built man, a bit coarse in contact, but he was a high-class specialist. I knew him well. We had worked together for several years in the Polish Ship Rescue. He had begun his career by recovering the wreckage of sunken vessels in the port of Gdynia and Gdansk and wherever it was needed, and I began mine many years later.

The pilot efficiently kept the machine in one place above the ship so that the boatswain could safely land on a small patch of the upper deck measuring about four square meters. It was the most difficult for him because there was no one to receive him. So everything depended on the pilot. The elevator was descending quickly, the first attempt was unsuccessful. The bosun with his feet pushed off the bulwarks behind which he was supposed to stand, but the wind jerked him and he found himself beyond the deck. The lifeguard pulled him two meters up, a small correction, and he landed safely on the deck. Then he quickly released the rope from the elevator, which was already gliding up for me.

I sat down on the floor, fastened the hook on the harness, stretched my legs outward and, holding on to the handle, signaled with my hand that I was ready. The taut line lifted me up a little, the elevator arm moved forward and I was already behind the helicopter, dangling over the ship. The helicopter rescuer lowered me quickly, but so precisely that I didn't really have time to think about whether I would hit on the first try.

"Anna Broere, and underneath the home port of Dordrecht," I read the inscription on its stern. The deck with the boatswain standing on it was approaching rapidly. I could see him shouting something to me, but I heard nothing - the sound of chopper blades working and the sound of the wind were drowning out his voice. I tried to figure out what he meant. "There" he was pointing with his hand behind me. I turned my head and saw the mast collapse at the bow, sliding across the ice to the first hold, where it lost momentum, stopping on the deck, tangled in steel ropes.

I was getting closer, I could see the static line touching the deck. The boatswain grabbed my harness, and I was already standing next to him. I released the hook immediately and it soared up for the next sail man. At the end they dropped off Motorcycle, which stood next to us after a while. Finally, our bags placed in the net landed.

Everything went quickly and smoothly, the helicopter crew showed full professionalism. It was impressive for anyone who knew how difficult the operation was.

We signalized with a thumb gesture that everything was OK. The helicopter turned and took off. We were alone.

First we went to the wheelhouse to establish communication with the PSR Coordination Center in Gdynia. A lamp and a radio worked - the crew, leaving the ship, had left a working generator. "Why?" the thought rattled in my head.

We entered the ship's bridge. The first impression I got was that nothing had happened there. All devices were on - the radar was working, the rudder pointer was in the center, and the engine control levers were in the "stop" position. We quickly recognized the remaining indicators and glanced at the unfolded map.

"Last position taken forty minutes ago," Alek said to us. He grabbed the radio handset and called the PSR base on an emergency channel reserved only for us.

"Center. Center. This is 'Anna Broere' - over."

"This is Center speaking. I hear you."

"I report that we are already on the ship and proceed to action."

"You are to connect with "Jantar" (a PSR ocean-rescue tug) ... - A moment of break - "the voice is fading," Alek said. "Yes, I can hear you," he called after a moment into the cellular radio.

"... which has already left Świnoujście and is on its way to you," we heard further.

"Captain K. from "Koral" is taking over command of the operation on the spot," I heard the dispatcher's voice. "Koral" will get to you in twelve hours."

"Koral, Koral, this is Anna Broere - over," the First officer called.

"Anna Broere, this is Koral," said Captain P.

"Alek, how's the situation?" the question was asked. The captain already knew who was on "Anna".

"Bad, very bad, the wind is pushing us ashore. There are still three hundred meters left, I'm just taking position. We have five to eight meters under the keel," he called out to us at the same time. "Flood the tanks quickly. All that are empty, we're about to run aground!"

"Anchors cannot be thrown, and the main engine can't be started even in an emergency!" He called into the microphone.

"I understand," replied the captain of Koral.

"Tumak (a PSR rescue ship) is closest to you, but it will not make it either, it left Gdynia half an hour ago," he added. "It is impossible to go to the bow, and from the stern side, there is "Halny", which is also flowing towards you ...

"It won't get closer, it's too shallow," I heard before I left the wheelhouse.

We went downstairs to look for the ballast maneuvering building. Driven by instinct and experience, we quickly found an office which was its center. We burst into it. Right in front of us, we saw a large closet, resembling an ordinary piano, but instead of keys, it had a lot of pressure indicators, knobs for turning the pumps on and off, lights signaling their work, as well as black lines painted between them, symbolizing the pipes through which water flowed. Rectangles meant individual tanks. It was all integrated into the sketch of the ship.

Above, where there are usually some ornamental patterns on the piano, there was a second diagram of "Anna Broere", on which were painted small rectangles symbolizing the tanks of the ship. In each of them, the indicator glowing green showed us whether and how much water was there. At the same time, a row of numbers was displayed next to it, informating about the amount of water in cubic meters. The ballast maneuvering building was constructed using the American method - "for a monkey", so as not to bother reading the instructions.

I looked at the gauges - left ballast tanks full. Fore, stern and starboard ones - empty. The drinking water tanks glowed blue.

"One bigger empty, two small ones full," I said to Motorcycle.

"Go downstairs to the engine room. We're turning on the pumps, make sure everything is OK."

I grabbed the phone hanging next to it, looked at the numbers and called the bridge:

"Alek," I called, "the right tanks empty, the left ones full, the forepeak[21] empty, and the stern ones too. Are you sure that I should flood the right tanks?" I asked.

"Yes. We are over the very bottom, flood everything you can."

"OK."

The bosun and I opened the tank dampers and turned on all the pumps - one by one.

---

[21] Forepeak - a watertight compartment locain a bow or stern of the ship.

"Will the aggregate withstand?" Jozwa was worried.

"I don't know," I replied, shaking my head while anxiously thinking about filling the right tanks. This would increase the list of the ship.

I watched the tanks fill with water quickly. Every now and then I looked anxiously at the tilt gauge above the board of the ballast maneuvering building. It is a circular device that looks like a wall clock, with a line drawn in the shape of a light semicircle at the bottom. In the middle of this line, there was a zero, above which the pointer hung vertically, and on the left and right there was a scale with the numbers "five", "ten" etc. up to forty-five degrees from the horizontal. No merchant ship could withstand such a great tilt and would overturn. Some of them capsize even at thirty-five degrees list. Here the pointer was at forty-eight degrees.

"The pointer has moved," said the boatswain, "the tilt is getting bigger. We can take a pratfall right away." He seeped the words through his throat without a hint of anxiety in his voice.

"We're not far from the shore, but the water is too cold for a bath," I muttered to myself, but the boatswain heard it anyway.

"Why don't we wear wetsuits?" It fell from his mouth. "Is that a question or a proposal?" I was wondering, but I replied:

"It's too early for that. Open and lock all exit doors so they won't close when we fall," I called to him without taking my eyes off the clinometer. With my feet I already felt that the tilt was on the edge of safety, it was only a matter of time - who first? Would the mass of chemical granules in the holds manage to move, or would we run aground?

The bosun started running toward the deck exit, and I swiftly opened the two large rectangular portholes on a in the maneuvering building - just in case.

Alek called.

"How is it going?" He asked.

"Almost full," I reported.

"Are you ready for an overturn?"

"Yes. I am. I can see the tilt getting bigger. We have already fifty-five degrees. Call to Motorcycle, to the engine room and tell him to go outside," I added.

"I already called, he's on the bridge. He says the pumps will turn off by themselves when the pressure rises."

"Ice coated the vents. Let's hope the deck doesn't get torn apart, in case the pumps don't turn off."

"I'm afraid of that, too," confirmed Alek, "but the air must be escaping somewhere," he added in a slightly surprised tone. "Turn off manually, don't refuel."

"I know, I will do so," I assured him.

The boatswain followed all the gauges.

"Don't turn off the phone, the probe shows me zero under the keel," Alek called hoarsely to the receiver that was dangling somewhere in the distance, when, leaning over, he looked at the probe. "We are about to run aground, watch out."

After a few minutes, we felt a tug. I turned off all the pumps. The tanks were almost full. I jumped outside and saw that the bow had already caught the bottom. The wind and the waves started to turn us. The icy part of the bow and a large tilt to the starboard, or maybe some sandy shoal, made the bow lean against the bottom, and the stern of the ship drifted further towards the shore. After another ten minutes, we were firmly leaned against the bottom with the keel[22].

---

[22] Keel - a longitudinal binding of the ship's hull.

The stern looked towards the shore, which was several dozen meters away from us.

It happened. The Anna Broere ran aground, tilting to the starboard. We returned to the bridge. I took out of a tube, a firefighting ship plan. On each ship, two or four large pipes painted red are attached to the superstructure in easily accessible places outside, in which the plan of the ship and the crew list are placed. This is used in the event of a ship fire. The firefighters need to know the layout and how many crew members are on the ship. I spread the map out on the navigation table and we got familiar with the layout. There was also a crew list - eleven. Most of the crew had been taken over by the Polish ship M/S "Garwolin", supporting "Anna Broere" after it had sent an SOS.

Motorcycle came to us.

"Come with me. We will check if the bilges[23] are dry."

I went with him to the engine room to check if there was water there.

We were walking down the corridor. We went downstairs, then turned left. I chose the wrong door and we entered the storage room.

"No, it's not that way. Another door, a second corridor and a descent to the engine room," he said.

We went inside. Motorcycle went to the generator to check the parameters, and I went down. I walked around everything and went down again, all the way to the bottom of the bilge. Behind me, the motionless engine, the heart of the ship - like remorse seemed to say, "What have you done to me?" It was impossible to go any lower - probably. Maybe from the bow side, but so far it was impossible. A

---

[23] Bilge - the lowest point inside the hull of a ship not separated internally by watertight bulkheads which collect dirt.

little uplifted, I returned to the top of the engine room. We entered the MCC[24] and I called the bridge:

"Alek, bilges clean, no water."

"Okay, come back, new people have to be hired. They'll be there in a dozen or so minutes."

"OK, we're going back."

On the way back, we checked every room we came across. Everything was open, but there were no signs of panic. We entered the mess and from there we went to the kitchen.

"See the kitchen plates, still warm," I said to Motorcycle.

"I wonder why they left the ship so quickly."

So, I'm not the only who had such insights?

On the bridge, Alek was just finishing a conversation with the Coordination Center of Maritime Rescue. And the boatswain and I were checking what rescue equipment was left on the ship. One lifeboat was unusable due to the inclination, the other - icy. The two port and starboard life rafts remained in their places.

OK, that's enough if that's the case. The rescue wetsuits were in an open warehouse - it was obvious they had an excess of them, but we hoped we didn't need them.

Alek nervously searched for the shipping log.

"It's not fucking here!" He roared.

"Are you surprised?" I asked. "Probably the captain took it."

"Listen up!" Alek said with a hint of excitement. "I got to know what's what. In the morning the captain of "Anna" sent an SOS. He said that they had a large tilt to starboard, because waves and splashes

---

[24] MCC - a room on a ship, most often in the engine room compartment, where the main engine and auxiliary machinery controls are kept.

of water in the twenty-degree frost had iced the ship, creating a cap of ice. The weight of this ice caused a great tilt - they tried to balance the ship with ballast, but at some point a critical situation occurred. The ship's list increased sharply, and it grew deeper and deeper. As they had loose cargo in the holds, they were afraid that the ship might have tipped over at any moment and they sent an SOS."

"Anna Broere, Anna Broere," the PSR base called again, cutting him off.

After the conversation was over, Alek continued:

"A group of chemists from the Central Chemical Rescue Station in Plock will arrive on the ship. They'll be tomorrow at noon. What for? I don't know. There's something fishy here," he added with concern in his voice, looking at us.

I took the boatswain and we went to do a reconnaissance of the entire ship. We started with the bridge.

The first cabin from the bridge was the captain's lounge. It wasn't closed so we went in. It was quite a big room for such a ship. A couch, a table, armchairs, and some kind of cupboard-shaped piece of furniture with a large TV on it. I opened the little bottom door and I saw there a little fridge, well stocked with alcohol. There were some papers everywhere, on the table, the sideboard and the couch. I looked into the bedroom and bathroom - there was order in those rooms. On the bedside table stood framed photos of women with two children. The closet was full of personal clothes, there were also two bags and a nice suitcase. On the table in the bedroom there was a laptop and a figurine of a cathedral in Amsterdam.

There was a locker with keys on the sheet in the living room. I took a master key - a key with which one can open all doors on a ship.

"There must be a safe here somewhere," Jozwa said.

He looked into the second locker.

"It's open."

The safe was almost empty, a few loose sheets, a notebook with jottings, instructions and nothing else. We were hoping that maybe there was the logbook there, which we had been looking fruitlessly for on the bridge.

We went further. Opposite the captain's cabin was the Chief Mechanic's cabin. Then we looked into the crew cabins, all the doors were open. In each cabin, there were personal clothes and other things left, diverse trivia proving that recently these places had been bustling.

We went outside the ship and tried to go port side to the bow with the boatswain. It was impossible to walk on the ice in our shoes. The cargo holds were covered with a thick layer of ice that had stuck to the deck equipment to form sculpture-like forms. I glanced at the bow, there was a mast in the center. Now a thick layer of ice stretched from its base, wide at the bottom, spread from port to starboard and sliding up these ropes, mast, and ladder with metal rungs, tapering with every meter in height to, in the break place, spread its arms to form a triangular ice sail.

It was that parts of the mast, on which the signal lamps, the tube of the alarm siren and various types of blocks with ropes wound around them, which couldn't withstand the weight of the ice and, pulled down by its weight - broke.

Looking at the rest of the ice blocks, you could only guess what was hidden under them. The two large beasts on either side of the mast must have been the anchor winches, from which, in a strange cascade of undulating quasi-steps, the ice was flowing down onto the cargo hold covers, enveloping them in the death grip of hundreds of tons of frozen water. Then it flowed restlessly to the holds, to stop at the base of the superstructure and freeze there, increasing its mass along with the continuous splashes of water.

The ice blanket, having gotten to the superstructure, climbed upwards. Having reached the first portholes of the crew cabins, it stuck to them carefully on the right side, more exposed to the wind, which, taking the water away, threw it to the height of the bridge wing. There, at such a high frost, it immediately turned into a layer of ice, which was increasing in volume centimeter by centimeter. And so, from the bow to the stern, along the entire starboard, a mass of ice stuck to the ship. When the weight of the ice exceeded the static displacement of the ship, the craft began to tilt to one side, and in the holds, the loose cargo, in accordance with the laws of physics, also leveled its surface and thus contributed to the fact that the ship could no longer return to its previous, upright position. When the ballasting of the tanks no longer helped - I believed the crew did it - the tilt reached the critical moment, and its starboard deck sank into the water, the captain thought the ship might have capsized at any moment and called for help.

Some of the sailors were taken by "Garwolin", and others by the Navy rescue helicopter, the same one that had dropped us there. "The Dutch didn't risk and left the ship, and we? Are we risking more than they are?" I wondered, looking at the piles of ice in front of me.

We returned to the bridge.

"What's up?" I asked Alek. "After all, they didn't have to leave the ship. One or two of the crew members could stay and wait to see what's next."

"The captain decided so, probably in agreement with the shipowner. They abandoned the ship worth several million dollars, plus a cargo whose worth isn't known," Alek said with his nose stuck to the map.

"And what's in the holds?"

"I know as much as you do. Some chemicals for Plock, but what it is exactly, I have no idea."

"Why will a team of chemists come to the ship?" I said to Alek, wanting to share my doubts.

"You know ... The ship was carrying cargo for them, it's probably worth a lot of money and they've already paid for it."

"What guidelines did you get from Koral?" the Bosun interjected.

"We are to keep the generator working so that the ship is navigably and technically operational until their arrival. We take watch by turns every four hours."

"So I'm going to make some dinner," declared the Bosun and added with a sly smile: "Alek, ask Captain Koral if we can use the ship's supplies."

"Koral, Koral, here's Anna Broere," Alek called.

"Yes, I can hear you," answered Captain P.

"Listen. Can we use ship supplies? Both provisions as well as machine and other parts?"

"Yes, you have my permission to use everything on board. Of course, apart from the personal belongings of the crew," the captain of Koral gave his consent.

"That's what I'm talking about," said the boatswain.

"I'm coming with you," I said, sensing some trick.

The bosun headed towards the locked door, and I followed him. "When did he find out that the canteen is here?" I thought.

"As the only room in the superstructure," said the boatswain, "it is padlocked, it must be the canteen. The key is in the captain's cabin, we'll find it later," he added. "I didn't take cigarettes, I had no time, and here, there are some for sure," he explained.

"Sure, you have permission, so take it and poison yourself if you enjoy it," I teased him, but I knew it was easier for him to work, having cigarettes. I understood him - there are so little pleasant things available to a seaman on a ship.

At that time, Motorcycle descended to the engine room to observe the work of the aggregate.

We went down to the mess. I felt weird - I was on the foreign ship, on which recently, a few hours earlier, there had been the Dutch crew. They had abandoned the ship, or in fact, escaped, not using all the possibilities to save it. "Why?" I was wondering.

Alek called us from the bridge.

"What's going on?" The boatswain asked.

"I've just received the message that the Dutch crew is already leaving Poland - they are flying to Amsterdam by the next plane. I'm coming down to you."

After a while he joined us in the mess.

"So the ship belongs to the person who will save it," said the boatswain, "but it won't be easy."

He lit a cigarette. What a rogue, he's already visited the canteen and said nothing?" I thought and asked:

"What's interesting there?"

"Where?" Alek asked.

"As usual in a canteen - there is alcohol, candies and hygiene products, what else can be there?" The boatswain said.

"Cigarettes, man! I see that you are smoking, and you didn't have any. Do you also have some for me?" Alek asked.

"Of course, how could I not," he said and handed him two packs.

"Nobody expected such a gift for the New Year," I said.

"What are you talking about? About cigarettes?" The boatswain inquired.

"No, about the ship," I put him right.

Motorcycle, breathless, burst into the mess, shouting:

"Show me the plan of the engine room, especially of the cooling system of the emergency generator, I need to know where the pump is getting water from. From which side, the port or starboard.

If the Kingston[25] was on the tilt side, that is, starboard, it would probably have sucked in sand already," Jozwa said confidently. "If it suck in sand, the light and pleasures will be over. We will spend the New Year in the dark."

"No, it won't happen to us. There is also an emergency generator, but in the bow. I need to figure out how it can be turned on from the engine room and from where it gets water for cooling."

We leaned over the firefighting plan of the ship, but no such details could be read from it.

"Come on, let's find the papers," I said in a calm voice to tone down Motorcycle.

In the office, there were rows of thick binders with technical documents regarding the engine room arranged in alphabetical order. Motorcycle quickly found the right plans.

"It's on the port side," he said, "there will be work," he added sadly.

"It's only a matter of two to four hours for the ship to dig deeper into the bottom, and the water will build up a wall around it," I said to Motorcycle. "What's the type of the bottom below us?" I asked Alek.

---

[25] Kingston - a pipe through which water is discharged outside a ship.

"Clay and sand," was the short answer.

"We have to come up with something quickly. I'll call you when I find a way to bypass the chiller cooling system, and then we'll create a makeshift. Those Dutch people are dear guys, they have everything ordered," said Motorcycle, amazed by this discovery.

"Then act, and I'm finally going to cook something. It's already afternoon," said Jozwa. Apart from the coffee and cookies that were on the bridge, we hadn't eaten anything.

We went to the kitchen.

From there, you entered the store of the precooling room with shelves for food products.

"Take your pick. Whatever you want," the boatswain rejoiced.

"But we don't have time for cooking, we need some semi-finished product, you throw it into the water and it's ready," I cooled his cooking enthusiasm.

Opposite there were two doors to the icehouse. First I looked into the room on the left, it was a "light" locker. There were plenty of cold meats, cheeses, butter, vegetables and other food products placed on shelves.

"Come on to the second room." I looked at the temperature gauge: minus eighteen degrees.

"Wait, I'll get my jacket," said Jozwa, following my gaze and seeing the temperature. "There is no time," I replied and stepped inside.

I wasn't interested in frozen meat and fish, I was looking for ready-made frozen foods.

"There it is!" I took the frozen packages of the vegetable mix from the carton.

"Okay, that's good," said the bosun who was also checking what was in the cardboard boxes on the shelves. He came across lasagne, and I found some dumplings - or so I thought. He took also frozen baguettes and three chickens, stating it was for the next day.

"Okay, enough. We already have something to heat up."

I went back to the light locker and took out a slice of smoked salmon, eggs, some cooked meats, weenies, blue cheese.

"Delicious!" I was glad. "There will be a spread for the New Year. At least that will be our compensation for the lost time.

"I hope we can find champagne too. We need to ring in the New Year with dignity. But only with one glass each," he assured me.

"Alright. Prepare something here, and I'll do my rounds."

With a handheld probe - which I had found in the engine room - I measured the draft at several points and marked it on the ship's situational sketch. It was needed to check whether and what would be the difference after an hour. I took it all to the bridge to Alek.

"Don't go," he told me, "more people will arrive soon. They will come by helicopter. "Pasat" can't come to our stern, it's too shallow. Tomorrow will arrive "Halny" from Gorki Zachodnie, then "the brass" will case the joint and decide what to do next. As you can see, the weather has stabilized, the wind is dying down, and by tomorrow the tide will decrease and a few people will be brought. I'm curious how many sober people they will find on New Year's Eve - apart from those on duty on the rescue ships, but it's the end of shift tomorrow, so maybe they'll find some. They probably already know what's going on, especially the replacement from the crew of "Tumak". They said that tomorrow "Halny" would drop them off - it is taking all of them from Gdynia."

A telephone was built into the maneuvering panel by the levers. I chose nine with the keys - the number to the mess hall.

"Mess, this is the boatswain," I heard.

"And someone else could be there?" I replied. "If you're not in a hurry, come upstairs, we'll throw out the pilot ladders - just in case."

"OK, I'm coming."

From the wing behind the bridge next to the lifeboat davit, we lowered pilot ladders on the port and starboard. I knew Alek had been keeping a journal since our arrival. He wrote down all important activities in it. It was well after six o'clock, and dusk was falling when I remembered the phone call home. I rummaged in the bag. "Holy smoke! About ten calls from Kinga. I will regret it." I thought and called back.

"Kinga, darling, I could call you only now," I said. "I'm fine, it's OK."

"Yes, I know Richie. I couldn't reach you and called the PSR base. And you know what? Such a nice guy answered, I introduced myself using your surname, told him that I was your wife and I was worried because I had no message from you. He replied: 'Yes. I know Richie. He's aboard the Anna Broere ship, and he is safe and sound. Ma'am, they have a lot of work to do there, but he will call you - don't worry.' He also gave me New Years greetings and said that I could always call him and he would let you know at the earliest opportunity that I called. They sound off about you on every TV channel," she added excitedly. They show the ship from the shore. It looks like you are on the beach."

"Because that's true, honey. We are not far from the beach."

"You know, Richie, I'm not going anywhere, I'm staying at home. I've already called everyone with the information that you are gone, so I'm staying at home for New Year's Eve. They are a bit disappointed but understand that there is nothing that can be done about it. Chris even said: 'I saw the ship in the news. Why is Richard there? I always said that he is unlucky with these New Year's Eve parties, he is somewhere far away at the sea, and if he is in the hometown, he will end up on such a day somewhere on a ship, and so what that not far from the shore, if far from you and us. But don't worry, we'll drink to those at sea.' He tried to cheer me up. I told him they had come to pick you up in the morning and a helicopter had taken you from the house straight to the ship. He agreed with me that you had had no choice.

"How is Olenka?" I asked.

"She's playing with mom."

"You know what? I will persuade my parents to go to the pier to Sopot - let them welcome the New Year there. But then you will be sad to spend New Year's Eve alone at home."

"No, Richie I won't be alone. Magda is on her way to visit us, I will pick her up soon from the train station in Sopot."

"It's good that your sister is coming. I have to go. Kisses for you and Olenka. I'll call you tomorrow at noon. Bye."

"Bye. Take care of yourself, Richie. I love you."

I returned to the bridge in good time, because after ten minutes the helicopter arrived. Efficiently landed on the ship, Konrad - Chief Mechanic and Bartek - Second Mechanic. We all knew each other, both were from PSR. I was wondering how it had been possible to bring them, but they would probably tell me that later.

So we were all there. The skeleton crew had manned the ship, and we could wonder how to get rid of the ice and pull the craft out of the sand.

Chief Mechanic and Second Mechanic were briefly informed by Motorcycle about the situation. Now he had superiors and it was them who were to worry about what to do next.

Dinner was ready, so we sat down in the mess.

"Richie, what about the tanks?"

Before running aground, we managed to flood the tanks almost completely. We made it at the last minute. We were a bit afraid that the ship would overturn, but it was probably already scrubbing the bottom, so it worked. We also flooded one empty drinking water tank with seawater. It needs to be excluded from the system."

"It is thanks to Motorcycle, which in a flash looked around the system," Alek praised Motorcycle.

"Praise him on the menu," I added.

The Chief turned to Motorcycle:

"So what's the situation?"

"I haven't worked out the emergency pump yet, but I believe we need to be prepared to get it going. In my opinion, it draws water from the ballast tanks for cooling. Apparently the ship is adapted to navigation on the rivers of England, where it often settles on the bottom at low tide."

"OK - we'll try to figure it out. And what about the ice?" He asked Alek.

"I have already told the "Koral" crew to get us crampons for shoes, otherwise it would be impossible to walk on the ice. They said something about cooperation with the navy from Gdynia.

"We drank up the coffee that the boatswain had served us, and went off to work. Jozwa and I were supposed to empty all the cabins of personal belongings that the Dutch crew had left. We put everything into big bags, closed them, and on the top of them, we pasted a cardboard with the position and name of the sailor. We put all the bags into one of the cabins, and Alek closed and sealed it. "Maybe they will come back for them?" I thought. Then each of us took a cabin and put our modest things in them. Everything we needed was in the laundry storage room. Everyone took what he wanted. I took sheets, towels, soap, that was all I needed for a couple of days.

Night was approaching, it was already past ten. "Koral" anchored nearby us, and "Pasat" swung right behind it, but the landing was announced by the captain of "Koral" for the next day morning, so we could rest until then.

We all sat down to the New Year's Eve dinner prepared by the boatswain.

"Just don't let it occur to anyone to shoot rockets to welcome the New Year!" Alek warned us, biting smoked salmon with a baguette with garlic butter.

I reached into the jar of mushrooms in vinegar, eating a roll with blue cheese.

"How do these snails taste?" Konrad asked.

"What? What snails?" I picked up the jar, but there were inscriptions in Dutch. The gale of laughter didn't embarrass me at all.

"You can eat anything as long as it tastes like food," I retorted.

In the second room, Motorcycle tried to turn on the TV - he caught the TV1 channel.

Somehow the conversation at the table was hard going. Their were all far away with their thoughts, and so was I. My watch was to be at four in the morning, so I had time to sleep.

The Bosun put a bottle of champagne on the table.

One glass each for a New Year's toast, it will be enough for everyone," he assured us. After dinner, the four of us moved to the TV room - the rest went on watch.

Anyway, if someone wanted to drink more, it was impossible to keep someone from doing it, because in the TV room there was a self-service alcoholic bar with drinks on shelves. Well stocked - apart from canned beer there were vodka, whiskey, brandy and wine. Take your pick. Next to it, there was a notebook in which the Dutch sailors wrote down every portion of alcohol they drank. I was flipping through the pages, and there was an entry on the last page - one bottle of champagne and the date of the bosun-joker. It was his doing.

Alek was sitting nervously shifting in place - it was obvious that he wasn't watching the program on TV. Finally he got up saying:

"I'm going to the bridge. I'll descend at midnight."

"No, don't come down, we'll come to you," I assured him.

"Okay," he said and snuck upstairs.

It was less than an hour until midnight, so we took glass and champagne and went upstairs to the bridge. At midnight, we raised a toast, giving each other best wishes for the New Year, and then everyone went to his place. I went to take a nap in the cabin. I didn't have much time left, after four hours I was to start the watch. I fell asleep thinking about Kinga.

Chapter 13

Ice

There was an incredible uproar from the very morning. The chemists announced they would land on the ship. The team from "Koral" was getting ready to come, but we were happy because they were supposed to bring us a cook, so there would be a normal meal.

Alek on the bridge bent over backwards, trying to control all the people who were coming to him with various problems. We finally agreed the order.

"The helicopter with the chemists has already taken off, they are flying directly from Plock," he told us. "They will be in less than an hour, the helicopter pilot informed me by radio. Two people and some equipment," he added.

"Anna, Anna here is Koral. Prepare the pilot ladders."

"They are ready to use. Come from the port side, from the stern," Alek replied. "Go see them, there will be a few people," he said to us.

The boatswain who had left earlier shouted at us from the wing:

"What a circus! See what's happening on the shore!"

And there were several dozen people, including a TV crew shooting. They were screaming something and waving to us.

"I'll give them an interview right away. I wonder how much they pay," he said.

We already saw "Zephyr" approaching the lowered gangway. It stuck to it, and finally the crew members climbed onto the Anna's deck, one by one. Captain P. greeted us, wishing us well-being in the New Year. He knew us all. He ordered a meeting in the mess after half an hour - there would be a brainstorming session, then he would give instructions.

The cook ran to the kitchen to prepare a meal for us - coffee was made, and the breakfast buffet quickly appeared in the mess.

"Gentlemen," Captain P. said, "Anna Broere is ours, and we have to do everything we can to get it out of this cesspool that the Dutch crew had put it into. We developed an action plan overnight for a few days ahead. We have to get "Anna" before the weather changes. You know very well that the ship may not withstand the next storm. Therefore, we asked the navy in Gdynia for help."

Bullshit - as we found out later, it was an order from above, from the crisis management.

"As you probably know, in the port of Gdynia and Gdansk, two ships have problems with icing and our "rs" and PSR seamen work there. The Polish ship "Wladyslaw Broniewski" in the avanport in Gdynia has problems with icing. It tilted 35 degrees under the weight of the ice."

"That's news to me," said the boatswain.

Undaunted, Captain P. continued:

"The Navy will support us with two landing boats and any number of people to hack the ice. The first step is to get rid of all the ice - this is essential to get the ship off the shoal. "We know that much, too," I thought as I waited for him to say something about cargo and chemists.

"As you know, two chemists are about to arrive on the ship to supervise the cargo."

"For what?" Konrad interjected. "What is this load?"

"Components for the production of artificial fertilizers," answered P. "The chemists informed us that the load can't exceed a certain humidity standard and that they would control this process," he explained. "Something else?"

"Yes," said Jozwa. "Will we get crampons for shoes? Because we can't walk on ice."

"We have seven pairs for you - that was it in the warehouse that they opened for us in an emergency at the Alpine Club. We also have a few bags of a special mixture of salt and sand. If needed, they will provide us with more. Sprinkle it on the deck, it will be safer to walk over it. They already carry motor chainsaws, crowbars and axes to us, everything for the navy team. I think thirty sailors will be enough for a shift, more would just disturb themselves. We forge day and night continuously in three shifts. You are to supervise the work and maintain the ship ready for towing. At noon, two landing boats will moor to the side. I think that cooperation with the navy will be exemplary. Navy sappers are considering the possibility of using small explosives to crush ice. Calculations are now underway to make sure they won't damage the ship. Meanwhile on the Anna, everyone on board carries out their duties"

Everyone went to do his job.

The boatswain, Janusz and I as well as the new AB Edward from Jantar went to the TV room at the mini-bar to establish an action plan. We were supposed to work eight hours on watches by the next day, when they were to send us two more sailors, including a replacement for Alek. So the two of us would be on watch. There were enough cabins for everyone. We were drinking coffee without boosters - although as for the boatswain, I wouldn't bet dollars to doughnuts. His eyes were glowing too much, or maybe it just seemed to me.

"I'm hearing the helicopter," said our new AB Edek, looking up.

I turned my head in that direction. The familiar silhouette of a helicopter was quickly approaching the ship. After five minutes, we had two chemists on board and, surprisingly, one of them was a woman. Nice little blonde.

"I'm Krysia," she introduced herself with a smile, seeing our surprised faces. "Any problem?" She asked.

"No, no," Jozwa replied, "it's just that there are only few single cabins," he joked about her.

"I can dwell in the captain's cabin," she replied resolutely.

"No way. It's already taken, but we'll find another one," added Alek, looking at us suspiciously. "Take the lady to the third officer's cabin, and to Gregory, the other chemist, give the one next to it," he decided quickly, fearing further bosun's jokes. "Meeting on the bridge in half an hour," he said in their direction and disappeared.

"How was your flight?" I asked Krysia. She asked me to call her so.

"Heavy," she replied, "We were thrown for half the trip."

"How did they bring you to this action?" I asked. "Where are you from?"

"From Plock," she replied, "and they took us from the New Year's Eve ball. Gregory and I were at our Company Center. Separately," she added, seeing the face of the bosun. "It was fun," she continued, looking at Gregory, "but only until we found out that it was a real action, not an exercise. At first, when the gendarmes came for us, Gregory called to them: gentlemen, the masked ball is in the other room," she continued over the coffee, which we drank together.

"What load is that?" I tried to ask Krysia.

"Components for fertilizers," she replied, confirming Captain K.'s version, but her gaze got serious and fled to the side. "In Plock, we deal with these components at the stage of their further processing. We are also part of the chemical rescue team, hence our presence here," she explained. "I can't say anything more until we examine the load composition. We only know as much as it is written in the order specification," she added.

"At the moment, it is impossible to get into the hold. Maybe there are samples of it on the ship," said the boatswain, turning to Gregory. "Look wherever you want," he encouraged them.

Why did I believe her? To this day, it has bothered me. "Probably because she was a woman," I considered a few days later.

We went to forge ice in the stern so that the landing boats could moor to us. Horror - tour de force - on ice, of course - it was a pity that we were far away from the shore, a bit of sand would have been useful. The mixture brought by "Koral" was good, but for thin ice and flat ground, and here the ice was thick and the deck was tilted. Pickaxes and axes bounced off the ice like springs. "So hard ... The only solution is to use a chainsaw to cut this ice," I thought.

"Richie!" Alek yelled from the bridge, standing outside by the chimney. "The landing boats are coming!"

"I see!" I yelled back to him. We had cellular radios, but we tried not to use them, because as one wise guy from the office explained to us - conversation are eavesdropped by amateurs and others, but whom he meant, he didn't deign to say - journalists probably.

Naval landing ships from Gdynia were finally going to be useful for something specific. For us, staying here was work, not training, but for navy seamen it was probably some form of training exercises.

They were very close now. We saw people bustling on their deck, we could also hear the officers giving orders.

Jozef asked, turning his head towards me:

"What do you think, how big draft does it have?"

"Maybe a meter, maybe two," I replied, remembering the depth of "Anna" in the last probe survey. It depends on whether at the bow or stern. Otherwise it wouldn't be able to sail to us."

After the first landing barge had been moored, the second boat reached our port side, and so they stopped in the now calm waters of the Baltic Sea. The waves were small - how long this would last - it was unknown. The sea at this time of year had never been calm for too long, so we had to make the most of this time. The barges were a little smaller than the ship, but their stern decks were almost flush with each other. After a while, the first group of sailors went on the deck of the "Anna", each of them was holding a crowbar, a fire ax or quite a large survival shovel. You could see that the army was ready for any situation - including such one. They split up efficiently into smaller groups and started chopping, hammering and pounding the ice however and wherever it was possible. The noise, loud comments and shouts of commands effectively scared us away. The lieutenant in command of this group informed us that seamen from landing ships weren't allowed to get inside the ship.

"But this prohibition doesn't apply to me," he added quickly.

The cook prepared three large thermoses with coffee and tea for them. He assigned the seaman to serve, handing him paper cups and sugar, and he placed it all in the stern corridor.

"For meals, they will go to their place, to the landing ship," the lieutenant informed us.

Unfortunately, pounding and forging didn't do much. The crowbars, axes, and pickaxes bounced off the thick ice, and only the gas-powered saws delivered later cut the ice efficiently.

In the evening they broke through, making a narrow path to the bow, which we decided to free from the ice in the first place. For tomorrow, January 2, in the morning, Koral announced passing a tow line, and for that, anchor lifts were needed, so they had to be activated. The hours passed and we only met for meals in the mess, where there was a heated discussion.

Usually Alek, giving fresh news, set a stone rolling.

"I spoke to the Poseidon. The action plan is clear and accomplishable. They start tomorrow morning. The Koral tow line will be given to us by the Typhoon. It should be fixed on the bow. Then Koral will start digging a trench along which it will pull Anna to extract it."

"How can it dig a trench at the bottom of the sea? After all, it is not a dredger," Krysia was surprised.

"It can, it can. You'll see for yourself," Alek assured us. "I hope we can make it before the weather changes."

"Could the ship still tip over then?" Krysia asked.

"When a storm comes, all these things can happen, but we would evacuate you to land, don't be afraid."

"I'm not afraid, and I will stay until the ship is safe in the port," Krysia declared, looking at us aggressively.

"As long as you are here, aboard this ship, you will obey my orders as everyone else do, and if it is necessary to leave the ship, you will do it," Alek gave her no illusions as to who was in charge there.

After supper, I went to my cabin to take a nap. I put cotton in my ears, but it didn't help much - the noise continued to disturb my restful sleep. Every now and then I was woken up by the sounds of a chainsaw. They broke large chunks of ice with them. The night passed horribly. Sleepless, after the morning watch, I called Kinga.

"Richie!" she announced to me in an excited voice. "Christopher called to say that he has an off-roader and they are going with Ula to your beach to see the ship. I'm going with them, it's not far, only for two hours."

If I had known then what was going to happen to them, I would never have agreed to it. I said then:

"Okay, but don't count on me. I don't have time to wave or chat while you are there. I don't carry the phone with me so that it doesn't disturb me," I informed Kinga in advance.

"All right, beloved," she agreed meekly. "But when we're there, I'll call you, maybe you'll have some free time," she told me in a pleading voice. "Alright?" She asked, waiting for confirmation. Seeing "Typhoon" heading our way, I told her:

"Alright. I have to go, honey," I said and hung up.

By noon, the boatswain and I fastened the tow line. This was due to waiting for the entire bow of the ship, especially the windlasses, to be cleared of ice sufficiently to enable their activation.

The landing ships' sailors, when they found out that the PSR would pay them a reward for the job they did, worked even harder, and the topic of the day was the amount of the daily rate, which with time increased in proportion to the waning ice.

Bosman was pissed off.

"And we will receive nothing, as usual," he roared at dinner.

"They will give, apart from the normal rates, they will add something extra," Alek assured, but as it turned out later, the boatswain was right. They gave nothing.

Alek entrusted me with looking after the chemists. It was going to be quite interesting.

"What am I supposed to do?" I asked Krysia.

"Help us take cargo samples from each hold."

"I don't know if we will be able to do it, the holds are still icy."

"It is very important. You see, that's why they sent us here," Krysia assured me with seriousness in her eyes.

"I'm surprised they even sent you here - but since you're here, we'll try. Dress appropriately and come on."

"Bosun, how is it going?" I heard Alek's voice.

"Great. Koral is just positioning its stern towards our bow and is starting to pull out the tow line. But it is still far away, some two hundred meters or more."

"Report when the harness goes up."

"What's the harness?" asked Gregory, hearing the whole conversation.

"Two anchor chains to which the tow line is attached," I explained to him. "It looks like real suspenders," I added.

"OK," I heard the boatswain.

I looked at my watch. Kinga was probably already on the shore. I had some time before Krysia and Gregory were ready. I went aft to the upper deck to get a better view. The shore was close, very close. Some people climbed the ice and they were about forty meters from the ship. I easily recognized Kinga, Christopher and Ula. I waved my hand to them.

They finally saw me. Kinga was jumping with joy. Ula was snapping and Christopher was shooting with a camera. "Of course - it's an attraction for them," I thought. How did he get permission to drive onto the beach in the Jeep?" I was wondering.

I didn't have time for more. I returned to Krysia and Gregory, who were already waiting with some measures or something like that.

"Do you need to take cargo samples, or it is enough to put the sensors in the hold?"

"Both, and as soon as possible," Krysia was nervous.

"Okay, we're going."

The first hold from the bow was already somewhat free of ice. Maybe something could be done there.

I had studied the layout of the ship before, so I knew roughly needed locations. However, the ice covered all pipes, blocks, wheels and other devices, hiding their meaning from sight. "There's a feather in the side of the first hold, try to place your sensors in this way," I said, unscrewing the cap on the pipe. "What does it measure?" I asked Krysia.

She muttered something evasively. In the end, she graciously explained:

"Air, gas concentration in air."

"What gas?" I asked.

"Bi and tetra something," that was what I understood. "Damn, not only is it a long name, but it also doesn't mean anything to me," I thought.

"Alright, put that damn thing in the pipe and measure," I said to Gregory.

"These are the vents?" He asked.

"No," I replied. "The vents are higher up and they're completely icy."

"At least one in each hold could be cleared," he said.

"Okay," I said, "you keep measuring here, and I will try to do it."

I went to the seamen supervising mate and presented our request to him, simultaneously showing with my hand which vents I talked about. "But are these shapeless chunks of ice really vents?" I thought and went back to the chemists.

Gregory and Krysia kept looking at the gauges, writing everything down in a special notebook with an electronic system, which every now and then printed them some charts and numbers whose meaning was known only to them. After a while, the mate came to us saying that the vents were already cleared of ice. It was good, but we still had to get there, which was not so easy. The ship was still tilted heavily to starboard.

"Krysia," I said, "I'll put a safety belt with a rope on you and you will climb up somehow. Or maybe you'd rather walk around it everything and go down from the port side?"

"No, I can handle it," she assured me and Gregory, who surprisingly quite quickly and efficiently climbed to the top of the hold.

As I said, I did so and Krysia, with the help of Gregory and mine, reached the pipe that the sailors cleared. I was relieved to see that it was a vent.

"Is that really a vent?" Gregory asked.

"Yes. The vent has such a characteristic shape. The end of the pipe that comes out of the hold makes an arc and goes back down toward the deck," I explained to him.

"Then we'll measure here, but the pipe must be straight, otherwise we won't put the sensor in it," he said.

It took a while to cut it at the base of the hold and throw off the curved end.

After fifteen minutes they called out:

"Get us down."

Slowly, they went down on their rumps, lowering their valuable equipment on the safety line before that.

"We're going to the mess," Krysia said in a strangely strong voice, but her face seemed more radiant to me. "Load is okay. The company will be glad that it didn't throw the money down the drain. You just need to bring it to the port," I told Krysia.

"Yes, yes," she answered me as if going off topic, and called Janusz.

"Come down to us," she asked.

We made tea with the addition - fifty grams of rum from the bar landed in it with the help of the boatswain, despite the protests of Krysia and Gregory. I didn't protest at all, I was even pleased with it. Frost didn't decrease, it was about minus twelve degrees all the time.

"Alcohol doesn't warm a body," said Krysia. She was probably right, she was a chemist after all, and she was familiar with it.

"It doesn't warm you up," agreed the bosun, "but it tastes better," he added, sipping his tea.

"Why is he fooling around? He's not like that at all," the thought ran through my mind.

"Alek," Krysia began, "the measurement results are good, but they have to be repeated at least every four hours, and in every hold. The samples can wait until tomorrow morning. But on the condition that the measurements in the other hold are the same."

"I'm glad," said Alek. "Tomorrow it will be possible to take the cargo for research from the hold."

"Send these printouts by fax to the company," Krysia asked him.

"Okay, give me them and I will do it right away," he said and disappeared, going to the bridge.

We drank tea and headed for the second hold. On the way I went aft, but Kinga and all the company were gone. Relieved, I went back to work.

The night passed calmly, but still very noisy, because teams of sailors forging the ice were working near the superstructure, where I was my cabin.

Chapter 14

Leakage

In the morning, after my watch and breakfast, as usual, I went to my cabin to check my phone. "What the hell?" I thought, seeing probably twenty calls from Kinga. I thought something had happened, as she had never tried to contact me so intensely. I called back.

"Richie, dear, it's good that you are calling. I've been trying to contact with you since early morning," she said quickly in a nervous voice.

"What happened?"

"Early in the morning, around seven, I had a call, someone was asking for you."

"Who?" I interrupted her.

"I don't know. He told me to tell you the Fatman called and you'll know who he is. It was a strange conversation. Listen carefully. This Fatman asked:

"Is Richie there?"

"There isn't," I replied.

"Where is he?"

"On a ship that ran aground near Rozewie," I replied to him. And he said:

"Damn, and you are still at home?"

"And where I should be?" I asked because I didn't understand anything. "And what's going on?"

"You have family in the countryside, please go to them immediately! It is important - immediately. And please don't tell anyone that I called - just Richie. I suppose he doesn't know anything"

"What doesn't he know?" I asked.

"Please take the child and leave immediately," he repeated, "and I didn't call you or talk to you. This is not a joke! Please repeat our conversation to Richie as soon as possible. Goodbye," he said and hung up. I'm very nervous, I don't know what's going on, do you?

"Me neither, but something dawns on me. Listen carefully and do what I tell you without asking any questions. Pack your bags immediately and leave with Olenka and your parents - immediately. Call Christopher and tell him that he is to leave the Tri-City for a few days. Say that Fatman called and I tell you and him to leave, immediately! Without publicity or questions. Understand?"

"Got it, but what's going on?"

"No questions - leave immediately. I'll call you in a few hours - you're supposed to be with your parents then. It is very important - do what I tell you. Don't tell your parents. Don't tell anyone. Got it?"

"Yes, Richie. We're leaving now, don't yell at me."

"Sorry, but the situation is very serious, I can't tell you anything more. Just leave."

"And you?"

"I will arrive later, I have to go. Kisses. Bye," I said quickly and hung up. Fatman was my friend, we had known each other since school. He worked in the Naval Staff in Gdynia. If he called, he knew what he was saying.

I went straight to Krysia's cabin. I knocked.

"Come on in," I heard. I walked inside and got at her right away:

"Listen carefully - I'll tell you something. I'm a serious guy and I just had a weird phone call. My friend told my family to immediately leave the Tri-City for the countryside. I know you can't say anything, so don't say anything. Just nod your head to express yes or no and I'll pretend I can't see. Understand?!" I yelled at her.

She nodded.

"The cargo is dangerous," - a nod.

"Very," - yes again.

"It might explode," she shook her head.

"Poison," - a nod.

"All of us," - yes again.

"The whole neighborhood," - yes. I dwelled on the subject.

"The whole Tri-City," - yes.

"What it depends on?" I asked and here she couldn't nod to me, but she pointed with a finger at the porthole, from where only the waters of the Baltic Sea could be seen.

"On the water?" - a nod.

"Thanks. I wasn't here," I said and ran back to my cabin. I called Kinga.

"How is it going?" I asked.

"We're already packed and we're leaving soon. But what about my job?"

"You will send them a sick leave for Olenka," I said. "If there is someone," I added in my mind. "I'll get it over the phone."

"No, there's no need. I will handle it myself in the Old Town," she assured me. "How long should the sick leave be?"

"I already know everything. Listen: you are supposed to be in the village three to five days. Pass it on to Christopher. For now, you're safe, but it takes three to five days for the threat to pass completely. Understand?"

"Yes. Richie, what is this threat?"

"I can't say anything. Not now," I added. "I'll tell you when I get back."

"When?"

"In three or five days," I replied, and then bit my tongue. I said too much.

"Oh. Now I understand," she said, "the threat is your ship ... Yes, Richie?" I felt that she was waiting for the confirmation of her guesses.

"I know, darling, you're a smart girl. Gotta go, drive carefully," I said quickly to avoid further questions.

"Take care of yourself," I heard.

I sat down on the couch in my cabin for a while and thought about what to do with this information. Did Alek know about everything or not? Who knew about it and who didn't?

After a while, I concluded that only the chemists and I were the only persons on the ship who knew about it. And I wanted it to be so. If I told Alek, then I would have had to inform the boatswain, and if they knew about it, it would have been as if the whole crew had known about it, and then on the next day the whole Tri-City would have known about it too. And then what? Chaos, panic, and an investigation into the source of the leak. I couldn't expose the Fatman. "The Fatman called only today, why? Maybe because break in the weather is predicted for tomorrow," I speculated. It meant that if the ship capsized or broke, and the water got into the hold, there would have been a big hazard. If not an explosion one, then what?

"In contact with water, the cargo may dissolve - yes, it can, but only those who possibly come into contact with it will be at risk. No, that's not it," I considered further.

"Probably the load under the influence of water gives off poison gas, some kind of cloud that can be carried by the wind and poison everything that comes its way. This has got to be it. After all, I've seen the chemists wear chemical suits and oxygen masks. But Krysia said it was their standard equipment." Now all the puzzles are put together.

The Dutch knew the threat or found out about it later, and therefore none of them stayed on the ship.

That's why they brought us to the ship by helicopter so quickly.

Therefore, PSR[26] wants to save the ship at all costs. Leaving it to its own fate would definitely end in a disaster. Who of them knows about it? Probably just a handful of people.

Therefore, the navy is involved in this. In the event of a disaster, they will use chemical troops. That is why they brought chemists from

---

[26] PSR - Polish Ship Rescue.

Plock on the ship. That's why the Fatman called me - thanks to him, Lord!

"In what direction will the winds blow tomorrow? I must check if it is the direction of the announced winds that prompted the Fatman to make this call. I ran to the bridge.

"What are the forecasts for tomorrow?" I asked.

"Bad. Wind to six, northeast," Alek informed.

"So it will blow towards the Tri-City. It's bad, very bad," I replied.

"Yes. Koral has already started digging and it's doing fine, but the weather can cross it," Alek confirmed, but he didn't know I meant something else.

"What can happen?" I asked.

The PSR staff provides for the possibility of changing the position of "Anna" and pushing it more to the shore. A capsize is also possible. And it depends on how the load behaves. And the behavior of the load depends on the degree of its humidity. And the humidity - well ... too much of it ... on ..." he ended. "Koral" will keep "Anna" on the tow line during the storm, and it will be helped by "Poseidon", which announced its arrival for tomorrow at noon. I think we will endure this storm together. The only comfort is that the temperature has dropped from minus two to minus five degrees. During this time, landing ships of the Navy will unmoor from us and will be waiting at the nearest port. Only the PSR units will remain.

"What about the chemists?"

"They stay," said Alek shortly, "we need them."

I took the binoculars and looked at Koral, which on the short tow line was digging a ditch towards the Anna's bow. Koral was slightly more submerged than the Anna, so its propeller idling, was flushing clay and sand from the bottom, creating a hole under the hull. Slowly but surely, it shortened the tow line and pulled back as if following a string. It would continue to do so until its stern was under the Anna's bow. Two smaller PSR tugs helped it to go in the right direction. Simple but effective. Only the weather could prevent them from further work.

I went downstairs to help the boatswain unberth the landing ships from our side. They returned to the port, and with them came teams of sailors removing the ice from the ship. What a silence - this topic was discussed at the dinner, during which Alek announced the alarms.

"I'm asking you to take these exercises seriously," he said, "and it applies to all of you without exception."

The second key topic was the readiness of the engine room staff to start the main engine of "Anna" and the mastery of emergency systems of aggregates.

"These are my slobs," the bosun praised them in his style.

"Richie," I heard, eating the chicken, "will you come with us after lunch for measurements?" Krysia asked, breaking the silence that had prevailed between us after my visit to her cabin.

"Of course," I replied.

"Krysia, did you take aviomarin?" The boatswain mocked her.

"For what?"

"The storm is coming. If the ship sways, you'll get seasickness, and aviomarin helps," he assured her.

"I'm not afraid of swaying, I swam on a yacht."

"In little lakes?" The boatswain asked a bit harshly.

"Stop scaring Krysia," Alek interrupted, as always businesslike. "We're are aground, and the ship won't be swaying," he explained, turning his head towards Krysia. "What happens to guys when there's a woman on the ship?" I thought. "Normally there wouldn't be such conversations and jokes like that now." I returned to the cabin to call Kinga.

"We are already on the spot, everything is fine. The road was fairly passable," she informed me. "I'm very worried about you," she added in a shaky voice. "On the news, they talked about you and the storm."

"I'll be fine. I have emergency equipment at my disposal," I explained. "I will be home in three days. Tell everything in detail," I demanded from her.

I really liked when Kinga told me about everyday matters. She always did it with commitment and sprinkled such small things that I had no trouble imagining that I was there with them, participating in these events. Olenka was the apple of my eye. Kinga knew it perfectly well and dragged her home accounts. She had the gift of talking passionately about small, ordinary, domestic matters and each time she involved me in these activities, every now and then asking: "Richie, did I do the right thing? Or should I do this or that? Tell me please." I just liked it and probably subconsciously waited for such conversations. But now I didn't have much time, so I ended the conversation sooner than usual. Kinga also told me that Christopher and his family evacuated from Gdynia and he would be in the hideout until I canceled the alert, and that if I could, I should have called him.

I called after a while.

"What's happening? Speak!" He asked.

"Now I really can't. I'll tell you everything when I get back in a few days. Do you remember our games in the old shelter at the end of our estate?"

"I remember."

"Then you already know."

"Thanks, Richie."

"Christopher, I have to go."

"Take care," I heard on parting.

When we were kids, our whole gang played war. Christopher had old gas masks, which we put on while waiting for the kids from the other yard to attack. Such were the times - we were taught this at school. Who would have thought that twenty years later we would take advantage of these memories.

Coming back with Krysia and Gregory from the measurements, I already knew from them that the results in all holds were good and the cargo didn't change its structure and no chemical reactions took place in it.

"By the way, such filth should be transported in other ways," I said to them, "for example in plastic bags or barrels. There would be no danger of the cargo shifting and causing the ship to capsize," I pretended not to know about the actual threat this shit posed.

"Costs, dear, costs. This is the point," Gregory answered me. "Every mode of transport poses a potential hazard," he explained calmly, staring at the gauges. "Take, for example, sulfur and crude oil, or ordinary coal dust whose transport by ship is also hazardous.

Yes, he was right. Coal dust, when it absorbs moisture from the air or water enters it, turns into a semi-liquid pulp and is a lethal threat to the ship. This is how a Polish bulk carrier sank in the Mediterranean Sea, or even two - I don't remember. Ordinary grain transported in bulk can overturn a ship, not because of moisture and water, but because of the structure.

Here, however, the safety of cargo transport was kept. It was the human factor that didn't show responsibility, allowing the ship to ice up. They may not have known about the threat posed by this cargo, but that doesn't change their extreme irresponsibility. They could avoid icing by changing course. However, they were in such a hurry to make it to the port by New Year's Eve that they didn't do it. Then it was too late and we ended up losing the ship. Ships sink, it happens, but such cargoes shouldn't be transported on them precisely because of the sinking. The train wouldn't be lost, although, I'm not sure. It can also fall into the water from some bridge. You can't win", I thought as I waited for the measurements to end. Then they took more samples of the cargo with a telescopic tube that spread like a fishing rod with a suction cup at its end or something like that. They didn't need many samples. They put this filth in test tubes right away - marked it, described, and we came back. I could see they were satisfied, but I wasn't.

A bit cold, we returned to the mess hall for hot tea. Without alcohol, because then the boatswain had to oversee Koral's tow line in the bow.

"The cargo is normal, but the weather is not," Gregory was worried.

Krysia became more cautious in expressing her opinion about the cargo. She was probably bothered by the realization that I knew what it was all about.

"Cargo is not everything, the ship is important," I said. "I don't want to scare you, but you don't know what a storm can do with a ship aground. I know it because I have already experienced such an event, or actually two. Including one in winter, in Ustka."

"And the second one?" Krysia asked.

"The second one in a hot summer in Egypt, near Alexandria, where an American fifty-thousandth bulk carrier was thrown onto the beach. It had an engine failure and was drifting with the wind pushing it ashore. It sent an SOS and waited for help. We didn't manage to get to it before it was thrown aground, but we were first at its side anyway, despite the fact that there were probably three or four rescue tugs sailing there. The crew, however, didn't abandon it. It wasn't until later that they flew home, except for the two who stayed and sailed with us all the way to Tampa, Florida. We worked on the "no salvation - no payment" principle. Cool, yeah? But that's a story for later, now there is no time for the "sea stories" from the "sea romance" chapter. The only consolation is the fact," I continued the previous thread, "that the announced winds are not as strong as they are usually at this time of the year, and that we had enough time to prepare for such an eventuality. And we are well prepared, so keep your noses up," I calmed them down.

Ever since Alek assigned me to them, they had come to me with all their doubts and questions, sometimes very mundane. Gregory recently asked:

"Richie, in my and Krysia's bathroom, it stinks. What to do?"

"Don't meet in the bathroom, but in the cabin," I joked.

"Really!" Krysia bridled.

"Pour water over the scupper."

And seeing that he didn't understand, I added:

"The water drain in the shower must be flooded with water from time to time, then it won't stink. It stinks, because the ship has a large list," I explained.

Or Krysia:

"I can't regulate the airflow and it's too hot at night."

"And how do you sleep, naked or in pajamas?" I asked.

"Don't be silly!"

"Alright, come on. I'll see what I can do."

Another time, Krysia asked:

"Richie, do something with my bed, it is tilted so that it is impossible to sleep."

"I can't," I replied, "I am faithful to the chosen one of my heart."

"But that's not what I mean. It's just that the bed is inclined and it disturbs my sleep."

"Bunk. It's called a bunk," I corrected Krysia.

"What bunk?" she didn't understand.

"You don't say bed but bunk."

"Oh. I'll remember."

"Wait in the cabin, we'll do something about it in a moment."

After a while I took to her cabin a piece of hard board and a few blocks, which I placed under the mattress, and it was relatively even. I had done the same in my cabin before.

It started blowing harder and harder. The ship was silent, no one came out onto the deck. From time to time only a watchman flashed to the bow and back.

Alarm bells began to howl - the lifeboat alarm - we are leaving the ship. It was Alek who started the alarm training announced during dinner. I took the equipment and headed to the meeting point, which was the deck next to the lifeboat. After a while, everyone appeared, and no one was whining, groaning or criticizing. We realized that such a variant could also happen. Alek briefly and substantively discussed tasks with each of us. He devoted most of the time to the chemists. He explained that if the ship turned over, we would have to run to the stern. He showed how to put on a wetsuit to protect the body from the cold, how to possibly jump into the water, enter a life raft, and such general guidelines. As rescuers, chemists were familiarized with a method specific to all rescue services to protect their own lives, because in order to save someone, you must first be able to protect yourself.

After we dealt with it, he didn't give us free time but announced a training fire alarm.

"There is fire in the engine room," we heard over the radio. This was only our domain, chemists were given a medical task - to help the victims.

After less than two hours sounded a signal. We could go back to our activities. As usual, Krysia and Gregory joined me and the boatswain in the TV room. We drank tea with an addition, but this time it was lemon.

"You want tea?" Jozwa asked.

"Yes please."

"With or without the addition?" he clarified.

"Without!" Krysia exclaimed, but Gregory was nodding that it could be with the addition.

"I meant lemon," the bosun said to Krysia, smiling.

"With a lemon, it can be," she agreed, and she was given one. Into Gregory's tea, the boatswain poured fifty milliliters of rum.

"Do you always have alert trainings on board?" asked Gregory.

"Always, and it is a constant element of our work," explained the boatswain.

"And what is the most dangerous for people on board?" Krysia asked. She was sitting at the table, dressed in a white, thick sweater. Looking at me, she tried to act like she hadn't told me anything.

"No doubt a fire," I told her.

"Why? After all, you always have plenty of water," she was surprised.

"As you know, not everything can be extinguished with water, and the worst are drafts," said the boatswain, "then the fire spreads rapidly. A terrible sight ... I won't forget it for the rest of my life," he added.

"What happened? Speak!" Gregory urged him.

"I was on the "Typhoon" in Kolobrzeg, when we received a call that the ferry "Heweliusz" was on fire," began the story the boatswain. "You must have heard about it, unlucky ship," he muttered. "We had a fifteen-minute initial readiness then, the motorists started the engine in eight minutes - how they did it is still a mystery today. The ship's engine is not like a car engine, you can't just turn the key and start it," he explained to the chemists. "When we got there, 'Heweliusz' was burning strongly. The car deck of the ferry was on fire. The rescue operation was hindered by the wind and such a large wave that it was impossible to stick to it, which would have made it easier to extinguish the fire. I remember very well that we were standing on the deck of the Typhoon, while passing very close to the port side of the ferry and its foresheet[27], and I had to hide inside because the heat was coming from it. We were as close to its left side as possible, pouring water from cannons and from whatever we could onto that red-hot steel. I can still hear the hiss of water touching the side of the ferry. I don't wish anyone such views."

He got up, said "sorry" and left.

"What happened to him?" surprised, Gregory looked at me questioningly.

---

[27] Foresheet - a front wall of a superstructure (from a bow side).

"A few years later "Heweliusz" sank during a storm. He lost his friends on it. Despite so many years passed, he is still very troubled by it," I explained the behavior of the boatswain.

"Besides, such drastically dangerous rescue operations in which people die are never forgotten. You experience it later very much. You analyze your own behavior and that of others. And maybe if it was done like this, then ... Or otherwise, then ... Unfortunately, time cannot be turned back, so you have to train and train again. I told them so, but is it really true? After all, I do everything to forget about it as soon as possible, so that these thoughts don't torment me, and I don't have to get back to what happened. For them, it's just a story.

"Do you know what the statistics say?"

"No."

"The most dangerous profession in the world is seaman, and now you are also a seafaring brotherhood," I told fibs, "so go to sleep, because you have to get up in the morning."

"Just don't lock the cabin doors," added the bosun, who heard the last sentence on his return.

"So early? No way! We're not going!" They protested loudly.

"Richie, you promised to finish telling about this incident in Egypt," Krysia said, looking at me pleadingly.

"Go ahead, I'll listen too," added the bosun.

"Then give me a chilled beer, one won't hurt," I said.

The bosun brought a can of beer to each of us, so having no choice, I started to tell.

Chapter 15

M/V Manhattan

"A few years ago, when I was working at PSR, we were on Jantar ..."

"Koral's twin which is here with us?" Gregory interrupted me.

"Yes, the same.

...near Alexandria, where we towed an old passenger ship from Canada for scrap. After giving it to the local tugboats, we headed to the port for supplies. We spent a nice and beneficial few days at Siki Abd ar Rahman. The Old Man was instructed to head to Gibraltar, where our base was. With great regret, we left this nice port, where some of us made quite close acquaintances with local girls - mainly bodily.

The weather was quite windy, but after the Atlantic experience, it seemed to be a zephyr, and a warm one, because summer was just about to end.

The bridge watchmen picked up an SOS at around nine o'clock in the morning. The American bulk carrier m/v "Manhattan" called for help. It had an engine failure and was drifting ashore.

Later it turned out that he had been drifting for twenty hours, and during this time the crew tried to repair the engine, but to no avail.

This position showed we were sixty-eight miles from it. The captain gave the order: full speed ahead, course for the "Manhattan". The more than four hours that separated us might not have been enough for our arrival on time," was considered on the bridge of "Koral".

The Old Man gave it our position and arrival time - for encouragement and competition. We realized that there were other tugboats in the nearby port, or maybe even closer, that would come to the rescue.

But here applied the principle of "first come, first served" - this concerned only property, of course, because everyone is obliged to save life at sea.

Trade negotiations regarding the ship began between the PSR office in Gdynia and the American shipowner. As it turned out, the Manhattan was without a cargo. We will take people off it for free and drop them off at the nearest port, or transfer them ashore in some other way. But the ship is money and we had to earn it.

If the entire crew leaves a ship, it belongs to whoever saves it, but that was out of the question here. The captain of the bulk carrier had no intention of leaving it, so we had to get along. The port tugs had no chance to compete with "Jantar", which is a purebred ocean tug, designed specifically for this type of operation. I remembered the sight of the ship that hadn't been taken off the shoal. At the beginning, they set a rate for towing to the nearest port for renovation. However, as the situation grew hotter because the ship was drifting ashore faster than its captain had assumed, the talks shifted to another stage. An hour before our arrival, we already knew that we were closest and that we would be tasked with saving their asses. The next two tugs could arrive only after five hours. But they were low-power port tugs. Twenty minutes later the Manhattan reported that it was stranded. The anchors it dropped didn't stop the ship. Half an hour later we saw the craft. Too bad, it was so close. However, this fact changed the situation diametrically, both in terms of saving property and in terms of trade. The crew members were in no danger so far, so they waited calmly for us.

The PSR office in Gdynia finally got along with the shipowner. The captain of "Jantar" came down to us to the mess, where the crew gathered.

No salvation, no payment. If we pull it off the sand, we will tow it to Tampa, Florida. There will be no engine overhaul in a nearby repair shipyard, because it would still have to go to the dock. The American shipowner calculated that it would be cheaper if we towed it to him. These are the arrangements, so get ready and do what you need to do. We will give the tug line in fifteen minutes."

We came closer. What a view! A desert appeared to us. Yellow sand, undulating like sea waves, covered everything around. The wind created piles out of it, and quite high hills, the shape of which caught the eye. The sight of sand flowing down from the dune peaks looking as if someone had cut them off with a machete, was especially delightful. The sands flowed steeply down, to climb laboriously the next hill, carried by gusts of wind.

On a nearby hill, you could see the silhouettes of camels swaying rhythmically to the steps taken. They were approaching a place where, at the very bottom, was the silhouette of a ship. "It's in trouble," the rhythm of their movements seemed to say, "there might be some use of it, and maybe some money." And they moved on, led by curiosity and hope that the ship would collapse and bring benefits - or perhaps by a desire to help. The sun was shining over the dunes, and the hot, undulating air blurred the silhouettes, intensifying the impression that all we saw was a mirage.

However, the majestic silhouette of the Manhattan was really there, it was no illusion, and we had to deal with it.

Having gotten as close as possible, the captain decided to lower the fast lifeboat and drop off our crew onto the bulk carrier to receive and fix the tow line. For this job, he assigned the second mechanic, me and a carpenter.

"That for now," he said. "What to do next, we will decide later."

Equipped with means of communication and willingness, we set off with the roar of two Mercury engines.

The boat made an impression on everyone who saw it in action. Now, rearing up, it raced, foaming the water behind it in a high wave. After a while we found ourselves under the side of the bulk carrier from the land side, where the lowered gangway was waiting for us. I looked at the depth measure on the ship's side - nine meters. We quickly and efficiently climbed the high side of the bulk carrier, after which the boat set off for the connecting line needed to give the tow line. There would be no heaving line shooting. It's a pity - I always liked this view, it's such a typical sea spectacle.

The American crew greeted us with friendly words. They were mostly African Americans. From that moment on, the ship was under our command, and the crew was to assist us as much as possible. We had to hurry because the wind and waves could push the Manhattan ashore for good, and the sea currents could create the sand dyke around its side. Time is half the battle.

It hadn't swum at full speed, but had drifted, carried by the force of the wind, so it had run aground relatively shallow. It was under full ballast - this also would make it easier for us to take it off.

We started with getting acquainted with the work of windlasses. Both anchors were in the water. They had to be pulled out of there, and that might have been impossible.

I asked the American captain:

"Master, which of them went into the water first?"

"Left," he replied.

So we started taking the starboard anchor, from the sea side. The Manhattan seamen were assisting us by operating the windlasses.

At that time, the boat brought a thin connecting rope, which I hauled with the carpenter onto board. After it, the second, thicker one, a hook, then the Koral tug line. Now all we had to do was fasten it, and for that we needed an anchor chain.

After an hour the tow line was attached. The starboard anchor was pulled in, the port one stayed in the water. The captain of "Jantar" decided that there was no time to try to pull it out again and ordered to break the chain with flame. However, he assured the Manhattan captain that for an additional fee our diver would find it and we would retrieve it at a later time.

It was almost noon, the sun was shining, and sweat poured over our eyes and all over our bodies. Dressed as prescribed in work coveralls, helmets, and hard boots, we could hardly refrain from throwing it all off.

"Jantar" began to release the haul and move away from us.

"They'll try to pull it off without digging," said the Third.

"I can see," the carpenter replied.

After a while, black smoke began to come out of the tug's chimney. The engines worked at full power. The tug line nearly jumped out of the water, but didn't break. The piles of white water swirling behind the tug showed how hard the engine was working. Then the tug began to rotate from left to right, trying to move the bulk carrier's bow.

I looked down at its pear sticking out of the water.

"It doesn't even budge," I reported. And so it would be for the next few hours.

The Third started the watch at the tug line. The rest went to dinner.

The silhouettes of two port tugs appeared on the horizon. After lunch, they anchored not far from us. They would be waiting and watching the unfolding of events - in the hope that the Captain of "Jantar" would decide to ask them for help. Sure they would have been useful, but it costs money and that's why it was the final version in case we couldn't handle it ourselves. But if all the three ships couldn't handle it, they would have still had to pay for assistance. The Third struggled with ballasts, and the carpenter and I took turns keeping watch for two hours in the bow.

And so the night passed - in the morning the wind died down and the wave was smaller, but the sun was already warming up. From "Jantar" a boat came for the captain of the bulk carrier - just such a courtesy visit and probably the signing of some documents. Taking the opportunity, they brought us some personal belongings according to previously issued guidelines, who needed what.

I ordered shorts, sandals and sunglasses as well as T-shirts and creams.

"Jantar" once again tried to rotationally pull the bulk carrier into deep water.

The Third emptied the bow ballasts, and that helped. The Manhattan's pear began to move and the beak slowly headed towards the open sea.

After a while, it was already pointing straight towards the stern of Koral. But that's all. The stern of the bulk carrier was submerged more deeply, it sucked to the bottom and didn't yield.

From "Jantar" they called to me:

"Richie, you have a job," I heard the Chief.

"I've been working all the time," I replied.

"But now you're going to work for extra money," he laughed.

"If so, I'm on my way," I replied.

The Old Man agreed with the captain of the bulk carrier that we would pull out his anchor with a chain for five thousand bucks. "What do you think?" the Chief asked.

"I'm for and even against," I paraphrased a famous saying of an electrician from Gdansk Shipyard.

"We'd have to get it out anyway. We will be digging to the Manhattan, and the anchor lying down could damage our propeller," the Chief explained. "We'll come for you soon," he added.

"OK, I'm not going anywhere today."

I was the only diver with papers on this cruise on Jantar. Usually the crew is selected so that there are two of us. Robert at the last minute, due to family matters, resigned from this cruise and they send someone else. But don't worry, each of the crew was properly trained to serve a diver or scuba diver. The ship's equipment consisted of two underwater cameras - real wonders, transmitting the image directly to the ship's monitors. There was also a decompression chamber - but we always hoped it wasn't needed. Appropriate suits, air tanks for divers and scuba divers, and the rest is good will and the right skills.

They lowered the lifeboat from the tug boat, which was to sail around the bulk carrier and take depth measurements. The map showed that the shore there sloped gently into the water and only further away there was a greater fault, but the bottom was sandy. Fate was on our side - there were no rocks or coral. When I was back on board, I asked the Chief:

"Are there any sharks? The best in shark is a steak," I added jokingly. The Chief, however, without a smile, gave me a bag of orange shark powder.

I dressed in wetsuit - it was warm and the water was clear and blue with a touch of green. Moreover, it was very warm, so it was pleasant to immerse in it.

We got into the boat, where two oxygen cylinders were waiting for me. I put on the fins, they threw the cylinders on my back, I checked the air amount, put on the mask and jumped into the water.

I dove where the bow of the Manhattan had recently been. I had to find the end of the chain that had fallen to the bottom somewhere there. It wasn't deep, but the bottom couldn't be seen from the boat due to the sunlight reflecting off the water surface. However, it was enough to immerse yourself in it, and the beauty of the underwater world was revealed in all its glory. I kept swimming in circles looking for the chain. Then I swam in greater circles about three meters above the bottom to see better. I was tied to the boat with a lifeline, and the boat crew could see where I was by tracking the bubbles.

"There it is!" I thought. Finally I saw the chain lying, facing the hull of the bulk carrier. I came to the surface.

"Throw a buoy here," I said, "the chain is under me." The little red buoy landed in the water. "Now loosen the line. I will attach the buoy to the chain and, swimming over it, I will look for the anchor."

After ten minutes I was over the anchor, which was stuck in the ground at a depth of about thirty meters. Here they threw a second buoy into the water. I went down, scaring off fabulously colorful fish, shimmering with all shades of the rainbow and with a characteristic black stripe along the body. I had no idea what specie it was, maybe it was "Nemo"?

I passed the thin steel line through the anchor eye and got back upstairs. That was where my part ended - the rest belonged to the boatswain who was supposed to pull the anchor out of the bottom.

We returned to the "Jantar", unwinding the thin steel line from the drum, for which the impatient crew was already waiting. When I was resting on the deck, the captain came down to me.

"Richie, will you see the hull of the bulk carrier?"

"Sure. For me, it's like a free vacation."

Viewing the hull of the ship is already serious work, but I was expecting it. Before making a decision, the captain wanted to know as much as possible. We went back to the bulk carrier. I started with the bow, which was buoyant - the bottom here was not even, it stretched diagonally from the shore into the sea. Therefore, one part of the bulk carrier was submerged in the water and was buoyant, while the other was resting on the bottom. "Valuable information worth a lot of money," I thought.

The bottom of the bulk carrier was wide and flat to the stern, but its right side sat on the sand. I swam around it from the other side, all the way to the propeller.

The stern looked good. The right side of the ship settled in the sand. The rudder blade was immersed in it to a third of its height. The propeller blades touched the sand only with their tips. It would have been good to spin them, but it wasn't possible - they already knew that without a shipyard they wouldn't repair the engine.

I returned from the other side, but didn't dare to swim under the bottom of the ship and see from what point it touched the bottom of the sea. It was too big and probably unnecessary risk, because the information gathered so far should have been enough.

I put everything on a sketch in a special notebook for underwater writing and drawing. I looked at the pressure gauge and, seeing that I had already touched the reserve of air, surfaced and got on the boat.

"Go onto the ship, let the Old Man watch it, maybe he'll want me to check something else."

Of course, the captain didn't miss the chance that I was in the water. He came downstairs to me because it would have been weird for me to get onto the bridge in the wetsuit.

"Listen, Richie," he said. "What is the straight line distance from the bottom to the ship's side and how many degrees is the bottom slope? We will calculate where the hull meets the bottom."

"Okay, I will swim and measure. How should I measure the bottom slope?"

"Guesstimate," he replied.

I went down again, measured the distances and put it on the sketch. The bottom slope was about twenty degrees to my eye. I walked around for half an hour, then checked if there were any mechanical damages of the rudder and propeller. I wanted them to know that I worked hard for the bonus. On my way back, somewhere in the middle of the ship, I saw a larger free space beneath its bottom. The sand sparkled in the sunlight reaching there, so I approached that place carefully. I guesstimated: the free space between the hull and the bottom of the ship is one and a half meters wide, so I can fit. I wanted to see how far it reached. Gently wiggling my fins, I swam under the hull, but visibility decreased with every meter, and so did the width of the clearance between the ship's hull and the sand. After swimming about ten meters below the bottom of the Manhattan, I turned back. I saw what I wanted and there was no point in risking any further. I swam aft to check the rudder and propeller again. Being under the ship, I didn't know what was happening on the surface of the water. And there my fellow boatmates, slightly panicked, were looking for bubbles, which disappeared when I swam under the bottom of the ship. In addition, one of the sailors on the Manhattan spotted a shark.

"Shark! Shark!" He shouted, pointing to the sea. In the boat, they jumped to their feet, and the motorist was scanning the water with binoculars.

"There it is, you can see the fin!" He spoke in a slight squeaking voice with shock.

"Maybe it's not a man-eater." The helmsman said.

"Why don't you come closer and ask it?" Motorcycle got angry with him.

"Where is Richie?"

"The devil knows, you can't see the bubbles."

"There are bubbles, there are, you can see them," Motorcycle screamed. "He has swum towards the stern."

"Follow him," he said to the steersman.

Meanwhile, having looked at the rudder and the propeller, I was slowly rising to the surface. I saw that in the distance the boat was moving towards me, and Motorcycle was pointing at something with his hand. I looked in that direction and froze. "Shark..." I thought, seeing the fin gliding towards me twenty meters away. The boat was sailing to me at high speed. "What to do?" I was wondering. "After all, I'm not going to race against it, first come, first served, to the boat." I hid under the propeller, just in case. I waited calmly for events to unfold. I knew not all sharks are dangerous, and this one didn't look too big to me - it was about three meters long. When it was a few meters away from me, it turned left, cutting off my way.

I looked towards the shore, which was further away than the boat. Out of the corner of my eye, I saw a few kids floating on a car's inflated inner tube. They were about twenty meters away from me. I don't know if they saw a shark, but probably not, because they didn't run away to the beach, where three Bedouin tents and a few camels stood on the sand by the water. I couldn't swim there, I would have attracted the shark to the kids, besides the distance to them was greater than to the boat.

Doing a half-turn, I plunged deeper and hid between the rudder and the propeller that covered me completely. Standing with one foot on the propeller blade, I put the other one on the rudder shaft, and holding on to its body with my hand, I looked first left, then right, searching for a shark. I didn't see it anywhere. Suddenly, a shadow above began to slowly move from left to right. It was the shark that made the ellipses because it couldn't go around me, as is usual. Farther above my head I could see the bottom of our boat and the silhouettes of Motorcycle and helmsman staring deep into the water. "Damn, I'm not gonna wait here all day for the shark to go away, because it might not happen," I thought. Then I remembered about the package the Chief had given me. I had it attached to my left forearm with a bur. I pulled out the knife fastened to my right leg and tore the plastic bag with it. Waving my elbow lightly, I released the powder that spread quickly around me, coloring the water orange-yellow. Probably the shark didn't see me anymore, and neither did I see him. "Damn it, I'm coming up!" I thought and with the knife ready in my right hand, I dashed up towards where our lifeboat had just been. I surfaced next to them, and before I realized what was happening, they grabbed my arms and pulled me inside.

"You scared us so much!" The helmsman said reproachfully.

"You? What about me, I'm a dog? This beast was hunting me," I replied, looking around. The children were no longer in the water, they stood on the shore and waved at us anything they had. Some used sticks, the other, rags and handkerchiefs. Women stood nearby - like all mothers, they were afraid for their children.

The water around us, within a radius of several dozen meters, was colored with the shark repellent - at least that's what the producer said, placing the appropriate inscription on the packaging. Did it help? It is unknown, but we didn't see any sharks anymore.

As it turned out later, while I had been discussing the subject, the assistant cook on the Manhattan, while preparing the fish for dinner, had dumped half a bucket of guts and other fish waste before I went into the water. It must have lured this sweetheart, because they are particularly sensitive to such specifics as blood and fish guts, which they can smell from miles away.

We made our way back, sailing towards the bow, as far as the Manhattan pilot ladder. We saw there probably its entire crew, leaning over the side and looking down curiously.

I waved my hand at them and, still slightly out of breath, took off my diving mask. My friends took my cylinders off and I checked the pressure watch. I should have done it earlier, and I probably would have done it if it weren't for the shark. I wasn't swimming deep or too long, the decompression indicators were in the green zone.

"It's okay, we can go," I told the boatman. We were approaching the "Jantar", gliding quickly.

The Old Man was already trotting in place, waiting impatiently.

"What was going on there?" He asked as if he hadn't know, and yet they had reported to him about the shark right away.

"Eh, nothing special. A friend visited me, but I didn't like his teeth, so we parted quickly," I replied.

"Do you have that sketch?"

"I do."

"Give it to me."

I discussed the details with him.

"Captain," I reported, "I entered the free space under the hull, somewhere in the middle of the ship. But only in one place," I added, and found that the third of the ship bottom width was propped on the sand," I reported the bulk carrier inspection and was reamed by the Old Man. But then I heard:

"Thanks, but don't do that anymore. Now I know the situation, and we'll try a trick. You have a day off," he added, "be on the alert. You will be replaced on the Manhattan by Pawel."

"Okay," I confirmed and went to the mess for chocolate. I knew that there were two bars of dark chocolate waiting for me there - it is such a ritual, and according to the regulations, a bonus "for energy loss during diving".

For the rest of the day and night, I was loafing around on the Manhattan, getting acquainted with the ship and chatting with the crew. Hunky-dory, I deserved it. Into the mess where I was sitting, or rather a large living room, lined with some exotic wood, with leather sofas and huge comfortable armchairs in a stupid greenish color for a ship, burst the Third Officer.

"I got the news that the anchor with the chain is already on board our tug," he boasted before those seated. This news didn't make any impression on the crew. What difference did it make to them whether the ship had a second anchor now or not? They were just watching a movie they commented out loud and mundane things like the anchor only disturbed them. I understood them only a little because they spoke some weird slang, but I was sitting with them in the living room because my own cabin wasn't available at the moment.

For supper, the cook served us an American steak - as big as their trucks, and bloody as if they had just killed the bull, as well as a hefty portion of fries. The captain of the Manhattan, sprawled in the cavernous armchair, said:

"I didn't know that Poland has such large tugs."

And I suspect that he didn't even know that Poland has access to the sea. Or maybe he thought it was part of Russia - I have already met such people in America. They are only interested in the tip of their noses. Clearly pleased, he praised our actions. He was particularly impressed by the possibility of penetrating the bottom and the hull with a camera and a monitor. He tried to ask me about the condition of the rudder and propeller. But I told him nothing and sent him back to our Old Man. Clearly angry, he got up and left, and I got myself a second cup of coffee-covered ice cream - I didn't care about him. I didn't evaluate him highly, nor did his crew.

All night the "Jantar" pulled the tow line and used rotations, trying to move the bulk carrier's bow. It managed to do so to a small extent. In the morning it changed tactics. It began to dig a trench and approach the bow of the Manhattan. It was evident that it pulled the tow line strongly, because the distance to us was rapidly decreasing. Every now and then it returned to the previous position, checking if it had a clear path. Arduous work.

The next morning, it reached our bow. To everyone's surprise, the Old Man ordered the towline to be suspended, and the craft moored to our side with the stern. It looked funny. The massive bow of the bulk carrier covered the entire stern of our tug, which, positioned perpendicular to its side, looked like a scrag. Only when the engines roared and the water swirled under the side of the bulk carrier did everyone watch the tug boat washing out tons of sand, which, carried by a strong current, was depositing far beyond it. They realized that in this way it would wash out the sand from under the bulk carrier's side. Only then did they understand the Old Man's intentions and his way of freeing the ship.

After a few hours the Captain decided that it would be enough and he positioned the stern under our bow. But it was just an elimination heat. The prelude occured later when he put out the alert:

"Take your positions, we will take the bulk carrier off the shoal!"

We stood by on the bow. The tug line tightened slowly at first, then faster and faster. It was evident that "Jantar" was slowly reaching all its power.

"And nothing," said the carpenter.

"It's too early," I replied, "all the sand must be washed out from the bottom of the bulk carrier," I explained to him.

The Third and the Chief from the "Manhattan" fought with ballasts, trying to help "Jantar".

I looked out to sea - harbor tugs were swinging nearby. They still waited like vultures, perhaps over future carrion. But our beloved tug must have sensed that the competition was awake and did its best. Black smoke came from the chimney, the stern of the ship twitched in convulsions, and the tug line moaned dangerously.

"Will it break or resist?" Asked the carpenter who had participated in such an action for the first time. "How much time can the engine run at maximum speed?" He asked again.

Suddenly I felt the deck shifting under my feet. I shouted to "Jantar":

"We started moving!"

"Okay," the Old Man answered calmly.

The Manhattan began to move forward. At first very slowly, as if casually, then a little faster. "Jantar" was pulling to the max all the time, but simultaneously it loosened the tug line a little.

"It's already ours!" I heard the joyful voice of the Chief. "A little more, and it will have enough water under its keel," he added after a moment.

And then we felt a jerk and a whistle of the tug line being broken. Instinctively, I huddled behind the winch. Out of the corner of my eye I saw the carpenter lying flat on the deck. After a moment, he waved his hand at me, showing that he was fine. The

The Manhattan, while gliding in the gutter dug by our tug, came across a mound of sand, which it simply ran over, but this moment of braking caused the tow to be broken. Fortunately, in the place provided for this, and the entire blow of the broken steel rope, as thick as an adult man's arm, went into the water.

I looked overboard.

"We're still sailing!" I shouted into the cellular radio. "We passed, we are sailing!"

"Drop the second tow line," was the Old Man's command.

The carpenter and I quickly cut the bindings of the spare tug line, and it fell into the water with a loud clatter.

"The tug line in the water," I reported. The Jantar's second hauling winch had already tensed it, and the bulk carrier was still kept on a leash, like a dog on a collar pulling its limp body.

This was the last obstacle of the jealous Neptune from whom we seized its prey. After a few minutes the Manhattan was rocking in deep water.

"Drop the anchor," the Old Man said to us, and added, "we are at a safe distance from the land."

We hauled a black ball[28] to the top of the bow mast. On seeing it, the two port tugs sailed away, bidding us farewell with a fountain of water from cannons and loud sirens.

"*Au revoir*, friends!" The plume of water directed at us seemed to be saying.

Jantar answered them with a siren wailing: "*Au revoir* - maybe next time you will be luckier."

We made a short stop to roll up the broken tow line, and we continued our way to Gibraltar, because that was where the American crew wanted to get. Now they could book plane tickets. And we - order fuel and provisions for a jump across the Atlantic. And so began the second lap of the Manhattan cruise, but that's another story," I finished telling.

---

[28] Black ball - on a bow means that the vessel is at anchor.

Chapter 16

Action

The next day the wind was stronger. The sea state was predicted to be six to eight on the Beaufort scale[29]. The white breakers, however, didn't come aboard the Anna. We were lucky, Anna was stranded at such an angle to the wind that the waves crashed against its stern without doing any harm.

"If the wind doesn't change direction, it will only help us," we discussed the topic at breakfast.

Captain P. announced on the radio:

"We will try to take off "Anna", we have a favorable wind. We're just waiting for Poseidon, it'll be in two hours. Get ready."

"We've been ready for two days," said Alek.

As announced, after two hours "Poseidon" gave us its tug line.

---

[29] Beaufort scale - it is used to measure the wind strength.

Two large ocean tugs kept Anna on the tow lines. The machines started to work. Both tug lines, fully stretched, resounded with the melody of violin strings, which turned into a double bass tone.

One hour passed, nothing moved. The boatswain and I were standing in the bow a bit frozen, waiting for something to move.

"Have you felt it?" Jozwa suddenly called.

"No, nothing," I replied.

But he was right, I felt a slight tremor of the deck under my feet. It was a good sign. The bosun joyfully shouted:

"I can feel the hull vibrating! More power!"

Now everyone on Anna felt it move. It made a short leap forward and very slowly moved ahead.

"It's not going faster, that's bad," I said to the boatswain. We felt "Anna" straighten the silhouette. It was Alek who helped it return to a horizontal position with ballasts.

"They are dragging it along the bottom, just to the ditch dug by Koral and the landing barges," Jozwa said. Leaning overboard, he threw a piece of wood into the sea and watched it. But you couldn't see much, the wind was too strong. However, we were still sailing forward, or rather diagonally to the shore, so that the wind was blowing at our stern. The tugboats, dancing on the wave, struggled with the reluctant Anna.

"We have moved about fifty meters," we heard Alek reporting to Koral.

And here bad luck caught up with us. The tow line of the Poseidon broke. We just came across a sandbar, a mound of sand made by waves, against which Anna's bow rested, stopping. After another hour, we heard the captain's decision:

"Too bad. There is a too big wave for digging. We'll wait for the sea to calm down."

We waited another day and a half.

On the sixth day of the rescue operation, the morning greeted us with beautiful, sunny weather. A slight frost only added to the charm of the scenery viewed from the deck of "Anna". The shore came closer to us, thanks to the ice that accumulated during this time. It would have seemed that you could walk along it to the shore. However, a small strip of clear water behind our stern would have stopped those willing to go for a walk.

Before breakfast, Krysia and Gregory took measurements and cargo samples. I didn't assist them anymore, they were familiar with the ship enough to be able do it themselves.

"Everything is normal," Krysia reported to Alek.

Anna had practically no icing, here and there only blocks of ice hung on the superstructure, but all the necessary mechanisms and devices were free of it. In the morning two landing ships of the navy reached us. This time they moored to our sides, each on one side. They would support "Koral" and "Poseidon".

Koral kept digging the ditch as it approached Anna's bow. It was held on the tug line by the Poseidon in front of it, which was ready to help it at any moment in case it went aground itself. After lunch, Koral was already before our bow and was grinding the water with all its might.

Both landing boats, with their sterns deeply submerged and blunt bows raised, were also moving their propellers to push behind our stern the sand from under the seafloor that Koral was washing out.

"They are grinding and grinding this water. When will they start pulling?" asked Gregory.

"When the Old Man decides that this grinding is enough," the bosun replied shortly. "Phew, what a relief," I thought, "half the success is behind us. With the support that "Koral" has, it may be possible to get "Anna" off the shoal now. The first time it almost worked."

Finally, Captain P. issued an alert.

"Everyone, take your position," we heard the instructions issued by Alek.

We went with the boatswain to the bow.

"We have both anchors ready," reported the boatswain.

"Here we go," the captain gave the order to all ships.

I looked before the bow. Immediately behind it, there was "Koral", on the port and starboard side, two smaller tugs - "Halny" and "Typhoon" from PSR, and in the front, the Poseidon hold it on the long tow line. At our sides, there were two landing ships "Tumak".

"It's an entire armada," I said.

Koral began. It was pulling the tow line slowly.

"Halny and Typhoon full ahead, keep course," was heard from "Koral". And right after:

"Poseidon, start."

The tug line of the Poseidon could be seen straightening and emerging from the water. It was relatively short so that it could keep going in the right direction.

"Barges - full speed ahead."

Then Koral itself moved at full speed. "Anna" began to tremble - it was clearly felt how these enormous forces were shaking it.

"Forward, forward..." the boatswain was excited.

"Rotate, Poseidon," we heard Captain P.

Poseidon was moving left and right. And so all the ships worked ten, twenty minutes, half an hour.

Koral once went left, then right.

After a long while, it helped. "Anna" began to experience longitudinal convulsions. It went forward in short movements - just to the ditch.

"It's working!" Alek reported.

And then it moved forward. I looked to the side, where the Pasat held the landing barge with its tow line. Pulled sharply, it leaned to the side. I saw its captain fall out of the wheelhouse into the water. At the last moment he grabbed the bulwark. Luckily for him, the Pasat tug line didn't resist and broke. The tug straightened as quickly as it lay on the side. The captain was thrown back on deck, but without the coat he had been wearing. Our brave tug, swaying steadily, was spewing from the wheelhouse a mass of water that had burst in there.

As it turned out later, the tilt had been 120°. Another ship wouldn't recover from such a list, and the Pasat, apart from the navigational equipment in the wheelhouse destroyed by the water, didn't suffer any serious damage.

"Five, ten meters, now fifty meters," I was giving the distances.

I could feel the "Anna" swaying from side to side. It was a sign that it was in deep water.

"Two meters under the keel," Alek said with satisfaction.

"All machines stop!" ordered Captain P.

It was quiet! All the ships stopped their engines. I saw the tug lines slowly plunge into the water.

"Koral, full speed ahead," the further instructions were given. It is no problem for a tug to haul them all together.

"Poseidon, full speed ahead."

The ships were moving away from the shore.

"Poseidon, stop machines. Everyone free from the watch, go to the bridge," asked the captain of Koral.

Alek called everyone to the wheelhouse. Our entire team was gathering there.

"What a strange feeling, we're rocking," said Krysia, surprised.

The radio on the bridge was activated. You could hear all the captains congratulating each other in turn. There was something to congratulate, it was a difficult and dangerous rescue operation.

However, not everyone had known how dangerous it was. Probably I will never know who had known, and who hadn't, about the actual danger posed by "Anna Broere". We also saw a group of people on the shore waving their hands at us, shouting something.

Now we heard the captain from "Koral":

"Ladies," he remembered about Krysia, "and gentlemen, I would like to thank all of you for your efforts and sacrifice in this action. Thank you again, it was a masterpiece. It was nice working with you. On behalf of the PSR management, I invite everyone to the ceremonial banquet at the Naval Casino in Gdynia next Saturday at 7.00 p.m., of course with accompanying persons. Thanks again," he said and hung up.

"Saturday is the day after tomorrow. They want to celebrate quickly," said Jozwa ruthlessly.

"We take over the tug line from "Poseidon", which will lead us to the roadstead of the port in Gdansk," Alek announced. "We throw the "Koral" tow line and the mooring of the landing ships. Sea watches," he added. I saw that "Pasat" from Gdynia stayed to assist. The rest were slowly leaving for their ports. I went to the cabin and called Kinga.

"Kinga, honey, go home. We are already sailing to Gdansk."

"Yes, I know, Richie. Everyone here watched the coverage on TV. I'm happy and I'm ready. I was just waiting for your call. Today we are returning with Olenka to the house," she added.

"See you soon! Oh!" I added, "On Saturday we are going to a banquet on this occasion."

"Where? To Chris?"

"No. This time the banquet is organized by the PSR management. We are going to the Naval Casino in Gdynia."

I also called Christopher.

"I know, I know, I saw everything, I'll go home soon. And how are you? Is everything alright?"

"Yes," I replied, "I'll be home tomorrow. I'll call you," I said, and went downstairs to dinner.

There was a heated discussion during dinner.

"See how sure they were that they would take off "Anna" - they prepared the banquet for Saturday. They will probably be showered with medals," the boatswain taunted, it's not known whom.

"But you will come?" Alek asked.

"I will come, don't worry. I won't miss such an opportunity. Krysia and Gregory are also invited," he added, looking at them with an eloquent gaze. "Krysia, who will you go with? Maybe with me?" The boatswain joked.

"Of course, you have time for your loved ones to come to you. It's worth it, I assure you," Alek concluded the topic.

The rest of the way passed calmly and in fine weather. Immediately after arriving at the roadstead in Gdansk, we were able to delegate our duties to our substitutes. Admittedly, they rose to the occasion. When, in the roadstead of Gdansk, the manager of the PSR rescue base, brought by "Halny" to us, went on board, immediately after the congratulations, he announced to Krysia and Gregory:

"You have reserved rooms at the Gdynia Hotel on Kościuszko Square until Monday. And I arranged everything with your company, you have "business" days off. De-stress and we are waiting for you at the Navy casino," - he said and gave them and the rest of the crew personalized invitations to the casino.

"So he knew about the threat from Anna. It is his "de-stress" that has betrayed him," I thought as I accepted the invitation. I also wondered when they had managed to print them. However, when I saw a small anchor and the inscription "Printing house of the Navy" at the back, I stopped being surprised.

"You have a hotel room for me too?" The boatswain asked. "It doesn't have to be in Gdynia, it can be in Zakopane," he added maliciously.

Chapter 17

Banquet

Lying in the cabin, waiting for substitutes, I went back a year with my thoughts. Almost a year, because without a month. It was when I was returning from my contract and Kinga came to pick me up at the airport in Gdansk. She was standing in the terminal hall, at the check-in exit, beaming at my sight. In her hand she was holding one large red rose. Greeting me, she whispered: "We are going to have a baby." I was so surprised that I said:

"Yes? But why?"

"Because I'm pregnant, silly. Are you happy?" She asked.

"Yes, yes!" I assured her, but I wasn't sure about it.

She hugged me, kissing me greedily and stroking my face.

"I'm so happy to see you!"

I hugged her tightly.

"God, how I missed you!" She murmured in my ear.

Holding her hands, I pushed her back to shoulder length.

"Stand still, I want to look at you," I said. "Youu are so beautiful, wonderful! I love you!"

"I love you too. Let's go home, you crazy," she said and pulled me to the exit.

She probably sat behind the wheel of our car, thinking that after three months at the sea I forgot how to drive it. I was looking at her with the pleasure of a hungry wolf, or basically a sex-starved sailor. She must have felt my eyes on her because she blushed and asked:

"What, have I changed?"

"No, no," I assured, "you're just more mature."

"I'm, because there are three of us now," she added with a smile on her lips.

We got to the house. I was curious what our apartment looked like, but I didn't get disappointed. Everything was high-gloss polished. There were fresh flowers on the tables. In the living room, a set table awaited me, with a decoratively wrapped box on it.

"It's your Christmas gift. Open it," she asked and added: "Sit down, I'll make coffee."

I sat down and opened it, wondering what it was. Inside was a silver chain bracelet with my initials engraved on the outside and my blood type underneath.

"Do you like it, darling?" Kinga asked, looking at me with uncertainty in her eyes. I saw her face light up as I called out:

"It's lovely! I'm glad, I've always wanted something like this! I also have a gift for you," I said.

I took out a decorative box, knelt in front of Kinga, opened it and asked:

"Will you marry me?"

"Yes, beloved, yes!" she assured and after a moment she exclaimed:

"It's nice, beautiful! And what is this stone, cubic zirconia?"

I put a ring on her finger saying:

"No, sunshine, it's a diamond set in gold and platinum."

"Oh my God!" She sighed heavily. "How did you know my size?" She asked with curiosity in her voice.

"This is my sweet secret."

She hugged me and pulled into the bedroom. In the evening, refreshed, lying on the couch in the living room, I called to Kinga:

"I want a drink, you don't even know how much. Prepare something strong and tell."

"You know, Richie ... I didn't know that these three months would pass so quickly. When you went, I was shaken, but Natalka and my colleagues supported me. Every day work, home. It was worse on Sundays and Saturdays off - sometimes I went to the girls, other times they visited me, and it passed so. It was the worst at night. For the first month, I woke up and looked for you in bed. The terrible feeling - waking up with longing for you ... And then this realization reaching me that you are not here, that you are far away. Sometimes I cried in my sleep, I know this from Natalka, who heard my night sobs when she stayed overnigh. But habit is second nature to man, and when I came to terms with the situation, it was easier for me. Then - a bolt from the blue. I don't know how it could have happened," Kinga continued, "it was three weeks after you had left. I went to the doctor and he said I was pregnant. On the one hand, I was worried because you weren't here, and on the other, I was very happy because it is the fruit of our love. Part of you is growing inside me. After much thought, I decided not to tell you about it over the phone. I figured it would be better for you. You once told me that a sailor, when he is at sea, shouldn't be informed about things that are important to him and over which he cannot have any influence. Are you angry?" She asked.

"No, I'm not angry. You did the right thing. I would have thought about it all the time and been nervous."

I was counting mentally: three months at home plus three at sea - I may not be able to arrive on time for the childbirth. I have to figure out something. I asked:

"What did the doctor say?"

"Everything is fine, the baby is healthy and growing properly. I had an ultrasound scan but before that I told the doctor, 'Please don't reveal the sex of the baby. I want his father, who is at sea now, to be during it. He'll be back soon.' 'As you wish,' he replied. He is the attending physician, a nice old man with many years of experience. There is little that can surprise him in this regard.

Kinga, for some reason, gained confidence in him and she would have liked him to be in childbirth.

"And what do you want? A boy or a girl?"

"I want the baby to be healthy," I replied, "and besides, I'm different from most guys and I'd like our baby to be a girl." And so during the next visit, to my joy, the doctor said:

"It's definitely a girl."

All these news, going to the doctor, Kinga's preparation for childbirth was stuck in me like a chip. Everything seemed to be okay, I was happy like Kinga, I understood her dilemmas, or at least I tried to understand why she wanted ice cream in the middle of the night, and all those other whims. Or that we needed to buy shoes for the little girl immediately. I acted the way I did, because I had to, because it was the right thing to do, but nothing really happened inside me that touched me directly. I was beside in everything. I was stuck in it because I was a father. And what have should I done if I didn't feel like a father at all? It took me a long time to realize that we were going to have a baby. It was only when Kinga proudly showed me her growing belly and, placing my hands on it, I felt gentle kicks that something broke inside me. I felt like a future father. "How is it," I thought, "this little man in Kinga's belly is half of me? Which of my features will Aleksandra have?" Because that's how we decided to name our little daughter. "Nobody knows, just like nobody can predict what a child will inherit from their parents, and that's better," I thought, looking at the future mother bustling around the kitchen.

Time passed quickly, Kinga went to work for another month, and then she was at home. She had no complications, but the doctor told her:

"Mrs. Kinga, it will be better for you and your baby that you spend the rest of the time at home, this is your first pregnancy and you have to be careful. You're a fragile woman," he fawned over her, and that's because I greased his palm - and here he was wrong. Kinga, if necessary, was tough and firm.

"If you, doctor thinks so, that's good, maybe it will be better. But I don't have to lie down?" she wanted to make sure.

"No, no. But please don't lift anything, don't overstrain yourself, and keep smiling," he advised.

"I took time off at work - I found a replacement for one contract, so I stay at home for nine months," I counted at Kinga. "Three months now, three if I went on normal mode, and three if I came back from it. A little long, but I won't be idle, I will find myself some occupation for this time, somewhere close, but not at sea."

Little Aleksandra turned our whole life upside down.

"Ring, ring ..." I heard the bells. I gotta go. It was well in the afternoon when we got to the quay in Gdansk. There were substitutes waiting for us and a minibus to take us all home. The time we traveled to Gdynia passed quickly. I said goodbye to everyone, wished a nice rest, and crossed the gate with delight. Kinga greeted me at the door. I headed first to Olenka. She had slept when I had left and slept when I arrived. But that's okay, I took her in my arms and hugged her gently so as not to wake her up.

Only now did the air go out of me - I sat on the couch and said to Kinga:

"What a relief it is finally over."

"But you scared us! Was it necessary?" She asked.

"It was, believe me. The disaster of "Anna Broere" could end in a great tragedy for the entire neighborhood, including the Tri-City."

"Why?" Tell me.

"Anna was carrying some chemicals for the Chemical Plant in Plock. In themselves, they are not dangerous and pose no threat to anything. But when they are combined with water, a chemical reaction begins, which produces poisonous vapors. Very poisonous. They can be carried by the wind and everything in their reach dies out, including people.

"Oh my God!" She exclaimed. "Why didn't they warn anyone?"

"I don't know. But probably for the same reasons I didn't."

"You did it," she said, surprised.

"Yes, but I warned only you and Christopher. Think. New Year's Eve, balls, then the New Year. You know what would have happened. Panic and panic again, it's worse than ignorance. They took the risk, but they succeeded. I won't hold them to account.

We couldn't sleep for a long time that night, but for completely different reasons.

In the morning, I barely got up when Christopher burst in with a black Johnny in his hand.

"Listen, Richie. Say what the hell is going on, I couldn't sleep all night. After our conversation, I figured it was about gas."

"Not quite," I said, "more about poisonous fumes."

And I told him everything in detail.

"Yes, thanks. You did the right thing. It's just luck that you made it, it could have been otherwise. It is scary to imagine a black scenario of events."

"When you were in Karwia, you drove to the beach without any problems?" I asked, looking at him with a smile.

"Sure, there was no one but people like me. In the grove in front of the beach, we only saw stakes stuck in the ground with signs with the handwritten red inscription on them saying "danger zone", but I didn't associate it with your ship.

"No sense of responsibility at all," I continued, irritated. "Damn, this was really all the local authorities could do? Was this supposed to be a warning of the possibility of the greatest environmental catastrophe since the Second World War?" I asked Christopher.

"Such toxic chemicals, in such quantities shouldn't be transported at once," Christopher added. "I gotta go to work. I will call you and we'll drink to you, Richie."

I was loafing around at home until Saturday, and the only job I did was clearing snow. There were also pleasures, but it couldn't be called work. On Saturday morning I picked up the phone to call to the hotel, to Krysia. "Wait a minute, I don't know her surname. Damn, how is that possible?" I was wondering. But I called.

"I would like to talk to Ms Krystyna," I spoke as broken.

"Room number?" Asked the receptionist.

"I don't know."

"Surname?" She asked again.

"I don't know."

"Do you know how many Krystynas are here?"

"No, I don't. But maybe you know who I'm talking about, she is a heroine," I spoofed her, "a chemist who was on the ship that was sinking. What was its name? Oh, Anna Broere," I continued.

"Oh, yes, I know, I know." Her tone changed to quite friendly.

"I'm already connecting."

"Krysia D ... I'm listening," I heard her voice.

"It's me, your ship admirer," I introduced myself.

"Richie! You're fooling around again."

"Krysia, I wanted to remind you that today we have a ball and we are supposed to sit at one table. Do you remember?"

"Yes, of course."

"Kinga, my other half, and I will pick you up at the reception desk half an hour before the party," I added. "Gregory and his wife are going to meet with Alek," she explained to me.

"Well, it's a pity - your company is enough for us."

"But I won't be alone - my boyfriend came to see me."

"That's good, it'll be funnier. Hope we like each other."

"What did you say at the reception?" She asked.

"Oh, nothing special. I was looking for a certain heroine - a chemist, because it's embarrassing, but I didn't know your surname."

"I know yours. I asked Alek and he told me."

"Two to one for you," I replied.

"Why two for me and one for you?"

I noticed Kinga was closely following the conversation - "Oh, I should end the conversation," I thought and quickly explained:

"One for nodding and other for your surname, and for me one for finding you. I have to go, see you tonight."

"We await you," said Krysia.

"What's the secret?" Kinga asked immediately.

"No secret," - whether I liked it or not, I justified myself, "Krysia told me everything about the threat, without saying anything."

"How? How is it possible?" Kinga asked.

"I asked and she nodded, showing yes or no, and also pointed once."

"At what?"

"At the water."

"I don't understand. So I told Kinga in detail how I had learned about the threat from Krysia. That calmed her completely, but she took my hand and pulled me into the bedroom.

"Now I'll nod my head and point my finger," she mocked me.

Oh! Female perversity must always prevail. I didn't mind, so quickly, on the way, I threw off my clothes.

Kinga and I entered the hotel on time. Krysia was sitting on an armchair in the hall and was waving her hand at us. We greeted as if we hadn't seen each other for a year. I introduced Kinga, Krysia - Janek.

"So, we're going?" Krysia asked.

"Yes, come on. It is not far, but arriving a little earlier is well perceived.

The Navy casino was about a hundred meters away from the hotel. Girls in evening dresses looked great. Krysia wore a long black dress that contrasted with her blonde hair. She looked quite different now than on the ship, where she had worn jeans and sweaters concealing her slim figure. Now, in black high heels and the low-necked dress, she attracted the attention of the male part of hotel guests. Jan, her boyfriend, standing next to her, contrasted with her look, and was as if the opposite of her. A tall, stocky guy in a well-cut, tasteful suit, with a sunburned face and lightly grizzled hair.

My Kinga put on a New Year's Eve dress, which she was supposed to wear at the New Year's ball. She loved to wear dresses with a naked back and a large neckline - and that's how she was dressed this time. The dress was narrow, tight at the top, and flowing at the bottom. A red outfit, red high heels and a stylish handbag. Her hair was in a bun so that it exposed her swan neck, adorned with a chain of white gold, whose each link had shape of a small tear, and fastened at its end a large platinum tear containing a huge diamond that Beata had given me. It symbolized all the tears that Beata had shed in her golden prison. *For the clueless - Beata and the diamond is an insert from the book "Hold captive by Somali pirates" in which I describe how this diamond got into my possession.* In ears, Kinga had a set of earrings harmonizing with the rest of the jewelry. She looked lovely and as she walked to the exit, the desk clerk stared at her like a starving male at its prey. Kinga was also very inventive in dressing me up for this ball. New shirt, new suit, tie and shoes. It was more about wandering around the shops than renewing my wardrobe. But I didn't protest - if it pleased her, it pleased me too.

We took a taxi anyway. It would have been difficult for girls to walk in high heels, and besides it wasn't appropriate to get there on foot.

We got out in front of an old, stately, pre-war building with a bright facade and large, beautiful windows decorated with maritime ornaments. The building was situated in the center of Gdynia, right next to the beach, in the so-called poplar avenue. In front of the entrance there was a line of sailors who acted as an honor guard. They were dressed in gala navy blue uniforms with white uppers of boots and white soldier's leather belts wonderfully harmonizing with them. They allowed guests to enter only upon presentation of an invitation. They handed everyone a table number with the program of the ball. Before that, the representative officer asked:

"Excuse me, how many people?"

"Four," I replied. We got number eleven - an eight-seater table near the stage.

"I wonder who will be sitting with us," Krysia said. A beautifully set table with neatly arranged glass and cutlery awaited us. Janek gallantly moved a chair to Kinga, so I also moved one to Krystyna, tapping her slightly on the arm. We burst out laughing, which instantly relaxed the atmosphere.

"We won't behave like stiffs," Krysia took the initiative. "Gentlemen, pour into glasses, I've waited too long for this. I deserve it."

"Damn," I thought. I didn't know such Krysia. Janek knew - he poured white vodka into glasses and made a toast:

"To the sailors!"

"To those at sea," Krysia corrected him.

After a while I poured and I raised a toast:

"To the chemists!"

Without waiting for lofty preface, we placed the appetizers on the plates. We were sitting alone for now. The Navy casino ballroom was a spacious room, now beautifully decorated - it delighted with its appearance and rich decorations.

"Come on, let's read what attractions await us," said Kinga, taking the program I had in my hand. "Right, first greeting the guests. Then the representative part. What could it be?" she wondered. "The Navy's artistic performances and only then the dance part," she read with mock regret.

Two couples approached the table. An officer in uniform with the rank of captain, with a pretty brunette, and a couple of civilians.

"Can we join you?" The captain asked, holding our table number in his hand.

Jan and I got up, the ladies were sitting.

"Of course," Janek invited.

"We'll be glad to keep the Navy Company," I added.

Everyone shook hands, exchanging names. The captain's name was Roman and his wife's was Alina. The civilians were Slawek and Joanna. As on the ship, Krysia immediately announced:

"Call me Krysia."

Janek turned out to be a good "firefighter", because he poured everyone straight away, saying:

"According to the English custom, let's call each other by name".

"Sailors all over the world are on a first-name basis," added Roman.

"We have two sailors here," Krysia laughed, "unless Slawek or Joanna are involved in this profession."

"No. I work in a bank, and Joasia is a journalist. Thanks to her I'm here - she is accredited."

"And you?" He turned to Janek.

"What a coincidence - I'm here also thanks to the woman."

"Are you a sailor?" Roman asked slightly surprised, turning to Krysia.

"Yes, a six-day sailor, and on a daily basis I'm a chemist, just like Janek."

"Indeed, I saw you on Anna Broere when you walked in the hold. At first we wondered what the woman was doing there. Then we found out about the presence of the cargo specialist."

"Oh god, I'm so famous already?" She laughed. "But I didn't see you," she added.

"You didn't see me, because I was on the bridge of the landing craft that was next to you."

The ice was broken and I was no longer keeping track of who was saying what - everyone was talking.

The Naval Orchestra played a welcome anthem, and everyone fell silent. Several people entered the podium on the stage, some of them in uniform.

"They'll talk a little now," said Krysia.

A gas was started by the commander of the Navy, and then, one by one, the others talked. They thanked, praised and such crap.

It got interesting when the PSR director started listing the names of the seamen who first had landed on "Anna Broere".

He mentioned Alek, of course, and then the boatswain. They both rose from their chairs one by one and bowed to the gathered guests.

When he mentioned my name, I had to get up and bow to everyone. I felt like an idiot on a runway, but I saw that Kinga was bursting with pride. They clapped a little and I had peace.

"It's nice that we are sitting together," Joanna told me.

What she meant, I found out later.

Then Motorcycle. Krysia got up right after him. As if on command, everyone in the hall got up, even those on the podium, and only she got a standing ovation with shouts - "Bravo! Bravo!" Deservedly - she was the only raisin in this company.

Then others got up, and Roman rose too - as it turned out, he was the commander of the landing craft. When they finished reading out the long list of names of people with merits for this or that company, I breathed a sigh of relief.

The waitresses served our table efficiently, bringing various delicious treats every now and then.

There was the Navy band on the stage. I didn't pay attention to it and I only noticed the musicians when people bid farewell to them with applause. I was already after a few drinks - it was too fast for me. I was busy talking to Joanna the whole time. This conversation was very interesting.

She began by asking if I would give her an interview.

"Who do you work for?" I asked. Here she mentioned the name of a national newspaper.

"No," I replied, "there is no chance that they would print what you would hear from me."

I saw that she was speechless.

"Are you kidding?"

"No, I'm absolutely serious. I made the face of our CFO when you went to him for a salary increase."

"Please! If you have any interesting news, share them."

She quickly poured vodka into my glass.

"You want to get me drunk to make me docile?" I asked.

"Maybe a little," she replied with surprising sincerity, and with that she took me.

"I will give you an interview on one condition."

"What?"

"Learn where the "bonzos" from the Tri-City had fun on New Year's Eve."

"It's easy," she rejoiced.

"Well, then one more condition."

"Speak."

"Where they were four, five days after New Year's Eve."

"It's easy too."

"So we got a deal. If you learn it, come over for a coffee."

"Deal," she confirmed our agreement, kissing my cheek. She was satisfied with such conditions.

The orchestra started to play dance pieces and we started dancing. I danced the first and last dance with Kinga according to an unwritten agreement. I asked my deity and we glided onto the dance floor. There, hugging, we were dancing to a quiet piece.

"Look after me, darling, so that I don't drink for a while," I whispered in her ear.

"Dance, Richie, dance. Then you don't have to drink. It was simple advice and probably effective, but how to apply it when every now and then our table was approached by curious people who pulled us to the bar for a glass of vodka. They didn't come to me, but to our heroine, Krysia. She was the person which the guests in this room remembered, and I served as an "export reject". Krysia didn't go anywhere, it ill befitted the captain in the uniform, so I was left alone on the battlefield. It's a pity the boatswain wasn't with us.

We were all cool - being a little drunk, I asked all the ladies to dance in turn. Janek and Roman were great dancers, so they took turns dancing with Kinga.

"Phew, finally a break, I can rest."

The ladies sat down next to each other and discussed lively, and we went to the room to visit our friends. Everyone theirs. I took Janek with me, and Roman took the banker.

I started with Janusz, Gregory and the boatswain. Sitting with them for a moment, I took part in a heated discussion about the usefulness of amphibious ships in taking ships off the shoal.

"Come to the bar, I want the Cuba Libre," said the bosun and pulled us with himself.

"Jozwa, why are you fooling around? There is not enough alcohol on the table?" Alek was reluctant to go.

"Come on over for a drink. I promised, and now there is an opportunity," the boatswain didn't give up.

At the very beginning, we made a bet with the boatswain about how quickly the ice would disappear from the ship. Alek and I said that the sailors would be able to handle it in two or three days, and the boatswain - in a week. They forged ice for three days.

So we went. The bar wasn't crowded, because the prices were military here, you know - the senior officers earn quite a lot. Besides, there was plenty of vodka and wine on the tables.

We made our way to the bar on soft legs where, having collapsed on the bar stools, we immediately ordered everything we wanted.

"Bartender," called the boatswain to a pretty black girl who, with the eyes of a thoroughbred stockbroker, judged whether we were solvent and how much money she could get from us. "Please give the gentlemen everything they ask for." Then he turned to us: "drink what you want. It's on me," he assured.

"What's your name, ma'am?" Alek asked. Does he have to be such a formalist even at the bar?

"Mariola," the barmaid answered unembarrassed. She was used to the various quirks of tipsy customers, and that question was relatively pleasant.

And lest it occur to us to order just anything, she leaned over the bar and rested her ample breasts on its top. I noticed that all the male gazes were stuck between her breasts. The commander of the Navy, sitting next to me, made himself slimy from the impression. A moment more and he would have started clicking with excitement.

"Well, Mrs. Mariola, I would like a tequila with a bit of vermouth," with a hoarse voice and eyes fixed on, it is known where, Alek spoke.

Bosun ordered his Cuba Libre. Nothing made an impression on him - he had seen many beautiful bartenders in various bars around the world.

"Everything but Bacardi," he said to the bartender who wanted to make his favorite Cuba Libra with Bacardi. "Rum, Cuban rum, darling," he added.

"Whiskey with Coke," said Janek, trying not to look at the bartender's breasts lying in front of him and slightly moving.

"And what for you?" She asked me.

I leaned over to her in such a way as to be higher than her breasts and whispered in her ear:

"For me water with lime and a bit of cola. You can count as for whiskey."

"You're a nice guy," she replied with a smile, "thanks," and she went to her kingdom.

The commander, who was more tipsy than me, became intrusive and interrupted our conversation every now and then. We discussed loudly about the barmaid's bust and I'm sure that she heard everything. And this is because of her taunt to Janusz. Handing him a drink, she said:

"Are you hungry, sailor? There is not enough food on the table? Order more, there will surely be someone who will give you what you want."

We burst into laughter. A moment earlier Alek was whimpering to the boatswain:

"Ah, I would like to munch those tits!"

The commander called to us:

"Gentlemen, sailors, I'm also a sailor! Can I buy you a drink?"

"Sure," said the boatswain.

"But what?" Alek asked. "Because, as you can see, we don't drink anything. The naval brotherhood in the alcohol industry is picky and has strange tastes.

The bosun asked the commander:

"What do you do in the Navy?"

"I'm the commander of the amphibious assault fleet."

A little drunk, I asked the commander sitting next to me:

"Listen, is it true you were hiding anti-chemical sailors inside the ships?"

"I don't know anything about that," he replied.

"If you don't know, who is supposed to know? You're not the one giving the orders?" I followed up.

"Where were you on January 2nd and 5th?" I changed the subject.

"In Masuria. Why?"

"Nothing, nothing. I'm looking for someone from the Navy command who was then in the Tri-City. There are probably not many such people," I chattered on.

"What do you want, Richie?" said the boatswain, scowling at me.

"Justice that I don't see here."

Roman leaned over to me and whispered:

"This is the Deputy Commander of the Navy."

"So I've found the right person," I said. "It's always the same - if you don't know what it is about, it's probably about your own ass," I twisted the well-known saying a bit and looking at the commander, I added:

"You are lucky that there are still such sailors in this country - with and without uniforms."

"I know that he knows that I know - and that is what I've meant," I thought.

"Keep playing in ignorance," I turned to Janusz and the boatswain, and with the dignity of a drunkard I left, dragging Janek with me, who clearly wanted to luck into another drink.

"Janek," I lisped, "let's go to your girlfriend. You don't even know how great heroine Krysia is," and completely unnecessarily I added, "the bust is not everything."

On my way back to our table, I came across the Fatman. I didn't expect him to be there.

"Thanks, Fatman," I began, but he, seeing that I was drunk, put a finger to my lips and whispered softly:

"Don't say anything, then I can swear that I didn't tell anyone anything - got it?"

"Sure," I just said, and we split up like two strangers who met by accident. Until the end of the party, I didn't drink any more alcohol. Kinga, happy to see that she no longer had to watch over me, went crazy on the dance floor with Joasia and Krysia, doing some modern contortions in a circle with other couples. I was too tired to accompany them. I had the wonderful companion - Janek. He warmed up and bandied memories around, so time flew by. In the morning the guests started to scatter. We drove home by taxi, having said goodbye to the rest of the company.

I agreed with Joasia that when she found out something, she would call me.

The next four days, Kinga and I spent in our house. We sporadically went for a walk when the weather was nice. Sometimes I visited my neighbor for a little chat, then his wife hung out in the kitchen with Kinga.

On Wednesday, Joasia called:

"Richie, we can meet now, I know everything," she said in a mysterious tone.

"Okay, come see us in an evening."

"But only tomorrow, okay?"

"Alright, we are home anyway because of little Olenka," I replied.

Kinga, listening to our conversation, said with a slight anxiety in her voice:

"Richie, do you have to say everything?"

"I don't know yet if I will say anything," I explained to her, "but it will be nice to see them."

On Thursday evening Joasia and Slawek came by - with a bottle of champagne and flowers for Kinga.

"Nice, but is it necessary?" Kinga protested.

"Absolutely, there is a custom that when you visit someone for the first time, you should honor it. And the tradition should be cultivated so that it doesn't expire," said Joasia with a smile on her lips, and Slawek nodded to her like a parrot.

Kinga prepared the dinner, putting all her skills into it and using a trot from the TV program "You can cook too", where they showed step by step the entire cooking cycle. Of course, I pretended not to know about it. She had this program recorded and watched it when I went to my neighbor. But it turned out to be pointless as she boasted to his wife, she in turn, of course said it to her husband, which immediately blurted it out to me. However, this didn't detract from her contribution and commitment.

There were starters already on our table, so I opened the bottle of champagne that the guests brought, poured it, we sat down comfortably and I said to Joasia:

"Go ahead."

And she pulled out a recorder and turned it on.

"Wait a minute. This is how journalists start an interview?" I asked laughing. "Show me your journalist ID."

She looked at me suspiciously, not knowing if I was kidding her. But seeing that I grew serious, she got up from the table and went to her purse. After a while, she put the ID in front of my face. I looked at it carefully.

Kinga, knowing what would happen in a moment, took Slawek's arm and said:

"Come on, let me show you the house."

They left, and I seriously asked Joanna:

"Are you bound by journalistic secrecy? You don't disclose the source of the information?"

"Of course," she replied, and began to list articles about journalistic secrets.

Since this is a serious thing that I found out from serious people, please don't record it. And give me the text for authorization. You can note down and record everything from the open part."

"Fine, as you like."

"So according to the agreement: say what you found out."

"From what I learned, no one I asked about or spoke to was in the Tri-City from New Year's Eve to January 6."

"And what does it mean to you?"

"Nothing except that they like to have fun in the bosom of nature, somewhere in the woods or other attractive places."

"Who are you talking about?"

"About all mayors of Tricity cities and their deputies, voivode, voivodship marshal and some people from the front pages of newspapers, when it comes to politicians."

"Do any associations come to your mind?"

"No," she shrugged. "What do you need this information for?" She asked.

"You'll see later. Now say what interests you."

"Anything related to the Anna Broere rescue."

"Only?"

"This is what the report is supposed to be about."

"And why the Anne Broere was rescued, you don't want to know?"

"It's obvious," she replied.

"Why obvious?"

She looked at me suspiciously from over her notebook.

"Because it ran aground and had to be saved."

"It ran aground when we were already aboard it," I clarified.

"No. Richie, let's from the beginning."

"Okay, you ask, I answer."

"Why were you selected for this action?"

"Ask the management of my company about that."

"What?"

"Petronafta from Gdansk."

"I will ask. How long have you been a sailor?"

"For several years."

"Had you already taken part in similar campaigns before?"

"Yes. When I worked in the Polish Ship Rescue," I kept answering her until she asked:

"Did you know what load 'Anna' had?"

"I knew it had chemicals, but didn't know what until I got some information."

"What information?"

"About the dangers lurking in the Anna Broere's holds."

"What was that threat?"

"Tons of chemicals toxic to the environment and all living creatures."

She stiffened.

"How's that?" She asked.

"I'm not a chemist. I only know that if the ship sank, overturned or broke and the substances on the Anna Broere merged with the water, the escaping vapors would have destroyed the entire local population, including the inhabitants of the Tri-City, and the ecological catastrophe would have been unimaginable. Chernobyl is a piece of cake compared to that."

"This is certain information?" Joanna asked excitedly.

"Certain, but as far as I know, you still have a duty to verify it with other sources, and the strange absence of everyone who might have known what the load of "Anna" contained only confirms it."

"I also talked about the chemists on the ship, about the navy, about the amphibious ships hiding chemical defense teams inside, until Joasia's questions exhausted the topic.

Finally I said:

"I don't condemn the decision-makers and I don't judge their behavior, because I know what panic means, and such a panic would have broken out if they announced an evacuation."

"And where is the right of people to a reliable truth about the threat to their lives? Remember Chernobyl."

"Yes, but that's a different scale and there was nowhere to evacuate," I replied.

Kinga and Slawek came to the table and we didn't come back to the topic again. Until the end of supper, Joasia was thoughtful and absent. Apparently she was bothered by the information obtained.

After two days, she called me and asked:

"Richie, come to us for a return visit, the article is ready."

I came with Kinga and little Olenka to Joanna, who lived in Gdynia, near the beltway. The apartment wasn't too big, but neat and tastefully decorated.

The article was supposed to appear in the Monday edition of the newspaper. I didn't know on which page.

I read it carefully. Then Kinga read it with curiosity and said:

"I like it, but don't you reprimand our authorities too harshly?"

"I accept it entirely," I told Joasia.

The article was written with an edge, and in such a way that it didn't reveal who was the source of the acquired information and who talked about the rescue operation. It showed that the story was told by several people, each from a different perspective.

I asked Joasia:

"Did you have other sources and interview others?"

"Of course. Otherwise there would have been no chance of printing it. But you were the first to reveal the truth. Then it was easier."

"That's good," I just said and added, "there will be an uproar."

And it was. In the morning I ran to the kiosk and bought five newspapers. On the front page there was a large photo of the icy "Anna Broere" stranded. Above it, the dramatic title:

"Anna Broere - a disarmed bomb.

A whisker away from a tragedy. Who hid the truth about the cargo?"

And so on.

I read the article with Kinga. It was the same, nothing was changed in it.

We were sipping coffee when Christopher called:

"Richie, have you read the newspaper?"

"I've read it," I confirmed.

"I bet it's your job."

"You exaggerate," I replied, "this is journalists' doing, you know what they are like. They can sniff out everything, they just need to be directed."

And in line with the motto of our politicians, I said:

"I don't confirm and don't deny. But don't expect heads to roll. Winners are not accounted for," I added.

"Yes, you're right," he agreed with me.

On Thursday afternoon I was chatting with my neighbor in his dwelling, when Kinga informed me that Joasia was knocking on my door and calling me every now and then.

"Richie," Joanna cried in a desperate voice, "help me, come see me to the editorial office! I have already booked plane tickets for you for tomorrow morning, three tickets of course, and an overnight stay in Orbis."

"Or maybe first you will tell me why I should go with Kinga and the child to Warsaw?"

"They will go sightseeing and shopping, and you will come to my office for an hour. The editor-in-chief wants to meet you. I didn't reveal anything about you, except that I spoke to someone from "Anna Broere"."

"It's good, if you don't reveal my name."

"Richie, it makes no sense, when you show up here, it will be like having your name written on your forehead. After all, we have recordings of the entire "Anna" crew from the action."

"Yes, you're right. What am I supposed to do with you? I will ask Kinga if she wants to go on a trip to Warsaw, but only on Saturday, because Kinga works."

"Great, I'm waiting."

Kinga, of course, was willing to go. She immediately threw herself on my neck and called into the receiver to Joasia:

"We're going, of course we're going!" and she already started planning the schedule. "We'll fly on Friday night and be back on Sunday, great! I will buy new shoes for spring for me, and for you a cord jacket and jeans suiting it," she didn't forget about me. "Joanna, you should have contacted me directly about this trip to Warsaw! I hope we meet there."

"Will Richie arrive?" Joanna asked.

"Of course. Me too."

"I'll meet you in the hotel. At the expense of the company," Joanna assured. "I will get a babysitter for Olenka for this time."

"Wow! You're so sweet, you remember about everything!" Kinga rejoiced. "And is this babysitter decent?" asked with a note of concern in her voice.

"Don't worry, proven, from my extended family - a student of pedagogy."

"Richie won't stay long in the editorial office - the editor-in-chief wants to talk him into something, but he is very mysterious and he doesn't reveal anything to me. So, should I buy the tickets?" She asked again.

"Yes, for Friday afternoon, and return on Sunday."

"Then, I'm looking forward to meeting you. Our car will pick you up at the airport."

"Alright. See you."

"Warsaw, my capital, why are you shrouded in clouds?" Kinga joked, looking through the round window of the plane.

We checked in quickly and efficiently at the airport and entered the arrivals hall. Unexpectedly, Joasia was waiting for us there.

"Beloved," she greeted us with an expression of joy on her face, "you don't even know how happy I am. Welcome to the shark stronghold."

"Is anyone going to devour us here?" I asked on the way to the car.

"Everyone here wants to devour each other, and not only in my industry," she replied, looking at me eloquently.

The journey to the hotel was a nightmare - frequent stops at traffic lights and waiting in jams. However, in the end, less than an hour later, we got to the entrance of the Orbis hotel.

"So I'm leaving you, and I will come for you, Richie, tomorrow at three o'clock," said Joasia, holding Olenka, while Kinga and I were checking in at the reception desk.

"Alright, I'll be waiting. But don't leave yet, I have to ask you something."

"What's the matter?"

"Did you find out what's going on?"

"No, Richie. And it probably has nothing to do with my article."

"We'll find out about it on the spot," I replied to her.

Kinga and I settled down in a room - a typical Orbis standard. Then we went downstairs. She ordered dinner and I, coffee which I had missed. The evening passed quickly, and after sitting, bored in front of the TV, we went to sleep.

"What we do?" asked Kinga in the morning, eating hot dogs - an integral part of a hotel breakfast.

"You have complete freedom in choosing how to spend your time, I will adapt."

Olenka will be with us until the evening - I agreed with Joasia that Monika, this student, would come to Olenka in the afternoon when we went to dinner."

After breakfast, we set off to conquer Warsaw, or rather shopping centers and boutiques, only on the way seeing the city panorama from outside the taxi windows.

"Today only shopping, sightseeing tomorrow," Kinga assured me, "on Sunday there is no such traffic on the streets."

"Okay, okay, I'm not saying anything," I said.

"But you're looking like you're dissatisfied."

"Because I know we'll sleep until dinner tomorrow."

And so it was a day until afternoon. However, not everything went according to Kinga's plan. In shopping malls, the number of stores Kinga wanted to visit was beyond her capacity.

At that time, I was sitting with Olenka at a table, from time to time I only went inside when Kinga already noticed something. Usually, it was a well-thought-out and necessary purchase. I liked watching her enjoy shopping. No, she didn't spend a fortune, she always took the price into account and looked for things that were good and not overwhelmingly priced. We ate lunch in one of the restaurants in the city center.

When we returned to the hotel, tired of running, we immediately threw ourselves on the sack to rest.

I had two hours until the meeting at the editorial office. After refreshing myself, I waited for Joanna. She picked me up half an hour in advance.

"It's in case of traffic jams," she explained. "Although it is not far away, you should always take unforeseen circumstances into account," she jawed as if anxiously.

The editorial office was busy as if the newspaper was issued on Sunday. We went straight to the editor-in-chief's office. Nobody paid attention to me, which was good.

"Richard ...," Joasia introduced me, "and this is the editor-in-chief of the newspaper, MM," she added.

We were seated on comfortable sofas in a lounge.

"What would you like to drink?" The editor-in-chief asked me.

"White espresso coffee, please."

"I started first - extremely courteously:

"It is an honor for me to be hosted in such a venerable place."

"Don't exaggerate," the editor-in-chief protested, "it's an office like any other."

"Oh, that's not true, after all, this is where the awareness of society is formed, and current news, sensations and various opinions and comments are provided," I buttered him up.

"Mr. Richard. Although Joasia didn't tell me who is the author of the information for the article about "Anna", it wasn't difficult for me to guess that it is you."

"Please call me Richard," I suggested.

"While discussing the article, she told me about the banquet in the Navy casino - I associated the rest myself."

"Yes, it's obvious," I muttered.

MM didn't let go and continued:

"I saw you in the footage of the rescue operation. Do such situations happen often?"

"It's my job, and the sea doesn't spoil anyone, so there are many situations like this."

"As you probably know, there is a regional supplement to our newspaper, but it's missing something. There is no permanent maritime column in it. I've got a proposition for you. Due to your profession, you have the appropriate knowledge and memories that we can present to our readers. Joasia is delegated to maritime affairs and all related matters."

I looked at her with an angry bull look, but her eyes answered me with a smile that seemed to say, "I know you want this!"

"What would this cooperation be about?" I asked.

"You would be a regular collaborator supplying materials for Joasia, who would turn them into columns."

"But at sea, actions like that with Anna don't happen every day," I protested.

"We know, we know, but you have your and your colleagues' memories. It's enough to write them down, remember them, properly polish and the article is ready," he replied. "Krysia told me that you had told them such a story that the skin had gone numb on her back when she listened to you."

"Krysia is exaggerating, I'm not a writer," I defended myself, but already without much enthusiasm in my voice.

MM sensed it right away. Joasia too, because she said:

"Come on! We will make it. It would be a pity not to share such experience with our readers."

"Aren't you exaggerating? I'm not so sure if there are people who care about it."

"We won't print every day - periodically is enough."

"And what if I'm at the sea? After all, I work."

"It will be fresh news! Certainly your work is interesting enough to attract readers."

"I won't beat them with arguments," I thought, so I started from the different side:

"Okay, let's say I agree, because if I don't, you'll find a lot of others, so why not try. What will it look like? Speak."

"Take notes and write down memories during a cruise. When you are at home, you and Joanna will edit the text. You talk, she writes, and when you are at the sea, you write and she edits. You will surely find a form of cooperation that will satisfy you," explained MM.

The coffee was drunk and I cornered. So I tried to win something for myself.

"But I'll be using a pseudonym."

"No problem - most do."

"So, do you agree?"

"Alright," I replied, capitulating.

"The matter of the salary will be discussed with you by our financial director," added MM.

We said goodbye on good terms, promising to meet after a while.

I was given MM's business card, his private phone number, and an assurance that I could call whenever I needed to.

"Be tough when you talk to him," Joasia advised, laughing, as we walked down the corridor to his office.

"So maybe I should also take a lawyer," this time I joked.

On the way to "His Eminence Payer" I was properly instructed by Joanna, so that the conversation with the financial director was very pleasant. He offered standard rates, I agreed and it was done. The personal data and contract were to be delivered by Joasia, so we could come back.

I came back to the hotel alone, there was already impatient Kinga waiting for me. There was also Monika, who looked after the sleeping Olenka. After a while, refreshed, dressed in new clothes, I went out with Kinga for a dinner party. Before that, Joasia asked us:

"Where do you want to go? Maybe to one of the famous Warsaw restaurants?"

"No, we have plenty of these in our city," said Kinga, "maybe somewhere where it is interesting?"

"So to the Journalists' Club," Joanna suggested.

"Where is it?"

"At New World Street. We'll sit, talk, and dance."

"Okay, you choose."

So we took a taxi to New World Street. The club was located in the basement of an old Warsaw tenement house, in the very center of the capital. A two-level venue where everyone can find something for themselves. The interior made a positive impression on me - music was seeping from loudspeakers, and the DJ wipped up the mood every now and then by telling dirty tidbits before playing the next song. Joasia had booked a table, so we took a seat without any problems. The menu brought by a waiter showed quite decent dishes and surprisingly low prices - of course, for the center of Warsaw.

"Homemade dumplings?" I read the surprising proposition, "in a nightclub?"

I got surprised and turned my head towards Kinga. We've already had a hearty meal at the mall.

Despite the music playing, I had a fierce discussion with Joasia.

"You know what, I'm not entirely convinced of my suitability for writing or writing columns. Telling experiences with a group of friends is not the same as describing them. Then matter the mood, the fleeting moment you want to share with others, and the place you do it. Its impact on the return of memories and the desire to let go of the accumulated positive or negative emotions. Take for example a situation when I'm at work. It's everyday life there, and it as a rule, can be boring - for me, of course, because I'm familiar with it. For those I work with, too, and telling each other interesting events comes from wanting to pass the time rather than sharing experiences. Sometimes it is perceived differently among us, for example as an attempt to get above oneself, to show that I am or was better. It's good when some funny events intertwine in the sea stories, because then it is fun, but the stories are also intended to show the possible dangers awaiting seafarers. Lessons can be drawn from this, sometimes the ones that make the work easier, and other times such ones allowing to avoid real dangers. Various things happen. In the past, when a lot of alcohol flowed into sailors' throats, the fantasy in these stories grew, but now the ships are mostly "Non - Alcoholic Vessels" and, surprisingly, this is strictly followed, with some exceptions, such as drinking one beer or a dose of rum in tea," I fell silent, because Kinga and Slawek had just returned from the dancefloor.

"Why are you sitting? Come on dancing!" Kinga called.

"Wait, we'll go right away, we'll just finish the topic," Joanna replied, pointing to the plate. Kinga and Slawek, having had a drink, went back to the dance floor.

Under the influence of drugs, the stories took on colors and became more intimate. Stories were told that really happened, but they were colored. Nobody will tell you, being sober, about what it was like in the port pub or brothel. Likewise, no one will tell stories about other "wives" in other ports or about a lost life and the loss of a family because of being a sailor. I fell silent, a moment longer and I would have added that I am an example of this, and yet it is my private matter.

Joasia, after a moment of silence, said happily:

"See, Richie? We already have the first column. Don't be angry, but I recorded everything," she said and pointed to the recorder in a case lying on the table, which I had taken for a phone. "It'll be good material for the first article," she added, laughing.

"You tricky viper! Are we finally going to dance?" I asked, getting up from the chair.

The DJ was playing songs that I liked. Hits of the 1980s.

I took her hand and we went to the dance floor, where Kinga and Slawek were rock and rolling.

Everything in this book really happened. Time and some characters are fictional. The resemblance to other people and places is accidental and unintentional.

Endru Atros

www.ingramcontent.com/pod-product-compliance
Lightning Source LLC
Chambersburg PA
CBHW020843020726
47497CB00005B/1228